RISING DRAGONS OMNIBUS

OPHELIA BELL

Published by Ophelia Bell
UNITED STATES

ISBN-13: 978-1-955385-01-5

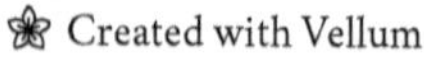 Created with Vellum

BREATH OF NIGHT

*R*owan rested on her barstool, sipping her tequila. There was a kind of depravity in seeking out a new lover. A desperation in the act of looking that she hated as much as she loved finding him. Bodies drifted by, carried by the colorful strobing lights and rhythmic music.

She preferred dark places like the club because her vibrant red hair didn't stand out quite so much. She'd grown up with an unusual set of features that doctors just explained away as a genetic anomaly. She wore colored contact lenses to avoid startling people with the strange, red color of her irises, but the hair color wasn't so easy to cover up. For some reason no dye would stick, but at least that part she could pass off as a fashion statement, and it did catch the attention of potential lovers. Not that it was difficult to catch their attention, with her unique looks. Even though most women looked at her like she was some kind of alien creature, the men were barely able to keep their dicks in their pants.

Some nights she'd come to this place just to watch, have a drink, and wonder at the eventual crumbling of the women's wills against the men who found them. What woman would let herself give in so completely to a man? She never would, and neither did she need to. She'd been drawn to lucrative financial opportunities from an early age, forced to find her own opportunities as an orphan. Now she enjoyed collecting rare, ancient carvings, a passion that had proved to be the only occupation that really fulfilled her.

She wore one small piece of her collection now—a tiny, red jade medallion with a dragon carved into it. It was set in gold and hung from a delicate chain around her neck resting just at the base of her throat. She touched it absently, believing she could feel some power in it, but knowing it was all her imagination. The only power was in her ability to seduce a man, but the right one had yet to present himself. She entertained herself watching the club patrons in the meantime.

A couple tumbled into a corner a few yards away and embraced. She watched covertly, entertained that they thought the corner was private even though it clearly wasn't.

The woman tilted her head back against the wall, inviting the man's lips to trace down her throat. She wore a tiny little dress that barely covered her. Easy access, Rowan supposed, taking a sip of her drink.

A dark shape sat down at the bar beside her. "A round of drinks says he'll fuck her right there," a rough, thickly accented voice said near her ear.

She didn't look at him, but her skin tingled in a way that let her know he was the one. Sexual premonition? Maybe. Whatever it was, she never needed much information to know a man was worth her attention. This one's voice—the gruff tone and foreign accent—were enough for her to know without even seeing him. And she smiled at the challenge he'd offered.

"Two shots of tequila says he goes down on her." She said

it without turning back to look at him, though she could feel his presence beside her.

"Oh, darling, that's cruel. To yourself, I mean. A man never goes down on a woman unless he loves her."

The small hairs on the back of her neck stood up when he said "darling".

"That is patently untrue."

The hot breath of his laugh caressed her shoulder. She heard him shift closer. Out of the corner of her eye she glimpsed a large, manicured, gold-ringed hand holding a glass. Ice clinked and the aroma of expensive whiskey hit her nostrils. She'd bet anything that the shiny watchband secured a Rolex to his wrist. None of it impressed her as much as his presence, so palpable he may as well have already been sinking inside her, right through her little black dress.

"You're right. I'd go down on you in a heartbeat and I don't even know your name."

Jesus, she was turned on just by his voice. She'd forgotten the couple in the corner, though she still kept her eyes fixed on them. Instead, she imagined she was that woman, and the man was her new friend.

The man had the woman turned around now, pressed against the wall, chest-first. His fingers tugged at the hem of her skirt, pushing it up above her hip. Not even the shadows could conceal the white, round shape of the woman's ass, a thin strip of dark fabric crossing one hip. That disappeared with a jerk of the man's hand.

Rowan felt the touch of a large, warm hand at her hip, a thumb grazing a pattern into the bare skin of her back just above the fabric of her low-cut dress. His touch was gentle and cool, but left a promise when he removed his hand. When his hand disappeared, he murmured behind her, "I think you owe me a drink."

"Wait for it," she said. Whether it was the way the man in

the corner was clutching the woman's ass, or some particular change in his posture, she had the sense of what he might do next. She had to restrain a laugh when he sank to his knees and buried his face between the woman's ass cheeks. Rowan could imagine the ecstatic sounds coming from the woman's throat by the way her chest thrust out and her head flew back, mouth open while the man tongued between her legs from behind.

"Did I call it or what?" she asked, turning around to gloat, only to be greeted by an empty barstool.

Obsessed was an understatement for her frame of mind the following week. Alternately pissed and confused, she sometimes wondered if she'd hallucinated the entire conversation, but that small patch of skin where he'd touched her still tingled. Finally after several sleepless nights imagining his shadowy presence behind her doing more than just talking, she resolved to go back to the bar, find him, and confront him about leaving her hanging. The only problem was that she'd never actually seen his face.

It might be futile. She had no idea whether he'd even be there again, much less talk to her. But in spite of all the pretty faces she *could* see in the bar—attractive men who she knew at a glance would happily go home with her—she could no longer settle. Where was he, and how in the world would she be able to tell if she'd even found him?

"Looking for someone?" The rough, accented voice sent a charge like a lightning bolt straight down her back. Rowan closed her eyes and savored the pleasant tingling sensation between her thighs for a second.

"Maybe I found him," she said, turning her head slightly.

There was no mistaking that voice and now that he was close again she recognized the mildly spicy scent of his aftershave. This time she'd be damned if she let him get away from her. She turned and looked up into dark eyes and an expression that gave new meaning to the term *smoldering*.

"I think you owe me an apology. And a drink," she said when she finally caught her breath.

He nodded. His eyes drifted lower, tracing the outline of her bosom while one large hand reached toward her, fingertips grazing along the contour of her waist and hip. The light contact through her dress may as well have been skin on skin the way the heat of him sank into her.

"I'm very sorry," he murmured. "But if I had stayed last week there would have been a second woman indecently exposed in the corner of the club. I pride myself on my ability to maintain control, but you…" The words trailed off and the muscles in his clean-shaved jaw flexed. His fingertips dug into her hip, subtly pulling her closer.

Rowan's lips curved into a pleased smile. That she could cause such a meticulously put together man to doubt his self control thrilled her. Something else about him excited her, too, but she couldn't put her finger on it. Something in those dark eyes of his seemed almost otherworldly, and he exuded the kind of sexual energy that usually attracted her to a man.

"That's a lousy excuse," she said. She resisted the tug of his hand even though it took all her willpower not to sink against him. Looking at him now, she wondered what ethnicity he was. The dark features and accent fit together in an alluring combination, but none of his clean angles gave her a clue. His accent was also hard for her to place. The scent of him was the worst culprit in enticing her to bury her face against his neck and just breathe him in. She decided that the other details didn't matter.

"How can I make it up to you?" he asked, settling his eyes back on hers.

"Start by telling me your name, maybe. Then buy me that drink. I'm Rowan."

"Rafe. And I have better tequila at home."

"If that's an invitation, then I accept." The words came out before she had the chance to censor herself. She had established personal rules when meeting new men, particularly in venues like the club she liked to frequent. Don't go home with them the first night was one of her first rules. But the enticement of expensive tequila along with a man who smelled as good as he did—and looked at her like he'd like to mount her right there, damning his own sensibilities—was enough to throw her judgment completely out of whack.

The sleek, black convertible Porsche that pulled up outside the club a moment later screamed wealth. The luxurious leather of the seats caressed the backs of her thighs when she sat. She lowered the visor to look in the small mirror in an effort to disguise her covert study of him after he shut her door and rounded to the driver's side. He moved with slow, easy grace, like a panther. As eager as he had sounded about getting her out of the club, now that he had her in his clutches he seemed intent on taking his time.

The idea of herself as his prey excited her. She normally couldn't stand domineering men, but so far he'd never once commanded her to do anything. He'd merely made a suggestion and she'd fallen right into his trap. Instead of struggling to get free, she had a strange urge to let him devour her.

"It's a chilly night, do you want the top up?"

"Cold never bothers me. Leave it down." In truth, she always ran a little warm, but tonight her blood felt like lava. When he put the car in gear and revved the engine he let his hand drift from his gearshift to brush the skin on her thigh.

He left his hand resting just above her knee, removing it only to shift gears as he drove.

She spent the first few minutes of the drive wishing he'd do more than caress that small patch of skin just on the inside of her thigh. When they were on the Coronado Bridge headed toward one of the richest neighborhoods in the city, her anxiety spiked enough to subdue her libido just a bit.

She became painfully aware that she might be getting in way over her head if a man as rich as he seemed to be was interested in her. Before she had a chance to comment, his hand began to slip up her thigh, the tips of his fingertips grazing her sensitive skin. She inhaled sharply at the intensity of his caress. His fingertips might have been live wires the way they caused a steady current of pleasure to sink through her skin. He didn't stop at the hem of her dress, either, but pushed past it.

The cool wind tugged at the wayward strands of hair that had escaped their binding. The breeze across her heated skin did nothing to cool her need. She sighed and spread her legs a little wider on the seat, aching for him to keep moving higher.

A low growl came from the driver's seat when his fingertips pushed past the barrier of her panties and slid between her wet folds. She tilted her head back and closed her eyes when he found her clit and began to stroke it. She was so lost to his touch she almost didn't register the question he asked her.

"Where do you come from, Rowan? Why haven't I met you before?"

"I—why would you? Oh God, don't stop."

When his hand disappeared, leaving her hot center cooling from the night wind, she opened her eyes.

Without looking at her, he asked, "Who are you?"

Confused and frustrated, she said, "I'm just Rowan. I

never knew who my parents were, so really I'm nobody. I promise I'm not a gold-digger, if that's what you're worried about. I have my own money."

Rafe laughed and darted a quick glance at her. His eyes sparkled. "It doesn't matter yet, but I will find out somehow, even if you can't tell me. I'm not worried about my money, either, even if you *were* a gold-digger, as you say, there are worse qualities than desiring wealth."

The depth of his interest should have disturbed her. The truth was she had tried to find out her parents' identities but had run into dead end after dead end, and nearly depleted all her savings in the process. She was still doing well enough financially to dig a little more, but had given up the search as a lost cause. Her parents hadn't wanted her, so why should she bother?

"Be my guest if you want to waste your time," she said. She shifted in her seat and tugged the hem of her dress back down, irritated by the remaining dampness between her thighs and the lingering ache he'd left by not finishing what he'd started.

She was on the verge of demanding he turn around and take her home when she noticed him shift in his seat. The slight movement brought to her attention the pronounced bulge straining at the front of his expensive trousers. She smiled at him when he caught her looking and reached across, placing her hand on his knee and sliding it up.

Rafe's right thigh flexed with the pressure he exerted on the accelerator. He took one hand off the wheel and placed it over hers, pressing her palm harder against him and tilting his hips.

Rowan's head buzzed from knowing she'd done this to him. She explored his hard length through the fabric, her pulse picking up with each increment of what she discovered was a very large cock, the head of which seemed to want to escape from his waistband.

With any other man, she might have unfastened his pants, unleashed his erection, and taken him into her mouth while he drove. But that would have been too easy and she had the urge to test her own limits almost as much as his.

CHAPTER THREE

The gated compound he drove into a few moments later was beyond the scope of what Rowan had expected. Rowan may not have been impressed by his attire earlier—many of the men she'd seen recently could afford an expensive suit and a nice watch and fancy car—but the scope of his wealth in light of where he lived made her reassess him yet again.

"Now it's my turn to ask, who are you? As young as you are, this has to be family money." *And whose family?* She'd heard of a rich drug lord who kept a house in the area, but Rafe didn't have the look of that kind of man. Not that she knew what that looked like.

Rafe cut the engine and delicately removed her hand from his crotch where she'd left it resting, forgotten in her interest with her new surroundings. He lifted her hand to his mouth and brushed his lips across her knuckles. "I'm older than I look, but yes, my family's wealth goes back for several generations. I've traced it to the Pharaohs."

Egyptian, she thought. That seemed to fit, even with his fair, smooth skin.

His look of a cat on the prowl was even more pronounced when he came around to open the door for her. Her heartbeat sped up when she stood and his hand shifted to her low back, pulling her to him. She stepped into his embrace, peering up into his dark eyes. His arousal pressed hot and hard against her belly.

She'd let him have her right here if he wanted. He seemed to sense it, and his gaze grew more heated. Both his hands rested gently on her shoulders and his thumbs traced the line of her jaw. He bent his head and pressed a gentle kiss against her lips. She opened up with a small moan, flicking her tongue out to taste him. The sweet taste of licorice met her tongue, along with the flavor of the whiskey he had been drinking at the club. His tongue was velvety softy when he teased back, but teasing was all he did. His hands tugged slightly at the clips that held her hair and a second later she felt the tightness of the bindings disappear and the heavy weight cascaded down her back.

Rafe pulled away with a smile, gazing at the mane of red tresses he'd released. "You have such gorgeous hair. You should always wear it loose."

Before she could thank him for the compliment, he wrapped his large hand around hers and led her up a long, stone path to the front of his house.

He hadn't been joking about *old money*, which was apparent from the decor inside his house. Rowan was no expert in antiquities, except where her particular niche of interest was concerned, but his collection would give any aficionado a field day, regardless of their interest.

She paused in the foyer before a life-size carved jade replica of the same figure that graced her throat. Her fingers went to her necklace involuntarily as she gazed at the huge red dragon before her. Something in its shape and sleek curves seemed so familiar.

"Don't worry, he's only a replica, but he is older than most."

"This is beautiful! And it must be valued in the millions."

Rafe pursed his lips. "On the antiquities market, perhaps. I don't sell pieces from my collection as a general rule, however. He was a gift to my parents from an old friend."

"Someone…*gave* this to your family?"

"Yes. But I can see what a connection you have with him. He's yours, if you'd like. A red dragon for a red enchantress."

She jerked her head around to stare at him in shock. "You can't be serious."

Rafe reached a hand up to hers where it was still tightly clutching her necklace. She let her fingers drop and he stepped closer to her. His fingertips lightly brushed her throat when he picked up the small medallion and inspected it.

"I believe he belongs to you, Rowan, but I have one condition."

He stood so close to her she could feel the heat radiating off him. His fingers let the pendant fall back against her throat but he kept contact, tracing her collarbone to her shoulder. The same little zings of electricity seemed to shoot into her skin wherever he touched.

Anything, she wanted to say, but the word caught in her throat. Anything to keep him touching her like this.

"He is yours, but he stays here, and you visit him frequently."

She swallowed and pulled back from his touch, suddenly needing a breath. Being close to Rafe was like standing next to a black hole and trying not to get sucked in. If she wasn't careful, she would lose herself completely.

"Are you thirsty?" he asked in a low voice. The reminder of his original offer only released her slightly from the pull of him.

"I could use a drink, yes." She didn't think it mattered what he served her now. She just needed something different to focus on for five minutes so she could come to her senses. She'd come with him merely seeking a night of sexual release. Not even three steps through his door, and she already found herself craving more than his attention. It wasn't even his obvious wealth that interested her, but the atmosphere in which he lived. Why did this huge house, decorated to the hilt with some of the oldest, priceless artifacts feel more like home to her than her comfortable Midtown apartment?

Impulsively, she kicked off her shoes in the entryway before following him barefoot through a wide, arched doorway into another room. This one at least had more modern furnishings, but they were no less exquisite in their craftsmanship. The value was in the artistry, not the age, she decided.

The allure of all these *things* he surrounded himself with was nothing compared to the draw of Rafe himself.

Rowan downed the tumbler of liquor in three quick gulps and contemplated leaving again. Her need to maintain control was quickly eroding amid her desire to let him take her to bed and keep her there forever.

He refilled her drink and studied her quietly while she moved to stand by a nearby bookcase, feigning interest in the leatherbound volumes on one shelf.

"You're afraid of me," he said. "Why?"

She sipped the smooth tequila this time and turned to face him. "I'm not afraid of you. Just my reaction to you. To everything." She let her eyes take in the rest of the room before settling on him again. "I never had this growing up, but…"

"Where did you grow up?" Rafe remained standing near the liquor cabinet, sipping his own drink

"Foster care, mostly, until I learned I had a knack for finding treasures in the most unlikely places. I have my own small collection like this, you know."

"We're alike in a lot of ways, I believe. You're a very special woman, Rowan. I think you know that, but what I don't think you know is precisely *how* special."

"I'm simply a confident woman who gets what she wants. That's all." She believed she enjoyed sex more than the average woman, too, but until today had always managed to keep her emotions out of the equation.

He smiled slowly and nodded. "Yes, but you are much more. Take out your contact lenses so you can see."

His request confused her. "But I need them *to* see."

"You don't. You're only hiding behind them because no one ever told you the truth of how beautiful you are. Did you ever wonder what it meant? What it is about you that causes men to fall at your feet and women to despise you? It's more than just your beauty."

His commentary chilled her. It was like he'd gotten deep into her head. He set his glass down and walked closer to stand just within reach.

"Let me see your eyes."

"Fine," she said. With two quick swipes of a fingertip, her flimsy disposable contacts fell to the carpet. She met his eyes, prepared for the startled horror she usually received when anyone saw the true blood-red of her irises.

Rafe only smiled, but before her eyes his own changed color, shifting from a steel gray to an almost bottomless, inky black with flecks of silver. The sense of falling was so pronounced as she gazed into those dark depths, she lost her balance.

He caught her and held her against his broad chest. He whispered into her ear, "Believe me, when I look in your eyes

I feel the same way, only touched by fire. You have no idea what you are, do you?"

Rowan didn't care anymore about his questions. Whoever, *whatever*, he was, that look had sent her past the brink. All she could do now was let herself fall and hope she emerged from the other side still sane.

She clutched the back of his neck and pulled him down into a deep kiss. The delicious taste of him tingled on her tongue when he let her invade his mouth. He gave as good, plunging back in return and pressing her hard against the bookcase.

Rafe's hands tangled in her hair then slid lower, tugging at the straps of her dress. He found the zipper at her back and tugged. Soon the tailored black silk was in a puddle at her bare feet, leaving her in matching black bra and panties.

Dissatisfied with only the touch of his hands, Rowan tugged at the buttons of his shirt. She needed to feel his skin against hers, but grew frustrated in the rush, gripped the front of his shirt, and ripped. The buttons went flying, pinging off the priceless objects in the room. A deep rumble rose from Rafe's chest when her hands slipped inside and splayed across the smooth, hard planes of his chest.

She slid her hands down his stomach and gripped his erection through his trousers, stroked up along the length until reaching his waist. With a few quick tugs she managed to unfasten his belt and pants without more damage to his clothing.

"Take these off and fuck me," she demanded.

Rafe's dark eyes flashed with a strange inner light she was sure must be her imagination. He quickly stripped the rest of the way and pressed against her again, but not before she got a good look at him from top to toe. Never had she seen a man so perfectly put together. *Godlike,* if she had to put a word to it. The sense of being consumed by some strange energy persisted as strongly as the feel of his mouth tasting her skin. He unfastened her bra with one quick motion and it fell to the floor.

He spun them both and pushed her against a ledge in a shallow alcove. A flower arrangement teetered and he picked it up and tossed behind him. The vase crashed into splinters on the floor, leaving colorful petals and green stalks in a pile of crystalline pieces.

Before she could react he'd turned her around and pressed himself against her from behind. She met her own eyes in the mirror on the wall and was startled to see the same strange flash of light she'd seen in his. She must be going crazy, but it happened again when Rafe shoved her hair aside and bent his head to her neck, kissed his way to her shoulder. Both his large hands cupped her breasts, squeezed and tweaked her nipples.

She braced herself against the marble-topped ledge in front of her to keep her balance, too overwhelmed by every touch to process the strangeness of him and her reaction to him.

Except it wasn't strange at all. It was exactly how it should be. The grip of his hand on her hip and the harsh rip when he divested her of her panties was perfect. The kneading clutch of his hands on her ass when he kneeled behind her, then spread her open and sank his tongue between her pulsing, swollen lips.

Even his tongue felt like it filled her completely and she cried out. She pushed back against him and raised her hands to brace herself against the mirror. Her eyes looked like fire now, glowing bright orange. *You have no idea what you are, do you?* His voice resonated in her mind for a fleeting moment then faded out beneath her harsh cries of ecstasy over the feel of his mouth and hands working her into a frenzy. His tongue felt impossibly long and agile as it plunged into her, his fingertips teased at both her clit and her ass.

Rowan lost herself completely, giving over to the sensations, falling into the heat of her own gaze. It was so good she hallucinated red smoke for breath as she panted against the mirror. The tingling rush of sensation quickly grew to a flood, inundating her with pleasure. She clawed at the glass as her entire body tensed with her climax. Her back arched and she cried out to the ceiling above her.

Dazed and still vibrating from the orgasm, she let him turn her to face him. She lifted her feet off the floor at his urging, wrapping both legs around his hips. His skin seemed to glow from within and she blinked for a second, sure she'd seen a forked tongue dart out to lick his lips before they were pressed hard to hers, his tongue penetrating her mouth as swiftly as his cock sank to the hilt into her still spasming pussy.

She writhed against him, meeting each plunging thrust with an eager surge of her hips. The heavy thickness of his shaft stretched her more than any other man ever had. She believed she had felt pleasure before, but the depths to which he could go were beyond anything she'd experienced. She clutched at him, every muscle tightening, her pussy clenching, seeking to pull him in even deeper, but he was already fucking her as deep as he could go.

Rafe pulled away for a breath and reached up to cup her face in both his palms. His eyes glowed with strange, ultraviolet light, and his face was not only seeping light from his pores, but bathed in an orange-red glow.

"You are like me, Rowan. You will never be alone again, I promise."

With that missive, his mouth crashed against hers again and he thrust violently into her. His cock seemed to swell and grow hotter inside her. With a heavy pulse the heat of his orgasm filled her and sent her rocketing to another crest.

She held him tightly and closed her eyes. His orgasm persisted, but the hot flow of it seemed to sink into every cell of her body, not just the tight, dark recesses of her womb.

Her body was on fire. From pleasure. From some unseen energy that infused her. Her eyes flew open and locked onto Rafe's. He watched with that strange, black gaze, smiling as though he were enthralled with her reaction to his climax.

After a moment, their breathing slowed and Rowan's heartbeat felt halfway normal again.

She let her hands slide away from his shoulders and he winced at her touch.

"What happened? Are you hurt?"

"Nothing a little breath won't cure. I see you found your talons." His fingers encircled her wrists and held her hands up for her to see. Shimmering, red scales had replaced her skin and instead of fingernails, she had long, sharp, black claws at the tips of each finger.

Rowan yelped in alarm and jerked backward, but there was nowhere to go and he held her tight.

"What the fuck did you do to me?"

"Calm down, love. This is only a glimpse of your true form. The young ones require an infusion of another's energy to unlock it. Have you never seen yourself like this before? Has it always been only your eyes and hair that were different?"

The slightest stroke of his steel-hard erection inside her sent a buzz of pleasure up through her body. How could she process having *talons* when he was fucking her like that?

"Here, turn around," he said, pulling out of her and lifting her off the small ledge she'd been perched on while they fucked. He turned her around to face the mirror.

The image that greeted her was alien and beautiful. The

edges of all her features were covered in the same shining red scales—at her hairline, along both sides of her neck, down the tops of her shoulders and arms, and down over her hips and thighs. Only her face and the front of her torso from breasts to crotch did she still have fair, normal skin showing through. And at the top of her forehead, extending in dark red coils were a pair of graceful horns, curving back and almost touching Rafe's chin behind her.

"Glorious," he said.

When she looked in the mirror at his reflection, a similar sight greeted her, except his features were framed in shining black scales, with a pair of large, deadly looking black horns sprouting from his head.

"What…what are we?"

"Darling, we are dragons." He said it softly, almost mournfully and his eyes grew sad for a split second before his features smoothed over. "Now, come to bed and I'll tell you everything."

They navigated their way around the minefield of broken crystal, leaving their clothing behind. His taloned hand gripped hers and led her toward a wide staircase off the other side of the foyer. When he turned, she caught a glimpse of the damage she'd caused to his back. Both his shoulders and ass were criss-crossed with bloody stripes.

"Jesus, Rafe! Why didn't you stop me?"

"Because you were enjoying it so much and I was at the point of no return, myself. It's nothing to worry about. I'd normally let it heal on its own, but there's one thing you can do."

Rowan see-sawed between mortification and confusion, but those feelings seemed inconsequential compared to the buzzing well of energy she seemed to have inside her. The urge to feel him in her again was overwhelming. And not just fucking her, either. She'd always taken more satisfaction from making men come, often not even caring whether she found her own release. Rafe, however, had given her more with that single orgasm of his than she'd enjoyed from all of the other men she'd been with. *Humans? I'm not like them, am I?*

"No, my love, you are not. We are a different race entirely." He hadn't spoken out loud, she was sure of it, yet it was unmistakably his voice she had just heard.

"You can hear my thoughts?"

"If you project with enough intent, yes. And you very much wanted an answer to that question. You can ask out loud, though. Anything you want to know, I will tell you. My staff are off for the weekend."

"You have a staff…of course."

"Someone has to polish the dragon."

She smiled in return to the smirk he cast over his shoulder.

"Alright, first question: How do I get my hands back? And I sure as hell can't go out in public with a pair of horns."

"It just takes a little concentration and some dragon magic. You'll be able to change your hair and eye color as it pleases you, too. You may need to build up more energy first, however."

"And how do I get the energy?"

"Darling, I believe you know the answer to that already."

He urged her through the door to a huge bedroom, closed it behind her, and stood facing her. He waggled his fingers in front of her face. "First, picture what you'd like them to look like."

"Just my hands, please." She made a cattish clawing motion at his face with her new talons that earned her a smile. Not only was he rakishly handsome when full of lust, but almost boyishly cute when he was amused. Her heartbeat fluttered at the contradiction.

"Right, now feel that warm burn of power I gave you, deep down inside."

"Hmm, how deep?" She quirked one eyebrow.

He stepped toward her and slid his now very human fingertips down her belly. "It may be here, or a bit lower. Shall I give you an anatomy lesson or do you want your hands back?"

She did feel the warm glow in her center, not unlike the sensation of a lingering orgasm, only much more subtle. When she focused on it while picturing her long, pale, and human fingertips, she could feel the energy surge forth and fill her limbs. A moment later the claws and scales disappeared. The weight of the horns left her head.

"So that's how it works!" she said. "Now turn around. I think I know what your back needs."

Rafe hesitated. "Healing breath has a trick to it, are you sure?"

"How am I supposed to learn if you won't let me make mistakes?"

He reluctantly turned. Rowan reached for the energy, enjoying the slight tingle that encompassed the flesh between her legs.

"Just be sure not to breathe fire on me by accident. Smoke is what you're aiming for."

Just as he said it, she clamped her hand over her mouth, cutting off the tiny gout of flame that had erupted from between her lips. In a muffled voice she said, "Okay, what's the trick?"

Rafe's shoulders shook with mirth. "Picture life, creation, sustaining powers. Avoid thoughts of destruction."

She rested her hands on his shoulders and focused, pulling on the now somewhat familiar well of energy, and expelling a breath. The red smoke spilled forth in a cloud.

"You can command it where to go, once it's left your body. Aim it at my scratches."

Wonders never ceased. With a thought, she did precisely what he said and watched in amazement as the smoke condensed against his wounds, tracing them like a series of small, delicate tongues and sealing each cut. When her breath dissipated, she smoothed her hands lightly over her handiwork. Not even a scar marred his skin.

Distracted by the feel of him under her palms, she continued caressing, moved closer and slid her hands down to cup his firm buttocks. He remained still, letting her explore. She pressed her breasts against his back and slid her hands around his waist, embracing him and pressing her cheek against his back.

"Thank you," she said.

He clasped her hands in his, drew one to his lips and laid a lingering kiss against her palm. He released her and she let her hands slide lower, over his muscular chest and stomach. The hot tip of his cock brushed her palm when she reached out from his midsection. Rafe let out a deep sigh as she caressed the velvet length of him. His balls were heavy and soft in her palm.

She ached for him again, but much more deeply than she had before. The understanding of a shared bond she had never had before with anyone frightened her a little bit, but also left her uncertain. Sex was one thing… the easy thing. This was the first time she'd ever been with a man who she hoped for more with. One night would never be enough.

He turned to her and kissed her, the strange forked tongue of his teasing into her mouth. She hadn't hallucinated any of it. Remembering her well of magic, she tried to mimic the shape and found it was natural to make her tongue like his. When the two tangled together, Rafe groaned out a deep laugh, then pulled away.

"You are a fast learner." The wistful look was back in his dark eyes, in spite of the smile on his face.

"What's wrong?" she asked. "You keep looking at me like I might die."

"I'm not worried about you dying. We have very long lives and are extremely hard to kill."

"Then what are you worried about?" She worried enough herself about giving in to him so completely. But who else was there for her in the world?

"You still have a lot to learn, my love. Don't worry, I mean to teach you everything."

The sad look was quickly replaced by one of playful determination. He gripped her by the ass and lifted her up.

Rowan laughed and responded by wrapping her arms and legs around him, letting him carry her to his bed.

CHAPTER FIVE

wo nights later Rowan awoke from the sweetest
dream of making love to Rafe. The bed beside her
was empty, but she heard the creak of a step followed by the
clinking sound of glass. Rowan sat up abruptly in the dark
and looked around, but he wasn't in the bed beside her, or
anywhere else in the room. There were no lights on and the
heavy curtains were drawn closed. She could still see clearly,
having learned to adjust her dragon sight to the lack of light.

She climbed out of bed, listening. There were definitely
voices coming from the first floor. A pair of male voices.

She threw on one of Rafe's shirts that was about three
sizes too big for her and nearly reached her knees. It smelled
delightfully of him. She crept to the door and opened it
slowly.

The sounds of their mingled voices became as clear as if
they were standing outside the door.

"…exist outside the purview of the Council. How do they
not know about her? She's just a baby. My parents kept me in
human form until I was sixteen. Most broodlings have to
wait longer before they are allowed to unleash their true

form. She's twenty-eight already, with no one to teach her who she is!"

"Rafe, friend. We'll figure this out. We always knew the Council couldn't be infallible. She's the proof. We can use her presence against them. Leverage to get us what we want."

"But what *do* we want? To mate with whomever we choose? We always both agreed they made the right decision on that. There are too few of us still—inbreeding would destroy the race."

"What we want is to abolish the sleep. It puts us at a weakness. The next generation shouldn't be at such a disadvantage. Her presence proves it's pointless. She's at full power, you said?"

"Sweet Mother, yes. She's more powerful than Geva. Only a purebred would be that powerful."

"Yet another reason to confront the Council. If there are other dragons outside the Brood that have bred while we slept, inbreeding wouldn't be a concern, particularly if they are as pure as she is."

"The Council won't see it that way. The law is the law to them, unless we convince them to change it, but that's one law that has stood for the last six generations."

Rowan sank down against the door jamb in the dark of the bedroom. Her gut tightened at everything she was hearing. They were talking about her. Rafe had called a friend to talk about *her*. Was he another dragon, this nameless voice below? He must be. None of the rest of it made sense, though. What was a Geva? It sounded like the name of a god, for all she knew.

"As long as she's better behaved than Geva, she'll be fine. She'll be free to find a human mate like the rest of us."

The sound of breaking glass made Rowan jerk in surprise.

"You don't understand, Kol. I have to have *her*. Not a human."

"You're in love with her."

"What? No… she's just… she's pure. Tell me why we shouldn't be able to breed?"

Tears streamed down her face and she swiped them away roughly with the cuff of the shirt she wore. She only half heard the talk that followed. Quiet words of comfort from the friend. More talk of bloodlines. But all he wanted her for was a broodmare?

"I love you, Rafe. But I can't do this."

She only hoped he heard her. She found a pair of sweat pants and a shirt, then grew frustrated with how they hindered her movement. The burn in her belly grew and she remembered the magic. If she could conjure her hands, she could conjure an outfit.

"Rowan wait!"

The door swung open and Rafe stood there, a larger, darker man behind him. She stood by the open window, clad in the red leather outfit she'd succeeded in conjuring for herself via some serious concentration and a lot of deep breathing. She was ready to jump out and see if she could actually convince herself to fly. Rafe had told her dragons could fly in their true forms, at least.

"I'm leaving. You and your *people* clearly have some issues to work out. I don't want any part of it."

"Rowan, stop." The deep, commanding voice of the other man actually pulled her back into the room. Jesus, it felt like a pair of hands were holding her, actually turning her around. She was helpless in the invisible clutches of this stranger.

He squeezed past Rafe's large figure in the doorway and came to stand in front of her. She had to crane her neck to look up at him.

"Sorry, I don't like having to do this, but I needed to be sure you wouldn't leave. Please stay and listen. We won't hurt you."

Rowan squirmed in the invisible grasp and finally nodded. "Fine, I'll stay." She shot a flaming look at Rafe, oddly satisfied when he ducked his head in response.

"My name is Kol," the man said. "I'm what you might call the head of security for the Dragon Brood. I care about keeping everyone safe. Every *dragon*. And every human bonded to us."

"Please let me go. I'm not going to give away any of your secrets. I just want my life to be my own."

The man's lips twisted ironically. He was impossibly pretty, even prettier than Rafe, if she had to quantify it, and his deep voice seemed to vibrate at a frequency that made her nipples hard. Yet the invisible grip on her body remained.

"We all want that. That's what we were talking about downstairs. What you heard. Freedom is what we all want. I want you to help us. Help our children be free to live."

"Why should I?"

The man glanced back at Rafe, who nodded at him. He turned back to look at her. His eyes were even deeper and blacker than Rafe's if that were possible. The hold he had on her finally released.

"Because even if he loves you, according to our *laws*, the two of you will never be allowed to mate or breed."

"Does he love me?" She glared at Rafe again. "Or am I just a vessel for his perfect babies?"

Kol looked uncomfortable. "That's not how it works with us. I promise. Rafe knows better than to mate another dragon. That's why he called me."

Rowan shot a look at Rafe, trying to discern any emotion in his placid expression. Did he love her, or was that just a ploy for Kol to get her to do what he wanted? "He called you because he wants to mate with me?"

Marriage, let alone children, had never been on her radar. She'd begun to think of Rafe as a potential partner. The potential for more than that wasn't something she'd thought about until now. Looking at him now, her gut twisted. She wanted it. And she wanted it with *him*.

"I want to," Rafe said. His dark-browed eyes seemed so forlorn. "There's more to mating than just intercourse. It requires specific intent and verbal consent, both to mate and to breed. Nothing we do is by accident. I could feel how much you wanted it the entire time, Rowan. And believe me I wanted to…"

"What would have happened if we did?" She directed her look at both men.

"You would mark each other. The mark binds you for life." Kol seemed oddly apprehensive and shot a look at Rafe. Rowan was sure they were hiding something by the sag of Kol's shoulders. "But our laws are clear, and part of my job is to enforce the laws, which I will do, if I have to."

"Why do I get the sense that you don't really enjoy your job?" Rowan asked with a tilt of her head. Kol was starting to grow on her a little.

"Because your existence proves what I've always suspected. The Council has been lying to us for centuries. Millennia."

Rowan looked at Rafe. "What happens if we try to be together? What will they do?"

Rafe's voice was strained, his face drawn with worry. "Likely they would take you and force you into hibernation for the next five centuries. When you woke up, I would be dead. It's their way of controlling our breeding cycle. Rowan, I'm already halfway through my life. I don't have five hundred years to wait. I'm expected to find a human woman to bond with, like the others, but you're the woman I want."

"You want me to breed with. So why the hell should I stay if it's just to be his broodmare?" She directed the question at Kol, but Rafe was the one who answered.

"Rowan, I don't care if we never reproduce. That's not why I want you. Did the last two days not tell you as much?" He started to step toward her. Kol held his friend back.

"Of course it is your choice," Kol said. "Leave and live as a human if you wish, but you can have no further contact with other dragons or I would have to turn you in to the Council. You'll be safer if only Rafe and I know you exist." He paused and stepped toward her, placing a large, warm hand on her shoulder. "Or stay and help us confront the Council with your existence. We have other friends who will help. As long as we stand together, I believe we can make a change."

Rafe seemed to lean toward her, intent on what she would say. She wanted him more than she'd wanted anything in her life. The past weekend had been overwhelming and enlightening and oh, so beautiful. Every lovemaking session had been even more spectacular than the last. Every waking moment when they weren't entwined had been spent with her asking question after question and him answering eagerly and honestly. At least she'd thought so. That first night she had known she would fall for him, and she had. Hard. But the thought of having an entire race—and her own happiness—dependent on her decision was an impossible situation, especially when his feelings for her still seemed so uncertain.

Her eyes welled with tears as she looked at him. Her gut knotted with anguish. "I'm sorry, this is too much for me to decide. Please forgive me."

Before they could respond, she looked back towards the

window. *Fly or die.* She leapt out, caught the strong gust of cool Pacific wind, and flew.

EPILOGUE

One week ago...

Rafe ran a shaky hand through his hair, cursing himself for his nerves. The red beauty was at the club again, for the third time in as many weeks. *His* club. This was his sanctuary, and one of the few assets from his inheritance that gave him true joy. Like every Shadow dragon, he was prone to dark moods, and lately they were brought on by his as yet unmet need to find a human mate.

The club was his father's gift to him, intended to help facilitate that very thing. Except none of the human women he'd met and seduced had interested him enough for more than a single night. They were beautiful, of course, and fulfilled his particular needs for fresh energy when he took them to his nearby penthouse and made love to them. They never left wanting, but Rafe himself was increasingly frustrated by the lack of a deeper connection with any of them.

Then *she* walked in one night, so vibrantly beautiful with her brilliant red hair and perfect shimmering skin, his heart nearly stopped. He watched her from the shadows that first night, disbelieving his eyes that a red dragon so exquisite could exist. The other dragons who frequented his club didn't seem to register her presence, and she seemed equally oblivious to them. It was the strangest thing to watch – as though they had selective blindness to each other.

Was she somehow charmed? If so, how was *he* able to see her for what she was when the others weren't? She wasn't from the recently ascended brood, that much he knew, which meant she'd been born outside the purview of the Council's laws, and was likely only exactly as old as she looked. If she hadn't hibernated with the rest of his brood, she may only have been born within the last few decades, while the other dragons in the place, himself included, were all at least half a millennium old.

That thought worried him. If he could see her for what she was, then whatever magic left her nature invisible to the other dragons must be weakening. If anyone with a need to earn praise from their autocratic Council discovered what she was, she would be in danger of losing her powers as punishment for simply being born outside their laws.

He'd observed her from afar for long enough, and had learned as much as he could about her without actually approaching her. She needed his protection, but he needed to know more about her than the fact that she had a preference for the most expensive tequila the bar stocked, and an equally discerning preference for the wealthiest human men – and occasionally the women – who frequented his establishment.

Tonight the atmosphere in the club was particularly charged, and the tequila was flowing. The wealthier residents of San Diego who had chosen to forego a trip to Tijuana in honor of Cinco de Mayo enjoyed the festive atmosphere at Rafe's Latin-themed club, the *Fuego Nocturno*. Energy was high, and escalated to an almost frenetically sexual pitch after she arrived, her aura pulsing with a particular craving tonight that Rafe recognized as the distinct aura of a Red on the hunt.

Around the Red, men and women gravitated toward each other with lust-filled gazes. One couple even disappeared into one of the dark alcoves that existed around the perimeter of the large room, tangled in a passionate embrace. It was only a semi-private spot that the other humans wouldn't be able to see into, but Rafe and any of the dragons in the place could easily view past the shadows with their preternatural senses.

The lovely Red's attention turned toward the couple with both amusement and arousal.

"Now's as good a time as any," Rafe muttered, steeling his resolve to step within the potent cloud of her seductive aura. He ignored the surge of lust that caused his entire body to flush from the close proximity to her. Sweet Mother, she was a powerful Red. Did she not know what kind of effect she had on the entire crowd? Briefly he was reminded of another Red he was well acquainted with. One of the young Court dragons, Geva, had once incited an orgy on the streets out of a misplaced sense of rebellion just before their generation went into hibernation five hundred years earlier. Not many reds were powerful enough to affect huge crowds into such profligate behavior.

He moved onto the bar stool beside her and his cock twitched and hardened, aiming in her direction like it were a dowsing rod seeking out the surest source of power. Out of the entire club, she was definitely the locus, and he marveled that none of the other half-dozen dragons had gravitated toward her. No doubt they were reaping the benefit of this young Red's overflowing energy, though. He glanced around and saw one of the other female dragons dancing in an almost lurid embrace between two human men. Another male dragon was seated in a booth with one woman writhing on his lap and two others flanking him while both his hands disappeared up their skirts.

Taking a deep breath, Rafe signaled the bartender who pulled a bottle of whiskey down from a high shelf and poured without having to be told what Rafe's preferred drink was. Rafe was idly grateful for his idea to make sure the staff was magically guarded against dragon magic, otherwise business would suffer on nights like tonight.

When he lifted his glass, the ice clinked and the woman's posture shifted, her awareness honing in on him with interest, though she didn't turn. She remained facing that steamy alcove with her elbow on the bar, one hand caressing the tumbler of amber liquid in front of her. She took it neat, he observed, appreciating the aroma of the exquisite añejo tequila, one of his own favorites, though not the best. The tequila was only the best he chose to invest in for the club – his personal collection included the true pinnacle of the liquor but it was too rare by far to share with the drunken masses.

Rafe directed his gaze to the scene unfolding in the dark alcove across the club. The woman's head was tilted back as she panted in ecstasy beneath the man's urgent touch. He squeezed her breasts while his tongue trailed up her bared throat and his mouth crashed down onto hers.

"A round of drinks says he'll fuck her right there," Rafe said, leaning close enough to capture a full lungful of his Red's delicious, spicy scent.

His Red? What was he thinking? Dragons couldn't interbreed. Except in very specific circumstances, it was the law. Humans were their mates of choice and had been since the very beginning. No, this Red could not be his, but he could at least entertain a brief game with her in the hopes of learning more about her.

"Two shots of tequila says he goes down on her," she replied.

Two shots of tequila if you let me go down on you, Rafe thought, intrigued by her counter-challenge and struggling even more to maintain control of himself. He ached to simply touch her, believing that if he did her skin might sear him, and he would love it. Instead, he reined in that urge, opting for a more casual reply.

"Oh, darling, that's cruel. To yourself, I mean. A man never goes down on a woman unless he loves her."

She let out a melodic laugh, turning her head slightly as though to look at him but not quite actually daring to do so.

"That is patently untrue," she said.

Rafe didn't argue the point. She was right, though he suspected that any man who'd had a taste of her must have at least left the encounter completely enraptured, if not actually in love. He shifted slightly closer so he could speak in a lower tone and still be heard over the pulsing music that surrounded them. His Red seemed to lean back ever so slightly as though gravitating toward him.

"You're right. I'd go down on you in a heartbeat and I don't even know your name."

She let out the softest breath at his confession and Rafe was nearly certain all the tiny hairs gracing the back of her neck stood on end. Her aura visibly brightened and the couple they were both observing switched positions.

The man flipped the woman around so that her arms were braced against the wall and her breasts pressed against it. Behind her, the man's hands pushed up her skirt. Rafe caught the briefest glimpse of the lacy edge of panties before the man made a fist and yanked hard, then tossed the destroyed bit of fabric to the floor. His hand roamed higher, up the woman's back as he pressed his crotch to her bare ass and ground into her hard.

The sight made Rafe's fingertips itch. He lifted one hand almost unconsciously, needing to simply touch his beautiful Red, to know whether his instinct would be true. When he made contact, she didn't set him on fire, but the burst of acute desire that flooded out of her made him struggle to breathe.

The man in the alcove reached down to unfasten his pants.

"I think you owe me a drink." It was an effort to get the words out around his urge to pull her back against him and grind his own hard cock into her ass in similar fashion. Rafe was a little disappointed because he'd begun imagining that *he* were that man and the woman was his Red. As he traced a small, secret pattern into the skin of her exposed lower back, he imagined sliding his tongue through her delicious, slick folds and having her cry out his name.

Abruptly, he realized what he'd just done with his fingertip and stared down at the tiny, proto-mark he'd given her, the magic faint, yet unmistakably signaling his claim on her. No, he couldn't have her, no matter how badly he wanted her. She was a dragon and they couldn't mate each other.

Cursing silently to himself, he left the barstool, cloaked in the silence his shadow powers allowed him, and retreated. It was from the solitude of his security booth that he saw the finale of the unknown couple's tryst and knew that his Red had indeed called it.

She had won their bet, but Rafe wasn't there to pay up.

He watched her depart after paying her bill, a look of utter bewilderment on her face. Around her all the other dragons paused as she made her way to the exit, turning their heads to follow her progress to the door.

In that moment, Rafe realized his mistake. Whatever magic that had protected her had been obliterated by his simple, impulsive touch. Now he had no choice but to find her again and make sure she remained safe.

Sweet Mother help him.

BREATH OF DESTINY

CHAPTER ONE

"**A**re we headed the right way?"

The words reached Geva's ears but he didn't quite hear them. He was too enthralled with the pleasing ivory column of Erika's neck and the slope of skin that led down, down, down, into the low-cut black shift she had donned before they'd left the luxury of the London hotel to brave a gray, windy afternoon.

Dress, she called it a dress, he corrected himself. His memory of dresses was a bit different from what she wore now—he preferred this mere slip of fabric that hugged every curve, cradled her full breasts, and showed an abundance of skin. Especially her glorious legs, tanned and muscular like a dragon woman's legs. Was she even human? He'd wondered it often, but seeing the other women she associated with he had to believe that human women in the current cycle were more attuned to their bodies than they had been when he was born.

He reached out a hand to caress the bare expanse of skin beneath her hem. The sharp smack of her hand made him look at her.

"You made me bring you out today, dummy. Tell me we're going the right way. And you're learning to drive. I can't stand driving on the wrong side of the street."

Chastised, he smiled at her and looked around.

The beasts Erika called *cars* sped down the lanes on either side of them. Gleaming, monolithic towers of glass drifted past, foreign and bizarre as they travelled through the city. Every so often he would recognize some small landmark or symbol on a sign, but other than that, his beloved city had become a stranger to him.

"It all looks different now, but the direction of the sun tells me we're headed in the right direction."

Soon the landscape changed. The bustling city with its alien structures replaced by smaller communities, then rolling green hillsides. The shine of a metropolis was a treasure trove to explore for a dragon like him, but the peace of the countryside let him breathe. He knew precisely where he was now, the landscape as familiar to him as the lush curves of Erika's body. They didn't have far to go.

Soon they approached a wide driveway, flanked by security booths. Erika provided identification to the man inside and they drove through.

The huge building they finally stopped before was one he knew well, inside and out. An imposing fountain in the forecourt spurted water out of a sextet of dragons' mouths into a pool below.

The most familiar was the emblem on the grand, polished sign that hung over the broad entryway. The stylized dragon caused a brief pang of homesickness in him. He didn't even need to read the strong type beside it. "Hayden Capital and Antiquities." He was home.

And yet he couldn't bring himself to get out of the car.

He considered himself the luckiest dragon of his generation, all of whom had slumbered along with him, deep in the depths of that jungle temple, until Erika and her team had completed the ritual to awaken them.

He'd never expected to awaken to such a beautiful, strong, and infuriating woman. One he desired to fuck as much as he desired to argue with her. Their latest argument had been about coming here today. Understandably she was more eager than he was. Everything was a new discovery for her, but finding out about his family's past wasn't going to be a happy moment for him. That his hibernation had ended meant his parents were dead now. Expired at the end of a life he believed he should have been a part of.

Dragon law had kept him away. Forced his generation into hibernation to lengthen their lives and preserve their bloodlines. And now they'd awakened to a vastly different world already inundated with humanity to such a degree that the dragons would be hard pressed to catch up.

The Council's magical restrictions on procreation seemed even more ludicrous now than they had when he was young. He felt it as keenly as his brethren—a kind of itch to get on with it, but with their hands significantly tied. Even though a dragon and his or her mate might both desire a child, wanting was only half the battle. The Council's magic meant it could take decades for a couple to conceive. Geva hadn't shared that detail with Erika, nor did he believe the others had with their mates. Human lives were normally so fleeting relative to a dragon's. There was no sense worrying them with it when they had his longer, dragon's lifespan to work with, his magic prolonging Erika's to match. Longer lives meant more opportunities.

Except the breeding restrictions and enforced hibernation had been instituted during a time when there was a real danger of dragon populations overtaking humans and beginning to view them as breeding stock. That was far from the case now.

Well, maybe not that far, considering Geva just wanted to stay in their hotel room and convince Erika to take his seed. He had no desire to mate with any other woman. But after the first attempt he wasn't sure how to broach the topic again. Apparently "let's make a baby now" wasn't an acceptable incentive to get Erika to agree to try. Even though trying was likely all it would be.

"You're still pissed about the baby thing, aren't you?" Erika asked. She shifted in her seat to face him.

Sweet Mother was she intuitive. "Yes. I don't understand the hesitance. A dragons' offspring are his greatest treasures. And most women want children. I want…" Heat flushed his cheeks and he glanced at her. He wanted more than anything for her to have *his* children. As passionate as they both were, they could produce a strong Red like him, or maybe a Gold. Those were the happiest dragon offspring. But after her response to his initial request, he hesitated. He also hated himself a little bit for being frightened of her. A human woman? Intimidating to *him*?

She brushed a palm down the side of his face and he closed his eyes, savoring her touch.

"Geva, I never wanted kids. I love my work too much. Maybe in a few years. Just not now."

Not now. The words stung but incited a blaze of desire in him that he couldn't explain. He wanted desperately to share his power with her, maybe to show her what their bond meant again and how beautiful it would be to have some tangible product of their union. He should just tell her why it was so important that they start soon, but he felt the need to convince her to want a child first.

With another swipe of her fingers through his hair, she was gone. She stepped out of the car and walked toward the entrance to the huge, stone building with the emblem of his mother emblazoned on its sign.

He watched her for a moment, admiring the flex of her calves and thighs beneath the short, black dress she wore. A gust of wind blew through and plastered the sheer fabric to her body. The visual made him go hard almost instantly. Then her impatient glower back at him made him question his sanity.

He grasped the lever to extricate himself from her vehicle and joined her. He slung an arm around her waist, only too conscious of the warmth of her body radiating through the slim scrap of fabric she'd covered herself with. It even penetrated the thicker wool of the modern, tailored suit he wore, causing his own skin to tingle pleasantly. Women in this cycle would be the death of him.

Erika would be the death of him. His cock twitched in agreement.

The interior of the castle that was his family's home centuries before was not quite the same as he remembered. True, the same pattern of polished marble shone beneath their feet, and the same grand, gilt details graced the walls and high ceilings, but as they climbed the wide, low steps that led from the foyer to the grand hall, the subtle differences became more apparent. The lights were first to capture his attention—the chandeliers that hung at intervals glowed much brighter than they ever had. They were as bright as the magic lights from the Temple he and his brethren had hibernated in for so long—a luxury dragons had to avoid when living among humans, but that humans had apparently caught up with. He wondered if there had been a dragon influencing the creation of these electric lights.

He'd encountered all these things over the last six months since awakening. *Technology* as she referred to it. He took it all in stride. In particular, he was fascinated with the tiny "gadgets" she used for her work and for communication with the others. He loved the sleek shine of them and their compact, symmetrical shapes. When Erika implied that the small object she called a "smartphone" was particularly valuable, his interest piqued, prompting a slew of questions. She finally had to resort to some not entirely unpleasant means to shut him up.

Seeing what he knew now to be surveillance cameras scattered around the place where he had come of age was jarring, however. When they reached the grand hall he stopped in his tracks. The hall was lined with cages, each one with a human standing calmly behind the bars, some having smiling conversations with other humans who stood on the outside. There were gaps midway down each cage where he could see exchanges being made.

"Are they prisoners?" he asked Erika in a low voice.

"No, sweetie. The place is a bank now. A very exclusive one, from the looks of things and how far we had to drive to get here. The cages are for protection. The clerks can come and go. Come on, let's find someone who can help."

Geva let her take him by the hand and lead him to one of the cages. He still marveled at the alien newness of the place in conjunction with its bone-deep familiarity.

"Welcome to Hayden Capital and Antiquities," a chipper male voice said, with only the barest hint of the familiar lilting accent Geva had grown up hearing. He looked away from the bank of huge, flickering screens on one wall that streamed numbers in a steady ribbon, each value he believed represented some form of wealth worth acquiring. He stored the information away to ponder later. Right now he was faced with an attractive, clean-cut young man with a mop of curly blond hair and blue eyes that took him in with a sense of familiarity Geva was unaccustomed to from humans.

"Good morning," Geva said, letting his lips curl into his most charming smile.

The man's eyelids fluttered when the breath carrying

Geva's words reached him. His pupils dilated and then his cheeks flushed brightly when his gaze flicked over to Erika. His eyes rested on her face for a split second before sinking lower. The man cleared his throat and tore his eyes from Erika's chest. He was flustered when he met Geva's gaze again, but made a concerted effort at formality, even going so far as to feign haughtiness.

"How may I help you today, sir?" The man's words came out in an almost seductive drawl. Geva hadn't intended his breath to be more than a calming influence. The reaction surprised him.

Erika muttered a curse. "Remember we're here on business," she said in a low tone. He got the sense she was trying to remind herself of that detail as much as him. He'd seen the way her nipples hardened and pushed against the fabric of her dress when the man's gaze rested there. He'd also seen the way the man had licked his lips at the sight of her. This might be a more rewarding outing than he'd thought.

He reached into his jacket pocket and pulled out the small, flat piece of metal that he'd acquired months ago, shortly after joining the world again after his centuries-long hibernation. The object had no intrinsic value. He'd been informed that the embossed figures on its surface were the true key to his legacy. He had expected an actual key to his family's treasures, something he could shove into a lock, just as he accessed Erika's pleasure on a regular basis. Things were very different now than they had been before he slept.

The man in the cage—"Benjamin," the tag pinned to his lapel proclaimed—took the key and studied it curiously. He glanced at Geva with a somewhat eager expression, picked up the nearby handset and placed it against his ear. After a brief exchange, he nodded, replaced the handset and pointed toward the side of the hall.

"Mr. Hayden, please walk to the double-doors. I will escort you down to the vault."

The man left his post and began traversing the open area behind the other cages. Geva turned in the indicated direction with Erika at his side.

"Hayden, huh?" Erika said. "You didn't tell me that was your name on the sign out front. What else don't I know about you?"

"It was a name my mother chose before I slept. The one she began using then. It's what's marked on this." He held his key out to her.

"Sir Gavin Hayden the Fourth," she read. "Gavin's a nice name. It'll take some getting used to, though. Are you royalty? By human standards, I mean."

"Hmm, minor nobility most likely. We used to seek ruling positions over humans, but it became problematic to maintain the relative anonymity we prefer. And please *don't* call me Gavin when we're alone. Mother was just trying to conform. I've grown to like Geva much more."

Erika gestured at the blond clerk who was scouting his way past the other clerks to meet them at the other side of the room. "Mister Helpful over there certainly knew who you were. That's a far stretch from anonymity for someone who's been out of the public eye for several lifetimes."

"It's his job to know who I am. This is my home. He is a bonded servant of my family. Employee is the right term now, I believe."

"Even your employees are marked?"

"Not as such, no. Their bond isn't permanent."

Benjamin stood waiting by the double-doors. Geva watched his eyes rove over both him and Erika and wondered if the young man had been acquainted with Geva's mother to be so eager. His mother had been striking in her human form. She had been a Green, but more passionate and desiring of power than her own parents. His human father had been an ideal mate, a true partner in all things, the way he hoped Erika would be to him.

"My condolences on your mother's passing, sir. She was well loved." The light flush that colored the back of Benjamin's neck betrayed his true feelings.

"You knew Geva—er—Gavin's mother? What was she like?" Erika asked, picking up her pace to walk beside the young man.

"Beautiful, and very generous. God may strike me down for saying this, but I daresay she was better loved than the Queen."

Erika faltered for a second. "Oh, you mean the Queen of England?"

Benjamin gave her a curious look. "What other Queen is there, ma'am?"

Geva smirked at Erika's amused expression, then bent to whisper in her ear. "Mother *was* our Queen, so it stands to reason."

Erika glanced ahead, but Benjamin had outpaced them and was now out of earshot.

"Your hierarchy confuses the hell out of me. How do you decide who's boss?" she murmured back.

"The Council makes the laws. The Queen is their enforcer, chosen by a combination of familial wealth, gender, and color. Racha was the highest-ranking Green female born to our generation, so they cultivated her as our next Queen. It fits her, but no other dragon could have ranked higher, either."

Benjamin turned and led them down a narrower passageway that Geva knew led to the Keep as well as the dungeon beneath the castle. He was eager to see what modern improvements they had made to the rest of the place. Another heavy door lay ahead, this time with a small, silver box set into the wall to the left of it.

"Swipe your key card and place your thumb like so," Benjamin said, demonstrating.

Geva pulled his key out of his pocket and inspected it. One edge was smoother than the other. He slid it through the groove of the metal box, observed the blinking light, then placed his thumb on the shiny glass window at the top of the box. A heavy click sounded from somewhere inside the door and Benjamin moved to let them through.

Geva became more impressed with the measures of security as he went, but kept his interest to himself. Everything he had seen so far represented his inheritance. He had expected his family's wealth to be his when he awoke. Before he slept he had lived with a sense of entitlement that had only gotten him into trouble. His mother had graciously tolerated his transgressions. His father had inflicted him with passionate lectures about being worthy of the legacy. He'd had centuries since then, during his hibernation, to let it all sink in. Now with the memories of his parents haunting him like ghosts as he traveled the halls of his childhood, he was determined to be a son worthy of those memories. And to be a mate worthy of the beautiful woman at his side.

They descended down the narrow, spiral stone steps into the dungeon.

Erika chuckled. "Deja vu. Are there sleeping dragons down below?"

"Not below," Benjamin said, surprising them both. "The living quarters are in the upper floors of this tower. Lord Hayden liked to call the bedroom 'where the dragon sleeps.' I believe that was his term of endearment for her Ladyship."

"Oh, that's sweet," Erika said, shooting Geva a playful look.

Geva smiled back at her, and when he looked away felt the pleasant squeeze of her hand through the trousers covering his ass. He tensed just slightly under the familiar caress, then let out a hiss of breath when her hand ventured further between his legs from behind. The pressure against the back of his balls sent a jolt into his cock, which became instantly rigid. Sweet Mother, the woman was testing him. He'd have taken her right there on the stairs if he wasn't trying to prove to himself he could assume the role of Lord here.

At yet another heavy door, Benjamin paused and waited for Geva to repeat the unlocking procedure. The young man's eyes widened when he caught a glimpse of Geva's groin. Erika's hand still rested against Geva's hip and she had a devious smile on her face. She was using his reactions to test the other man. Geva didn't exactly disapprove but his focus was faltering as a result.

He wasn't sure what to expect on the other side of the door. His memory of the dungeon was of a place filled with dark corners to hide in, and it had very rarely been used to house prisoners. Considering the level of security, he'd predicted they would find a majority of his family's collection. He wasn't wrong, but the elaborate arrangement of every priceless object was far more impressive than he could have imagined.

The doors of each jail cell had been removed, the small alcoves converted into elaborate displays organized by century.

As they stepped silently down the corridor, Erika gripped his hand, her fingers clasped tightly around his. Her breath sped up and Geva caught the sweet, warm scent of her sex. She was only that aromatic when she was ready to be fucked. And *very* ready if the pink glow of her skin indicated anything.

"This is all yours?" she said, her voice sounding like she had trouble finding the breath for words.

"It's ours," he replied, squeezing her hand.

They reached a wide chamber at the end that had an open staircase leading to the deeper dungeons. The chamber was filled with priceless objects from a time even before Geva had been born, and the pieces were arranged in the manner of a large and luxurious boudoir including rugs, cushions, tapestries, armoires, and chairs. A massive wooden bed featured prominently, the headboard taller than Geva.

Erika gasped. "Is that an original Byzantine bed? And in perfect condition, too. Oh, baby!"

She rushed toward it and brushed her hand reverently over the elaborately carved footboard, then up along one of the columns that supported a heavy red velvet canopy.

Geva had never seen the bed before, but then if his parents had always used parts of the dungeon in this manner, it was no wonder.

"Can I?" Erika asked, making as if to climb onto it. "I don't want to break it."

Benjamin nodded. "It is really quite a sturdy piece of furniture. It has easily held her Ladyship, his Lordship, and guests." Geva shot a surprised look at him and Benjamin stammered. "I—I mean her Ladyship and—oh, bugger."

"Exactly how close were you and my parents, Ben?"

"Ah—um—they were lovely, lovely people. Took me in and made me welcome. And—well, your mum—I should say it was quite a blow when they were killed. In the prime of their lives, too. I'll just—go now. Leave you two with the, er, bed."

Geva resisted the mirth that bubbled forth hearing the young man fumble for an explanation

"Do stay," Geva said, not looking at Benjamin, but watching Erika.

She kicked her shoes off and slid onto the bed, her eyelids fluttering as she sank back against the cushions and velvet. She made pleasant little noises of appreciation and looked for all the world like she didn't even need a partner. She watched him in return, turning on one side to face him and slide her hand down over her body as if to smooth her already wrinkle-free dress.

Instead, the tug of her fingers caused the skirt to slide up over her thighs a little higher until Geva could almost catch a glimpse of the lacy underthings she'd put on that morning. A garment so spare as to be almost pointless, aside from his arousal to see her wear it.

Benjamin was even more enthralled by the sight. Geva stepped over to him and slid his hand across the man's shoulders, then bent and murmured in his ear, "Shall we see if it's sturdy enough for us three?"

Erika was in heaven. The treasure trove of antiquities that Benjamin had led them to was even better than a wet dream. And the bed! It was in pristine condition from top to bottom. It had a real down-filled mattress and velvet bedding. The bedding may have been new, but it was still rich and luxurious and she wanted to be naked on it with Geva fucking her.

She'd all but forgotten about the young clerk who had led them down there. She glanced away from Geva and looked at him. Benjamin was certainly well-built, with broad shoulders, and a trim waist, but nowhere near as tall and imposing as Geva. He did have almost as impressive a bulge in the front of his trousers, however. He couldn't keep his eyes off her, and clenched them shut when Geva whispered something in his ear.

Erika leaned on one elbow and watched, enthralled by Geva's slow seduction. Benjamin had the look like he wanted to turn and run at first, but Geva kept whispering in his ear. Ben's pink tongue darted out and he licked his lips, then opened his eyes again.

The young man's posture tensed for a second, then relaxed as Geva began to undress him. Her lover's movements were gentle, but methodical. He stood behind Ben, tugged his jacket off his shoulders and slid his large hands across Ben's shoulders and down his arms. Cufflinks clinked to the floor and the shirt soon followed.

Geva bent his head to whisper something else in Ben's ear. Ben nodded and Geva looked at her.

"Your turn, my love."

He was making a game of it, and Erika was eager to play. Pleasant tingles raced over her skin and between her legs in anticipation.

She unbuttoned the front of her dress, taking her time to draw it out. Ben's breathing quickened with each inch of flesh she revealed to him. Geva augmented the teasing by beginning slow caresses with his hands up and down Ben's smooth, toned chest and abdomen.

Witnessing the increased flush of arousal in Ben under Geva's touch was far more erotic than she could have anticipated. She'd seen her lover with another man before. He'd seen her with another woman. But something was different about this encounter. Perhaps because their partner this time was human rather than dragon, and completely at their mercy.

Every few seconds Geva would glance back up at her and their gazes would lock. His caress on Ben's skin seemed like a signal to her. His large palm brushed down one of Ben's pectorals and he teased at the man's nipple. In reply, Erika slid her palm down her chest and cupped her breast, teasing her own nipple until it grew as hard as a small pebble beneath the black lace of her bra.

Geva repeated the action with his other hand, so both were now reached around Ben from behind, teasing his tight, pink nipples. The younger man sighed and tilted his head back against Geva's shoulder.

Erika repositioned onto her knees so she could continue the game. She cupped both breasts, pushing them together and squeezing her nipples a little harder. Ben let out a gasp and closed his eyes when Geva followed suit, taking her lead for a change. It was like Ben was a surrogate lover, but she could feel the intensity of sensation just as if Geva's hands were the ones touching her.

She unfastened the remaining buttons of her short dress, leaving herself exposed from the front. She spread her thighs just slightly and slid her palm down the center of her abdomen and over the tingling circle of the Mark Geva had given her during the ritual to awaken the dragons. When she reached her pubic mound, she cupped herself, letting her fingertips sink just a little past the edge of her panties into the slick wetness between her legs.

Geva's nostrils flared and his irises flashed red. His hand slid down and cupped Ben's bulging erection. He bent his head to trail small bites along the young man's neck and shoulder.

Ben moaned and his eyelids fluttered, but he kept them open, avidly watching to see what she would do next.

She reached between her breasts and popped the clasp of her bra. The two halves sprang apart, releasing her breasts to their view. She shrugged out of both bra and dress and cupped her breasts again, squeezing her nipples and thumbing them in slow circles. Her clit throbbed a heavy beat between her thighs.

Geva wrapped one large arm around Ben's chest and unfastened the man's trousers with the other hand. He let out an appreciative rumble when he reached inside and tugged Ben's erection from its confinement.

Ben let out a curse at the first tight stroke of Geva's

expert hand along his shaft. He turned his head to the side, a desperate look in his eyes. Geva accepted Ben's offered mouth, capturing it in a hungry, passionate kiss. He stroked him harder.

Even though he wasn't looking at her, Erika knew he was putting this show on for her benefit, and she loved it. But she wanted more.

Geva tore away from Ben's kiss. The red light flared in his eyes when he looked at her. In a gruff voice he spoke into Ben's ear. "She needs your tongue between those creamy thighs. And I need you to show me this ass."

Ben eagerly kicked off his shoes and dropped his pants. He came toward her with a cocky grin, like he'd just won a prize. "Scoot back," he said to her when he reached the bed.

"Oh, now you're in charge?" she challenged.

He looked a little uncertain and glanced over his shoulder to Geva, who was taking his sweet time undressing.

"You'd better get to work, Benjamin. Don't keep his Lordship waiting. Tell me, did you service the prior Lord and Lady like this, too?" She slid backward on the velvet bedcover as she spoke, encouraging the naked clerk to follow on hands and knees.

When she stopped, leaning back on elbows to watch him, he nodded. He placed a soft kiss against her inner thigh and answered in between more kisses as he traveled up her leg.

"Her Ladyship was a beautiful woman, like you. It was always a pleasure."

She watched the blond curls atop his head move closer. A lock of hair had fallen across his forehead and she brushed it back like she used to do with Eben. She liked to watch a man's face when he started licking between her thighs.

"And his Lordship?" she asked. Ben had reached her panties with his mouth and pressed a harder kiss against the soaked fabric, darting his tongue out to press against her swollen flesh and taste her through the lace.

"Strong and a little forceful."

Erika had trouble controlling her quickened breathing in response to his lips brushing against her pussy. God, would he just take them off her already?

Finally he reached up and tugged at the stretchy lace of the waist and pulled them off, down her hips and thighs.

"Forceful. Did he hurt you?"

"Never. Every moment with them was heaven. I like it a little rough." He looked up at her, his eyes dancing with excitement. "He had a tattoo like this, too," he commented. He bent his head and pressed his lips against her dragon mark.

The tattoo tingled hotly from the contact and Geva let out a low growl, meeting her eyes. His scales were starting to show faintly. He must be hungry for her Nirvana, though she couldn't imagine how, considering the marathon of fucking they'd done in the hotel since they'd arrived in London the week before. In spite of that, her pussy was wet and eager for Ben to have his fill of her.

"Did you let him fuck you?" Erika asked through a haze of pleasure when he began stroking her soaked clit with his thumb. Her gaze followed Geva as he climbed naked onto the bed behind Ben.

Geva's thick erection bobbed as he settled himself and swept his palms down the length of Ben's back and over his ass.

Ben raised his head to look at her and she forced herself to look away from what Geva was doing to meet his eyes. Now it was Ben who tested her resolve, sliding two fingers deep into her clenching slit and pressing his thumb hard against her clit.

"I love getting fucked," he murmured. The words trailed

off into a low moan when Geva dipped his head. Erika caught a glimpse of a forked red tongue snaking out to tease at Ben's ass. She almost wished she could watch from another angle, but what Ben had begun doing to her pussy felt way too amazing.

"Oh, God that's it. Eat me like that."

"Like what?" Ben pulled back with a sly smile.

"Like you're starving for my pussy," she growled. She gripped his head in both hands and shoved his face back between her thighs. He let out a brief laugh against her wet lips, then a gasp of hot breath escaped him.

Her eyes shot back to Geva, who was attentively working fingers in and out of Ben's ass while he stroked the man's cock and balls from behind with the other hand.

The heat in Geva's gaze warmed her with lust as strong as the talented tongue working her clit. The brief divide she'd felt after their heated conversation that morning no longer existed. She wished Ben weren't there and Geva was about to plunge his cock into her, rather than the other man's ready ass. She craved the velvet breadth of him ramming her in his half-changed dragon form, the red monolith of his sex shooting thick, molten spunk so deep she could taste it. And for a brief, irrational second she wished for that seed to take root.

The merest thought of it caused a near-orgasmic spasm to course through her body. Geva's eyes widened, his pupils as red as blood. He plunged his entire length into Ben's ass in one quick, violent stroke.

Ben let out a strangled cry against her pussy and paused briefly, resting his forehead against her belly and squeezing her hips tightly.

"Are you alright?" she breathed.

He nodded and smiled blissfully at her. "Better now. Much better." He bent his head again and tongued and sucked at her pussy with abandon. The plunging force of Geva behind him forced Ben to brace himself with one hand against her breast. His other hand still had three fingers sunk deep into her, steadily fucking.

Erika mewled with pleasure when his pinky finger pressed rigidly against her slick, tight asshole and slipped inside. The tight friction of that tiny invasion made her want even more and she bucked her hips up to meet his thrusting motions, urging him deeper still.

Ben's hair was a chaotic tangle of gold where it bobbed between her thighs. He wore some kind of strange medallion that he'd shoved around to his back so it didn't interfere. The metallic emblem caught her eye briefly, but before she could ponder it further, Geva's free hand gripped her foot where it rested on Ben's shoulder and squeezed.

His red-maned form was bent over Ben's back, thrusting urgently while he pumped Ben's cock. The contact of his thumb against the ball of her foot sent a jolt of pure pleasure through her. She nearly forgot it was another man attending to her pleasure, so lost was she in Geva's passionate, red gaze.

Ben's tongue and steady fucking with his fingers faltered only briefly when Geva's eyes closed and he threw his head back with an ecstatic roar. Another hard thrust and her red dragon lover's entire body clenched and quivered with the force of his orgasm. Erika could imagine the hot pulse of cum Ben was feeling, pushing him into his own stuttering climax. He lost the ability to move for a second, but the curl of his fingers inside her and the press of his lips against her clit were enough to light the blaze of her own orgasm. It burned a scorching fire through her body from her spasming center outward, appearing as a shimmering glow that passed from her mark, moving as though seeking her lover. A similar light flowed from Geva toward her. They passed through Ben and mingled finally in a throbbing pulse at the medallion around his throat.

The dragon shape in the center of the pendant shone like a beacon for a moment before fading back to cold metal. Erika blinked up at Geva in surprise. He rested a hand on it and gave her a little nod that meant, *I'll tell you later.* He slowly eased back from Ben then let himself collapse beside Erika. Ben fell to the other side, one arm draped across her thighs and his forehead pressed against her hip.

Geva dozed amid the luxuriant velvet of the bed, only partly unconscious and still buzzed from the infusion of energy of his two lovers. He could taste them both as distinct as two flavors mingling in his mouth. Erika's a rich, earthy flavor that seemed to underscore everything in his life lately, and Benjamin's a brighter, crisper flavor. They mixed into a delicious combination that would easily arouse him again if he let it. Erika's warm body shifted against his and he opened his eyes a crack to see her rise up, bracing one hand against his chest. She was smiling and flushed. The sparkle in her eye made his heartbeat speed up.

Her scent surrounded him like a pleasant cloud when she leaned over and pressed her lips against his. Geva parted his lips to taste her, letting her in for a deeper kiss and drifting his fingertips over her hip. His eyes opened fully when she pulled back.

"Can we keep him?" she whispered, glancing at the snoozing Benjamin on the other side of her.

"He is already ours," Geva said. "Inherited from my mother, like all bonded humans after one of us dies."

"Doesn't he have a choice?" Erika asked, her brows creasing with concern.

"Of course, but most choose to keep their positions. It's only mates that don't have a choice." Geva paused when another thought occurred to him. "Or did you mean to have the bond made permanent? I could, but...no, it's too soon yet. Perhaps in time."

Erika reached out and touched the medallion that rested in the center of Benjamin's chest, rising and falling slowly with each of the blond's sleeping breaths. "A talisman, huh? A stand-in for the mark?"

"It's a less permanent bond. Not as powerful, and it doesn't allow for full knowledge of our world, but it does provide some advantages depending on how close the bonded human was to the dragon."

"I get the sense he was very loyal to your parents. Tell me, do you know how they died?"

"Making love, most likely."

Erika lay down against him again, her head resting against his shoulder. Benjamin shifted in his sleep and wrapped an arm around her, nuzzled against her neck, took a deep breath, then relaxed back into slumber again. Geva knew the comfort of her scent in sleep.

"Making love killed them?"

Geva chuckled. "No, but at the end of our lives, we can choose to just let our energy fade away until we're no more, or channel our last remaining living power into a vessel for the next generation. Most mated couples make a pact as such. There will be documentation in the lower dungeon. A letter from Mother explaining where she channeled their energy at the end."

He glanced at Benjamin, but the younger man was still sleeping soundly, drooling slightly on the back of Erika's shoulder. He smirked, and wondered how long the man had served his parents. It could have been decades or only a few years. Even without a mated bond, dragon magic could make a person seem ageless.

The itch to find his legacy had seeped into Geva's blood since arriving here, and now replaced the languid buzz from the sex. As always, Erika seemed attuned to his mood and gently nudged Benjamin awake. He blinked sleepily and nodded, rising.

"This is as far as I go with you two," Benjamin said. He gestured to a nondescript door nearby. "The loo is through there. The staircase will take you down to the lower dungeon." He let out an involuntary snicker.

Geva raised a brow. Benjamin responded with a twitch of his shoulder. "His Lordship joked about sending your mother down to the dungeon on occasion. I always pictured leather contraptions bolted to the walls and torture devices, but was never allowed inside. Not once in thirty-five years."

Erika cocked her head while fastening the buttons of her dress. "How old are you, Ben?"

He looked abashed and stammered for a second. He glanced between both Geva and Erika. "Ah, right, you would know about the Lord and Lady's unique status. I took over as their body man for my mum after she passed, when I was twenty-five. That was thirty-five years ago."

Without missing a beat, Erika said, "Well, I look forward to a long relationship. You are always welcome." She bent over to pull on her shoes, giving both men a generous eyeful of cleavage.

Geva was grateful for Erika's noncommittal reaction, and how deftly she managed to distract Benjamin from his embarrassment. Benjamin headed back up after explaining he would meet them in the upper tower that evening. After he departed, they headed down to the lower vault.

Like the rest of the manor Geva had seen, the lower

dungeon was different from what he remembered. The walls were more polished, with electric lights at intervals. It wasn't the dank, dreary dungeon he used to hide in as a child. Yet another secure door blocked their path at the bottom of the spiral staircase, this one with familiar old runes carved in the stone in the spot where the other doors had held an electronic lock.

"What does it say?" Erika asked, brushing her finger over the worn, recessed figures.

"Take a breath," he said with a smile. "Something Mother used to say to me when I threw tantrums as a dragonling."

"You mean to tell me you weren't a perfectly behaved little angel as a child?" She batted her eyelashes at him innocently

"Dragons rarely change their colors," he replied, with an impish smile.

He instinctively felt for the well of fresh energy from their lovemaking session above, and breathed a cloud of red smoke into the door latch. The door opened inward without a touch. Bright lights came on, illuminating sealed glass cases that displayed his family's most valuable artifacts. Objects that had not seen un-mated human eyes for centuries and more. The walls of the room were all polished granite, the floors the same, buffed to a high shine with not a single speck of dust present. It had to have been magically sealed since his mother's death to have remained so clean inside.

A beep and a whir sounded from the far end of the room. Geva strode with Erika by his side to an alcove amid the cases, within which rested an object similar to the modern gadgets Erika had introduced him to.

"It's an IBM," Erika said in amazement. "An older model. I wish Corey were here, but maybe we can make some sense of it without him. It has to be nearly thirty years old… almost before my time."

Geva blinked at the string of characters that flashed green across the dark screen. He smiled. "Mother's color," he said.

Erika glanced at him and shook her head. "Most of these things came in green back then," she said. "Green or gold on black. Sometimes white or even blue. This is all gibberish, though."

Geva nudged her aside. "It's perfectly legible. Mother always insisted on having the most modern contraptions. You would have loved her."

"What does it say?"

"Dragon secrets," he said with a smirk, earning him an elbow to the ribs. "It's mostly a recounting of their lives since my hibernation. This isn't the only vault of treasures, just the most valuable ones." He rested his finger on one of the keys and the text began to flow slowly up the screen. The flow of words paused when he lifted his finger off the button. "Here she talks about a Benjamin—*brilliant inventor*—she says. Do you think she means our Benjamin?"

Erika gave him a quizzical look. "It sounded like our Ben was born in fifty-five—definitely proof that humans age well around you guys. Does she give a timeline?"

"Hmm, met in seventeen fifty-three. I guess that was a few years early."

"Geva, that's about two centuries too early. She's talking about Benjamin *Franklin*. You have a lot of reading to do on the last five centuries, sweetie."

He laughed, but resolved to spend some more time hunting for collections of the videos and books she had shown him so far to catch up on all he'd missed. At least he'd focus on the things his parents had lived through so he would have some frame of reference.

He kept skimming, pausing every few lines to read off a name for Erika. Each one impressed him more than the last. He paused and swallowed harshly at the emotions that welled up. Partly lingering sadness at not being able to introduce his mother to the amazing woman who stood at his side, and partly profound irritation that every generation still had to follow the Council's ridiculous laws of hibernation.

"What is it?" Erika asked, tracing gentle fingertips through the hair at his temple.

He shook his head, blinking back tears and clearing his throat.

She moved closer and urged his arm around her, embracing him and resting her cheek against his chest. He lowered his nose to the top of her head and took a deep breath, letting the scent of her ease his brief anguish.

"My father would have loved you," Erika whispered in the middle of his silence. "I miss him so much now. I'd never be able to keep you a secret from him, either, I don't care if we would've broken laws to tell him."

Geva kissed the top of her head and moved on, scrolling further. Judging by the date at the top of each entry he was close to reaching the current year. Only a few decades to go.

A few lines made him stop abruptly and backtrack. His stomach clenched at what he'd read. He scrolled forward quickly to the very end of the entries, then back again. He pushed Erika gently away so he could look more closely.

"Sweet Mother," he whispered, and began reading out loud to Erika.

"Your father brought a new friend to the Manor tonight. Or, rather, a very, very old friend. I had not seen Warik since my youth in Greenland where we were raised together as dragonlings. After all the centuries he has never mated. Eternally alone, he promised he would stay after we parted, but as the Queen my responsibilities were to the Brood. I had to take a human mate. I pray that will change in your time. I love your father, but would have chosen

differently had I had the option. In a perfect world perhaps I could have even had them both.

"Your father is thick as thieves with Warik, even after a few days and knowing my history with him. Your father was never a jealous man, which is an excellent quality in a mate. We have enjoyed the centuries largely in each other's exclusive company, except for the occasional diversion—Benjamin being the latest. Do take good care of Benjamin, he is dear to us."

"Wow," Erika breathed when Geva paused.

His mind reeled at what he'd already read. He had to have her hear it all before he would believe it, however.

"Can you re-read his name?" Erika asked.

Geva did, pronouncing all five syllables for her, rather than the shortened version as he'd read it. *Aiwarikar.* He watched her brow crease the way it always did when she was reaching back into the wellspring of history she kept locked away in her mind. "Is it familiar to you? I suppose it does sound like your own name a bit. *Erika.*"

"Yes, but I don't think it's important to the story. Just an interesting tidbit, considering the timing. He was pretty damn famous figure if he is who I believe."

"She skips ahead several years here," he said, and continued reading. Erika's fingernails began to dig into his arm before he was finished.

"I am the example held up by the Council for the rest of the Brood to follow. I have failed in my duty but do not regret it. Warik and Bertram are beside me in this as well. When the child—your half-sister—is born, Warik and I have resolved to spend our last remaining power to bind her magic, then hide her from the Coun-cil. If they find her and take her, they will execute us and she will be forced to live as an Unbound. We will not relegate her to slavery. It is near time for the Awakening, but there is no more time for us. Please, my dearest son, find your sister and help her learn her heritage. Keep her safe and perhaps appeal to the Council to change

their laws. Warik and I had no blood relations in common, and we will give her every last drop of our love and passion upon her birth. It will be with your father's last breath that he sees her safe somewhere far from here, where the Council will not look. He hasn't told me where that will be, but the Verdanith can find her. Just find a way to make the Council let you use it without betraying your sister's existence. We mean to name her Rowan, a name that is as much a human name as it represents her dragon legacy, and that is all that I can tell you."

"Is that the end?"

"She says she loves me and to never compromise destiny for someone else's rules."

Geva's head spun. He looked around the room but there was nowhere to sit. Then he remembered one of the last things he had read. He rushed to the glass cases, frantically looking for it.

"Tell me what it is, I can help," Erika said.

Geva shot the words over his shoulder. "The Verdanith, it's a wedge-shaped piece of a disc carved from jade, about the size of my hand. Green like those characters on the screen."

"Here!" Erika tapped at the latch of a case near the center of the room. "What is it?"

"My sister's salvation."

CHAPTER FOUR

The two of them spent the afternoon moving out of the hotel and into the living quarters at the Manor, which had taken a single trip considering the sparse belongings they carried with them.

In spite of her nomadic tendencies, Erika wasn't a stranger to living rich like this—she'd grown up wealthy, after all—but after roughing it in the field for her studies and then work her entire adult life, it felt indulgent to be immersed in the luxury of royalty. After six months of living like an academic, with late nights in labs and hotel rooms—a situation Erika was accustomed to—this situation was suddenly very domestic and took a lot of getting used to.

Settling into a shared domicile that *wasn't* temporary felt odd. Deciding on a bathroom. Deciding on shared closet space. Not that Geva had that much in the way of clothing aside from the single suit they'd bought for him the week before, and the odd necessities. It helped that it was all as foreign to him as it was to her, at least, in spite of it being his family home.

He'd developed a rather odd attachment to Erika's bath

products over the last six months. To the point she had to scramble to order more. She'd been relieved to discover the obscure organic-only company was still in business. Then winced at their increased prices. But how do you keep a dragon happy? Especially if he wants expensive bath products.

It was both irritating and comforting. She didn't have an issue finding him bath products, and she loved his presence, particularly how eager he was to tell her everything he knew about the era he'd lived in. She'd really have loved to chat with his mother, though. The woman who'd actually *lived* through the last five hundred years.

For the first few months since she'd found Geva, she and her team had lost sleep finalizing their paper, then published to outstanding response. It had earned them lucrative grants and a brief moment in the academic limelight. In the past they would have been reeling from the attention, but in light of their fresh secrets the entire team was ready to slink back into the shadows and enjoy their true accomplishment out of the public eye.

She and the others had had to drastically alter their paper before publishing, but the Queen had allowed the collection of a handful of priceless objects to be taken and displayed.

Now she and Geva sat at their dinner table, basking in the moonlight that came through the tall window of the Manor's East Tower and the flickering candlelight that Ben had provided. The flames of the candles were nothing compared to the object that captured their attention now that they were done eating.

Erika stared at the carved jade fragment they'd brought up from the vault earlier. There was something incredibly familiar about it, but she couldn't put her finger on it. She'd seen so many jade dragon artifacts over the six months since their expedition, they all bled together.

This particular object resembled the other artifacts in some way, yet there was something different about it. When she touched it, she felt a pulse of power, the same as she'd felt at each of the doors she'd touched within the Temple—particularly the one that led her to Geva.

The slab of green jade sparkled in the center of the table now, monolithic in its significance in spite of its wedge shape only being half the size of a dinner plate. Erika chewed on her lower lip. Geva kept pulling at the cowlick on the side of his forehead where his right horn normally appeared when he was half-shifted during sex.

"We need to call the Queen," he said.

By his inflection she took his meaning: *She* needed to call *Corey*. His reluctance to show his face to the Queen was almost comical considering how imposing a man he was in general. Yet there was no denying the Queen's distrust of him, even after her show of support. Erika wondered if it was due to his lineage or for some other reason. She definitely didn't believe Geva's assertion that it was because he'd acted out when he was younger.

"And what would you like me to tell Corey?"

Geva glared at her for a second, then sighed. "The entire Court has to agree to the assembly of the Verdanith for it to happen."

"So, why won't you ask?"

"It's a matter of propriety. No one ever wants to be the first to ask. It makes us seem desperate. It's just…customary for things to happen this way."

"Well, you need to get over your adherence to custom."

"It's not that easy. The Council is *very* strict where custom is concerned. If we don't observe the required process, we could fail."

"So, I'll just call the others and ask…" She paused when he began shaking his head. "What?"

"They won't say anything. It's like a contest. You have no idea how competitive we are, do you?"

"But they're my *friends!*"

"What your friends believe will have no effect. What the other members of the Court believe will, and we are far from united, in the Queen's eyes. But if we can win over the Queen, we will have a true advantage."

Erika found that hard to believe, considering how tight-knit she was with her team, but then she hadn't spent much time with the other members of the Dragon Court since they'd left the Temple.

"And we can't outright say we need it to help find your sister, either. So what's our alternative?"

His jaw clenched and he gave her a sidelong look before averting his eyes. "We have to convince her we want it to assist in conceiving. That's the reason everyone else will likely use. Once the Queen hears from all of us—sees we are united—she will take the request to the Council."

She was about to ask how the hell it could help with that, but held her tongue. If it could help them locate Geva's sister, she shouldn't be surprised.

"So, what works? What did your ancestors do to convince the Council?"

"They've never said yes."

Erika couldn't quite believe what she was about to suggest. "What if we steal the pieces? Wait, don't answer that, it's a dumb idea. We'd completely compromise your sister if we did that."

"It's also impossible. You saw the security to get into our vault. The others would have similar measures in place. The Queen might not report us over it, but the Council would definitely know who'd stolen it. It's really a simple request. We will sacrifice rank by making the request prematurely, but the others will follow suit quickly."

"So, we convince the Queen we want to have a baby. I'm a pretty decent actress when I want to be." Even though it would be a blatant lie, she'd compromised her principles for less. "Besides, it's Corey we'll be talking to. I've known him for years, he's got a huge soft spot for me."

Geva looked more optimistic at that. "Alright. Shall I join you for the picture palaver?"

Erika stood up and bent to kiss him. "Video conference," she corrected, pulling back and squeezing his cheeks between the thumb and fingers of one hand until his lips scrunched together. "Yes, I think it would be a good show of intent if you were with me, don't you? Corey likes you."

Geva's eyelids lowered just slightly and his expression grew thoughtful, a look Erika had grown accustomed to over the past few months, and it made her grow a little warm between the thighs every time. She resisted the temptation to climb onto his lap and take advantage of his infinite libido. It was a particular challenge tonight, too. Ever since their tryst with Benjamin that morning, she'd been aware of a subtle shift in the dynamic between Geva and herself. As if they were even more attuned to each other's emotions. He'd been agitated to distraction about the bomb his mother's journals had dropped, but rather than withdraw from her, he'd been more amorous to the point of desperation, like he was driven by raw need for her Nirvana.

"Come on. The sooner we get this done, the sooner we can find your sister."

Erika retreated to the ornate bathroom attached to what Ben had informed her were her 'quarters,' though she and Geva had decided to share the smaller, more intimate bedroom on the opposite side of the floor. She wasn't oblivious to Geva's wistful glance when she nudged him toward the other bathroom, giving the excuse of not wanting any distractions because they were on a timetable.

The truth was they hadn't been apart for almost six months since she and her team had completed the ritual to awaken the dragons. They had spent a brief and luxurious week in a Monastery on a remote island in the South China Sea—a place Erika had thought of as a sort of halfway house for dragons. The the human occupants of the Monastery might have been a sect of Buddhist monks, but it had soon become apparent that they were all very aware of who their new visitors were. It also became apparent that several of the long-term residents of the Monastery were a servant-class of dragons who hadn't been part of the Brood that slept in the temple.

These dragon monks had piqued Erika's curiosity, but when asked, Geva had evaded the question. Even after needling him about it he finally whispered that they didn't talk about the *Unbound.* She resolved to get the answers out of him one way or the other, and hearing that term again in his mother's journal added another piece to the puzzle.

The rest of their time before moving to London had been spent traveling back to the Temple, collecting more data and a few artifacts. When she and her team were busy preparing their paper, she had corresponded with her team remotely from a collection of hotels around the world, in cities where other experts existed who could validate the authenticity of their artifacts. It had been the Queen, Racha, who had dictated the terms of their use of the data they had collected from the Temple and she had reviewed and signed off on the final submission of the paper to the most elite journals in Erika's field.

The only time she and Geva had been out of sight of each other since they'd left the Temple had been during the secret meeting he and the other Court dragons had attended, high atop the mountain on that tiny island. The Council had important things to say that the human mates couldn't be privy to, but it just made Erika wonder who this elusive Council was.

Geva hadn't been inclined to share the details of that meeting at first, only saying that they had accomplished more than he'd expected. All she'd figured out was that 'dragon law' required the Court and the Brood along with it to disperse to the four corners of the Earth. The reasoning for that was vague, but Camille had suggested their laws assigned each dragon a jurisdiction. Geva had confirmed that suggestion when they moved to London.

He was literally royalty, in the dragon sense, and his 'kingdom', as it were, encompassed all of the United Kingdom and Scandinavia.

The locales of the others began to make more sense to her after that, though there were really *six* corners to the Earth if their assignments were any indication. She'd begun to see the pattern with them as well. The number six kept recurring. Six dragon colors, six ultimate matings among her team, six separate fragments of the magical artifact they were trying to assemble.

Six generations, Geva had said, since they'd been forced into these cycles. He'd only said it once, then grew broody and muttered something about how six was enough. Erika had been reminded of her father complaining about politics not long before he died.

She stepped under the steaming water of the shower with a sense of sadness and a sudden pang of homesickness. Not for the huge, empty house she'd left behind in Boston when she started college, but for the memory of that same house when her father was alive and it still felt like home to her. She longed to share the success of her discovery with her father.

At first it was a sense of pride and excitement over confirming what her father had always believed was the truth but had never proved. Today, however, she had the strongest wish that Geva and her father had had the chance to meet. It was absurd to think she saw aspects of her father in her lover. She was probably projecting due to having too much time on her hands now and feeling particularly sentimental.

"My legacy is your destiny," she remembered her father saying when she was a teenager testing her boundaries and rebelling against his need to share his life's work with her. *"You'll understand when you have your own child. The need to pass this on will become a priority. I won't live forever, Erika."*

She'd of course rolled her eyes at that comment. Gabriel Rosencrans was strength personified—immortal in her own eyes. Now she realized he'd been making more frequent comments about his own mortality at the time. It wasn't until the cancer had advanced beyond his ability to hide it that he finally told her he was dying.

And to think if he'd found the Temple and mated a dragon he might have lived. Here she was instead, carrying on her father's work but with no young, bright, inquisitive mind to impart any of that wisdom to. It had never occurred to her what she might have meant to her father until now. She'd filled his shoes in so many ways. Could she follow in those footsteps, too? And not just in the sense of an academic sharing her knowledge with younger peers, but that of a parent influencing the mind of her own child.

Geva wanted it. Of course, it was instinctual for dragons. There were so few of them left in the world and so little time relative to their life spans and the schedule their laws imposed on them. Was she being selfish withholding that from him?

They still had time by her own standards. Decades, even. Was it selfish for her to want to wait just a little longer? *Yeah, but for how long?* The next big discovery could have her in the field hunting for a decade for all she knew. She had just assumed he would come with her. Would he? *Could* he?

The conception and nurturing of her work involved objects that had been hidden for centuries and were crying out to be found. What was a decade of study and searching in the scheme of ageless antiquities? Especially now that she had a seemingly infinite amount of time in which to find more lost treasures if her link to Geva really did what he said it would. She had no reason to doubt him.

She stepped out of the shower and wrapped a towel around her torso. Swiping the steam away from the mirror, she scowled at her reflection. A few years for her to regain her balance after the last six months. That shouldn't be unreasonable to ask. With that thought she forced herself to stop thinking about it.

She had a tricky meeting in store for her and was determined to make it productive, which meant looking the part of someone who recognized not only the power she had, but the power of the person she'd be talking to. Even if Corey generally answered to her in the world of jungle treks and ancient digs, in the dragon world he was technically her superior now. The shift in hierarchy definitely wasn't lost on her.

Finding Geva's sister had to be a priority now. The girl's existence was a fresh mystery for her to solve and the prospect excited her as much as learning what this Verdanith artifact could really do once whole again. She wondered if the rest of her team even had the thing on their radar or if they were too busy enjoying the lull after submitting their paper to even think about it.

Hair and makeup done, she donned a low-cut red blouse and gray pencil skirt. Red flattered her, she decided, looking at the whole package in the full-length mirror. It never hurt to give Corey a little visual candy either. He may be a gentleman when it came to talking to women, but that didn't mean he wasn't a red-blooded man who appreciated beauty and sensuality. If anything, he'd been even more overt in his appreciation since becoming the Queen's consort, as if he'd needed permission from a strong woman to let himself out of that reserved shell of his.

Geva was already standing by the office window when she made it down. She paused in the doorway for a second, taking him in. "Wow, you really aren't screwing around, are you? Did Benjamin help?"

"I can dress myself, you know," he said with mock offense, but lowered his eyes and then smiled and nodded. "I called him when you abandoned me to my own devices. The suit was Warik's—father's would be too small and the one I bought last week was…not suitable for wearing after this morning."

"And the hair…?" Erika gestured wide-eyed at the now short-cropped russet hair on his head. It was a far cry from the tousled red mane she was used to.

Geva self-consciously ran a hand through his gelled hair, causing it to rise into spikes. He grimaced at his hand and tugged a handkerchief out of his pocket to wipe off the sticky residue. "I want to look professional. Serious. This is impor-tant. *Rowan* is important."

Erika smiled and stepped closer to comb her fingers through his hair, straightening it with a few swipes. "And green eyes, too," she said, peering up into his eyes that were normally a dull brown. "Be still my heart."

"Mother's color. It seemed right to honor her in some way when I'm about to appeal to her successor for help." His gaze lingered on hers, perhaps seeking approval.

Even in high heels she still had to stand on tip-toe to kiss him. She caressed his cheek and gave him a swift peck, pulling away before she could get sucked into the passionate whirlwind that was their sex life. She had work to do. Not her favorite kind of work, but perhaps even more important.

She took a deep breath and turned back to the desk, mentally preparing herself for the posturing and competitive volley she knew would happen once she was face-to-face with Corey.

Too big for his britches, she thought before reprimanding herself. If anything, her old friend's new role seemed to agree with him. He was finally in charge of a group of people who *had* to do what he told them. A rather large group, at that, comprising the entire tech team of the Aris Technical Corporation the new Queen was CEO of.

With a swipe of the mouse, the wide, flat monitor of her computer came to life, the camera scanning her features and logging her in via facial recognition. The video conference app activated from her vocal command, transferring her desktop along with her figure to one half of the massive flatscreen on the office wall. The outline of an anonymous avatar was displayed in the inactive half of the call.

"Jesus, your parents didn't fuck around with tech," Erika commented.

"Mother was always ahead of the trends, particularly if she could make money with them, but it was Benjamin who did all this. Part of Mother's final instructions to him."

"Dial Aris Tech," Erika said out loud. Geva came around to her side of the desk and stood within the camera's wide frame just behind her. Her skin tingled at the brief, delicate warmth of his fingertips through the thin fabric of her blouse when he brushed her hip. She caught a glimpse in the widescreen of both of his hands starting to reach for her then clench into fists before he shoved them deep into the pockets of his trousers.

A terse, female voice answered. "Good morning, Aris Technical Corporation. How may I direct your call?"

"Hayden Antiquities calling for Mr. Monaghan."

"Thank you. One moment."

A split second later, Corey's handsome, smirking face appeared, filling the void in the other half of the screen. "Somehow I knew it would be you, Erika. Geva. And judging from the getup, this is a business call, am I right?" He eyed them both from the top down.

Erika hadn't known quite what to expect, but the last thing on her list was the sight of Corey in a suit and tie, seated comfortably in what looked like the corner office of a skyscraper. The late afternoon vista of the Boston Harbor out Corey's expansive windows caused a fresh pang of homesickness to twist in her belly. She quickly gathered her wits.

"You in a tie. Wow, Racha's really turned you around, hasn't she? Nice view."

Corey chuckled. "It's my job to look the part for clients, but since it's just you…" He stood and slipped out of his jacket, loosened his tie, and rolled up his shirt sleeves. "That better?" His bright smile caused the corners of his eyes to crinkle attractively, the only remnant that showed his age. All in all he actually looked younger and more at ease than usual. He leaned forward onto the desk, an expectant look on his face. Somehow he still looked slightly amused at receiving the call.

"Spit it out," he said.

"Geva and I would like to formally submit our petition to —ah—assemble the Verdanith."

Corey nodded solemnly. "Geva probably knows that as the Queen's proxy I have to ask you a few questions. But we can save some time if you just answer one. Why?""

"Jesus, Corey. What do you think? I've been in the field for years. My time's running out. I want to carry on my father's legacy."

"Hunting for things that don't exist? No offense, Geva."

"No! I want to…" She swallowed. She'd never had issues lying to get what she wanted, but this particular excuse lodged in her throat. "I want a… a daughter to carry on Dad's legacy."

"I knew it!" Corey sat back in his chair, then pointed at her. "But I don't believe you. The others I believed. Hallie was obvious. Would you believe Camille wants to see if it'll give her twins? One from each of them. Dimitri made the best case—honoring his brother, of course."

Erika blinked in surprise that bordered on humiliation. They had all called already? "What about Kris and Issa?" she asked dumbly.

Corey waved his hand dismissively. "They don't really need it, as much magic as they have between them. Kris still called as a courtesy."

Geva's voice broke through behind her. "Prismatics have never had the same fertility issues as the rest of us."

"Ah, is that it?" Corey asked. "I wondered. But as much as I love you two, Racha—the Queen, I mean—well, she doesn't trust you, Geva. I think she irrationally mistrusts Reds in general and there's no talking her out of it."

"Her father was a Red," Geva grumbled.

"Does she trust me?" Erika asked, irritated.

"Alone, yes. But as a couple she naturally assumes Geva's the one in control. I tried to convince her otherwise, but…" He shrugged.

"So, convince her! You have her trust, and you trust me, don't you, Corey?" Erika asked, growing agitated at his flippant attitude.

He grabbed a baseball off his desk and started tossing it into the air and catching it. Erika got the feeling he enjoyed having the upper hand for a change and wondered if he'd secretly hated having to answer to her since working together. But he still had to answer to Racha.

Corey caught the ball and held it. His expression grew more serious when he looked at her. "I won't lie to you, Erika. I know you and I think it's a huge stretch asking me to believe that you ever wanted kids. If Geva really *was* the alpha in your relationship I might, but look at the two of you." He gestured toward them.

Shit. He was right. They hadn't thought this through very well at all, had they? Given Geva's intense personality, he might have been able to convince Corey if they'd spoken one-on-one. But Erika had already blown it merely by taking the initiative, something that was second nature to her.

Geva seemed to sense her agitation and shifted closer. He pulled his hands out of his pockets and smoothed one palm up her back. The touch calmed her, but she was out of ideas.

Corey's smirk returned, mischievous now and entirely infuriating. "I'll throw you a bone. Convince *me* you want it and I'll tell the Queen."

"How the fuck am I supposed to do that if you know me so well already?" Erika snapped. "Jesus, Corey, after everything we've been through, do you have to hold out on me like this?"

With a raised eyebrow, Corey glanced past Erika at Geva, his expression seemed to ask, *"Is this what you have to deal with?"*

"He can't lie to the Queen, you know that," Geva said. "If he doesn't believe what he tells her, she'll know." His hand had drifted down her hip and squeezed comfortingly. The firm touch was just enough to send a pleasant warmth into her core.

Erika sighed. "I know. What do you suggest, Corey?"

"Well, you could tell me what you really want with it. You always have an ulterior motive when it comes to hunting for ancient treasures, after all. Or…Convince me you want the pieces reunited for the stated reason, the same reason all the others want it to happen. To help you get pregnant."

"I can't do that. Not if my word isn't good enough." She knew better than to try, even. He was so good at reading her, if he even caught her in a lie…

"Oh, I think you should at least try. You know I'm from a big family. You've even met some of them. I have…" He held up a hand, counting his fingers. "Six nieces and six nephews. Kids are amazing. Believe me, Racha and I want this to happen as much as the rest, but it has to be unanimous among the Court before it has a chance of being approved by the Council. Tell me you never even *thought* about it. Not once when that huge Red's cock was buried inside you. Tell me it never crossed your mind to share something that profound with him in the last six months."

Geva's touch had grown distracting, the heat of his caress against her back sinking into her skin as deeply as Corey's words into her mind.

"What are you saying?"

"I'm saying *show me* how much you want it. Let me see the intent for myself." He began unbuttoning his shirt.

When it was halfway open, displaying the dark hair on his muscular chest, he pulled it apart. The large, green emblem etched into his left pectoral glowed slightly.

He leaned forward and touched the glowing dragon mark, his expression fierce and intimidating. "*This* is what it looks like when you're trying like hell to make it happen. When you're primed and willing. Show me yours."

"Show you my mark? *Now?*" Hers never glowed except right as she orgasmed. The glow never lingered.

"Yeah," he said with a devious smile. "I showed you mine…"

Geva's lips nuzzled against her ear. "Show him, love." He

had one hand gripping her hip, the other splayed across her stomach with his thumb casually caressing the side of her breast. "If I tease you enough, we can make him believe it," Geva whispered. When he pressed his steel-hard length against her backside she was done for.

"Oh, God. Alright, *alright.*"

Corey sat back with a self-satisfied smirk. "And go slow, if you don't mind."

She glared at him. "Am I looking at the same man who refused to believe, or even participate in the ritual until he had no other choice?"

"Call me a convert. Either way, I guess I just have a thing for getting spun up just before I go see my girl. Not that I need the incentive of course... Racha just likes it if I'm especially needy. Come on, I've seen you two going at it a few times already. Make it worth my time. And trust me, I *will* know if you're faking it."

"Christ," Erika muttered, but she'd already begun to glaze over from Geva's attentive touch that had moved from teasing caresses below her breast, to a hand slipping inside her blouse and fingers squeezing her nipple.

He pushed her hair aside and nipped at the column of her throat. He tugged the hem of her skirt up and slipped one hand beneath it from behind, rumbled a deep sound of interest at the sparse strip of lace he encountered before sliding his fingers between her legs.

"You and your panties. I wish I could see you in these and nothing else," he murmured behind her.

Erika moaned as he deftly worked her clit between his fingertips. She bent forward, bracing her hands on the surface of her desk. She met Corey's eyes in the video.

"Fuck you, Corey."

"Oh, you must hate this, but trust me I'm doing you a favor. All it takes is wanting it just enough."

She caught a glimpse of her own captured video feed, as it displayed her flushed cheeks and her teeth biting hard against her lower lip while Geva attended her from behind. He still watched over her shoulder with his hand between her legs.

He stopped stroking her abruptly and grinned, then reached around her waist and yanked at the front of her shirt. The tiny red buttons flew off and her blouse hung open. He grasped the edges of her lacy bra and tugged down, letting her full breasts spill over the top.

"He wants a show," he rumbled, tugging mercilessly at her nipples until she pressed her ass back against his erection.

"That's right I do," Corey said.

Erika watched the monitor distractedly, half aware of both sides of the exchange, but not quite comprehending either enough for anything to register. Only Geva's hands on her skin and his breath in her ear mattered to her.

"Get rid of the skirt," Corey said in a thick voice. He took a long swallow from a glass of water and scooted forward in his chair. He hadn't buttoned up his shirt and Erika fixated on the glowing emblem on one side of his chest. *All it takes is wanting it just enough.* How much was enough?

She didn't argue when Geva unzipped her skirt and shoved it down off her hips. Her panties went next, leaving her only in her destroyed blouse and dislodged bra.

"Tsk tsk," Corey said, catching a glimpse of her mark just above her pubic bone. "I don't see it glowing. You're going to have to do better than that. Much better."

"You like getting off to watching me squirm, is that it?" she asked.

He raised both hands. "Hey, no getting off on this side of the call. I'm just waiting for you to prove yourself. You want some help? Maybe the idea of your Red's hot, potent spunk shooting into your wet snatch and taking root will get you hot enough to want it. He looks virile enough. It's just the stupid magic that keeps him from knocking you up. How many times have you fucked him already? I know for a fact none of you bother with birth control anymore. Doesn't it excite you just a little bit to feel like you're throwing caution to the wind every time? That it *might just happen* but you don't really care because dragon law says you can't if you don't want it enough."

God, he knew her well. And she did feel that way, now that she watched Geva quickly strip behind her. He gleamed a little redder than usual and her pussy clenched in anticipation. He would shift completely if she asked him to, but she wanted his hands on her still, his lips against her throat. And most of all she wanted that beautiful cock buried in her. Fucking her.

It might have occurred to her to put a condom on him once after they left the Temple, but the truth was she had always enjoyed the thrill until the other day when he'd first broached the topic of actually conceiving. Now that the idea was a pure and present concept hanging between them she felt hotter, needier than she ever had.

"That's right, Erika. He hasn't even made you come yet. You do want it, don't you?"

She tore her eyes away from the image of Geva behind her, and the distraction of his reverent kneading of her ass. She shuddered when he pressed his cock between her creamy folds and slid in deep.

She looked back at the screen in a daze. Corey's eyes were fixed on a location at the lower edge, near the desk. She followed the direction of his gaze and saw herself in disarray, bent over the desk, breasts pushed up obscenely high and hard nipples pointing directly at the camera. But below all that was her mark, glowing bright, neon red and pulsing with each thrust of Geva's cock deep into her.

"Oh, that's right you fucking *stud*. Fuck her good. Sink that shaft into her hard. Make sure it goes deep so all your hot come gets up inside her." Corey bit his lip and clenched his brow, his eyes now watching Geva's fingertips dance over Erika's clit, halfway obscuring the embarrassing brightness of her mark.

She wondered with the tiny part of her brain that was coherent whether Geva had noticed, but decided she didn't really care. She loved him, she wanted him, and she wanted more than anything to have something even more tangible to prove everything she felt, and to prove to herself that her life had some meaning beyond her work. That something beautiful and real could come out of the depth of feelings they shared, the all-consuming passion that gripped them in moments like this, would be a miracle.

"Yes," she whispered, and then moaned at the deep thrust of his cock and the way the thickening, ridged head of it rubbed along the sensitive walls of her tight channel. He paused at the apex of his passage and their eyes met in the video reflection in the widescreen above them.

Geva's brows drew together in confusion, and then he saw the glowing mark above the dark triangle of hair between her thighs. He buried his head against her neck, inhaling the scent of her hair and skin like he always did, but this time he let out a slight laugh combined with a moan and began fucking her in earnest.

"You want this?" he asked, sounding almost like he didn't believe her. "You want my seed to grow, you want...my child?"

"Oh, baby. I didn't think I did, but I do. I do. Fuck me harder. Make it happen."

Geva growled behind her, the urgency of his thrusts growing more intense. His skin seemed white hot against hers. He gripped the back of her neck and pushed, forcing her to bend further over the desk until her cheek was pressed flat against the polished antique wood, her breasts squashed against the blotter that protected the surface. She reached hands out to grip the edges, and darted a look at the desktop monitor that was still just within sight the way she had her head tilted. The monitor still displayed the images that were reflected in the widescreen above them. She smiled when she saw Geva's half-shifted form behind her, his eyes glowing red and his skin erupting into jeweled scales. His huge horns cast shadows against the wall behind him. He was magnificent like this. And he was hers.

His cock pressed even tighter and hotter into her, stretching her with each violent thrust. Her eyelids fluttered closed from the pleasure. He was keeping her on the edge to draw it out, she thought.

Corey smiled smugly in the monitor, the only thing she could see from her restricted vantage point. Just before his half of the screen went blank and she lapsed into the distracted spasms of a body-gripping orgasm, she heard him murmur, "You're welcome."

CHAPTER FIVE

*C*orey sat back in his leather desk chair staring at the now blank screen in front of him. In spite of the cool air in his office he was sweating and his dick was impossibly hard. Jesus, the two of them could set off fire alarms as hot as they were. He'd enjoyed inciting them, forcing Erika to give in just once and see her lose control to the point of confessing a deep desire he believed she'd always had. He still remembered a time when he'd imagined being that man with his cock buried balls-deep into her, her harsh cries carrying those words to his ears.

He'd never have satisfied her, though. It was a fact he'd figured out early on in their friendship. He loved powerful, self-assured women, but Erika had the kind of personality that needed a more flexible man. Corey could never have been that man for her, so he'd left Eben to it. Flexible seemed to be in Eben's repertoire. And in Geva's.

That didn't mean he couldn't appreciate watching her fall apart when the right man fucked her. *Dragon,* he corrected himself. He'd been doing that a lot lately but wondered if it really mattered. They weren't really all that different from humans.

He clutched his baseball in one fist, picturing Erika's gradual crumbling. He felt a little guilty, but she had needed the wake-up call. She was near thirty. If she didn't figure it out soon, she'd be in denial for the rest of her life. And they didn't have time if what he'd learned so far was true. None of them would take in the first year. Not one of the brood would conceive a child no matter how much they wanted it.

As the Queen's proxy he knew the requirements. The Council strictly monitored and rationed magic to the brood. The magic they needed to conceive. The idea disgusted him, but he was loyal to Racha first, so he couldn't tell them. He could only hope they stood together to make the Council change that one ridiculous law.

In the meantime, Corey was forced to watch all of them try to prove their need to procreate. They all wanted it, but come next year, there would be no new dragons unless they could convince the Council to let them assemble the Verdanith. Making the artifact whole again would take the power out of the hands of the Council and give it back to the Brood.

Maybe Racha was right, though. Maybe it took enough raw need between two partners. He had enough right now after watching that display.

He buttoned up his shirt and tightened his tie, then grabbed a stack of random files to hold in front of his crotch before leaving his office.

"Mr. Monaghan," his secretary started in surprise when he opened the door.

"I have a meeting with Ms. Aris. Hold my calls."

"Yes sir."

The elevator took him up the one floor to her office. Six

seconds was how long it took. He'd counted it multiple times, and counted again. How else do you pass the infinity it takes you to get to the woman you love?

The doors opened directly into her lobby. No hallways existed on the top floor. Her secretary, a bright young woman named Heather, lit up when she saw him.

"Is she busy?" he asked.

"No sir. Go right in." She beamed at him and he tried to ignore the way her eyes drifted up and down him a few times before he passed through the doors.

"Racha Aris, CEO" was plastered on the heavy wood door.

She sat at her desk, intently reading something—most likely the latest financial reports for the company she had inherited from her father when he had died, and assumed control of six months ago. She'd slipped into the role her father had filled with very little effort aside from Corey's explanations of how the modern world worked. He felt a little ineffectual now, to be honest. She was blindingly intelligent, he'd realized quickly once they were out in the world. She picked up on everything—social nuances, technical jargon, even the subtleties of corporate slang that irritated him to no end.

She didn't move from her position when he entered the office, but there was an almost imperceptible shift in her posture once he was there. Their game, he thought. She would ignore him until he forced her to pay attention.

"Erika called."

Racha's head jerked up and she stared at him. Jesus, she was beautiful. Her green eyes were wide and expectant, her hair caught up in a pair of carved jade combs, with dark curls escaping. It was the end of the day and she was just a little oblivious of her appearance on days when she had few meetings, like today.

"You're carrying files. You couldn't e-mail me their location?"

"You're observant," he said.

"What did Erika say?"

"She was calling to petition, like the others."

Racha laughed. "You must be joking."

"No, and she was convincing. Very convincing."

Racha's eyes drifted back down to the manila folder he held in front of his hips. Her posture shifted again as she swiveled to face him. She crossed her legs and he admired the way her snug skirt rode up her thighs a tiny bit.

"So we have five petitions for my brother to take to the Council. The Council controls the sixth, so we just hope for now that they'll approve. Shall we celebrate?" She glanced to the wet bar on the other side of her office, but Corey had in mind some other lubrication to enjoy besides the expensive liquor she kept available for clients.

"Yeah… I think we should." His voice came out rough. He walked into the room with purpose, and tossed the folders onto her desk a second before he knelt in front of her. She was flushed already, her eyes wide when he slipped his hands up her thighs and pushed them apart maybe a little too force- fully. But he needed her and was too impatient to be gentle.

He shoved his hands up beneath her skirt, found the waistband of her panties, and tugged hard. She lifted up just enough for him to pull them down. Her shoes went along with the expensive lingerie she liked and he shoved her skirt higher, pulling her hips forward.

"She always gets you worked up." She threaded her fingers through his hair and bent to kiss him.

"Powerful women get me hot. You like it," he murmured against her lips.

"I love it."

While they kissed he let his fingertips slide between her

thighs. With his other hand he unbuttoned her blouse and unhooked the lacy little front-hook bra she wore.

Pleasing her was the apex of his day. Since learning who she was and the scope of her family's influence he'd been intimidated, but this was one situation where he still felt in control. Being the master of her pleasure was the thing he'd craved and now he had it, every day. He'd arrived at her office earlier than usual today, but needed this as much as he knew she did.

"I love you," she breathed. He smiled around her nipple and enjoyed the harsh exhalation when he plunged two fingers into the scalding wet depths of her pussy and began rubbing her clit with his thumb. He'd make her come at least once before he gave himself to her. It was his way of asserting himself and she'd yet to complain about it. Today he had a lot of himself to give.

She cried out and pulled his hair, tugging his face back up to hers to kiss him savagely while her orgasm shook her. He quickly lifted her out of her chair and shoved the objects on her desk aside to make room.

The glow from her climax hadn't subsided yet when he sank into heaven a moment later, his hard, aching cock throbbing in contact with the wet sheathe of her pussy. He kissed her while he fucked her, only half conscious of her hands busily unfastening the buttons of his shirt and pushing it off him. His pants fell forgotten around his ankles. Nothing remained besides the godforsaken tie around his neck. The tie had an abstract green pattern that now draped across her breasts as he bent over her, burying himself inside her sweet depths over and over.

He came hard. His body shuddered and tensed. He took a breath and met her gaze. She smiled up at him in that worshipful way she had during these moments. Her hand grazed the glowing mark on his chest.

"Maybe this time?" she said, hopefully.

"I'm not done yet," he said, beginning to slowly fuck her again. He intended to give it all to her today before he stopped. Every last drop. The way she tilted her head back and sighed when he moved inside her again just made him hotter. Her bare, creamy breasts bounced slightly with each thrust and she reached behind her head to grip the edge of her desk for leverage. Her strong legs wrapped around his hips, pulling him into her with rhythmic tugs. She wasn't done yet, either.

By the time they *were* done, he'd climbed halfway onto her desk and her head and shoulders were draped over the other side, her slender legs both hooked over his shoulders while he fucked her into oblivion.

He pulled her up and shifted them both back to her desk chair, where he seated himself with her tucked onto his lap.

"Maybe this time," he murmured into her neck, darting his tongue out to taste the sheen of sweat that coated her skin. She ran both hands down his cheeks and pulled him in for a deep kiss. When she drew back, her expression was resolute.

"It could take decades, but we have time."

"You don't sound like you believe that," he said, caressing her pale thigh where it rested across his.

"The sooner we conceive the more time we have with our children after. The hibernation comes so quickly. I was a late child. I just remember seeing how distraught my parents were when I had to leave. Or my mother, at least. Father was away at the time."

"Fucked up law, if you ask me," he said. Corey rarely articulated his opinion of dragon law, but this was one he firmly believed to be bullshit.

"I don't make the laws. You know that."

"That doesn't mean I have to like it," he said, but he did

know. Even though she was the Queen, her role was more of an enforcer than anything. Her brother was the one with the Council's ear. Now with the entire Court in agreement that the Verdanith should be assembled, he hoped something might change. He'd at least like to surprise his mother with one more grandchild before she gave up on him entirely.

Racha's desk phone trilled, its red light flashing. The sound jolted them both out of their intimate moment. She sighed and kissed him quickly, then leaned to answer the call.

"Ms. Aris, your four o'clock is here."

"Thank you. I'll be right there." She slid off his lap. With a breath, her clothing shifted and rematerialized in perfect organization, her mussed hair adjusted itself into a perfect coif on her head. She still looked flushed and satisfied when she turned to survey Corey, still sitting naked in her chair with his pants around his ankles.

"You should sit in on this meeting. Not naked, though."

Corey stood and dressed. "It's your father's publicist, right?"

"Yes, but that's not why I'm meeting with her. She was Father's mate at the end of his life."

"You don't sound enthusiastic about meeting her."

Racha's shoulders tensed, but she was already striding toward the door after confirming he'd put himself back together sufficiently to greet a guest. "She's *not* my mother."

Corey wanted to ask more questions, but she'd already opened the office door and was walking back toward him with her guest behind her. Corey quickly swiped a hand through his hair, then did a double take when he saw the lovely woman behind his lover.

He'd have known the confident carriage anywhere, even without seeing her face and the head of blonde waves that spilled over her shoulders. She had haunted his dreams for a year until he'd finally allowed himself to move on.

"Ms. Jillian Valenti, allow me to introduce you to Mr. Corey Monaghan, our Chief Technical Officer."

"Hello, Corey. Long time, no see."

"Hello, Jill."

CHAPTER SIX

*E*rika roused herself from a lazy nap to find Geva seated near the bed, naked and watching her with a sleepy smile. The new haircut threw her. She was used to his insanely red hair that grazed his shoulders. Now he actually looked kind of respectable, not the wild dragon man she'd fallen for.

She still loved the look. Especially when he greeted her naked like this.

"It glows even when you sleep." He glanced at her lower abdomen.

Her mark tingled in response to his appraisal. Heat rose to her cheeks and she pulled the sheet up to her navel. "That must make you very happy."

"Insanely." He grinned. "Aren't you?"

She sighed. "It's complicated. I don't deny the desire is there, and obviously it's very real if my mark is telling the truth. But it's been six months since we got back. I'm itching for a new expedition. A baby would complicate my work."

"More than I've complicated it?"

"Maybe. At least I can take you with me. That is, if you

can go." There were all kinds of arguments to the contrary. She'd known plenty of archaeologists who had raised kids in the field. Even given birth in the field. She could be hardcore like that. But didn't she owe it to her kid to be more responsible?

"We do have a new expedition—the one to find my sister." Geva gave her an expectant look. She wasn't completely oblivious to his need to please her. She adored it, if she were being honest. The way he'd couched this particular plea made her love him more, but it was still too complicated.

"Which we can't begin until we get that artifact assembled. Will it just tell us where she is, do you think?"

"Our legends say once it's assembled it must be taken to the Mother's birth place and affixed to her shrine. Then She will speak to us, bestowing the wisdom we seek." He propped his elbows on his knees, ready to give her any other incentive she needed. She felt suddenly self-conscious that a man like *him* was looking to her for help and validation.

"Your mother or *the* Mother?"

"The Mother."

Erika's gears began to turn. A true expedition, provided the Council approved. Nothing else mattered to her in moments when she had a clear objective.

"Where's this shrine?"

"Only the Council knows the precise location, but there's sufficient available lore for us to find it without their help."

Erika snorted. Of course only they knew. She enjoyed how Geva seemed to grow more excited at her own enthusiasm.

"Well, first things first. Let me call Corey back and find out if he has any news. It's already been a week." She snatched her phone from the bedside table.

Her friend answered on the third ring with a grumbly, "Monaghan."

"Hey, Cor. What happened to your secretary?"

She heard a curse on the other end of the call. "Jesus, Erika. I was planning on calling you when I woke up. You're probably the most impatient woman I know. I have no idea how that man lives with you."

Erika glanced at Geva who was laughing quietly. She'd forgotten how keen his hearing was. She glared at him and he mouthed "sorry" to her. "Where are you, Cor?"

A deep sigh met her ear through her phone. "I'm not at the office… It is only 4 AM on the East Coast, you know? It's not like I was sleeping anyway. My calls are usually forwarded directly to my cell when I'm offsite."

"Sorry I woke you."

"Fuck you, you aren't sorry for anything. I'll just get right to it anyway. I have good news and bad news. Mostly bad news."

Erika tensed. Corey didn't sound optimistic and considering his 'yes man' attitude, his tone worried her. "What is it?"

"The Council approved our request."

"That's incredible! When should we bring you our piece of the artifact?"

"Not so fast… We're missing a fragment. We thought the Council had the sixth, but it turns out they don't. They lost it centuries ago."

Centuries ago? Her blood went cold at the implications, but her brain immediately kicked in to compensate. 'Centuries ago' was her favorite phrase. It normally made her a little wet to hear, but this time the situation was more complicated. She averted her eyes from Geva's. An expedition was what that meant, but she knew she shouldn't be happy about a delay in finding Geva's sister. Either way, she needed to make sure Geva heard from someone else's mouth what they needed to do, no matter how sharp his hearing was.

"I'm putting you on speaker. Say that again." She tapped the screen of her phone and set it down on the bedside table.

"I said, the goddamn *Council* has *lost* the sixth piece of the fucking artifact. Racha's gone to meet with her brother to try to figure out what to do about it. And we have other problems, too."

"Do they affect us finding the damn thing?" Geva asked.

Erika raised an eyebrow at his outburst. He was actually starting to sound a little like her.

"Not exactly, but they may affect how the Court proceeds. I believe you want the Verdanith for the reason you asked for it, but I know you, Erika. I know there's another reason."

She started to object but he cut her off.

"Don't tell me. It's none of my business. If you're keeping it on the down low, I believe you have a good reason so it's best if I *not* know considering who I live with. I'd be obligated to tell her, and she'd be required to tell the Council. I'm having a tricky enough time handling damage control for the other members of the Court. And for our own issues."

Erika sat back against her pillows and met Geva's gaze with raised eyebrows. This oughta be interesting.

"Care to share?" she asked her phone.

"No time right now. But whatever it is you guys are dealing with, trust me you're not alone. We have to choose our battles with the Council, but if there's anything you can do to work on locating the lost fragment, please try. I'll send you what details I can on its last known location. This is your realm of expertise at least, so we're counting on you. Maybe Dimitri can help, too."

"Of course. I'll do whatever I can."

"Good," he said. "And Erika?"

"Yeah?"

"I think we need to be prepared for the worst if Racha and Kris can't get the Council to see reason."

"I thought you said they approved?"

"It's about more than the artifact. It's about their entire way of life. Just prepare yourselves."

Erika turned to look at Geva. Her red lover had a look of intense interest on his face.

"Do you know what the fuck Corey's talking about?"

He smiled at her. "My people's outmoded conventions are a way of the past, my love."

Erika laughed. "Is that your way of telling me times are changing?"

"I love how concise you can be."

"You haven't seen me give a lecture yet. My students hate me."

"Teach me, sweet Erika. I will listen."

BREATH OF MEMORY

CHAPTER ONE

Corey, like a good Catholic boy, tended to flagellate himself a little too often over his conflict. He recognized his issues, but it didn't stop the self-torture. It wasn't even about being Catholic. He told himself that over and over. He was just trying to be honorable. He loved Racha more than he'd loved any woman—except for one.

So when his ex, Jill, came into Racha's office and said hello like they'd never said goodbye, his entire world was turned on its head.

He could still remember the flavor of her essence on his tongue, like it hadn't been a year and a half since he'd last been with her, enticing her back into his bedroom one morning and shoving his tongue deep between her legs. Like she hadn't called him the next day to tell him it was over because she'd met someone else.

That memory turned the remembered flavor of her sweet climax bitter on his lips.

Yet here she was, beautiful as ever and talking to his mate. And Racha, ever the professional, was carrying on the conversation as though it were business as usual.

"Ms. Valenti, I understand you worked very closely with my father before he died. I'd love to hear everything."

Corey had taken up a spot just behind Racha's chair, leaning against a heavy bookcase and watching Jill suspiciously. She darted a quick look at him, which he returned as impassively as possible.

"Yes. I've worked here for about a year and a half since he hired me as PR Director. It is lovely to finally meet you. I have to say you don't resemble your father at all."

"No, I take after Mother more. Forgive me for being so forward, but I gather you and my father had a relationship that went beyond the professional?"

Jill flushed at that, and Corey was sure he caught a slight bite to Racha's words. He had never discussed her family with her before, aside from her younger brother, Kris, who he considered a good friend. Racha's last comment before admitting Aris Tech's as yet unnamed PR Director—and her father's former lover—to her office had spoken volumes. *"She's not my mother."*

Jill seemed to catch the tenuousness of the conversation and answered delicately. "Aris could be persuasive. It was always in his nature to get what he wanted." Jill glanced at Corey again with a slightly apologetic expression.

Corey swallowed and averted his eyes. So that's who the richer man had been. He'd had no idea of his usurper's identity. Only that the last time he'd laid eyes on Jill was as she climbed into a sleek limousine after a banquet he and Erika's team had attended not long before their expedition. He hadn't seen the man she had been with.

"Why did you stay after he died," Corey blurted. "I mean, if you loved the man, surely it would be too difficult to be faced with his memory every day."

Jill flinched at his comment, laced as it was with accusation. Escape was precisely what Corey had done when he lost

Jill. He'd left town a couple weeks later and spent the next year with Erika and the others hunting for the ancient temple where he finally met the love of his life, a woman worthy of replacing Jill. Racha glanced over her shoulder at him with a hard look, then took a deep breath and seemed to brace herself when she turned back to Jill.

"My father was never an easy man to live with. He and Mother were estranged for a significant portion of my life, but somehow he always went back to her.

"He told me when we met that his wife had died. Or should I say mate? I know how…*unique* Aris was. You don't have to hide anything from me."

"Yes, she died a little more than twenty-five years ago."

Jill shifted in her seat, her eyebrows drawing together. In a near whisper she said, "He always used to talk about how his days were numbered, but that his daughter would take over for him after he was gone. He seemed so vibrant and full of life at the end, even. So… *young*. He never told me how old he really was until the end."

Racha stood from her desk chair and crossed the room to pour three drinks from the crystal decanter on the bar. She added an extra measure to one, then turned and handed one to Jill. She handed the fuller one to Corey, giving him a resigned look and surreptitiously caressing his wrist when she passed by. The touch did little to calm him.

"Come sit," she said, inviting Jill to the comfortable sitting area near the window. The sun streamed through behind her, casting her perfect delicate skin into a golden glow.

Jill sat beside her and took a hesitant sip of her drink.

Seeing the two of them facing each other—Racha's dark, otherworldly beauty facing the golden light of Jill's angelic features—Corey's heart seemed to split. God forgive him, he still loved her.

He almost didn't hear the rest of her story, as enthralled

as he was just watching the two of them. But when Jill turned her back to Racha and lifted up her hair to display the back of her neck, he snapped back to attention. What had she just said? "Marked."

Just beneath her hairline on the back of her neck was a red, disc-shaped tattoo, identical to his own, aside from the color. It pulsed with a steady inner glow.

"Fuck me," Corey muttered. "The bastard mated you."

He immediately felt like an ass for referring to Racha's father that way, but the fucker had stolen his girl. Of course it wasn't lost on him that the man had also *fathered* the woman he loved now.

Jill let her hair fall back to her shoulders in a sweep of shining gold and turned back around. Her blue eyes were shining when she met his gaze.

He had an overwhelming urge to walk over and kiss her. To offer forgiveness and ask her to come back to him. But Corey's life was a lot more complicated now. Between loving the Dragon Queen and his new role as Chief Technical Officer of one of the most profitable technical corporations in the world, he didn't have room to consider reconnecting with an old lover.

Still, he knew how Reds worked—if Racha's father had wanted Jill badly enough, there wasn't much she could have done to resist his seduction. Perhaps he could forgive her someday, but the wound was still too raw, even after all this time. And even worse, the vivid memory of the last time they made love kept replaying through his mind. Right now he just needed to put as much space between the two of them as possible.

While Jill stood and straightened her tailored suit, Corey headed to the door. Racha's voice held him back.

"Corey, take Jill down to the marketing wing and show her our new plan."

He glanced back and was confused by the curious look Racha gave him when she stood. She seemed flushed again, like she was primed for sex, even though they'd finished a very satisfying session only moments before Jill had arrived.

Jill stepped forward as if to follow Corey, but Racha gently gripped her arm. "Wait…"

The moment seemed to slow to a pregnant crawl as Corey watched Racha pull Jill into a tender embrace, holding Corey's gaze the entire time. Racha slid a hand down Jill's back, but stopped just shy of impropriety. Her thumb rested just over a spot that Corey knew Jill loved to have caressed.

With that one subtle touch, Jill tilted toward Racha. Racha leaned in, pulled Jill's head toward hers and kissed her deeply.

The sight made Corey's blood grow hot. It was as though Racha had seen into his mind and was now acting out his own fantasy. Her enjoyment of it was so plain he believed he could taste Jill himself, which only enhanced his longing.

Just a kiss. That seemed to go on forever. He imagined himself holding Jill, sliding his own tongue between those supple lips, the way she would feel and taste, the warmth of her soft curves pressed against his hard body. And he imagined where he would take it next.

As if reading his mind, Racha slid her hand up Jill's side and cupped her breast, grazed a thumb across the tip that jutted against the sheer fabric of her blouse. Jill tensed and moaned against Racha's mouth.

Corey was about to either get in on the action or call a stop to it to preserve his sanity when Racha pulled away.

Without a word, Jill turned and followed him into the elevator, dazed from the experience. Corey punched the button for the marketing floor.

Once the doors closed, Corey hazarded a glance at Jill.

She leaned against the handrail in the elevator, flushed and rubbing her lips thoughtfully.

"She's… powerful," Jill said, then looked at him. "You're hers, aren't you?"

"Yes."

"It's a little ironic, don't you think?"

"What do you mean?"

"That I left you for her father and now that he's gone, here you are, mated to her."

"I moved on." The statement wasn't precisely a lie. He *had* moved on, but sometimes life had a funny way of bringing a person full circle.

"But you came back."

Yes, he had, and here they were, standing side-by-side in the enclosure of the elevator. He was immersed in the famil-iar, citrusy scent of her. Her chest rose and fell with deep breaths as though she were trying to calm herself down. The pale silk of her blouse was translucent enough for him to see the pattern of lace of her bra. His gaze drifted higher—her top button had come unfastened, affording him a view of the top of one full breast. He licked his lips, imagining pressing them against the soft skin, tugging the shirt open and making her moan when he took her nipple into his mouth and sucked.

He shifted closer and turned his head to try to smell her hair.

Jill's head turned toward him a fraction, just enough for him to know without a doubt that she was aware of him. Her shirt fell open just a little more, the silk sliding along the creamy skin of her chest before draping wide and displaying the lace-fringed swell of her breasts.

Hail Mary, full of grace…

His conscience was busy doing a panicked backpedaling, trying to keep his libido under control. Though he didn't precisely agree with Jill's observation of his relationship with Racha, it was still the truth. He belonged to her. He'd left the temple six months before as the Dragon Queen's Consort. Inheritance or not, he and Jill were coworkers now and he had to keep things professional. Racha was the woman he was committed to now. Jill had given up that opportunity more than a year earlier.

He repeated the words like the Catechism. Why wasn't he touching her? Because she'd given up. She'd left him. He'd moved on. He was with someone else. Someone who had just given him an incredibly erotic scene to ponder that would be stuck in his head for the rest of his life. And now Jill was standing alone with him in a tiny, mirror-walled room and he was struggling not to kiss her just the way Racha had.

His phone vibrated in his pocket. The familiar rhythm told him it was a text from Racha. He glanced at the screen and immediately smacked the STOP button on the elevator's panel.

"What is it?" Jill asked. Her hands gripped the rails, her eyes wide with alarm.

"Worship her the way you worship me," the text read.

"Corey! Is something happening?"

He stared at the screen, trying to make sense of it. The prickle at the back of his neck reminded him of the camera in the corner. He twisted his head around to stare up at the mirrored corner of the elevator. The camera was on the other side of the glass, hidden but watching. Racha was watching. And fuck if that didn't turn him on more.

He turned back to Jill. "Forgive me, baby, for I have to sin."

$\mathcal{J}$ill's breath left her lungs in a gasp against Corey's mouth. Confused by the sudden kiss, she pressed both hands against his chest. Her palms slid up over his shoulders, reveled in the familiarity of his hard muscles underneath the crisp cotton of his dress shirt. The intensity of the kiss left her breathless. Her fingers tangled in his hair and she arched against him. So much the same, but so different. So demanding.

It was like they'd never been apart. The same charge of passion was there. His beautiful hands were on her body, his tongue in her mouth. The memory of Aris had faded, but the guilt over hurting Corey hadn't.

She let the memory linger in the back of her mind until it wouldn't let her enjoy his kiss. Until the buzz of her dead dragon lover's energy that still infused her was too strong and made her stop.

Corey came back in more passionate than before. Both his hands gripped the sides of her head and his mouth was intent on devouring her. Something about his touch... every skimming caress of his fingers… made the specter of Aris recede just a little. But never completely.

Aris's seduction was still clear in in her memory. Along with her betrayal of the man she loved.

The one who was now gripping her ass and pressing himself against her. He said nothing, too occupied with teasing his tongue into her mouth. He tugged impatiently at her blouse until his fingers found the buttons and unfastened them. She was too dazed to help, but marveled at how little he'd changed. He'd been an impatient lover, but never to the point of ripping her clothes.

She wished he would now, though. She needed him to tear them to shreds and fuck her.

"Corey…"

He tugged her lacy bra down to release one breast. "What?" He blurted out the question in a gruff tone just before latching onto her nipple.

"Oh… *God yes.*"

Her head knocked back against the wall when he freed her other breast and teased that nipple with his thumb. The entire world seemed to be spinning except for the parts of her body he was touching. Her nipples, her stomach, her knee, her thigh.

His fingers slid up her inner thigh while his mouth still sucked eagerly at both her breasts in turn.

Goddamn her for comparing him to Aris, but she did. Aris had been perfectly accommodating to her every need. Anticipating her moods to the point of infuriation. He'd been a surprise at every turn, and she had loved him.

Corey was his impulsive self, at least now that Racha had set him loose. The whispered words between Jill and Racha hadn't meant much to her until now. "He will worship the both of us."

She wondered how he would feel if he knew what Racha had said to her. Not that she cared when he had her pressed against the back of the elevator. The mirrored walls showed every angle of their tangled embrace. It seemed lurid to her own eyes when she wrapped her legs around his waist and pulled him to her. Her skirt rode up, displaying the tops of her stockings. His hard cock was pressed solidly between her thighs, the front of his trousers rubbing against her hot center.

"Too much for you?" he asked, his lips twisted in that half smile of challenge that she knew so well.

"Fuck you," she said.

He laughed and slipped down to his knees, leaving her perched on the rail of the elevator with her legs spread. She almost dropped her legs but paused when she felt the tease of his tongue against her panties. Her head flew back again, forgetting the wall and knocking into it with a bang.

"Holy fuck, men like you should be regulated."

"Mmhmm" was all he said when he pressed his mouth against her pussy. He grazed his teeth across the fabric with a growl. Jill was sure he would rip her panties off with his teeth. Instead, he stood and pulled her tight against him, capturing her mouth in a rough kiss. With his tongue doing its masterful plunging sweep between her lips, he tugged the hem of her skirt up until the cold steel of the handrail pressed against her backside. His hand was between her thighs again, pushing beyond the edge of her panties and sliding between her slick folds.

Her lips tingled when he pulled away from the kiss. The look of lustful determination on his face was almost more arousing than his touch. She remembered that look and how it almost always preceded the most satisfying and surprising sex they'd ever had.

He spun her around and pressed her against the side of the elevator, the hand rail the only barrier between her flesh and the polished glass. She braced her palms against the glass. Her eyes met his in the reflection briefly before his gaze drifted down to her exposed breasts. He cupped both breasts in his hands and teased her nipples until they were almost too sensitive and she was out of her mind from the pleasure. She pressed her ass back against him, her core aching to have him. Her blouse had fallen off one shoulder and he drifted his lips across the pale skin, up the side of her throat until he nuzzled against the back of her ear.

He slid back down to his knees behind her and she watched their reflection, almost as though she were an outside observer. The scene brought back the urgency of their sex life when they'd been together. The way he'd seemed like he could never get enough of her. He shoved her skirt up until it was rucked around her waist, and tugged her panties down, grazing his teeth over her skin in a path that followed the lacy fabric down across the swell of her ass. With both hands gripping her hips, he urged her back against his eager mouth. She gripped the handrail and bent over, adjusted her stance to spread her legs wider and give him access.

His hot breath gusted against her swollen flesh. She thought she heard a whispered prayer behind her just a moment before his tongue slicked gloriously between her pussy lips all the way from her clit up the crease of her spread ass cheeks, then back down. He paused long enough to plunge his tongue inside her in several swift strokes before descending back to her clit and sucking.

She was lost in a haze of pleasure, on the verge of orgasm when he stood again and urged her upright. Her cheeks were flushed, her lips parted from steady, shallow pants. He stood at her side, his erection pressed against her hip, but he seemed more concerned with touching her all over than with fucking her. One of his large hands gripped her ass cheek, his fingertips digging in briefly, then slipping between again. She shuddered and leaned her shoulder against his chest when he slipped two fingers deep inside her. His other hand slipped between her thighs from the front and began mercilessly stroking her clit.

"Touch your nipples, Jill," he whispered. "Goddamn you look beautiful when you're about to come."

She lifted shaking hands and clutched both breasts, squeezing and tugging at her nipples until twin little spikes of pain shot through her. The hand between her thighs worked her in a steady rhythm. The fingers plunging into her from behind shifted, sweeping a slick stripe of her juices back between her ass cheeks and teasing at the tight opening.

"Oh, God yes," she murmured. She gasped and leaned harder against him when he pushed beyond the barrier, his finger fucking into her ass and sending jolts of pleasure through her. Her clit was a tingling mass of sweet sensation that seemed to increase in potency with every stroke of his fingers. When the rush of her climax broke through, she released her breasts and turned her head. He read her pleading look and claimed her mouth in a hungry kiss she used to ride out the waves and to muffle her own harsh gasps.

He held her in his arms afterward, waiting out the aftershocks that even the slightest touch seemed to incite. She pressed her face against his chest, reveling in the scent of him. A new scent was mingled with his familiar musk, however, and she abruptly pulled away when it registered what it was. She'd had a good breath full of Racha's lovely scent when they had kissed. It wasn't a perfume so much as a natural, verdant aroma that evoked memories of summer for her. It was all over him, too.

He didn't belong to Jill anymore. She didn't belong to anyone now, and that fact had never been quite so apparent as it was at that moment, with Corey standing on the other side of the elevator with his hands in his pockets. He was only a few feet away but may as well have been on another planet. He watched her reflection silently while she straightened her clothes. Why hadn't he fucked her? He'd always been keener on her pleasure first, but always took his own. And his erection was very apparent still, its thick ridge visible behind the front of his trousers.

The buzz of a phone sounded and he pulled his hand out of his pocket to look at the screen. A small smile curled the corners of his mouth and he glanced up at the corner of the elevator. He made a casual salute to whatever it was. A camera? Had someone been *watching* the entire time?

"You've got to be fucking kidding me," she muttered. She disengaged the STOP button with a rough gesture and the elevator car lurched back into motion.

He gave her a perplexed look. "What is it?"

"This was all a fucking game to you, wasn't it? You and her."

"I don't play games, Jill. Neither does she."

"But she was watching us, wasn't she? The entire time. How many women have you gotten off in this elevator while she watched? I know you always enjoyed watching, too... I guess you finally found your true match, huh?"

The doors opened on her floor and she was out like a shot, heading down the hallway to the sanctity of her office.

"Jill!" Corey called after her. He didn't run to catch up, though. She supposed letting the employees see their CTO running after her would have been a little conspicuous, but he did speed up when she reached her office. He slammed a hand against her door to prevent her from closing and locking it.

"Jill, we need to talk."

She gave up trying to keep him out and turned away, taking refuge behind her desk.

"You couldn't have tried that before your tongue was buried in my snatch again? Jesus Christ, Corey. Don't you get that I still love you? I never stopped, even when I was with him. I wanted him to bring you in, too, but didn't think you'd be too keen on sharing."

"You'd have been right." He shut the door gently behind him and lingered, facing away from her for a second before turning and looking at her.

"So what the fuck was that?" She pointed in the direction of the elevator. "You get to share me with her now, in some twisted voyeuristic game you two play?"

"It isn't a game. Christ, Jill, you're the only other woman I'd ever consider going down that road with. I was on the verge of going nuts standing in that elevator with you and not touching you. I'd never have done it without her knowing about it."

Jill dug her nails into the blotter on her desk. The meeting should have been simple. She'd gone in expecting to complete the formality of having Aris's daughter accept Jill as her inheritance from her father. Corey's presence had thrown her, however, and she'd never managed to actually broach the topic. Her mind still spun from the last hour or so. Seeing him again was the least of it.

She struggled to keep the tears at bay and turned to face the window behind her desk. Corey made no sound, but a moment later she could feel his warm presence close behind her.

"I missed you," he said.

She clenched her eyes shut tightly. "I'm sorry," she said.

"Was he good to you, at least?"

She nodded, staring blankly out at the view of the harbor

beyond her window. "I loved him like crazy. But the day he died I dreamed about you."

"You broke my heart."

"You left the country before I could explain. Then took your sweet time coming back."

"What was there to say? You told me you loved me one day and the next you were with him."

The day in question was still vivid in her mind. Making love with Corey the morning before beginning her new job. They'd begun making plans, excited about their future. He'd invited her to meet his mother that weekend.

In the span of twenty-four hours everything had changed, but any words she gave him now would fall flat.

Max Aris had happened. He'd had an inexorable pull on her the moment she'd shaken his hand and gazed into eyes the most impossible shade of dark blue. It wasn't that Corey meant any less to her, but the sheer presence of Aris had overwhelmed her to the point that he became the sole focus of every single thought, whether it was about her work for him, or the lightest touch of his fingertips at her waist when they exited the elevator together. He'd taken her to dinner that night to celebrate her first day, then had seduced her so thoroughly she'd never left.

"He didn't give you a choice, did he?" Corey asked, bringing her back to the moment.

"It wasn't his breath, if that's what you're wondering. He showed me what he could do a few times, after I found out what he was, but he never used it on me. I made the choice because I think deep down you needed me too much. I was willing to compromise in our relationship because I loved you. He offered me a relationship that never required a compromise. He gave me almost everything I wanted."

"You're delusional if you think you didn't compromise."

"You found your match, Corey. If I had stayed with you,

that never would have happened. I can see that she's good for you. When I'm gone, you'll have her." She let out a long breath. "I want you to be happy."

His hand gripped her shoulder and spun her around. "What the fuck are you talking about? I'm not a fucking fool, Jill. So why the hell does it sound like you're about to die or something?"

"Because I am." Tears rose to her eyes again and she let them spill over unchecked. "I should have died with him, you know that, right? Or at least soon after. That's how it works with their kind. When she goes, you will, too, and you won't even object."

He stared at her in horror.

"Corey, don't tell me she hasn't told you."

"She has, but she also told me we had centuries before we had to worry about it. Now you're telling me it's happening to you?"

"I would be dead now, except he did something at the end. The last time we…" Her breath caught in her throat and came out as a sob. "Last time we made love, I knew it would be the last time. I was ready to die with him. But at the last moment it was like every ounce of his power filled me. He said he'd given me a gift and made me promise I would be happy, but he died in my arms before he could tell me what it was. I— I think what he gave me was time to find you again. Except I can't have you, and without Racha's acceptance of me as her inheritance it's all over."

"The hell it's over. She'll accept you."

"But will you?"

CHAPTER THREE

Corey met Jill's pleading gaze and felt his heart breaking all over again. He'd let her go finally a year earlier. Moved on, but now here she was, begging for his acceptance. For the life of him, he couldn't bring himself to give it to her yet, even though he wanted nothing more than to hold her in his arms and tell her it would all be okay.

"You can't even answer me, can you?" Jill asked.

"There's got to be an alternative," he said. There was always an alternative where dragons were concerned. "Trust me, I'll find it."

He was walking to the door when she called out. "Corey, I meant it when I said I still love you. I'm not trying to get between the two of you, but you need to know."

He suppressed an urge to turn and look back at her again.

"I still love you, too. That's the problem," he said to the door, then opened it and walked out.

~

HE WENT BACK to his own office to clean up and get ready to leave for the day. The sunset was reflecting off the sides of the buildings outside his window, casting the space in an orange glow. He stood gazing out at the waning light, trying to get his thoughts in order. He didn't turn when he heard his door open and close behind him.

Racha's lovely, delicate scent washed around him before her hand rested on his arm. He could just make out her reflection in the glass and caught her concerned expression. He closed his eyes and inhaled. After just a moment in her presence, his body relaxed and his thoughts seemed to clear.

"Do you do that on purpose?" he asked. "Breathe when you think I'm stressed."

"I don't like seeing you distressed. Why didn't you tell me you had a history with her?"

"Because it was just that… history."

"She is my inheritance. At least part of it. The most valuable part of it. But if she distresses you, I will reject her."

"But she'll die if you don't accept her. Is there something else we can do?"

Racha's hand slipped into his, cool and soft and so delicate. He closed his fingers tightly around hers, knowing she could handle it. His insides were a tangle of emotional knots over seeing Jill, tasting her, enjoying giving her pleasure again, then learning how dire her circumstances were. He'd have behaved differently in the elevator had he known.

"Corey, you know our bond lets me feel some of what you feel. Are you sure you want to give her up?"

"I can't be around her when I'm bound to you. It's torture. Knowing she was with your father instead of me."

"Very well. The Second Shadow lives in Kol's region. He's been resistant to finding a mate. I spoke to Kol a few weeks ago and he suggested this dragon might need a temporary change of locale, too."

He felt dirty, bargaining for Jill's life like this, for her ownership, essentially. If he were man enough he'd have forgiven her, accepted her. But at what cost? Would he be compromising his relationship with Racha for this old lover who had left him?

It was better this way. Jill would live, and she'd already exhibited a penchant for dragons, so perhaps this Shadow would make her as happy as Racha's father had.

"I want to meet him first before we decide."

She squeezed his hand. "I'll make the call tonight, but you'll have to handle the rest as my proxy. I have to meet with my brother and the Council in two days. I'm leaving tomorrow."

Right. After Jill's appearance he'd nearly forgotten about dragon politics. The Queen had to appear in person to petition the Council to assemble the Verdanith that would refocus the Council's magic and improve the race's fertility.

"I'll take care of it. Let's go home."

MAKING love to Racha always felt like a walk through summer rain. She quenched his heat with steady, unrelenting attention until he succumbed and let her inundate him entirely with her touch. While he was amorous and urgent during the day in her office, she repaid him with gentle and thorough attention at night in their bed. They were languid and unhurried. When they climaxed, the glow of power spreading between them nearly blinded him and washed their bedroom in pulsing light for several moments until it subsided. Only the faint pulsing green of his mark was still visible.

She didn't say it, but he knew she thought it. *Maybe this time.* They both knew better. Until the Verdanith was assembled, they wouldn't conceive. Jill's situation was a much more immediate concern. While Racha was gone dealing with politics, he'd be here preparing to send his old lover into the arms of another dragon.

"You're thinking about Jill, aren't you?"

"You're smarter than you are pretty, which makes you a fucking off-the-charts genius."

Her tousled black head rose up into his line of vision, silhouetted in the glow of moonlight that came through the window of their penthouse apartment. The side of her face caught the moonlight and seemed to shimmer slightly, the faint outlines of her usually invisible scales catching the light.

"Please be sure about this, Corey. The transfer of the bond is a tricky one. I won't be able to complete it since I'll be away, so you'll have to do it for me. Your mark gives you the authority and the power to do it. But if you're not completely committed to the transaction it could backfire."

"Shhh. I'm committed."

She looked skeptical. "You haven't even asked what you have to do to complete it."

"Some dragon ritual, I guess…" He started to shrug when it hit him what the last dragon ritual he'd encountered had involved. He took a deep breath. "Alright, let me guess… Dragon number two… Second Shadow or whatever he is… has to fuck me in the ass to take possession of Jill."

Racha snickered softly and slid atop him, laying prone on his chest with her chin resting on her hands. "No. Well, not unless you want him to. But the three of you do have to make love together."

His traitorous cock twitched at that comment and she raised an eyebrow. "You felt that?" he asked uncertainly.

"Maybe." She shifted her hips until her thigh brushed against his cock. The soft warmth of her skin aroused him enough that there could be no mistaking how much he wanted her again. She shifted again, pressed her hands into his chest and rose up. The tip of his cock was still pressed just in the right place and she sighed when the hard length of him pushed into her with just a little rise of his hips. Her eyelids fluttered in that way they did when she was enjoying herself. He sat up and embraced her, lowering his mouth to her breast and teasing his tongue and lips around one nipple until it perked up in response.

She continued talking in between the fucking. "If you enjoy it, all the better, but you will have to relinquish control to the other dragon after you find your Nirvana. When he releases his magic into her, she'll be primed for his mark. After he marks her, my father's mark will disappear, and the exchange is complete."

"And if you were here, you'd complete this exchange… with the other dragon." It was a struggle for him to maintain the thread of their conversation amid the tight clenching pull of her muscles around his cock, but he managed.

"It would be business." Her words came out in a purr. "Nothing like this."

"Am I enough for you?" he asked. He trailed his fingertips down the length of her spine, marveling at her texture. The velveteen feel of her scales was always present, even if he couldn't see them. She relaxed and released her magic for a second, letting her skin go all dragon. Even the tight sheathe of her core seemed to tighten and change texture, though not in an unpleasant way. He fucked her harder, enjoying the friction. She'd expressed a need to be scratched in that form, and he'd done it many times. She'd have crushed him if she changed completely, but still seemed to get the same pleasure out of having his hands on her true skin, even if the rest of her was still human-shaped.

He raked his short fingernails down her back and back up, and continued along every inch of skin he could reach until she vibrated with satisfaction. Her skin went back to its pale human sheen and he gripped her hips, urging her up and down on his shaft.

"As long as you do that, yes." She grinned at him, but her smile faded quickly and she paused in her motions. She wrapped herself around him, arms and legs both embracing his torso while her head rested on his shoulder. "It's just that she was Father's. I believed when I was young that I'd never want anything from him. That I'd reject it the way he always seemed to keep rejecting my mother. But here I am, taking his place. And he's left me one of the most amazing treasures, but I have to give her away."

"She made the choice. She can't stand to be around me, anyway." And he couldn't stand to not have this. Racha's lovemaking had become a drug to him. He feared losing it. Losing her love. And would do anything in his power to preserve what they had.

"Am I enough for you, my love?" she asked.

"More than enough."

"I can tell you still love her, yet you're insisting on this. Why?"

He let his hands pause in their caresses. He rested them at her waist and lay back again, pressing his head back into the pillow. He'd asked himself the same question all day, and there was only one answer.

"I can't love you both. And I can't lose you."

"You admit that you love her," Racha whispered.

"I want you. Every fucking moment."

Racha's face pinched as though she were irritated by his response. "And I want you, but giving her away isn't easy for me, either. I could feel your draw to her today—the pull was strong enough that it only took a nudge from me for you to have your way with her in the elevator." She rose up along the length of his cock and sank back down. The sensation left him giddy. She did it again until he held her still, his fingertips sinking into the flesh of her thighs.

"That's why I have to let her go. I can handle the transfer. Then it'll just be you and me. The way it needs to be." He cupped her face between both his hands and looked her in the eye. "We were meant to be together, you and I. She let me go, so I'm letting her go."

"Very well. I just hope you're not doing this to punish her for hurting you."

"I'm doing this to save her life. That's all."

THE SMALL CAFE Corey arranged the meeting at was virtually empty during a midday lull. Patrons were beginning to trickle in slowly. Jill had hesitantly accepted the invitation after his insistence that he had an alternative that would keep her alive. Corey hadn't told her she'd be meeting that alternative today, however. And with luck and some clever persuasion, she'd be out of the woods by the end of the night.

The dragon arrived first, as Corey had arranged, and there was no mistaking him. Large and dark-haired, he was clean-cut like a man who cared about appearances. Corey didn't so much, given his mood, but he'd made sure to shave that morning. Like Racha had said, this was a business transaction, so a professional attitude seemed appropriate. It was a struggle for him to think of it that way, but if he tried hard enough maybe he'd be able to convince himself.

He took the dragon in with one quick glance. His size and obvious power might have been intimidating if it weren't for the broody look on the man's face. Something Corey could identify with. Their eyes met and the dragon nodded solemnly. He stepped across the threshold and walked toward Corey.

The clang of something metal being dropped on a hard floor resounded around him when Corey stood to shake hands with the man. He shot a glance at the embarrassed barista behind the counter. The pretty young woman blushed brightly after looking at the two of them and turned away.

The dragon chuckled. "It happens when we go out in public sometimes. Animals flee… humans get more clumsy. Mass hysteria. I'm Rafe. And you must be the Queen's Consort, Corey."

They sat and the flustered barista brought over the cappuccinos Corey had ordered earlier. She'd regained her composure but couldn't keep her eyes off Rafe. The dragon barely seemed to notice.

"Kol tells me you have a dire situation and need my help."

Corey was happy to get straight to it. "Racha's father mated a woman before he died, he kept her alive with… ah…"

Rafe nodded. "With the last vestiges of his power at the end. That is how we generally go, given the choice. We infuse some object, or even a person, with our remaining life essence, generally as a gift for our offspring when they come out of hibernation. I take it the Queen won't accept the inheritance?"

"She will. But I won't."

Rafe's dark brows drew together. He took a sip of his coffee and studied Corey. "Two women—one a dragon queen. Most men would be over the edge with eagerness. Why aren't you?"

Corey had hoped to not have to get into the details, so he hedged. "I believe the Queen deserves my undivided attention."

Rafe raised an eyebrow. "Either this woman is too awful or too perfect. If she was mated to Aris, I doubt it's the former. I'd be honored to take her, but I don't believe you really want to give her away."

Corey was about to object when the subject of their conversation walked in. Jill paused in the doorway. When Corey saw her, the room seemed to close in on him. Her golden waves draped over bare shoulders in the summer dress she wore. She'd been out in the sun today for a bit. He could tell from the flush of heat on her cheeks that caused the smattering of freckles across her nose to stand out.

Rafe turned to look at her, too, and turned back with a hard look. "You are a fool if you're giving her up."

"It has to happen." He stood to greet Jill. She came forward and accepted his embrace and the kiss on her cheek. She seemed to linger in his arms for a second before pulling away. She looked at Rafe, who had stood and was looking expectant.

"Jill, this is Rafe."

"You're the dragon who's going to save my life, aren't you? Because this asshole can't find the guts to do it himself."

Rafe grinned and looked at Corey. "See. She's attuned to the situation as well as I am."

"It's not open for discussion," Corey said, sitting down again. "Are you both amenable?" he asked when they were all seated and Jill had made her order from the perplexed barista who'd decided to attend to them personally.

Rafe and Jill looked at each other and some silent message seemed to pass between them. Corey tried not to be irritated by the way the other man was looking at her. He could tell Rafe found Jill attractive, but the dragon still seemed somewhat resigned to the transaction, which puzzled Corey.

"Yes," they said in unison.

"Let's just get this over with," Jill said, grabbing her purse and tossing a tip on the table.

∼

JILL PRESSED her hand against Corey's chest before he could get into the limo with them. "I need a few minutes alone with him if you don't mind. I get what you're trying to do, but if you're in the middle of us the entire time, it will never work. Okay?"

She pushed back a little harder when his expression grew dark. He glanced behind her into the interior of the limo… his limo… that was ready to carry her to her salvation, and her demise, all at once. She may live, but what good was a life when the man she loved rejected her? She would willingly give herself to this other dragon, not only to save her own life, but to make Corey happy. He didn't want her enough to keep her, but he loved her enough to save her. She had to accept that.

"Take a cab, Corey. We'll meet you there, alright?"

Finally he nodded and stepped back.

The air conditioned interior of the limo made her skin prickle instantly into goosebumps. It felt good after the summer heat outside.

"He loves you too much," Rafe said unexpectedly. She stared at him.

"He's afraid of me now. I hurt him, so I deserve it."

"I need you to know something before we do this." Rafe glanced out the window, then back at her. The limo lurched slightly, pushing her closer to him. He caught her, his hands warm and soft on her skin. Their faces were millimeters apart. He could have kissed her, but he just shifted back in the seat.

"What is it?"

"I'm in love with a dragon. This… transaction is a way to keep the Council off my back. A formality. Marriage of convenience if you want to call it that. I suspect that's what it would be for you, too."

Jill sank back against the leather seat and sighed. "You're right. Don't get me wrong, you seem great. More than great, but no. I'm still in love with that bastard. Tell me about your dragon lover?"

She shifted in her seat to look at him. His brow clenched in dismay for a second. "She's lost. I need to find her. It was part of my bargain with the Queen. If I do this… with you… she'll help me find Rowan. She asked that I not tell her mate about it until it was over."

"Rowan? That's a beautiful name. Have you known each other long?"

Rafe shifted, looking embarrassed. "We were together for only a few days before she disappeared, but she's like no other woman. No offense… you are beautiful. I understand why Aris loved you and circumstances being different I would not hesitate."

"But you are hesitating…"

"She's very young, and not accustomed to dragon conventions. If I'm mated to you, what will she think when I find her?"

"Listen, Rafe. Once this is done, let's just agree to go our separate ways. You can find Rowan and I'll… find someone."

"That's not good enough." He startled her with his conviction.

"Why not?"

"You were mated to Aris. That ranks you just below a Queen. I'm not good enough for you, but you don't seem to realize that. The only situation worthy of you would be exactly what you want. And I mean to make that happen." He raised a hand up and she held completely still while he let one knuckle graze along the edge of her jaw and down the side of her neck.

The intensity of his gaze held her in thrall, the gentleness of his touch left her breathless. "How?" she asked, catching her breath when he placed an open palm against her chest, just above her breastbone. Her eyes fluttered closed at the feel of him. He shifted closer and let his hand slide back up until he cupped the back of her head, large fingers twining through her hair. His lips grazed her temple.

"You'll see, but I mean to enjoy the process regardless. To enjoy you just enough to make Corey believe he's succeeded. He has to be reminded how it feels to lose you."

CHAPTER FOUR

Corey beat them to the apartment he shared with Racha, which surprised him. He wondered what the two of them were talking about and felt a surge of jealousy. Jesus, he shouldn't be feeling that way if he was giving her away. He hated the fact that she didn't even have a choice in the matter, thanks to Aris. Jill's life depended on being possessed. Being owned. The mark was a brand and at the moment it was a time bomb for her. If he didn't go through with it she would die.

He wished like hell that Racha was here. Her calming breath could get him through the ordeal. He walked into their bedroom, made sure things were in order. It was ridiculous because he'd already gone through the motions earlier. He hadn't expected the two of them to go off alone, though. They would arrive eventually. Jill's life still depended on this.

Soon his cell phone buzzed. It was a message from the door man letting him know he had guests. He responded, then opened the door and went to pour drinks. He tried his best not to think about what might happen after.

The pair entered, Rafe's large arm solidly draped around Jill's waist. She looked a little flushed, too, like he'd already been all over her for the entire ride. The idea infuriated Corey enough to make him doubt his sanity. He slammed the bottle down a little too hard on the counter and shoved the drinks toward them.

Christ he needed to keep himself under control if he was going to go through with this.

"Thank you," Jill said, smiling in that way that always made him want to fuck her. She took a sip and licked her lips.

Rafe walked up behind her and whispered something in her ear. Her eyelids lowered and she smiled and nodded.

"Corey, show me where we're doing this. I'd like a moment alone, if that's all right."

Her plaintive tone settled his mood a little. She sounded almost as nervous as he felt.

"This way," he said, leading her to the bedroom.

"A camera?" she asked, noting the live feed of the room displayed on the widescreen television that hung from the wall facing the bed.

"Racha insisted. She'll be joining us remotely." He was at least grateful for that fact. Racha had given him the option and he had accepted, somewhat relieved to have her be involved, even if she couldn't participate directly. He left the room and closed the door behind him.

"Did I hear correctly?" Rafe asked when Corey rejoined him in the main room. "Will the Queen be with us via conference?"

"She considers it a business transaction, so yes." Corey poured himself another drink, trying to ignore the slight smirk on the dragon's lips.

"Giving up a treasure so valuable, I understand. She wants to make sure Jill is well cared for."

"So do I," Corey said.

"Good. It needs to be clear that we both have Jill's interests at heart before we begin. I will do everything in my power to see that she's happy with the results."

"I want nothing less."

"Of course," Rafe said. His dark eyes narrowed, as though assessing the veracity of Corey's remark. "Do you think Jill will like living in San Diego?"

Corey's hackles rose at the suggestion of Rafe taking her away with him. "The way I understood it, you would be relocating here."

Rafe shrugged. "Of course it is up to her. On the way over she suggested she might like some new scenery."

Corey's attention was drawn to the closed bedroom door when he heard Racha's familiar voice bleeding through. A moment later the door opened and Jill stood there, looking apprehensive. She'd taken off her shoes and brushed her hair. Behind her, the large screen on the wall displayed the beautiful features of the woman he was really doing this for, yet he couldn't take his eyes off Jill. Her skin was flushed and beautiful. Some unseen breeze caused a wisp of hair to trail across her cheek.

If this was a business transaction, why could he suddenly taste her on his lips again? It had only been a couple days since he'd had the pleasure of her flavor on his tongue, but he craved her again as strongly as he craved Racha. His face heated and he looked behind Jill at the screen on the wall.

"Corey, you know what needs to be done. It is all up to you now," Racha said. She walked past the camera and it panned to follow her. She was wearing the same wispy gown she'd worn that first day they had met in the temple. The day he learned she would have died rather than coerce him into making love with her. With her back to him, she tugged at the clip in her hair, letting her shiny black curls fall down over her shoulders. Soon she wasn't alone in the frame. Two men who looked vaguely familiar flanked her at the foot of a large bed. They were nude from the waist up, with heavily muscled torsos, deep tans, and shaved heads. They both had banded tattoos around their forearms that shimmered with colorless power. Their eyes were both unnatural shades—one red, the other gold.

"Who are they?" he asked, his jaw clenching.

"I thought it might make it easier for you if we fulfilled two of your fantasies at once. These are my brother's teachers from the Monastery. Darius and Zak. They will do anything you ask. You can watch while you handle our other business."

Corey remembered the men now. Or dragons—because that's what they were—only they were shackled by magic to prevent them from shifting. The two men were the bastard children of other dragons, born centuries earlier without the sanction of the Council and compelled into servitude to punish their parents for breaking dragon law. Oddly, they were referred to as "Unbound" even though they were clearly the opposite. But he supposed the term referred more to their state at birth than what they had become.

At the moment they both stood placidly by Racha's side, but every so often the younger of the two—Zak—would steal a glance at the tiny video in the corner that showed their own room to him. Perhaps Zak enjoyed watching, too. The proposition itself was not something Corey had expected, but Racha knew him well. Perhaps it was the time he spent serving as cameraman during Erika's expedition. Having to spend the entire ritual watching the other members of Erika's team couple in various configurations had given him an appreciation for the cinematic and he'd discovered he enjoyed directing. The moment in the elevator with Jill had been the first time he'd been on the other end of the camera, expected to perform, however.

This time it went both ways.

He crossed his arms and walked into the room, pausing to stand so that his upper body filled the entire frame of video of their room that took up one corner of his screen. "Are you really doing this for me, Racha? Or is it to sate your own curiosity? You enjoyed watching me with Jill the other day, didn't you?"

He had yet to share Racha with anyone. So far he'd been her sole lover and he'd sensed her need to experience more variety. He'd been oblivious to it for months until she'd caught him watching his secret stash of videos from the ritual. Her insatiable need had nearly overwhelmed him at the time, and it made him realize that while he may satisfy her emotionally, being the lover of a dragon woman was exhausting.

Racha's cheeks flushed. "Yes. I didn't want to miss this, but I also didn't want to watch alone. I've spent much of my energy these last few days shifting so I can fly between the island and the city. But I realized I prefer not to replenish my magic without you present, even if we aren't sharing each other. This was the only alternative."

"Where are you now?" he asked. "That doesn't look like the Monastery."

"It's a hotel in Singapore that belongs to Issa's family. I can call her to join, if you'd like."

"I believe three is enough." Corey glanced behind him at Rafe and Jill who both stood watching with interest. When Racha's attention fell on Rafe, the large man knelt and lowered his gaze.

"Greetings, Your Grace," he said.

"Hello, Rafe. I haven't forgotten our agreement, but it will take more time." She looked back at Corey. "Before we begin,

I need to let you know, the Council approved assembly of the Verdanith, but there is a problem."

"What is it? Erika will want to know, and so will the others."

"The final piece is missing. It was lost in the sixth century when it was entrusted to a line of nobles bonded to a dragon who died prematurely. The dragon herself bore no children, but the bond to her mate may have been passed down through subsequent generations. It wasn't uncommon for human mates of previous generations to have children with their human lovers as well as the dragon they were bonded to. If he did, he would have passed on his bond to his human children."

"If there's any information on when and where it was last seen, Erika can find it. Send me everything."

"I will. Shall we begin?" A hint of eager anticipation tinged her voice, reflecting Corey's own emotions acutely.

Corey beckoned to Jill who walked slowly to him. "Are you all right with this?" he said softly, placing his hands against her shoulders.

"It may be the last time I'm with you. So, yes."

"Even though I'm going to watch him fuck you?" He glanced at Rafe who had stood again and now leaned against the closed bedroom door, waiting and watching. His hands clenched involuntarily, squeezing her shoulders tightly.

"Maybe you'd better ask yourself the same question," Jill said. "Are you all right with this? With watching him with me? It does feel a little like karma to me, you know. Getting to watch her lose her mind the way I did the other day. I'm just a little sad I don't get to watch you do it to her."

Corey suppressed a flinch and released her shoulders. "Come here and watch with me." He gripped her hand in his and pulled her in front of him, so that they both faced the screen and his hands rested lightly on her hips. As an afterthought he glanced at Rafe. "You can take off your clothes and wait on the bed." The larger man nodded and complied, but Corey's attention was back on Jill and Racha. The two women watched each other silently, both seeming to anticipate what he might say next.

"You heard what she said, Racha. Let's watch the two of them take their time with you until you lose your mind. I think you owe her that, don't you?"

Racha's eyes flashed green, betraying her excitement. With the barest glance, Zak was at her side, his mouth pressed against her throat. He tugged the strap of her dress off her shoulder and pushed it down her arm with a slow caress of his palm. The bodice of it clung briefly to her erect nipple before falling in a smooth sweep to drape below one pert breast.

Darius knelt in front of her, pulling the dress the rest of the way off. He leaned in and latched his mouth on one nipple while Zak cupped her other in his hand and squeezed its dark pink tip. Racha tilted her head back and moaned. She accepted Zak's kiss hungrily and let the two men lower her to the bed.

Corey's mouth watered when Racha's shift in position gave him a perfect view of the slick, pink folds between her thighs. The sight was obscured by a head and a thick set of shoulders sinking down and pulling her across the bed until her ass reached the edge. Darius pressed his mouth against her.

"I want her on her knees," Corey said. Without a response, the figures on the screen shifted positions. "It's time for you to suck some dragon cock, baby."

Zak settled in front of Racha and she worked his shaft with both her mouth and hands. Darius knelt behind her with his tongue buried between her legs, working her pussy with methodical precision.

Satisfied that Racha was being attended to, Corey looked down at Jill.

Jill's breath came more quickly, the rise and fall of her chest beneath Corey's line of sight capturing his attention. He buried his face in her hair and inhaled. Jesus, she felt so good pressed against him, her supple ass just brushing the straining front of his trousers. He wanted to make her cry out again like he had in the elevator. To make her lose herself to pleasure under his touch. He had to let her watch for just a little longer while Racha crumbled on the other side of the world.

Jill seemed to have other ideas, however, as evidenced by her grip on his hand, pulling it up her stomach to her breast.

"Are you ready for me to take care of you, baby?" he murmured in her ear. He slipped his other hand up and cupped both her breasts, brushing his thumbs across their tips. She arched into his touch with a sigh, still responsive to him, even after all this time.

She turned to face Corey and looked over his shoulder at Rafe where he lay on the bed. "I want him, too," she said.

"The lady's wish is my command," the dragon said. He moved around them and stood behind Jill, obscuring a good portion of the scene unfolding on-screen until he knelt behind Jill, sliding both hands down her back as he went.

Jill's attention seemed to falter. She glanced back at the screen, seemed briefly enthralled by the sight of Racha getting her sweet, pink pussy tongued from behind. Then in a blink her fingers were tangled in Corey's hair, urging him down to her mouth. There was nothing slow and deliberate about her kiss. She devoured him with her urgency, her teeth grazing his lips and her tongue plunging insistently into his mouth.

Corey groaned against the crush of her, trying to follow the course of events with half his attention, but failing miserably. She was warm and soft and needy in his arms, rapidly undressing him, pushing his shirt off his shoulders and tugging at his belt until his hard length was gloriously sliding through her hand. The sweet friction of her touch brought back every second of their fevered lovemaking before he'd lost her. The wet heat of her kiss and the tight grip of her hand around his throbbing shaft made something in his mind snap.

He was only dimly aware of Rafe removing Jill's clothes, and soon she was naked, her ass gripped in both his hands, her breasts soft against his chest. Another hand brushed his, reminding him of the other man in the room but Corey was too overwhelmed with need for Jill—for Racha—for them both to even care. Corey looked at the screen, his sanity shifting to pure erotic need when he saw Racha, front on with her thighs straddling Zak's mouth, her hips undulating and her expression a glaze of pure ecstasy. He knew precisely how amazing it was to have her pussy poised above his lips just so. She tilted forward resting her palms against Zak's ribs. She held Corey's gaze with only a flutter of her dark lashes as Darius sank his cock into her from behind.

"Oh, fuck, I've gotta be inside you." Corey wasn't sure which of the women he was directing the plea to. He'd happily have had them both in that moment. Racha's cries from the screen became more intense and primal. Corey urged Jill to turn around again so she could witness the moment when Racha flew to pieces.

CHAPTER FIVE

"Watch with me, baby," Corey's rough voice spoke in Jill's ear. The caress of his breath sent a pleasant tingle down her neck. He urged her to turn, then pulled her back against him as he sat on the foot of the bed.

Her entire body was awash in sensation. She'd craved getting him naked since first seeing him again. Now she had him and it was glorious. His mouth pressed against her throat, the sound of his voice murmuring incoherent words of lustful appreciation. His hips shifted against her ass, pushing the hot, hard length of his cock against her back.

Before Jill could reposition herself to fuck him, Rafe knelt in front of her. He was large, naked and still amazingly calm. The only signal that he was enjoying himself was the presence of his proud, thick shaft jutting at her from between his thighs. He gripped her hips and lifted her like she weighed nothing. He set her back down slowly. Corey's cock was unmistakably pressed against her center, and he thrust home hard enough to make her cry out. Her voice was a harsh echo to the sounds of Racha emanating around them. She leaned back against his chest, her head resting on his shoulder, struggling to catch her breath amid the pleasure.

Rafe slid his large hands up her legs, urging her to drape them over his shoulders. His thick, forked dragon tongue lashed out, tasting her drenched core and tickling between her folds. He leaned closer, pressing soft, hungry lips to her, swirling his tongue in a frenzied pattern while Corey thrust into her. Corey gripped her chin and turned her head to kiss her, his own tongue attending her mouth as thoroughly as Rafe's attended her pussy.

She twined the fingers of each hand into the hair of two different men, nearly lost, floating against the tenuous tethers both men had on her pleasure. Except she was more aware now than ever of the words Corey kept repeating.

"Oh, God help me I love you so much. So much." Sometimes he spoke the words louder, sometimes they were a mere whisper in her ear. In the middle of her haze of pleasure she realized he was directing the words at the screen when he raised his voice.

She opened her eyes and was greeted with the image of a shimmering green goddess entangled with two men. She only barely recognized the half-shifted form of a dragon in the throes of lust. The only time she'd seen one had been her old lover, and the sight before her was every bit as beautiful, though different.

Racha had shifted positions again. The image of the trio on the screen mirrored Jill's and the two men with her. Her eyes locked with the Queen's. Racha shuddered and a shimmer of light coursed over her skin.

At the same instant, Corey's cock surged hard and hot inside Jill. Rafe's mouth disappeared from between her thighs, but she was too enthralled with what she was witnessing on-screen to be upset. She was only grateful when Corey's fingers pressed between her thighs, picking up where Rafe left off. The familiarity of his touch and the sound of his voice in her ear sent her to the brink.

With one more whispered "I love you, Jill," she hurtled beyond. She rode him harder, ignoring the painful grip his fingers had on her hips, too hyperaware of the pulse of his cock shooting hot seed into her. She yelled his name and heard it in another voice coming from all around her, resonating with an odd power. The sound subsided, leaving her confused. She had only a moment to wonder what had happened.

Corey turned them both and pulled out of her only briefly, leaving her with a dull, throbbing ache between her thighs. She needed more. He pushed her down against the mattress and slid into her again, the stroke slow and deliberate this time, his eyes locked with hers and filled with the same overdue rejoicing she felt welling up inside her. His entire body was covered with a sheen of sweat. As he fucked her, he gradually became wild and more intense than she'd ever seen him. He pulled her legs up against his shoulders and fucked her as though their lives depended on it.

A tiny voice inside her—her last vestige of rational thought—said, *your life does depend on it.*

They came together a second time and he collapsed to the side, holding her tightly with his chest pressed against her back. She reveled in the familiar feel of him. His whispered words sent her back to their last day together before she'd met Aris, to the way Corey had whispered them for the first time after making love that long-ago morning. It had been the perfect beginning to what ended up being the most bittersweet day of her life. Now that he was hers again, if only for a few moments, she intended to enjoy it. She had no idea where Rafe had gone, and didn't care. The screen on the wall had grown silent and still, but neither of them looked at it.

Corey remained pressed against her from behind. His embrace loosened after a moment and his hands slid down over her body. He traced her curves, the hard and soft of bone and muscle, her slick center, wet with their combined remnants of lust. She twisted around until she faced him. She admired his naked body with open appreciation, so familiar and so long missed. She remembered every tattoo, every scar, and found new ones whose stories she wished to know, but after tonight they'd be done for good. She had no idea how much time they had before Rafe returned to complete the exchange, or whatever he had planned, but she intended to take advantage of every second she could.

She slipped her knee across his waist, kneeling astride him. He placed his hands on her thighs and she gripped them, twining her fingers through his and pushing both his hands above his head.

"No touching. I just want to feel you fucking me one last time, please."

He relented, relaxing and letting her make love to him. She began with slow, steady strokes, intent on feeling every thick inch of him rubbing against her slick, tight sheath. Only a few strokes and she was riding him in a frenzied rhythm, chasing the delicious sensation of the peak she remembered reaching with him that morning so long ago. He groaned and his back arched. He thrust back, pistoning into her hard and at just the right angle to bring tears of pleasure to her eyes. The hot rush of his orgasm shot into her and her entire body tingled from head to toe.

"Oh, God yes," she moaned. "I love you," she managed to gasp through the hitching breath of her climax. The finality of it gripped her suddenly and her chest constricted. Her voice cracked and her words mixed with sobs of sadness and grief. "I don't want to lose you again, Corey. Please don't make me leave."

"Shh. He sat up and wrapped his arms around her. "I think it's too late to change our minds," he said.

"On the contrary," Rafe's deep, accented voice came from the doorway. He was dressed again, though when he'd done that, Jill couldn't be sure. "You've taken possession of the lovely Jill so thoroughly, it's way too late for me to get involved. She's yours now, brother."

Corey's hard erection was still deep inside Jill, and seemed to show no sign of subsiding. The glowing pulse of the dragon mark on his chest cast his face into an eerie, green glow. Jill gradually began to notice an odd stinging sensation on the back of her neck. They both turned their heads to look at Rafe, uncomprehending.

"What the hell are you talking about?" Corey asked. "Racha told me this was how it works. I make love to her first, then give her to you to seal the deal."

"True enough. That would have worked, if that had been what you did. You should understand dragon magic by now. Your *intent* is half of the power. If you had truly intended to give her up, I'd have taken her after your first Nirvana. I'd have given her my Nirvana, infused her with my energy, then taken over Aris's mark by giving her my own. Except it seems the Queen left you with more than enough power to take her yourself. Not surprising, all things considered. If the Queen had intended to give her up, she'd never have left it up to you—a man so in love he has no control over the power he wields."

Corey shifted beneath her, started to move her off his lap, but Jill objected. "Wait, Corey. He's right." She wrapped her legs around him and tightened her muscles around his half-hard cock. It thickened and pulsed inside her, sending a brief jolt of pleasure through her lower body. She placed her palm against the glowing mark on his chest. "I've never seen one glow so brightly. Except for my own the day after Aris died.

And as good as making love with you felt before, it never felt so good we didn't need a breather in between."

His hands rested limply on her thighs, the confusion on his face transforming into panic. He let out an agonized groan and pushed her away harshly. She remained kneeling at the end of the bed while he scrambled out and fumbled for his clothes.

"This isn't what was supposed to happen," Corey said. He shoved his feet into the legs of his trousers and yanked them up.

The harsh bite of his words made Jill flinch after the beautiful things he'd been saying while they made love. The TV screen on the wall was blank, the call having ended. She remembered Racha calling Corey's name over and over again, but they hadn't been coherent enough to pause what they were doing long enough to find out what she wanted. How long had it been since they'd lost themselves that first time?

"What the fuck did I do wrong?" Corey bellowed at Rafe. "I followed instructions... you were there. You should have stopped me!"

Rafe sat casually on the end of the bed. He reached a hand out and laid it gently on Jill's shoulder, startling her from her wide-eyed shock at Corey's behavior.

"Darling, show him your mark."

She nodded and bent her head, pulling damp hair away from her sweaty neck. Rafe's strong, sure touch brushed against her skin as he took over, holding her thick golden strands up and away from her skin. She had no idea what they were seeing, but the feel of it told her something about her mark—Aris's mark—had changed. Her hands shook and she gripped them into tight fists to hold them still.

"Jesus Christ, it looks like mine."

"I know it does," Jill whispered. "Except mine's red."

"No, Jill. It isn't. It looks *exactly* like mine. It's even bigger than it was before. And glowing like fucking kryptonite. Rafe, you can't take over now?" His voice was almost a plea, but also had a touch of resignation to it.

Jill turned to look at the black-haired dragon, but knew the answer without him saying it. Their conversation in the limo came back to her. This was what he had planned, all along.

"Could you have stopped him?" Jill asked. "After the first time."

"Yes, but my loyalty is to the Queen. She knew Corey would never have gone through with it completely if she were here making love to him, too. His draw to her power is too strong. But she never intended to give you up."

"Why not?"

"Because you're carrying her father's child."

"That's bullshit," Corey said. "The man's been dead for months."

Jill blinked at him, then closed her eyes, unwilling to witness the conflict of desperation and confusion he was displaying.

"It isn't," she whispered. She opened her eyes again and looked at Rafe. "That's what Aris did with his magic at the end. Just before he died and all his power went into me, he told me he gave me a gift." She placed her hands over her flat belly.

"It's magic similar to what young dragons endure during the hibernation," Rafe said. "We are aware during that time, but we don't age." He leaned down and pulled her hands away from her midsection. A gust of shadow expelled from his mouth and settled on her skin, tingling and cool. It luminesced, briefly betraying a large dragon mark around her navel that she'd never known existed.

"The child must be kept secret. In fact, you should stay

hidden until the Verdanith is assembled, too. If the Council learns Aris's last mate is still alive, they may wonder why and come looking for you." Rafe said. "When the Verdanith is whole, the Queen will unlock the magic so the child can grow again. If you appear to conceive too soon and the Council finds out, they'll label the child Unbound and take it away. If it appears to be a product of a fresh union, you'll be safer."

A pained look crossed his face and Jill lifted a hand to cup his cheek. "That's why you're looking for Rowan, isn't it? She's…Unbound. Is that so bad a thing? The men with Racha were like that, weren't they?"

"Yes, and I promise you, as loyal as they are to dragon law, they would sacrifice their own lives for the chance to fly again. The sex is the only remnant of dragon life they get to keep. Forget shifting, forget mating and family, forget any kind of wealth whatsoever. The things that make us who we are would be stripped from this child and from Rowan, their magic trapped inside the way we are trapped in stone for half our natural lives. But I would gladly be Unbound if it meant the right to choose how to live and whom to love. When I find her, we're never letting our children near the Council or their blasted laws."

"We will help. Won't we, Corey?"

She looked around and found Corey standing by the window, still shirtless and staring out at the sunset.

"The baby's a dragon, isn't it?" Corey asked without turning to look at them. "How are we supposed to hide that fact from the Council after it's born?"

"The same way you just managed to override Aris's mark. The Queen has enough power to make you her surrogate. Not many dragons can accomplish that. Purebreds like her can. or prismatics like her brother."

Corey met Jill's gaze finally. She resisted the urge to apologize to him again. She'd said she was sorry and for a brief interlude that evening she believed he'd forgiven her. Now he looked at her curiously, his expression almost eager. It caused a swell of hope to fill her chest.

"That's actually possible? For me and Jill to have a child together—one like Racha?"

"If the three of you want it, yes. At least once the Verdanith is assembled. It's the key to all of this working out for us."

THE VERDANITH WAS THE KEY. For more than just their fertility issues. Corey's eyes narrowed. "This artifact is going to help you find this other dragon somehow, isn't it? What else can it do?"

"The Verdanith acts as a focus for power, so there are many possibilities," Rafe said. "But to prove to the Council our laws need to change, I need to find Rowan before the the artifact is assembled and the Council finds her with it. She's stayed hidden her entire life, which means her parents must have sacrificed their last remnants of power to protect her. But now that she's discovered her nature, it won't take them long to learn of her existence."

"Why the hell would the Council let this thing be assembled if it takes power away from them?"

"The Council is the reason we can use magic in the first place. They channel the Mother's gifts to all of us, and they're the reason we can even take these forms. Like it or not, we need them, but millenia ago, they learned the concentrated flow of their power into dragonkind made things too easy for us to assert our dominance over humanity."

He cupped his hands around his mouth and exhaled a breath. A dark, shimmering cloud emerged and coalesced into a perfect small sphere. While Corey watched, it floated slowly through the air straight at his chest.

"The Verdanith merely concentrates the flow of power. Think of it as a prism. If the prism is in fragments, the sunlight is scattered, lacking focus and causing the beams to illuminate more dispersed areas."

Before the sphere reached Corey, Rafe expelled another breath that arranged itself in a shimmering grid in the path of the sphere. The sphere passed through, splitting into pieces that bounced with stinging collisions against his skin, each piece dissipating after impact.

"Things are different now—dragonkind is different. Once the Verdanith is assembled, the concentrated flow of magic will return. The intent of our magic may be different than what you witnessed, but it would require less time and effort to achieve what we want, including making children."

Rafe placed a large, gentle hand against Jill's bare stomach. "Changing our laws is another story entirely, however, but this is the first step to prove to the Council how different our goals are than they were three millennia ago."

"What were they then?" Corey asked. He remembered his first impression of dragons when he'd met Racha and imagined a throng of horny, flying beasts taking over the world and turning humanity into a horde of sex-crazed breeding stock. He knew better than that now.

Rafe grinned. "Burning villages, stealing livestock, demanding virgin sacrifices in exchange for our protection of a kingdom's citizens. Essentially wreaking general mayhem and fear among humans in order to force them to give up their most prized sons and daughters to serve our *particular* appetites. That is, until the dragon and human populations became unbalanced. After the Council dismantled the Verdanith and scattered its pieces, it became safer for us to hide among humans because they stopped hunting us out of fear. Over the centuries it became preferable. Now I don't believe there's a dragon alive who would do things differently. Humanity is no longer in danger of extinction at the hand of dragonkind. Quite the contrary—our numbers have dwindled to a dangerous level. If we want to survive, the hibernation needs to be abolished and we need to be allowed the power to breed at a faster rate. This would mean forgiveness for all the Unbound dragons in the world, in the process."

"Does Racha know this? She's never expressed any other agenda besides assembling the thing so we can start a family."

"She does, but she wouldn't speak about it, even to you. Her knowledge of Aris's unborn child is enough of a risk without her suggesting treason. She's the Queen, so her position is difficult. She must protect and see to the needs of the brood while upholding our highest laws. When you do talk to her, be careful what you say. Not out of any mistrust, mind you. Just don't put her in a position that might force her to betray the Court's confidence."

Corey raked his fingers through his hair and looked at Jill. She sat rubbing the back of her neck, lost in her own thoughts and seemingly oblivious to how alluring she looked. She was still naked with her hair a glorious tangled halo around her head and the sheets of the bed crumpled around her hips. He'd always loved how she looked when freshly fucked, but quashed the returning urge to make love to her yet again.

He had to talk to Racha again before he could figure out what to do. His motivation for sending Jill away seemed meaningless now, but if he had jeopardized Racha's feelings in any way, he would never forgive himself for losing so much control. It would be a challenge to never openly mention Jill's child, or once it was born, to pretend it was *his* and not Racha's father's. Could he even pull that off? Could he introduce another man's offspring to his mother as her grandchild?

At least he wasn't alone in his own uncertainty. The other members of Erika's team and their Court lovers all had either alluded to or outright confessed that they had different agendas for wanting the Verdanith assembled. After hearing Rafe's story, he was sure many more of the Brood probably had similar ideas. The best thing he could do was to help Racha manage things until Erika found the final piece. The first way to accomplish that was to make sure Jill was safe and comfortable.

The decision made, he finally found the calm determination he needed to move forward. This was something Racha needed him to do, and he'd grown comfortable with that pattern of action over the past six months, helping her get settled in her position as CEO of her father's company. Doing the same for Jill should be no different, though he was still apprehensive about it. As enthusiastic as Racha had been on-screen earlier, she'd cut the feed before he could find out if he'd damaged their relationship by not following through the way he'd said he would.

"Rafe, did you speak to Racha at all after..." He struggled to find the words. *After I failed to do as she asked.*

"I did. She was due to speak with the Council again and gave her regrets. She said to tell you she misses you." He stood and walked toward the open door. Partway there he turned back, as though he'd remembered something else. "Jealousy is rarely an emotion dragons feel, you know. We're more inclined toward indifference when our feelings are hurt, which can be more damaging. Mostly we are accepting and fearless. Queens are trained to be that way, of course, but that mark of yours and the power you spent today tells me you mean more to her than you realize. It tells me Jill means just as much to you. The sooner you give yourself up to those feelings, the better off you will be."

Rafe slipped his jacket over his shoulders, then gave Corey a salute as he walked out the door. "Good luck, friend. I have to go talk to a Guardian."

CHAPTER SIX

Jill stood in the bathroom with a hand mirror aimed at the back of her neck, trying to see the mark that tingled there. The blazing green glow caught the reflection and she held the mirror still, staring in wonder at the new mark that had replaced the small red medallion-shape Aris had given her over a year ago.

She'd loved the tiny magical tattoo and made a point to wear her hair up when she was with him. It had only been about the size of a silver dollar, situated just at the base of her hairline. The new mark was an almost identical pattern, but now reached all the way across to each shoulder and from her hairline down to the small, protruding knob of her vertebra between her shoulders.

How the hell had Corey done it? He wasn't even a dragon. Everything that had happened after their last go-round was a blur. She'd struggled to process it all, but the realization that Aris's child now resided inside her had overwhelmed every other emotion or thought. With a valiant effort of will, she had succeeded in holding her tears at bay. Partly happiness over having a part of him to hold onto, partly in grief over

Corey's sudden and unexpected rejection after everything he had said.

"Goddamn you!" She smashed the hand mirror against the counter, surprising herself with the strength and ferocity of her anger. The sight of all the slivers of glass reflecting her shattered life made her double over and sob harder.

A pair of strong arms slipped around her from behind. She sank back, lost and in need of the comfort, but tensed and spun when she realized who it must be.

"You succeeded in destroying me, are you happy now?" she yelled, punching her fists into Corey's chest. "I'm getting the fuck out of here. Tell Racha I'm sorry. I'll talk to her about the baby when she's back."

She pulled against his embrace, but he refused to release her. His jaw was set, his eyes hard and determined. "You're not leaving, Jill."

"*Don't* fucking tell me what to do, you bastard. I went through this goddamn day to have one last moment of joy before you threw me away. I believed I deserved it, but you couldn't even let me have that. You fucking ruined it because now I'm stuck with a man who only pretends to love me. Rafe would have never pretended, but he'd at least respect me."

"Jill, it isn't about you and me, I promise you. You have to stay. I'll leave you alone if that's what you want. You don't even have to see me. But for the safety of your baby, Racha would want you here."

She'd heard enough of the conversation to know he was right and sagged against him. She hated how sweet he was being now, especially because of how easily she responded to his comfort. It was just their bond. The Godforsaken dragon bond they had, as if he were her mate. For life.

"I've got to get the fuck away from you." She turned and

ran, picking up her scattered clothing and purse on her way through the bedroom.

"Jill!" His quick footsteps followed her to the landing of the balcony outside the master bedroom.

"Shut up! I'm not leaving. Just… leave me alone alright? And show me where I can stay." She still refused to look at him, and headed to one of the guest rooms he indicated—the farthest from where they'd been today. She shut herself in and locked the door, then collapsed into a crying mess on the bed.

It was the middle of the night when she calmed down enough to venture out. When she opened the door she found a pair of suitcases outside with a note taped to them. "Food in fridge. Gone to Mom's. Call me."

"Man of few words. What's new, asshole."

She lugged her suitcases into the room and tossed them on the bed. Inside she found all her favorite clothes. Not the things she'd always worn with Aris. He had preferred her in more elegant attire than jeans and a t-shirt. No, her suitcases were packed with the things she'd worn with Corey. Clothes she hadn't worn *since* Corey, as a matter of fact. She dug through, increasingly astounded at his choices. She found the one set of lingerie he'd said was his favorite—red lace that he told her made her fair skin and blond hair seem surreal to him. The pair of jeans he liked her in most. The socks he said he'd hated, but knew she loved because they were so comfortable. She'd worn red more often with him because he told her the one time how good she looked in it. She'd worn red for Aris, too, because it matched her mark, but every time she did, she thought of Corey.

The last thing he'd ever given her was tucked at the bottom of the second suitcase. A red silk scarf with brilliant embroidery that he'd picked up in China after he'd left. It had been months since she had ended things with him when she received it. She'd hidden it, still in the package, in her underwear drawer along with his note.

She unfolded the fabric and a small slip of paper fluttered to the floor. She knew what it said before picking it up to read it. *The world and circumstances might tear us away from those we love, but I will always have faith that love is possible.*

She wiped tears from her eyes and lay the scarf on the bed, then went to shower.

After finding more than enough food in the well-stocked kitchen on the first floor, she went back to bed. Loneliness had become a habit for her since Aris died, but she'd had her own apartment to comfort her then. All her own belongings —knicknacks collected over the years. Here she only had darkness and unfamiliar sounds. She longed for home, but more than that she longed for a pair of strong arms to hold her. A solid body to weigh down the other side of the bed. Firm hands to touch her.

She scrambled out of the blankets and felt around the end of the bed for the one thing she thought would comfort her. The silk brushed against her fingers and she grabbed it.

She lay back down with the scarf crumpled under her cheek and breathed deeply. She imagined she could smell him on it. Maybe he had worn it for a little while as he wrote that note. Maybe he'd even carried it on him for a time until he could find a place to mail it. She tried to imagine everything he'd experienced since they'd parted, including how he and Racha had met. A seduction like Aris's seduction of her? She doubted Corey would have fallen for that like she had. Yet he and Racha were together, and he was tearing himself to pieces over his love for her… a mere human.

No. Corey wouldn't have given in unless he believed he could love Racha. She must have done something spectacular to accomplish that. Jill respected Racha for capturing his attention. Of course the Dragon Queen had to be the least pretentious woman Jill had ever met, in spite of how beautiful she was. That would have attracted Corey, too. And she was a good kisser.

Jill rolled over onto her back, remembering the kiss. She'd been surprised, of course. She'd gone to meet the new boss. The daughter of her old lover, and the person who could keep her alive. It had been business in her mind. The kiss Racha had given her at the end of their conversation had been her undoing. It left her vulnerable to Corey, moments later in the elevator. And all that followed.

But that kiss had been so sweet, so gentle. Such a perfect mix of urgent need and love. Acceptance and fearlessness. Racha had sensed her hesitation and pulled away, but Jill had been left with the feeling of being intimate with Aris again, along with an old lover and a new one. All three of them rolled into one kiss.

She fell asleep with her thumb caressing the same nipple Racha had touched, in an effort to evoke that same feeling again. Acceptance. Fearlessness.

Jill called in sick to work on Monday. She didn't want to chance seeing Corey, but had what she needed where she was. She'd texted him that she needed her laptop, and at some point in the early morning he'd delivered it without her knowing. She could work anywhere, provided she had an internet connection.

Being confined at the moment suited her, at least as long as he was avoiding her. In a day or two she'd hopefully be brave enough to slink back to reality, but for now her mind was entirely occupied with old memories and thoughts of a child she'd already carried for months but who still wouldn't have a chance at life unless she stayed put.

Corey remained absent for the next week. Some mornings she'd wake up and find gifts with short notes. Hollow gestures, she thought, as she stared at each one when she found them. Her favorite eggs Benedict from the restaurant they'd eaten at after making love all night their first weekend together.

One evening she only vacated the main room long enough to work out and shower, but came back to a bowl of chocolate-covered peanut butter pretzels and a bottle of champagne. Their celebration the night before their last morning together.

She finally remembered the camera in the bedroom that first night and wondered if there were others around the apartment. He must be watching her to know her every movement during the day. It didn't bother her. She'd always been private about her personal life, but he *was* her personal life, and they'd shared everything when they were together.

The realization was cathartic for her. She didn't go looking for the cameras, though. She did other things.

She masturbated in the shower that night, thinking about him watching her. She did it with no fanfare, losing herself quickly to the feel of her fingers between her legs, swiftly rubbing, and her soapy caress of her nipples.

She went to bed and fell asleep almost instantly after that, smug and satisfied.

The next day, she was determined to walk around naked all day. She put her hair up first, knowing he'd be able to see her mark as clear as day. Halfway through the day she got bored and fell asleep on the sofa after getting herself off again.

The following morning she awoke to a steaming break-fast of artisan sausages and potatoes. The note was pinned with a toothpick into one of the sausages. *Don't you do anything but masturbate all day?*

She flipped the piece of paper over and wrote back. "Only when you're watching." She snagged one of the sausages in her bare fingertips and took a huge bite, letting the juices run down her chin. She ate the rest of her breakfast with her fingers, enjoying the hedonistic quality of torturing him just a little. She briefly contemplated doing other things with the last sausage. She even went so far as to trace its tip over her nipples and trail the greasy length down her belly, but the first salty taste her pussy had of it told her it was a bad idea, so she just ate it instead. She added to the note, "More food to masturbate with, please."

Breakfast the next day consisted of a basket of fruit. She looked through it, finding bananas, mangos, strawberries. And a large cucumber. The obvious divergence from the theme made her laugh. *"Don't go hungry, please,"* was all the note said.

She took her time with the fruit, though. She pulled out a bowl, trimmed the berries, peeled the bananas, cut the mangos. The cucumber she washed but left alone otherwise.

Sitting in her chair she picked each piece, tested it for stability once with her mouth, then worked it into her pussy as slowly as possible. She rubbed her clit with it for good measure before tossing it into the bowl. She had no idea whether he'd follow through with this little game, but if he was willing to follow her leads, she'd follow his and hope he was up to the contest.

Each sliver of fruit went into a new bowl after visiting her deepest depths. She saved the cucumber for last.

She kissed it once for effect, and licked its tip before placing it against her spread labia. The thing was easily as thick as Corey, though shaped differently. She wished for the curve of his cock, but she'd have to make do with this inanimate object. The memory of Aris's cock popped into her head just then. He'd had an oddly straight and symmetrical cock, but had wielded it like a weapon. She always had the sense of herself as his opponent whose weaknesses had yet to be revealed when they were in bed together. But he'd known exactly what to do with his cock.

Corey, on the other hand, was made just right to start with. She fit his cock like a glove, every inch of him always felt amazing inside her no matter how he moved.

She shifted the cucumber so it pressed against her most sensitive places, mimicking what Aris might do, but still wishing for Corey. A slight rub, teasing at her slick folds, sliding up to swirl tiny circles around her clit, then back down again. First the tip in, testing like a hot bath. Then going for broke and plunging in all the way, making her cry out.

"Oh fuck!" She hadn't meant to actually say it out loud, but she was so surprised at the way it made her feel, she couldn't help it. But it felt good. And she hadn't had something that solid and thick inside her for days. Fuck strawberries. Her fingers were more adept. The cucumber might not feel just like him, but it would make her come. She gripped her breast when the surge began. "Oh fuck. Oh yeah. Ah. Corey! Corey!" It was all incoherent syllables to her, though they came back to her a moment later. She pulled the cucumber out of her and tossed it into the bowl. What the fuck had she been thinking? Masturbating in front of him with fruit. Boredom was making her a little bit crazy. She sat up and looked at the bowl. What was he gonna do, *eat it?* Eat the fruit that she'd done the deed with while thinking of him. Okay...worse things could happen, and the thought did arouse her.

She shoved the bowl of illicit produce into the fridge and went to take another shower, making a point to cleanse even the deepest crevices. "Don't want any fruit diseases," she muttered while aiming the showerhead up her vagina.

She shouldn't make him eat it. The thought occurred to

her in the middle of the night after she woke up. She ran down to the kitchen, but the bowl was gone already.

She stared into the empty fridge, muttering a curse.

The next day her breakfast was a fruit salad, with ... diced cucumber. The note read, *Just thought I'd share, since you were so generous.*

She succumbed to her curiosity for only a moment. Maybe he'd made it from fresh fruit? She took one bite then tossed the rest in the trash.

Boredom was the worse prison than simply being confined. The intense longing she felt for him in the midst of it was torture. She wasn't strong. Not enough to resist him. His little gifts over the last week left her with no doubt that he still wanted her. And she was still living alone in the apartment he shared with his new lover. She assumed he'd have let her know the moment he learned Racha was returning.

She did nothing the next day. Ignored his breakfast and his message. Whatever it was, she wanted something different. She wanted him. She wanted him enough to close the curtains and live in the dark for a day, trying to convince herself *not* to want him.

The next morning she went downstairs to make coffee. No new gifts rested on the counter. Maybe he'd gotten the hint finally. But what was the hint? That she didn't need him, when clearly she did?

She stared into her coffee, willing herself not to cry.

"Jill."

His voice startled her. She looked into the shadows beyond the counter. He stood too far away, in the dimly lit entrance of the apartment, but it was him.

"Corey?"

"Hey, baby..."

She set her coffee on the counter, nearly missing the edge. Her heart pounded. "I missed you."

He took a few hesitant steps into the apartment. "I missed you, too."

"Is the Council looking for me, do you know?"

Corey pursed his lips. "I haven't heard from Racha since we were together."

"Do you want me to leave?"

His face constricted in such a conflicted expression, she felt sorry for him.

"She hasn't called you yet... not in all this time?"

"I'm not trying to keep you prisoner or anything. I'm just... worried. It's been two weeks since... Since I bonded you. I didn't want you to leave before she got back and we decided how to keep the Council off our backs."

"I will stay here for a million years if it means keeping my baby safe. And a million more if it means you forgive me enough to love me again."

He walked toward her, a clever smile on his face. A moment later his hands slid down her back and pulled her to him. She trembled in his grip. God, he felt good. His body's warmth, the hardness of every angle she could feel through his clothes.

"I never stopped loving you, Jill. Never. If you want his child, I'll do everything in my power to keep you safe. Dragons or no dragons."

"You taste like bananas today," Corey teased. He resisted the urge to stay in position and give Jill another orgasm with his tongue. She hadn't tasted like bananas, but she'd tasted amazing. Every time. And every time he'd mentioned fruit during the past two days, she disappeared to her shower immediately afterward. It gave him the time to try to call Racha.

Where the fuck was she? He was beyond worried. Their feed had cut out after him fucking Jill and telling her he loved her. Which was no lie, but his other lover had been watching. Or might have been. Jesus, he needed to talk to her.

Giving in to Jill's teasing over the subsequent two weeks had been second nature, but he sensed Jill was just as worried. He finally decided the best thing was to confide in Jill. Except that only worried Jill more, which was the last thing he wanted to do.

The remnants of his latest tryst with Jill were strewn around the kitchen. His shirt, her panties. All the rest of her clothes for that matter.

The scattered clothes reminded him of how much he loved her naked, and how much he'd discouraged Racha of exactly the same thing from the very start. He'd made so many mistakes with Racha. Impulsively, he grabbed his phone and sent her a text. *I want you naked. As often as possible. Fuck the temple. When are you coming home?*

He found Jill in her shower. He stood for a moment outside the enclosure, just watching water slide down her back. She looked back at him and smiled, then turned away. She spread her thighs and tilted her hips, letting the stream of the shower cascade between her thighs.

He shed the rest of his clothes and stepped inside the wide enclosure.

Jill pressed against him instantly when he embraced her under the water. She released a long breath and rested her head against his shoulder.

"Have you heard from her?"

The same worry over not hearing from Racha had tinged Jill's mood during their lovemaking since he'd come home.

"Baby, she's okay," Corey said, turning her to face him.

"I'm worried about her, too. Mostly because you're different now. You love her."

"She's easy to love." He reached for the body wash and squirted a dollop into his palm behind her back.

"Unlike me?"

"Maybe, but the effort is worth it." He lathered the soap and smoothed it down her back, pausing at her ass and clutching both plump cheeks. He'd enjoyed every inch of her multiple times in the last day, marveling at all the little similarities and differences to Racha. She slipped her arms around his neck and pulled him down to meet her lips. A soft moan escaped her throat when his hands slipped between them and he rubbed soapy palms over her breasts, swirling the slick suds in circles around both nipples. They hardened instantly.

The stream of water disappeared from his back, but before he could turn to find out why, a second pair of naked breasts pressed against him from behind. A familiar pair of slender arms slipped around his waist in a tight embrace and he relaxed, the worry from the last few days disappearing instantly. She'd come home to him finally.

"I missed you," he said over his shoulder.

"I would have called, but the Council isn't always flexible. Kris and I were talking to them for several days straight. Now I just need a taste of you."

He caught Jill slipping away shyly and gripped her hand, pulling her against him again. "Not so fast. If I'm stuck with you both, I'd like to enjoy it at least once."

He turned in Racha's arms and pulled both women closer beneath the steady stream of the shower. Racha reached for Jill and the two women came together in a tender embrace, their wet mouths colliding and hands sliding down across shimmering curves.

"I should get a camera…" Corey murmured. He stepped back, taking in the two of them.

"The hell you should." Jill flashed him an irritated look. "You should come here." She gripped him by the back of the neck and pulled him down to kiss her again. When he pulled away, Jill had a mischievous glint in her eyes. "It's my turn to watch," she said. "Give her what she needs."

"My pleasure." He lifted Racha off her feet and turned, pressing her against the tiled wall. She wrapped her legs around his hips and sighed as he positioned the tip of his hard cock between her thighs. He slid deep inside with one slow thrust.

Her tight, hot sheath felt amazing, but it wasn't quite enough for his current appetite. He beckoned to Jill. Now that he had her back, he couldn't bring himself to stop touching her. "I need you, too."

Racha braced her hands against his shoulders and began riding him, her breath coming in soft pants against his ear. She turned her head and reached for Jill, too. "*We* need you," she corrected. As the women's lips slid together, Corey pressed Racha harder against the wall so that her ass rested on the tiled ledge. He braced one hand flat for leverage to fuck her deeper. He reached for Jill, cupped her breast with his free hand, slid wet fingertips down her stomach to the thatch of dark blond curls between her thighs. She leaned closer, moaning against Racha's mouth when his fingertips slid between her hot, slick folds, slippery from her arousal more than from the water.

The women parted, gasping harsh breaths in tandem. Jill leaned back against the wet wall next to Racha. She tilted her head back and closed her eyes in pleasure when he sank two fingers into her and rubbed her throbbing clit with his thumb.

"Fuck, you both feel so good," Corey said.

The pitch of Racha's moans changed, the clench of her muscles around his cock urging him to the point of no return. Her hips undulated, forcing him deeper with each thrust until he was sure he'd drown in her. He kept his eyes on Jill's face, then skimmed a glance down to where her hands cupped her own breasts and she steadily swirled fingertips over her nipples.

"Come for me," he urged. "That's right. Oh, fuck yeah."

His cock spasmed, the tightening of Racha's pussy and her cries of pleasure pulling his orgasm from him. His fingers faltered between Jill's thighs when the blinding rush of ecstasy washed through him. She arched her back and clung to him suddenly. Her hips jerked against his hand and she gripped his wrist, riding her own orgasm and soaking his fingers with her slick juices. The glow of the magic shimmered on their skin, the pale green light seeming to emanate from both women's pores.

Jill's mouth crashed against his, her tongue plunging into his mouth in a hungry search. Abruptly she stopped and sought out Racha, who responded in kind.

"Maybe you two just made a brother for my baby," she said breathlessly. "Maybe all you need is a little extra power when you try."

Corey met Racha's gaze and nodded. "We can hope. Either way, I'm happy to keep trying with that extra help."

The women slipped away from him then, leaving the steamy shower to dry off. He leaned against the shower wall, letting the water beat on the back of his neck and sighing deeply. He turned to look out the door in time to see them hugging tightly, no animosity at all between them—only acceptance.

For the first time in a long time, he felt like he was on his way to unmitigated joy. "No thanks to yourself," he whispered.

BREATH OF INNOCENCE

$\mathcal{A}$ shift in balance of the large yacht woke Camille from a sound sleep, which was unusual. She usually slept like a baby when they were out on the open water of the South Pacific.

There it was again, the subtle rock of the boat, like a swell had hit it. The weather report had promised calm seas for the next week.

The calm of night and the warmth of two bodies had lulled Camille to sleep hours earlier. The large cabin of the yacht with its massive bed was illuminated only by the thin wash of moonlight that found its way through the narrow portholes and the still faint glow of her dragon mark.

Roka's steady breathing halted abruptly and he tensed beside her for only a split second before he shot out of bed as quiet and quick as a breath.

Camille sat up. "What is it?"

The deck above their heads shuddered as though something immense had fallen on it.

"Stay here," Roka said. The gleam of his white hair receded quickly down the corridor, the rest of his muscular bulk cast in shadow. He disappeared up the hatch to the upper deck.

Camille nudged the sleeping Eben and saw that he was already awake, his eyes wide. "What the fuck is out there?" he whispered. Soon, he was out of bed, though moving more slowly than their dragon lover.

"Stay here," he said to Camille.

"The hell I'm staying here alone, you ass." She followed him, ignoring the exasperated look he cast back at her before heading up the steps.

They found Roka on the helipad, kneeling over something. Whatever it was, it wasn't moving.

"How the hell did he get here?" Eben said.

Camille cautiously moved closer, and could make out the pale form of a large, naked man, prone on the deck. His eyelids fluttered and he groaned.

"Sweet Mother. Where did you fly from? What happened to you? Rafe?" Roka shook the man's body. The slight jostling caused a sickly glow to emanate from the man and he convulsed, his skin erupting briefly into shining, jewel-like black scales before receding again to human-looking skin.

"Magic … almost… dry. Can't keep… body…"

Camille barely made out the words, but she inferred enough to guess what was wrong. "He needs energy, doesn't he? Who is he?"

"No time," Roka said. "It will be quicker for you, my love. He needs human Nirvana."

That detail was clear to her from the convulsions, but it took her a second to register Roka's suggestion. She was simultaneously shocked and aroused, particularly when she glanced at Eben and saw his intrigued smile.

"You want me to just… right *now*?" She kept her eyes on Eben's face, watched him raise one eyebrow in slight challenge as if to say, *If you don't, I will.*

The man convulsed again and his body contorted.

"You could wait until he loses the last of his magic and is forced back into his true form. He's about my size."

Camille wasn't oblivious to the facetious tone that bled through Roka's obvious concern. She nodded, her heartbeat speeding up with anticipation. She'd be damned if she'd give Eben the satisfaction of one-upping her. "All right. Just… hold him down and, well, you know what to do."

She moved to straddle the spasming shape while Roka grabbed the man's arms from above and pinned his hands over his head. Eben took his place behind her at his feet.

"What's his name?" Camille asked, looking into Roka's silvery eyes.

"Rafe," he answered. "He is Kol's Second."

"Kol's stupid second, if you ask me," she muttered. She placed her hands against his chest and peered into his contorted face. Dark, pleading eyes opened to stare back at her.

"Please…" he whispered.

"It's alright, Rafe. I'm going to take care of you."

She rested her bare hips atop his, her backside just barely brushing his flaccid cock. She rose up and shifted a little lower so that her bare, sensitive lips pressed lightly against his hardening length. She was acutely conscious of the silken heat of his skin between her thighs and his quickened breathing. Barely half erect, Rafe's thick shaft was easily as large as Roka's, the shadow of which twitched as her pale dragon lover watched her prepare to fuck this near perfect stranger.

With both hands, she clutched her breasts, pinching her nipples until they stood up in hard peaks. Little zings of pleasure shot between her legs, wet warmth spreading. She shifted her hips just enough to give Rafe a taste of slick friction. His eyelids fluttered and his hips tilted up in response.

Bracing her hands on the deck beside his head, she lowered herself to his chest, whispering her lips across his mouth and rubbing her breasts against his torso. She slid up, until both her soft orbs caressed the sides of neck and jaw. She twisted to let one nipple brush over his lips, and then the other way, aiming the other breast across his jaw toward his mouth. The soft contact sent electric pleasure through her body.

A long, forked tongue lashed out at her, startling her when it wrapped around her nipple and pulled the hardened flesh into his mouth. His hips bucked up harder. She moaned at both the smack of hot, thick flesh between her thighs and the tingling pull of his mouth against her nipple.

He sucked hard, as though he thought he could pull her climax straight through her nipple in some hungry infantile fashion. If only it were that easy, she thought, but the sensation reignited the longing that had visited her frequently over the past several months.

She was dimly aware of Eben's chuckle from behind her.

"He's ready. And so are you, from the looks of it," he said.

Rafe's body shifted, tightened in a struggle to get free of the two men holding him down, but they held tight.

Camille knew from the heavy throb between her thighs that they were both indeed ready, but Rafe seemed disinclined to release her from his mouth. She pulled away forcefully and he craned his neck to follow as she shifted back down.

With one hand, she groped between her thighs and found him, long and thick and as hard as polished stone.

She sighed when she sank down on his shaft, holding Roka's gaze the entire time. He seemed to be able to read the pleasure as if it were plain on her face. It may have been, but every time she'd had another dragon deep inside her like this, it was as though they revisited their first time together.

This poor, exceedingly reckless dragon between her legs needed her now, however. If the situation had been different, she would have given a piece of her Nirvana to Roka, too. Unfortunately, Rafe was so far gone, once probably wouldn't be nearly enough.

Rafe jacked his hips up against her and let out a guttural roar. He pistoned into her slick depths hard enough to make her teeth knock together and she braced herself against his chest, clutching at him for stability.

Roka held his arms from the top, but Eben apparently had other ideas.

She couldn't see behind her, but felt Eben's solid, warm body slip up against her back, his hands circling around to cup her breasts. He nuzzled against her ear. "Let's give him a double dose."

The familiar feel of his talented fingers between her thighs made her moan in pleasure. He found the throbbing bundle of nerves and teased it in tiny circles. His other hand groped between them, repeatedly slicking bits of her juices between her ass cheeks. He tested once, slid a fingertip two knuckles deep, then urged her to lean over further.

She did, bracing her hands on the deck again, struggling to stay alert in spite of the return of Rafe's mouth hungrily sucking at her breasts and Eben's gentle prodding at her ass. The urgency of the moment infused Camille with an energy she hadn't felt before, and an urgent desire to provide Rafe with the much needed infusion of Nirvana.

In spite of the care he took in getting her ready, Eben's first thrust beyond her tight barrier made her cry out from the sudden painful stretch. The sensation subsided quickly into a familiar pleasurable feeling of being too full. She attempted to move her hips, but Eben held them tightly in both hands while he fucked her. He'd released Rafe's legs so the man was now free to thrust up into her from beneath, each push of his thick length into her coinciding with a ripple of dark scales appearing in place of his fairer skin.

She was nearly out of her mind with the pleasure when the hot, pungent scent of Roka inundated her from the front. It only took a brush of the velvet tip of his cock against her lips, the salty-sweet flavor of him slick against her flesh, for her tongue to dart out instinctively to taste. She opened her mouth, welcoming the length of him as he slid deep until she tensed and nearly gagged. He gently gripped her head and she opened her eyes, trying to get her bearings. He was right where he'd been, just behind Rafe's head, but had released his arms. So that's whose hands were needfully groping her breasts now while Roka fucked her mouth.

Her orgasm crashed through her like an avalanche of pure, unadulterated pleasure. The white blaze of her mark illuminated all four of them, pulsing with the waves of power that traveled from her and into the body of Rafe beneath her. There was an odd sensation of resistance from Roka. He wanted it, but refused to take it, letting his friend have all her Nirvana instead. She would happily take his, however.

She sucked and licked, the shaking remnants of her orgasm making her desperate for the cleansing wash of Roka's energy. His thrusts between her lips changed tempo and the telltale growl began deep in his chest. His fingertips dug a little deeper into the back of her neck, holding her head so he could control the depth of his cock. She closed her eyes, relaxed her throat, and pushed back against Eben, the only real motion she could control.

The twin shafts piercing her body's other end hadn't stopped moving. Eben's hands gripped her hips like a vise as he yelled out and plunged in deep, holding her tight against him while he shot hot pulses deep into her ass. He didn't move when he was finished, but instead reached around between her thighs and began toying with her clit again, urging her to another climax.

Roka bellowed at the sky as his thick, hot spunk shot down her throat. He pulled away from her slowly, leaving his hands gently cupping her head, thumbs caressing her cheeks. He grazed one thumb across her cum-slick mouth, the light caress teasing the magic-infused fluid along her lips, the energy it contained even more potent than his breath.

She lurched from the slam of Rafe's cock into her pussy and his body arched beneath her. The rough friction made her cry out, from pleasure, not pain. Roka chose that moment to lean down and capture her mouth with his, teasing his tongue gently against hers in odd contrast to the utter possession she'd felt with his cock in her mouth a moment earlier. Her second climax washed over her with a gust of Roka's breath, sinking through her from her head to the tips of her toes. The shimmer of it cascaded into Rafe and he went limp, panting and lolling his head to one side.

Eben slipped out of her after leaving a soft kiss on her shoulder and collapsed in an exhausted heap to one side. Roka knelt placidly above Rafe's head, looking down at the man.

Camille sank flush against Rafe's chest, too spent to move even enough to extract his still erect cock from inside her. It was a comforting sensation, at least, even if it didn't belong to one of the men she loved.

The sheer size of him became apparent once her grasp of reality returned. Still joined at the hips, her head rested comfortable on his chest, the steady thud of his heartbeat loud in her ear. It was so much like making love to Roka, she almost forgot he was a stranger. The feeling persisted when he wrapped both solid arms around her, let out a deep, satisfied sigh, and kissed the top of her head.

"Not quite the welcome I was expecting," he murmured. "But thank you."

The sound of Roka's laugh from somewhere too far to be this new lover's voice reminded her of the truth. Camille sat up abruptly, gasping at the fresh pressure of the hard cock inside her. She met Rafe's sated gaze, taking in the slightly amused smile, uncertain whether she should be offended or not.

"You're welcome…ah…" She glanced down between them uncertainly. He was still very ready, and the truth was she probably had a few more rounds in her, too. But the fact remained, he was a stranger and she was not mated to him.

He shook his head and reached out to grip her hips and lift her off. "As much as I would love another *dose*, as your lovely man said, I have more important things to discuss."

Roka's voice cut through the dark again. "Such as why you're showing up on our boat in the middle of the night with no warning, nearly capsizing us in the process?"

Camille moved to Roka's side and settled against his large, naked warmth. It was a chilly night, though unseasonably warm for mid-July in the southern hemisphere, but she'd been less sensitive to extreme temperatures since becoming a dragon's mate. Still, the heat of Roka's body was a comfort.

Rafe sat up and looked around. He grunted in amusement. "It would take a dragon the size of Kol to capsize this monster. Clever idea, though, a boat. It must make it easier to fly when you want, being so remote. It took me nearly three weeks to find you out here."

Roka's torso tensed against her and his hand squeezed her thigh involuntarily. "Please tell me you haven't been flying non-stop for three weeks. Though I guess that would explain why you were so unstable when shifting. Most dragons know better than to go that long without replenishing their energy. How long has it been for you, my friend?"

"Nearly a month," Rafe said. His expression grew shadowed. "That's why I'm here. The last woman I was with is missing." He seemed to hesitate, the next words caught halfway past his lips. "She's a dragon, and a purebred who never knew her true nature until I found her. She ran before I had the chance to teach her everything she needs to know. I need your help finding her." The repressed anguish in his words made Camille's heart clench in sympathy. Rafe was very clearly in love with this woman. The thought of ever losing either Roka or Eben terrified Camille, but she had no reason to fear that happening. At least she hoped not.

"But surely the Verdanith can help…" Roka began.

Rafe cut him off. "Even if I were allowed to use it first, I can't risk the time it will take, nor risk the Council finding her first once it's assembled. No doubt you know by now that there's a piece missing. It will take time to locate. I've already wasted enough time coming here, but Kol won't allow me to do this alone. And with our combined powers, we should be able to track her more quickly than they can find the lost fragment of the Verdanith. I absolutely have to find her before the Council has a chance to discover she exists, and once the Verdanith is assembled it won't be long before they know."

"She is Unbound," Roka said in a hushed tone.

Rafe didn't answer, but the worried look in his eyes told Camille that Roka was right. She suddenly wished there were more she could do to comfort the man, but she wasn't the woman he loved. The fact that he'd gone so long without seeking out a human simply for the sake of replenishment spoke volumes about his feelings for this woman.

"Stay here and rest until you're ready to leave," she said. "I think our bed is big enough for one more, if you need to top off."

Rafe gave her a perplexed look, then his eyes widened slightly when he caught on. She was sure he must have blushed but couldn't see it in the shadows.

"This isn't something I normally do," he said apologetically. "Before I met her, I might spend one night with a woman every few days and that was enough to keep me going. I'm not used to storing up more energy than I need to last until the next tryst. But I haven't had the stomach for them since I met her. The hunt has become too tedious. You are too generous to offer."

"She is," Eben said, giving her a look that made her skin prickle in irritation. He always seemed to get a little bent out of shape if she initiated with anyone other than him.

"You were on the verge of offering, too," she said to Eben, her voice honey-smooth. "You've been sizing him up, wondering what it might feel like sandwiched between a Shadow and a Guardian. I love you because we have so much in common, you know. At least I don't mind sharing."

With an exasperated shake of his head, Roka stood and beckoned to Rafe to follow him. "Sometimes being mated can be just as tedious, brother," he said. He chuckled at the rude gestures Camille and Eben both directed at him.

Eben stood, gave Camille a resigned look, and followed the two dragons.

Camille watched the trio of perfectly toned, naked bodies saunter across the deck and disappear down the ladder to the lower deck. She marveled at the contrast between the two men she spent virtually all her time with. Eben was definitely the jealous type, but it was as though he were only selectively so. As long as it was Roka's idea, he was on board, but they hadn't actually shared her with another since the ritual six months earlier.

In spite of maintaining a kind of status quo among their trio, Eben had become oddly distant lately. When the three made love, he tended to become withdrawn for a brief span afterward, seeking out solitude and leaving her alone with Roka to wonder whether they had done something wrong. Earlier that night was the first in several that she'd awoken to both warm, male bodies in her bed, but they had also fallen asleep without making love. It was a rare occurrence, but it happened, particularly if she fell asleep early. She had learned later from Eben that Roka had forbidden him to wake her, "Because that kind of peace is too lovely to disrupt."

She understood the sentiment, having woken on many occasions to see the two of them, serene in their slumber. Serene was a bit of an overstatement, however. Eben talked in his sleep, and Roka had a habit of embracing her in the middle of the night and nuzzling her neck until she was mad with need. He swore every morning that he didn't remember doing it.

Camille had no compunction against waking either of them for sex, at least, and had yet to hear a complaint. She had been doing it more often lately. A series of vivid dreams had begun to visit her nightly for the last couple months, ever since Roka had broached the topic of starting a family. Dreams of a baby suckling at her breast, a tiny, beautiful bundle in her arms with golden hair like Eben's and silver eyes like Roka's. She would wake from them so overwhelmed with need she was sometimes blind to which one she turned to first.

Eben had been noncommittal about the family idea initially, but the last time she'd awoken him in the dark of night he had responded to her with an urgency that matched her own. Afterward he had held her in a desperate embrace, refusing to let her go even after her soft protests.

When the chilly ocean air finally began to affect her

enough to give her goose bumps, she stood and descended into the warmer confines of the lower deck. Eben could be remote when it came to his feelings, particularly where she was concerned, so she was at a loss as to how she should get him to open up. Roka, on the other hand, was open and honest to a fault, and didn't seem to grasp Eben's reticence. She would have to figure out some way to get through to Eben and find out what it was that bothered him. Perhaps when they docked in Sydney, the three of them could have a night out before Roka was back at work managing the Australian branch of Kol's security firm.

The lowest ranking of the Court dragons, Roka had been granted the least desirable territory, but relished it even as spread out as it was. Camille loved the scenery herself, and loved being able to travel at a moment's notice between New Zealand, Australia, and Africa. They'd chosen the yacht for precisely the reason Rafe had suggested. Not only was sailing preferable to being trapped on an airplane to travel between the cities within Roka's territory, it allowed him the opportunity to fly when he liked without the worry of being seen. Their travels the past six months tended to take them across the Indian Ocean frequently, with stops in port to refuel and restock, as well as check in with Kol's bonded staff.

She had hoped this lull in their travels would give both men a chance to unwind and relax. It had worked for Roka, but Eben had just grown quieter with each day. Now she wondered if it might not be better for the two of them to have some time alone.

CHAPTER TWO

*S*andwiched *between a Shadow and a Guardian.* Eben could think of worse things, but Camille had been wrong. So wrong. He loved sharing her with Roka, but some nights wished like hell for the dragon to go flying just to give the two of them time alone. But on the nights Roka would shift, Camille would whoop in excitement when he bent his bulky form to allow her to climb on. After the first few flights, Eben began to beg off. He'd go back to their bed, embrace her pillow, and fall asleep with the scent of her in his nostrils.

It wasn't even sex he wanted from her—just her undivided attention, something he had yet to be graced with since the ritual had begun. Hell, he even missed the little moments they'd had during their jungle trek before they found the temple, if they could be called "moments." The stolen glances when they'd meet eyes for a split second across the campsite, before hastily looking away and trying to pretend they weren't both too terrified to talk to each other. At least those moments had been theirs and theirs alone. He had never been so turned inside-out over a woman before.

Now there was another face in the mix and he had no idea what it meant. Another dragon who could snap him like a twig if he said the wrong thing, not that he'd ever seen a hint of animosity in Roka. If anything, Eben was the one prone to violence. The large, platinum-haired dragon seemed to have a calming effect on everyone around him. When they would go out on the town in Sydney, Roka could stall a bar fight merely by being present.

Rafe didn't seem calm, however, in spite of the air being obviously permeated with Roka's breath. Eben had grown accustomed to the delicate scent of it, like the faint scent of Camille that lingered on his own skin even after he'd bathed. Roka's breath had the same effect on Eben as Camille's aroma—a kind of subdued longing, though lately Camille's scent evoked a much more potent flavor of need. A craving he couldn't fully grasp, but that he desperately needed to sate.

The Shadow was clothed now, in a black t-shirt and black jeans. Roka hadn't bothered conjuring clothes for himself, lately preferring to experience the variety of human-made garments he could find. He now sat comfortably across their breakfast table from Rafe in a white terrycloth robe, sipping coffee. Heavy cream and sugar, Eben knew. He guessed the Shadow took his black. He poured himself a cup and carried it back down to the cabin so he could shower and dress.

Several minutes later, Camille's figure appeared ghost-like through the steam that coated the shower door. She stood outside it for a moment, seeming to hesitate.

"Can I join you?" she asked in a soft voice that instantly made him feel guilty for being an ass to her earlier.

"Please." The word came out scratchy, like a desperate plea from a dying man to be put out of his misery.

She entered and stood beneath the rain shower in the center of the enclosure. He didn't move, remaining against the hot jets that sprayed water from the side of the shower. The sight of her naked body calmed more than it aroused him. He watched her wet her hair and tilt her face up into the water. He was fascinated by the way it streamed down over her skin in wet sheets, cascading off her nipples in thicker streams, pooling slightly at her navel before spreading through the trimmed vee of dark gold between her thighs. He could watch her all day, just like this, and never get tired of it.

She moved toward him, a quizzical smile on her face. Eben's heart raced the closer she got. God, why did her proximity always affect him so acutely? He watched her lips move but couldn't register her words, he was so enthralled. Her blue eyes widened and her brows arched higher, questioning. Finally he snapped back to his senses.

"Uh, yeah, here's the soap," he said, handing the bottle of body wash to her.

Camille's brows drew together. "Are you all right? You've been acting strange lately."

He kept his face a mute mask and shook his head. "I'm fine."

She pursed her lips. "I don't believe you."

The floral scent of the body wash filled the steamy enclosure when she squeezed a measure into her palm and handed the bottle back to him.

"Believe what you want. I'm fine."

"*Fine.* Get my back, will you?" She turned away from him and shifted backward almost unbearably close. Close enough for her ass to brush against the erection he hadn't realized he even had until the slightest touch of her made it painfully apparent. She had to know how she affected him. Once he'd made his feelings known to her that night in the temple, she'd seemed more intuitive. Maybe she had always been that way but her shyness beforehand made it impossible to tell.

Christ, he wanted her now, but he wanted more than just to get his rocks off with her underneath him. He wanted to witness her enjoyment of his touch and know it was only his touch she was enjoying. To give her pleasure and know every little sound and twitch she made were only because of the things he did to her.

He gently picked up the wet rope of her long hair and draped it over her shoulder. The soap slicked down her back in a fragrant lather. He moved his hands in slow circles, massaging her neck, her shoulders, then lower. She let out a soft sigh of contentment and leaned back farther. Any closer and she'd be flush against him. He slipped one hand between the cleft of her ass and delicately cleaned there, too. Knowing she was probably still tender, he refrained from touching her more than necessary.

Silently, he moved around her and let the spray from the side rinse her back. He took over washing the front as slowly and methodically as the back, starting again at her neck and shoulders. The contortions they put her in during sex weren't comfortable—he'd experienced some of them himself. This was the first time he'd had sole access to her after the fact, however, and he intended to enjoy it for as long as possible.

He cupped both soapy breasts in his palms, kneading them in slow, gentle circles. He didn't mean to tease, but it was second nature to try to elicit a response from her this way. It always worked. Her eyelids fluttered closed and she moaned, arching against his touch. The weight of them in his hands along with the soft, quick pants from between her lips was the best combined experience. He brushed thumbs over both nipples and watched her face, fascinated by the ripple of enjoyment that passed across her features.

He reached to the side and aimed one of the other myriad nozzles at her to rinse the suds off. When he glanced back, her eyes were open and watching him with a mixture of love, lust, and confusion. Was she feeling the same things he was? An unusual sense of discovery that they'd never experienced before? They had made love before without Roka getting involved, but never without him in the room. His presence had been ubiquitous from the very beginning.

This felt very different. This singular focus they had for each other. It would end soon, but he intended to savor it.

She tilted her head back when he moved closer, and accepted his mouth with hers. Her lips were wet and tasted a little soapy, but her tongue was as sweet and velvet soft as always. Eben lingered, absorbing her need like a sponge until he felt saturated. He released her and bent to her breasts, taking her nipples between his lips one at a time, sucking them into pebble-hard peaks.

Her fingernails raked through his hair, scoring his scalp and pulling him closer. "Oh, Eben. You know I love you, don't you? I've always loved you."

The words had the force of cleansing fire, but they weren't enough to sear away his worry. They only served to reveal his weakness, and it was too stark to deny. He loved her. He always had, and sharing her had become a heavy yet necessary burden.

He claimed her mouth again and pushed her hard against the thick glass at the back of the shower. With both hands, he gripped her thighs and lifted her up. Her skin made rough skidding sounds against the glass as he slid her higher until her legs could wrap around his waist.

"Yes," she whispered when he pressed his throbbing tip against her hot core. *"I want you. Always."*

He slid deep, his hips rocking hard against hers. Her slick heat was so welcome. After the cold air on the deck above, the shower's heat had done little to warm him. Her warmth seeped into him with each steady thrust, with each tight squeeze of her muscles, urging him deeper. She clutched at his head, pulled him to her again. Her lips traced silent affirmations against his jaw, his mouth. Their tongues slid together in an intimate dance, articulating the things they felt, but had no words to adequately convey.

They climaxed together, shuddering, clutching, clinging to the last drops of pleasure. Their mouths bit and sucked, seemed to drain each other dry like parched wanderers in a desert being dragged away from the long sought oasis.

He refused to release her, however. He punched the knobs for the shower, turning everything off.

"You can put me down now," Camille said, pushing away just enough to look him in the eye.

"Do you want me to put you down?"

She shook her head and wrapped her arms around his neck. He grabbed a couple towels with his free hand and draped one over her shoulders. At the bed, he climbed on slowly, scooting on his knees until he could lay her down against the pillows, following so that their hips never parted. He intended to keep making love to her for as long as possible, to take advantage of this window of opportunity to have her all to himself, even though the steady, throbbing glow of her mark made it agonizingly apparent that she would never be wholly his, ever.

"WHAT IS IT?" Rafe asked, his brow creasing with concern when Roka hadn't spoken in several moments.

Roka met his friend's gaze and studied him for a moment. The Shadow knew the trials of love well enough, but he had yet to forge the kind of bond with another that Roka had with Eben and Camille. He might understand, and after the story Rafe had shared, Roka believed he could share his own in confidence.

"It's the bond I have with them. It was unconventional to begin with, but at least the Council has no laws against us mating with two humans upon awakening. Issa refused to take him."

"Was there something wrong with him?" Rafe asked.

"Nothing at all, save his love for Camille. In spite of my bond with him, which is mutually satisfying, I think he still prefers her."

"You have the power to release them, you know. Or to simply let them be together and get out of their way."

"In theory, yes…" Roka glanced toward the narrow stairwell that led down to the lower deck where the master bedroom was. It was impossible to ignore the combination of emotions welling up from beneath him. His connection to the pair was strong. Everything they felt, he received a concentrated taste of. Camille's worry for Eben. Eben's desperate need for her love. They were sharing something now that he didn't think he could compete with, nor did he believe he should.

"But…" Rafe raised his eyebrows expectantly.

"But they are *mine*." Roka's teeth clenched and he pounded the heavy table with one fist for emphasis. The wood creaked under the strain. "His connection to me may not be very deep yet, but we are both lost without her."

"You understand my predicament, then," Rafe said.

"Yes. I understand well. You should rest now. There's a spare cabin below. We will fly at dusk."

Rafe nodded and stood.

"Rafe, if she offers again…" Roka began.

"I will decline, for his sake, and for yours."

Roka nodded and watched his friend descend to the lower

deck. He sat in silence for a moment, then stood and left the shelter of the interior to stand at the railing facing the bow. Dawn was creeping over the horizon ahead of him, chasing the night across the sky. There was nothing like being out in the middle of nowhere, being able to witness these moments. Shifts in the universe, another cycle beginning while the prior ended. The continuous flow of it, persisting uninterrupted, for eons.

In some ways he regretted his own interruption. The enforced hibernation. Time had stood still for him and his brethren for five hundred years. Their own cycles arrested for reasons most of them had forgotten, yet took for granted as necessary. After Rafe's visit tonight he agreed that their laws needed to change, but also felt a little guilty. Had it not been for those laws, he never would have been the Guardian that night in the temple. Never would have been the object of Camille's innocent affection. Perhaps it didn't matter, though. Perhaps fate would have brought them together no matter what. He had to believe that, if he were going to help Rafe with his quest.

The sun finally peeked its shining head over the horizon. The surface of the water became a vast ocean of pure gold that made him long yet again for a child with similar qualities. He didn't wish for a White like himself. Only the Virgin's Guardian ever rose above the rank of servant and protector. He wished for a child as full of wide-eyed eagerness and wonder at every new experience that Camille possessed, and one with the same fearless curiosity as Eben. Sweet Mother help him, but he loved them both so much. It pained him to know that one of them might ever be unhappy.

The flood of emotions he'd channeled from them all morning subsided as the sun's full glory finally birthed itself from beyond the edge of the Earth. It hung there in proud challenge to the shadows that fast retreated to the other side of the world. With a silent greeting, Roka turned and went back inside.

He let them sleep for a little while longer, finding comfort in his own thoughts. There was something to be said for true solitude like this, and he hadn't had it since being frozen in jade in the temple. He didn't miss it, but being presented with it now, he relished it. The other two were a constant presence in his life, his thoughts, his bed. He was truly happy, a feeling he never imagined he would feel during all those centuries of guarding his race's treasures. Camille had chosen him, and everything else had followed.

His bond with Eben, though solid, felt tenuous at the moment, when the man's desperate craving for Camille was too apparent to deny and drowned out all else. Roka had considered taking one or both of them along on this quest he was embarking on with Rafe to find the lost purebred his friend loved. He had second thoughts now. As much as it would hurt to leave them behind, it seemed that was the best choice. He knew the perils of where he and Rafe had to travel. Camille and Eben could handle it, he was sure, but he doubted Eben would object to staying, and Eben would be able to convince Camille it was the best plan.

He wandered into the galley and perused their food stores. They were well stocked for weeks, but it would only take a day for them to sail back to Sydney after he left. The skeleton crew they had brought with them was made up of competent and loyal employees bonded to Kol's family. Roka had yet to hire any of his own and bond them to be loyal to him. He preferred the freedom of only being responsible for himself and the two humans he loved, but knew that would likely change before long.

He tied his hair back into a tail and began cooking, the best way he'd discovered of rousing the two of them from sleep without actually climbing into bed with them and trying more intrusive means. He didn't wish to intrude on them this morning after the taste of their true feelings he'd had earlier. He only wished he'd understood before now what was troubling Eben so he could have found a way to fix it.

Within half an hour, the aroma of fresh baking quiche filled the yacht, luring his lovers to the upper deck. Camille appeared first, sleepy eyed with golden hair trailing in tangled strands over bare, sun-kissed shoulders. The spare top she wore rode up enough to display her tan abdomen and a small glimpse of the glowing mark that adorned her belly. The evidence of her readiness to procreate always incited a surge of need in Roka, but he quelled it this morning. The contrasting absence of the glow in Eben's mark was as much of a signal to their conflict as their emotions. It would do Roka no good to tell them their own feelings if they couldn't articulate it themselves, however.

"You should be sainted," Camille mumbled around mouthfuls of food a few moments later. "This is the best breakfast I've ever had."

"After your performance last night, I'm not surprised," Roka said.

"So, how is your friend doing? Is he recovered?"

"Well enough to travel."

"I hope he smartens up and learns to ask for help before it's too late next time," Camille said.

"We won't have to worry about that because I'll be accompanying him."

Eben, silent until that moment, looked up from his meal. "You're leaving?" His tone was partly excitement, partly apprehension. When their gazes met, Roka nodded.

"But we're going with you, right?" Camille asked uncertainly. She was intuitive, but disbelief could breed denial and override any certainty she had of the truth.

Eben answered for him, still holding Roka's gaze. "No, he's not taking us. Do you want to tell us what this is about? I only heard the bit he told us on the helipad. Something about finding a lost dragon, right? An Unbound?"

"Yes. She must be kept safe from the Council until we can convince them to change our laws. They won't be able to find her until the Verdanith is assembled so we have that in our favor, but we can't very well resist helping look for the lost fragment after begging them to reassemble it. And we do want it assembled, don't we?" His inflection didn't exactly frame it as a question, and he directed the statement at Eben, more than Camille.

"Of course we do!" Camille answered.

Eben remained silent.

"But…" Camille began, gazing off into the distance as she pondered some plan. "We can look for the fragment. Erika's probably going to call us, anyway, depending on what kind of information they already have. We can make sure to 'help' just enough to give you more time to find her. Where do you think she is? I mean… do you have leads?"

Half the tension Roka had been holding in his shoulders left him at her eager response. Camille did relish uncovering a mystery. So did Eben, and the two had been too long away from an expedition like this. Perhaps that's all they needed to sort out their issues—clearly one brief night alone together hadn't been enough to resolve things between them.

"Rowan is a young dragon and just learned her true nature. When I was her age my parents had already released the binding on my magic so I could shift. I spent the first year after I came of age simply stretching my wings like all young dragons do. There are places we go when we do so."

"Dragon teen hangouts?" Camille said with a smile. "Did you hook up with girl dragons and make out and stuff?"

"That wasn't encouraged, but it did happen. Not to me. I

was more focused on the challenge of flying as far and fast as I could. Learning what I could do with my new body—I was already well acquainted with my human body."

Eben finally showed an interest in the topic. "Where are these places and how do you know where to go first?"

"They're scattered around the globe. Remote, unpopulated areas. Mostly mountaintops that have been imbued with magic over several millennia. It's become a custom for every new dragon to leave a bit of their magic behind, and the power has built up. Humans can't sense it, but it acts as a beacon to young dragons. We'll backtrack to where Rafe lost her and find the closest location from there. With luck the two of us will be fast enough to catch up with her before it's too late."

Camille whooped in excitement and bounced out of her chair. Her ebullient nature always amazed Roka and the enthusiasm she showed now reaffirmed that he had made the right decision. Even Eben's mood seemed vastly improved— he smiled at Camille, watching her dance her way to the kitchen with her dishes. She danced back, hopped into Roka's lap and kissed him soundly.

"I'm going to miss you so much," she said, cupping his cheeks between both her hands.

Roka briefly considered urging them back down to the bedroom and spending the rest of the day making love before he and Rafe had to leave. He sensed that Eben would be happy with the idea, too, but not for the same reason Roka wanted to do it. He absently brushed his palm across her belly and she gripped it and held it over her glowing mark.

Camille leaned her head close to his and whispered in his ear. "You do what needs doing. We have all the time in the world for this."

With that she was dancing over to Eben, singing a song

about expeditions and swaying her hips to her own little beat. She straddled Eben's lap, wrapped her arms around his neck and kissed him. The kiss lingered a bit longer than the one she'd given Roka and a brief sense of triumph washed through Roka—a feeling he knew didn't originate from inside himself.

Yes, my loves, you will have each other alone for a time, while I ensure my love-sick friend doesn't self-destruct. Take care of each other.

The pair of dragons shifted at sunset. Their gleaming scales caught the orange glow to the west. The boat listed dangerously under their combined weight until Rafe lumbered to the opposite side of the heli-pad. They stretched their wings, testing the air currents, which were strong that evening.

They had already said their farewells, but Camille walked over to Roka again, struggling to hold back tears. He lowered his head and exhaled, encompassing her in a cloud of pale, calming breath. She wrapped her hands around his horns and rested her cheek against the smooth dip between his heavy ridged brows.

"You two take care of each other, all right? We'll meet you at the Monastery in a few weeks, hopefully."

She could feel the words rumbling forth from his chest when he spoke, the sounds resonating around her. "Take care of Eben. He needs you."

"We both need you," she said softly.

He let out a soft gust of breath, the warm cloud brushed up against her back. "I will be back with you soon."

She stepped back and watched, mesmerized by his magnificence as he spread his wings. With only a couple strokes he was airborne and flying, his white scales catching the remnants of the dying sunset as he flew into it. The yacht listed once then settled as Rafe took flight. Rafe's darker shape caught up with Roka's pale silhouette. When the pair were abreast, they let out a roar at the descending orb of the sun. The sound resonated through Camille's body, leaving her tingling from head to toe.

They were almost dots against the horizon when Eben wrapped his arms around her. She sank back against him, but even his warmth couldn't ease her worry.

"They'll be fine," Eben said. "They're dragon elite, pretty much, you know that, right?"

She shook her head and craned her head back to look up at him. "What do you mean?"

"He never told you?"

"Told me what?"

"C'mon, let me make you dinner while the captain gets us moving."

Eben talked while he cooked. Camille perched on a barstool watching. She'd never been quite so spoiled as she was living with the two men. They rarely gave her a chance to cater to their needs in this way. The things she *did* do for them didn't seem like they required such a reward—she felt just as spoiled in their bed as out of it. She didn't argue, though, particularly not now because Eben actually seemed to have relaxed somewhat now that it was just the two of them.

"Shadows are like soldiers, in a way," he was saying, and paused, thinking. "Only more like special forces commanders. There aren't that many of them. Rafe said that Kol's mother was the only female Shadow ever born, and there are only about a dozen all together. They're the biggest dragons, too."

Camille snickered. "I beg to differ."

Eben caught her eye and smiled back. "Yeah, well, apparently male Guardians can be the exception to that rule. But when they're young they train together—the Shadows and the Guardians. Like, hard-core, walk-through-fire type training. Literally. It makes them pretty indestructible."

"And cocky."

"My point is that the two of them together… there's probably nothing they can't do." He paused his cooking and set a glass of wine in front of her. Leaning with his hands against the counter across from her, he looked into her eyes earnestly. "They're going to be fine."

"Please tell me you miss him as much as I do," Camille said softly.

Eben pursed his lips and turned back to the pan on the stove. He shrugged. "Of course I do. What we have is pretty damn amazing."

"If you feel that way then why have you been in such a shit mood the last couple weeks? Ever since we learned the Council approved assembly of the Verdanith. Today's the first day I've seen you actually look kind of content."

He dished out their food and carried two plates to the table. She followed him with their wine. "Last night was good, that's all," he said.

"This morning, you mean. And I don't see how it was any different than other nights." The truth was, she had a good idea why it was different, but wanted to hear him admit to it. *Tell me the truth. Tell me you hate sharing me with someone else.* Was it validation she was looking for? She didn't think so. It was honesty, because even if Eben confessed he felt that way, Camille had a strong feeling that was only the tip of the iceberg with him. He'd had an open relationship with Erika before Camille had met him. He'd also been just as enthusiastic about making love with Roka as she was, a sight she enjoyed watching as much as she enjoyed being the center of their attention.

Eben didn't answer her at first. When he finally spoke again it was to talk about their travel plans and to speculate what they would need to do to locate the missing fragment of the Verdanith. Camille was too tired to push the issue of his mood, so indulged his change of subject.

As it turned out, Erika didn't contact them immediately. Late the next day they made it back to their high-rise apartment in Sydney. Camille was reviewing her translations from the temple when the call finally came. They would fly to Singapore and from there, Kris and Issa would meet them and fly them to the Monastery.

"Did she say what she needed us for?" Camille asked after Eben ended the call.

"It's mostly you she needs. There are ancient texts in the vault at the Monastery. Accounts of the lineages and bonds of the previous Court dragons who each Verdanith fragment belonged to. They actually wrote all this shit down back then. It's in a dialect older than the Unbound that serve the Monastery, so you're the only person who is capable of translating it in detail."

Camille raised her eyebrows. "That'd have to be Dark Ages or older if it predates any living dragons who would be able to translate it." She fidgeted in her seat and rubbed her palms on her khaki-clad thighs. Eben eyed her in amusement. "What? I'm just eager to get started. I'm better at translating ancient dragon dialects than your wonky moods, so let's get going already."

～

IF IT WEREN'T for the incessant white glow of Camille's dragon mark, Eben could have pretended life was perfect. He didn't begrudge her the obvious desire she had to have a baby. In fact, he believed she'd be a fantastic mother and could easily imagine her boundless curiosity and enthusiasm affecting the child in what could only be a positive way. He just didn't see where he would fit in the whole arrangement. He could deal with three. Sharing her with Roka had never been an issue, even though now that it was just the two of them he relished having her to himself. And the truth was, he missed Roka every bit as much as Camille did. Two more giving lovers he could never imagine he would have, and the Guardian generally provided a mellow counterpoint to Camille's vibrance, giving her something different to focus on during the rare moments when Eben wished for solitude.

But he felt like a fraud every time he saw that mark and knew his own still lay dark and unresponsive. She had to have noticed it. He knew Roka had, but the Guardian had avoided mentioning it. One advantage of the marks, however, was that with the magic infusing him he had no concerns about accidentally getting her pregnant. Even though he knew she would be over the moon if it happened, his lack of true desire for a child was the perfect form of birth control. Too bad the dragons couldn't bottle that magic and sell it world-wide. They'd make millions.

Eben looked forward to their trip to the Monastery. Erika would understand how he felt, at least. Maybe she'd even be able to help him put the whole situation into perspective, or at least figure out how to explain himself to Camille. The leader of their little group had been his best friend and lover for years before they'd discovered their dragon mates. She probably knew him better than anyone, the same way he knew her. They'd both professed early on to not wanting kids until their careers were well established and they'd done all the living they could do. At twenty-eight, Eben felt that he had barely even scratched the surface. Now that they had centuries, he saw no point in rushing.

Camille was her effervescent self, bouncing off the walls while she packed, her chipper excitement infectious to the point that he felt just a little buzzed himself.

"I wonder if they've found her yet," she said as she rolled her cotton panties into tight little bundles and stuffed them in the trekking backpack she preferred to travel with.

Eben looked up from his own more haphazard packing. "She had a few weeks' head start on them, but Rafe said she was new to being a dragon. Hopefully if they haven't, they will soon."

"Just as long as that doofus of a Shadow doesn't run himself dry again," Camille said with a sardonic look. Her expression darkened as another thought crossed her mind. "You don't think Roka would…you know."

Eben blinked at the suggestion. The possibility had never occurred to him. "You know he would if he had to. You did it —and you loved it. So don't tell me you're jealous."

"I loved it because you were both right there with me. The poor guy looked like he was dying, and if I could help somehow, I had to."

"Well, let me put it this way, if it were you out there with him and he needed it, would you?"

Camille pursed her lips and cast her eyes down to the khaki shorts clutched in her hands. "Yeah. I did love it, and not just because you were both there. There was something different about Rafe that made the whole experience feel… I don't know… more dire. We don't make love with each other for survival. When he had his mouth on me it felt like he needed something only I could give him. Like his sole sustenance came from me alone."

Her pretty blue eyes met his, wide and intense, and just a

little bit fearful. Maybe she thought her confession would upset him.

Eben rounded the bed and cupped her face in both his hands, tilting her head to look at him. "We both need you to sustain us, Cammy. Trust me, I don't know what I would do without you. I'd be lost, and I think Roka would, too."

"But that's different. It's entirely mutual, that need. With Rafe it was like he was helpless. I didn't *need* to do what I did, I only did it because he needed what I could give him. Having another person's survival in your power like that, it made me feel like I really had a purpose, you know?"

Eben eyed her curiously, his brows drawing together. "Somehow I don't think you're trying to tell me you want to be with him again. So what are you saying, Cammy?"

She pulled away, the press of her lips signaling her irritation that he'd yet again misread her signals. "I know you don't want a baby, so it doesn't really matter, does it? You and I could start now, if you did want one. It's the dragons who have fertility issues, not us. But you don't want it, and Roka won't go through with it once we can unless all three of us are all in."

So that's what it was about. She had most definitely noticed and it had probably been eating at her for weeks. Eben's teeth ground together and he forced himself to relax. He shook his head slightly. "I don't know what to tell you. I can't force myself to want something like that. I'm sorry."

Camille didn't respond, but her jerkier movements as she packed indicated that he'd be better off leaving her be for now.

She barely spoke to him during their trip, instead staying hyperfocused on her translation notes that she carried with her. Her mood only improved once they reached Singapore and stood on the roof of a massive high-rise hotel waiting for their ride to the mountainous jungle island where the Monastery lay.

He barely saw them as they flew closer, their underbellies shimmering with reflective magic that rendered them nearly invisible to observers from the ground. He heard them loud and clear, however, the flap of their expansive wings as loud as a ship's mainsail whipping in a heavy wind. He recognized the pair even before they shifted, but was confused at who had arrived to take them to the island.

"Geva. Kris," he nodded at the gigantic pair of dragons in greeting. Camille had opted for a more affectionate greeting and was hugging them both, peppering their ridged brows with kisses and stroking their horns. Geva purred at her in response.

Kris shifted, the prismatic scales that covered his large shape fading into smooth, tattooed skin. He stepped close to Eben and pulled him into a warm embrace. "Greetings, brother. It's been too long."

Eben returned the hug, only slightly aware of Kris's naked state, but more interested in having another question answered. "Where is Issa? I thought the two of you would be meeting us." He tried to camouflage the disappointment in his tone with genuine interest, but Kris's eyebrows raised briefly.

"She couldn't make the trip. Other responsibilities at the moment." Kris shifted his gaze halfway through the statement, glancing at Camille, then accepting another embrace and giving her a peck on the cheek.

"What kind of responsibilities?" Camille asked.

Kris only shrugged. "Council stuff."

Eben narrowed his eyes. As cagey as his friend could be about dragon politics, something in his demeanor seemed off. Issa had been Eben's first experience with a dragon. He'd awoken her from her frozen slumber in the Temple, and that brief connection they had shared still lingered. It was in no way as intense as the connections he'd forged with Roka and Camille, but he still considered her one of his closest friends among the dragons.

In truth, they had all been more intimate with each other than Eben ever had with his human friends. Kris's lingering touch during their hug was enough of an indication that he hadn't forgotten and the affection hadn't subsided. It was a comfortable mental zone for Eben, that level of friendly affection that could lead wherever they chose to take it with no worries of emotion complicating the scenario. The anticipation of their stay at the Monastery suddenly aroused him in a manner not unlike his excitement as a kid whenever he was about to leave for summer camp. Even though he and Camille had just ended a very relaxing vacation and he knew this was a working trip, he looked forward to spending time with everyone in a spot where there were no secrets and inhibitions didn't exist. That was his hope, at least, but a glance at Camille's closed expression made him wonder if he might be wrong entirely.

"Shall we?" Kris said, pulling Camille by the hand to Geva and giving her a leg up to climb onto Geva's wide, ruby-scaled shoulders. Then he shifted again and bent down for Eben to climb on his back.

Erika was there to greet them when they landed, a wide, excited smile on her pretty face. Eben felt himself grinning like an idiot to see her again. The second he reached her he pulled her into a tight embrace, reveling in the familiar feel and smell of her. Her soft curves were always at odds with the dusty scent of her skin, like she'd been digging in dirt. It was a scent that was wholly Erika.

"God, I missed you," she said into his ear. "How's life treating you guys?" She pulled away and looked up into his face, then at Camille. "Where is Roka, anyway? You didn't say why he didn't come."

Camille recited their scripted answer nonchalantly. "Kol needed his help with something, and when the boss calls, you don't say no." It was the perfect answer, particularly considering they had jumped at Erika's call and were here now.

Camille followed Erika without a glance back at Eben. Before he could hoist his backpack onto his shoulders again, Geva had grabbed it and effortlessly slung it over his shoulder, draping his free arm across Eben's shoulders.

"She looks a little tense, my friend, are you not satisfying her with the big guy gone? Come to that, *you* look tense. Maybe the two of you should come to the baths with us after you get settled in, unwind a bit before you get to work and get your issues out in the open."

In spite of trying, Eben couldn't hide the tension. Dragons were so goddamn perceptive it wasn't funny. Now Geva was doing that thing he did with his tickling breath raising goose bumps on Eben's neck and raising other parts of him in response. He chuckled and shook his head. "Man, are you persistent. I don't think I can talk about it right now, though, and I doubt Camille wants to, either."

Geva dropped his arm and shrugged. "Suit yourself, but you know where we'll be. Erika's been in the vaults all day. As much as I love the dusty, dirty version of her, getting her wet is always the highlight of my day. I'm sure you would agree?"

Eben would be hard pressed to forget how enthusiastic Erika had been when they were lovers, but at that moment a different visual popped into his head. Camille's suntanned thighs spread wide in his mind's eye, the dark golden fringe between them framing the glistening pink of the treasures therein. He was painfully aware of the fact that they hadn't made love as frequently since the night before Roka had departed. Could he convince her to go join Erika and Geva tonight?

He found her in the sparsely furnished room they had been assigned, across the hall from Erika and Geva's room. His gut tangled with conflict over how to even approach her now. There was nothing he could say at this stage to make her come around. They clearly wanted different things and that understanding tore him to pieces. He'd only just discovered how much he loved her and now she had pulled away. He just hoped it wasn't an irrevocable distance that lingered between them.

Stripping down to his skin, he picked up the plain linen drawstring pants that were left for them to wear during their stay so they blended in better with the permanent residents. "I'm going up to the baths to join Erika and Geva before dinner. Want to come?"

Camille was busy brushing and rebraiding her mass of golden waves. She had already changed into her own Spartan underthings, the pants riding low on her hips and the round swell of her breasts pushing the split neck of the shirt wide. The loose robe that would cover everything hung on a hook nearby. She was going braless like she tended to do more often lately, the sight of her nipples pricking at the soft linen a tantalizing treat for his eyes to feast on.

She glanced at him, her gaze skimming down his naked body. Her eyes had that hungry look she would get whenever she was particularly horny. Eben wondered if Geva had gotten to her, too. The man did like to tease them with his breath, get them worked up and then sit back to see what they would do. Except she always gave him a look just like it whenever he took off his clothes. It was usually followed up with a sly smile, then some particularly lewd proposition would spill from her lips, the naughtiest and most arousing contradiction to her angelic features.

She didn't say anything close to what he hoped to hear. She clenched her eyes shut and screwed up her face. "I don't think so. I want to get to work for a bit. You go have fun."

You go have fun. And what the hell did she mean by that? They were here to work, for one thing, but there was no reason to rush it, particularly since they had agreed to deliberately take their time with the research so that Roka and Rafe would have a good head start on finding Rafe's lover.

Whether or not she meant for him to have the kind of fun he had hoped she'd join him for, he couldn't be sure. He pondered her comment while padding barefoot along the stone paths that meandered around the lush, meticulously kept grounds of the Monastery.

The slightly citrusy aroma of the baths hit his nostrils long before he reached the cozy outbuilding. The squat, square structure was built of worn stone, smoothed by centuries of weather and use, and the lovely scented steam that billowed out the door only managed to remind him of their brief respite at the Monastery after they had completed the ritual and left the Temple months earlier. It had been the most relaxing session of lovemaking he'd ever had, with the aromatic herbs the monks added to the water, the heat that encompassed them, and the slow languid, fucking the three of them had engaged in for what had seemed like hours without stopping. He'd never felt so intimately bound to any other person as he had been to Camille and Roka during that afternoon. It almost felt sacrilegious to step into the baths without them, but he needed time to think.

CHAPTER FOUR

ithin a day, Roka was too far from Eben and Camille to pick up on their varying moods. The two dragons flew west into the night, timing each leg of their trip to pause at a remote, unpopulated location to rest. Rafe insisted on pushing forward even during daylight, particularly when they were approaching the coast of Africa.

"*We can replenish at one of the villages on the coast,*" Roka projected as they flew. "*You need it worse than I do, brother.*"

"*We need to keep going. We already had to backtrack to catch any sign of her. I won't stop until we see another.*"

While they weren't exactly hot on Rowan's trail, they had seen signs of her stopping in a handful of locations, most of which were inactive volcanoes that were frequent waypoints for young dragons stretching their wings. They could fly for days at a stretch without rest, but Rafe's energy reserves wouldn't keep up with this pace for long. If he had mated soon after awakening in the temple, the regular infusions of energy from a partner would have allowed him to fly for a month or more with little rest, though it would severely deplete his energy. Roka preferred not to take the risk of not stopping, but his friend was adamant.

The temporary power link they had forged for the trip enhanced their tracking abilities, and also gave Roka a strong sense of how quickly Rafe's power began to dwindle as their trip progressed. He almost hoped his friend didn't sense the shimmering trail of a female dragon's power he could see as clear as a shaft of sunlight ahead of them.

Rafe let out an excited roar and began to fly faster. *"A fresh trail. It must be hers!"* He banked to the left and dipped lower in the sky, hurtling downward for several hundred yards before leveling off again and soaring forward on an invisible current of air.

Roka sped up to follow. They would have to teach her to cover her tracks once they found her, but the intensity of the energy she'd left behind signaled that they were getting closer. The wind whipped past him as he descended to catch up with Rafe.

Miles ahead, the majestic white monolith of another dormant volcano lay, holding court over the lush green of a vast jungle. He remembered this place vividly from his own youth. It was the pinnacle of the African landscape, and served as a beacon to adolescent dragons on their quests for independence after learning to fly. He hoped Rafe's Red would be here so he could return to his mates. The distance from Camille and Eben left a void inside that was more than just his depleted energy reserves. He still had enough energy from them to last him several more weeks, but that wouldn't preserve his mood any if Rafe continued with such single-minded and obdurate persistence.

Kilimanjaro loomed closer with each strong stroke of Roka's wings, and the magic grew stronger. It was as distinct a signature as if they had found her footprints, particularly since it was the most prominent trail. It had been centuries since Roka's generation had traveled these skies. While he could pick up faint remnants of those long ago trips, they had faded to a ghost of their original potency. Rowan's magic was impossible for them to miss.

Rafe picked up his pace and Roka surged ahead to stay even with his friend. When the deep, shadowed circle of the volcano's dark caldera came into view, Rafe began to descend, carving a wide arc around and circling in a spiral closer to the ground with each circuit. There was no sign of their quarry aside from the potent residue of her magic glimmering in ethereal streams and undulating waves in mid-air. As Roka got closer, he could see the depressions of taloned footprints in the snow below them. Rafe followed the visible trail, skimming along only a few dozen yards above the ground, but Roka knew they had missed her yet again. Hopefully only by a brief interval this time. At least they were at a good place to rest before they pushed on, and there were small villages below the mountain where the pair could replenish their energy.

Roka landed heavily, the powdery snow puffing up around him. It was nearly dusk, so they would have to wait a bit longer before descending down to the level of human view.

Rafe, however, stalked around the area in frustration. He nosed at the deepest depression at the end of the trail of footprints and growled. Rowan had clearly taken off from that point to fly again.

"She's only a few days ahead of us, friend. We will catch her soon. Rest for a moment and then we can head into the jungle for some respite and to refill your reserves."

"I told you I will not stop until we find her!"

"You told me you would stop when we saw another sign of her. This is that sign. You will kill yourself if you don't rest and replenish."

"You don't need to follow me now that I have a clear, fresh trail."

Roka watched in astonishment as Rafe swished his tail around and leapt into the sky again, his wings quivering with the effort. He doubted his friend even had enough magic left in his reserves to shift if he wanted to, which wouldn't do if he fell unconscious in a populated area. The villages below the mountain were long known to be bonded to lower ranking local dragons, and since Africa was technically part of Roka's territory, he could visit them when in need. They had need now, but Rafe wasn't seeing reason. He would need to be able to shift before entering the villages. The indigenous peoples' legends spoke of occasional visits by magical people from the mountain. However, if they showed up in their true forms they would likely terrify the people.

With a burst of energy, Roka surged into the sky, angry at his friend's stubbornness. He easily caught up to Rafe and gripped him by the tail with one large taloned foreclaw. Rafe faltered, but kept going.

"You are a fool. If you don't stop, you're going to force ME to take care of you. Trust me, I still have the strength to pin you down and give you what you need, whether you like it or not."

He had hoped it wouldn't come to threats. It would have been preferable for them to replenish their reserves from several willing humans, but sharing their own Nirvanas would serve the same purpose. The disadvantage of that scenario would be leaving a stronger signature behind, something Shadows and Guardians both were trained not to do. Plus, the magic that seeped through them from the ether during their climaxes would leave them both marked with traces of each other. Rafe was his friend, and while that level of intimacy between dragons was not unheard of, it could affect the balance of power in the dragon hierarchy. But he was a Court dragon and technically Rafe's superior.

He had been careful not to touch Rafe during their encounter on the yacht, allowing Eben and Camille to provide him with the energy Rafe needed. The only dragon they all had no hesitation about coupling with was the Catalyst, but Kris was the anomaly among dragons. He absorbed, and only gave when it was absolutely necessary. Other dragons only had sparse control over how much energy they could keep back.

Roka had no compunctions against asserting his rank. He would give all his energy to Rafe if he had to, and likely some of it would be pulled from the lingering magic Rafe's lover had left behind on this mountaintop. He clamped another talon on Rafe's hind leg.

The Shadow roared in indignation and banked in the air, turning and battering his wings hard against Roka to get him to let go. His tail and leg twisted in Roka's grasp. Roka released him but only so he could quickly clasp his talons around Rafe's black-scaled foreclaws. With white wings flapping to keep him airborne, he hooked his legs around Rafe's and swiped his tail around to hold his friend against him by the waist. He clamped his jaw down on Rafe's neck hard enough to bruise and immobilize, but not hard enough to puncture the dragon's nearly impenetrable scaled hide. The sharp contact with the pressure point rendered Rafe unable to fly, his wings going slack. Roka beat his wings harder to keep them from plummeting to the ground and lowered them both slowly to the deep bed of snow in the crater below them.

"Take it because you need it," Roka said, tickling the back of Rafe's neck with his tongue.

Rafe groaned at the contact with the erogenous pressure point Roka's teeth and tongue were assaulting—a spot it was only accepted for a high-ranking dragon to use to assert dominion over one of lower rank.

Roka was already primed himself, the anticipation and his own need rising in him at the contact with the black dragon and the taste of Rafe's growing submission against his tongue. He had never coupled in full dragon form before and the novelty of it aroused him further.

Rafe's black wings splayed against the snow and Roka pressed against him. Roka's erection blazed between them, the full length of it emerging from its protective scaled sheathe between his thighs.

"Sweet Mother, you don't actually mean *to fuck me, do you?"* Rafe's eyes widened as he struggled in Roka's grasp.

"If you don't let me, I'll sit on top of you and give it to you like this." Roka shifted his hips back and rubbed his thick length between Rafe's scaled thighs. The soft, hot friction sent an electric tingle through his cock and into his groin. He stroked again, closer to the seam that marked the opening of the pouch where Rafe's cock hid. The bulge swelled slightly and Rafe groaned.

Rafe twisted his hips away, his rear talons clawing ineffectually at Roka's thighs. Abruptly, the figure beneath Roka shimmered and shrank.

So Rafe did have enough energy to shift after all.

Roka lost his grip on Rafe's human form, but only for an instant. He, too, shifted, more quickly and smoothly than Rafe had. The dark-haired Shadow stumbled and fell to his knees, his human body appeared strong enough, but shook from the effort of the change. He wasn't quite as bad off as he had been that night when he had arrived unannounced on their boat, too depleted to maintain his human form for long if they hadn't helped him. He clearly wasn't far from that point now, though. His skin still shimmered darkly with the mirage of scales trying to emerge again.

Rafe hung his head, clutching snow into his fists. He appeared to be shivering, but Roka knew it wasn't from cold.

In spite of them both being stark naked, extreme temperatures had no effect on them in either form.

"You know what will happen if we don't do this," Roka said. "Your baser urges will take over, you will go insane, your dragon instincts compelling you to devour any living thing that crosses your path just for sustenance. Occasionally you will want to fuck, but only helpless human virgins will be able to satisfy you and there are far too few of those in this world we live in now. You will seek dominion over humanity and you will destroy everything our race has worked for over the last few millennia. Why are you being such a fool?"

"I will die without her anyway."

"But will you let yourself die before you even find her? We will find her, I can promise you that. Let me help you so you can keep going. Once you are past this we are going down the mountain to find a better source."

For the first time Roka regretted not asking Camille and Eben to come with them. At the very least, they would have had willing and available partners to keep the dragons going, even if it meant carrying more supplies.

Rafe sat back on his heels, arms hanging limply at his sides. Roka stood before him, looking down in sympathy at the pleading look his friend gave him.

"Help me, please," Rafe whispered.

Roka knelt in front of his friend and reached for him. Rafe let himself be pulled into the guardian's embrace and wrapped his arms around Roka in desperation. The intensity with which Rafe surrendered was nearly heartbreaking in its contrast to his resistance a moment earlier. Rafe's hot, soft mouth sought out Roka's, Rafe's hands reaching up to tangle in Roka's long, sleek hair. Roka gasped at the invasion of tongue and the clash of their teeth. His cock surged back to life and he groaned when Rafe gripped it tightly, stroking insistently. Rushing would do neither of them any good, however. The more they let the well of magic build up before releasing their Nirvana, the more energy the other would have access to. Not to mention, the more pleasurable the experience would be.

"Slow down," Roka whispered, pulling Rafe's hand away from his cock. "You want to be strong when we find her, don't you?"

"I need a taste now," Rafe growled. "I'm losing it." His skin shimmered with the emergence of obsidian scales that didn't subside, and shimmering black horns coiled up from his brow, their shine reflecting the blood-red of the sunset so vividly Roka almost wondered if his friend had spontaneously changed colors.

Roka pushed him back down to the ground and followed, sliding his tongue between Rafe's lips in a promise of what was to come.

"I will take care of you," Roka said, sliding down Rafe's body, the wet trail of his tongue turning to crackling ice as he went. The snow beneath them had melted and frozen again, leaving them in a slippery depression. Roka dug his toes in for purchase, like it was sand on a beach, and took Rafe fully into his mouth. At the same time, Roka gripped his own cock and stroked, his rising need acting as a magnet to the residual magic in the air. There was always more of it, the trails of invisible power a web that linked them all to their origin. To The Mother, wherever she existed. The power was doled out in strictly governed rations by the Council, who acted as conduits between Her infinite power and the rest of the race. He couldn't think about those lingering issues now, however. He focused on simply absorbing what he could to give it to his friend tonight.

Rafe's hips bucked against him and Roka gripped the other man tightly behind his knees, pushing his legs wide, his knees against his chest. Rafe allowed himself to be handled, giving over fully to Roka.

The thick, hot length of Rafe's cock throbbed in Roka's mouth. The Shadow was already on the verge of orgasm, so Roka pulled back, watching the glistening column slap back against Rafe's stomach, his saliva hardening into a crystalline mesh for only a second before melting away again due to the man's increasing heat. Rafe's heavy sac tightened beneath Roka's kiss. The Shadow sighed and placed both large hands on Roka's head when he darted his long tongue out to lick and suck each delicate globe into his mouth. Rafe jerked at the subsequent invasion of Roka's tongue between his ass cheeks and deeper. Roka gripped his thighs tighter to hold him still.

"Oh, fuck, I need you. I'll take anything you can give me. Everything. Please just give it to me!"

Roka's mouth quirked as he looked up at Rafe. He loved the man's desperation and would have enjoyed a little bit of torture at this point, something he knew Eben loved to have inflicted on him. But Roka knew better in this case. Rafe truly did need what he was about to receive. Satisfied his friend was slick enough to accommodate Roka, he pressed his cock to Rafe's ass and pushed. Rafe's head flew back into the snowy ground and he cried out as Roka sank in to his hot depths. Rafe's tight opening clenched and pulled, constricting so hard Roka almost lost his mind. Then his friend relaxed and Roka pulled out slowly. He groaned as the tightness returned, clutching at the tip of his cock. Roka spread his knees to gain better traction in the ice and dug his bare feet deeper. The cold cut of the rough snow was the perfect counterpoint to the hot pleasure surging into him in the form of the magic his desire attracted. He fucked harder and the wind kicked up around them both, as though their need created a pocket of low pressure, sucking every bit of spare power to them in a swirling cyclone. Roka's hair whipped around his face violently, but he could still see Rafe's back arch up in ecstasy, his dark eyes locked in a needful gaze on Roka's face.

The power flowed through him in a tingling deluge, but seemed to catch, as it always did, just at the base of his spine. He held back, on the verge of a mind-blowing orgasm but waiting as long as he could until the energy reached the point of overflowing. It was always that sensation of being too full that he loved. Full of power as tangible and unrelenting as the squeeze of Rafe's ass around his shaft, but this time it pushed harder at his restraint, as though Rafe's empty well was a vacuum seeking to be filled. When it reached that point, Roka held his breath and stopped abruptly, every muscle quivering. He leaned over Rafe, bracing both hands on either side of his friend's torso.

Rafe's face was illuminated by the spill of glowing magic emanating from Roka's eyes, white hot and bright as the sun. The dark-eyed face rose up, hands clasped the back of Roka's neck. Roka let himself be pulled down, the kiss a hungry signal of encouragement. Roka groaned against the kiss and pumped his hips. Once—the plunge of his cock so deep his hips clapped against Rafe's as loud as thunder. Twice—the friction against Roka's cock lit a fire that quickly seared through the barrier between the magic and his will to hold it back. The third stroke sent him over and he plunged his cock deep, dimly aware of the harsh cry coming from his throat as he came in hot spasms. He lost himself to the flush of all that power singing through him as brisk and violent as wind whipping through a canyon, carrying him soaring along with it. He let the magic carry him as he had the strong currents of air and magic they had flown upon to reach this place. When it began to subside, he let himself drift back to solid ground, to the feel of the warm body beneath him, arms wrapped around him and skin shimmering with fresh power.

He pulled back slowly and collapsed to the side, relishing the cold crunch of the snow beneath him, helping to regulate his heated temperature.

"Was it too much for you?" he asked, taking note of Rafe's dazed and lethargic expression. His friend looked a little drunk. The lack of focus when Rafe sat up and turned to face him only served to emphasize that impression.

Rafe let out a low chuckle. "You didn't even come close to what she can do, my friend. It's like she's *made* of the stuff. Her trail may seem strong here, but she's much farther ahead than the remnants of her magic would lead you to believe. That small taste of her magic was the best thing I could have had tonight though, so thank you for that."

Roka raised up on an elbow. "You said she was inexperienced, that you unlocked her magic. Was she a virgin, then?"

"No. At least not physically. She'd only been with human men before. I've been wondering about it ever since, but even she didn't know her origins—who her real parents were, and for good reason. Someone wanted her hidden badly enough to bind her magic so that even she wasn't aware of it. But it only took one look at her for me to know. It wasn't magic I sensed, but some other, more subtle energy she had, that I've only seen in other dragons." Rafe paused, his eyes skimming over Roka's face and body.

Roka looked down at himself, conscious of the details his friend was taking in. His hair and eyes weren't the least of it. They all had a bearing and attitude that made them stand out even next to the most striking humans, regardless of how they concealed it through magic. A dragon whose magic was bound would not stand out to an unobservant dragon, but a Shadow like Rafe would be attuned to those kinds of subtle cues.

"Your curiosity got the better of you, I take it," Roka said. He understood the way a Shadow worked. Anything that had the scent of a secret caught their attention to the point they couldn't let it go until they uncovered every nuance and shed a light in every dark corner.

"I took a chance. The first time we made love, I could feel her magic reaching out, trying to break free. It was my first time with another dragon. I had no idea what would happen. It blew my mind and I nearly shifted completely the first time. I didn't even have to reach Nirvana before she was pulling every bit of magic I had in reserve. I don't think she even realized what she was capable of."

"Fucking you felt something like that," Roka said. "Well, almost. With Eben and Cammy, it feels like they're merely open to me, ready to give but not devouring me in return. Your need almost broke me."

"I'm sorry," Rafe said, eyeing Roka's groin again.

"Don't be. You needed it and I was happy to give." He lay back against the snow, staring at the star-speckled sky. It was full night, but the white of the snow made it seem unnaturally bright, particularly since Rafe's skin still emitted a luminescent glow.

Rafe sighed deeply. Roka sensed a hint of tension in his friend a second before the caress began. The light brush of a hand at his hip startled him because Rafe hadn't moved from his slouching seated position, arms resting on his knees. Roka glanced at him and their gazes met again, Rafe's dark eyes flashing with violet magic. Roka closed his eyes and let out a low moan when the warmth of an invisible palm cupped his balls and squeezed gently.

The Shadow's signal was wordless, a mere nudge of that incorporeal hand urging him onto his side. Then Rafe's real hands were on him, growing more urgent with each touch. An arm slipped across Roka's hip, a hand gripping his erection tightly and stroking, then pushing him onto his stomach. The cold snow bit into his cheek, but the rough friction only stimulated his aroused flesh more. He spread his legs at Rafe's urging and raised his hips up slightly. The caress and squeeze of hands magnified as though there were several exploring his body at once. One pair on his ass, kneading and invading with gentle prodding. Another pair between his thighs, stroking his cock and balls. Yet another caressing the rest of him. He was still acutely aware of Rafe's presence behind him, readying him for fucking. The simultaneous sensations were akin to the cyclone he'd been in earlier. Magic quickly coalesced around them, surging through him with every stroke of the shadowy hands.

Sweet Mother, he'd heard what Shadows could do but had never experienced it himself. The plunge into the abyss was simultaneously instantaneous and everlasting, his climax stronger than before, now that Rafe channeled the Nirvana from the intricate, ethereal web of power that surrounded them. For one surreal moment he was sure the glow that emanated from them and reflected off the snow was the sun breaking over the horizon, that they'd been tangled up with each other for hours, riding the waves of Nirvana together.

If the young Red they searched for had made Rafe feel better than this, it was no wonder he was so desperate to find her.

CHAPTER FIVE

Camille found it comforting to work by lantern light and spent her evenings in the dark, ancient vaults of the Monastery as much to work as to avoid Eben's increasingly contradictory moods. The cool, shadowy space, combined with the sweet, dusty scent of the tomes in front of her lent a nostalgia to the process. It helped that she was dressed in the simple, timeless linen undergarments and draped in the lightweight robes that all the monks wore. The clothing was so voluminous that it easily concealed her figure, the only telling attribute of her gender her long, blond hair bound in its perpetual braid.

The thick rope of it fell over her shoulder and brushed across the faded page of calligraphy in front of her. She blinked and rubbed her eyes, wondering what time it was, but she hadn't bothered to bring a watch to the vaults with her, or any other piece of technology for that matter. The most modern thing she had was her simple loose-leaf notebook and mechanical pencil that she used to transcribe her translations.

Erika and Geva had done some initial work before she

had arrived, identifying the most likely sources of useful details by the gilded artwork they contained. It was Camille's job now to decipher the stories that went along with those drawings and illuminated text. She was abstractly reminded of the night in the temple when she had uncovered the purpose of the ritual. Only this time she felt oddly devoid of the desire that had driven her that long ago night to sacrifice her maidenhead to the inanimate figure of Roka, the Guardian.

The realization of her lack of libido depressed her. She thought of what she had said to Eben the night they had arrived here, and was gripped with an irrational pang of jealousy. It was her own fault if she drove him back into Erika's arms. Erika would probably understand how he felt. The very vocal leader of their team hadn't been shy about sharing her philosophies of life, one of which was that life was too short to spawn offspring who might hate you anyway. It made no sense because Erika had loved her own father fiercely, from what Camille could tell in other, more maudlin moments during their quest. Either way, a woman as driven and ambitious as Erika would undoubtedly prefer a childless life.

Camille, on the other hand, had always wanted kids. She'd been the only child of a Nebraska farmer and his high-school sweetheart. She had wondered why her parents never had more, until her mother confessed to having complications after Camille's birth that required her to have a hysterectomy. In a sense, Camille had been blessed because she'd grown up with foster brothers and sisters—her parents' attempt at sharing their love and their need to nurture a younger generation. She was still close with many of those surrogate siblings, though she hadn't spoken to any of them in almost a year.

It had been an entire year, she suddenly realized. A year

since Erika had assembled her team to begin the search for the temple. A year since Eben had walked into that bar where they had met and proceeded to torture her with his tense silence until he finally confessed he had loved her all along but was too overwhelmed by it to even speak to her. He'd been giving her the silent treatment for the last three weeks again, but for entirely different reasons. She just hoped like hell the reasons wouldn't end up destroying them.

Camille shook her head to dispel the unsavory thoughts and focused more closely on the ancient text in front of her, turning the pages with gentle reverence. The third volume of the stack of tomes she was researching came from an Italian village during the middle ages. The text was difficult to read, but she found the gilded decorations around it gave her clues to its context. She had always loved illuminated manuscripts. So much that they had been the topic of her master's thesis. But these were far older than any others on record. Though they resembled some that she had studied as an undergrad, the language was far different from the Latin that graced the pages of the manuscripts she had studied in college.

She turned the page and stared at the twin dragons that graced the margins of the page. The top of the page had a vivid green symbol that she quickly sketched into her own notebook. It was a circle, with six dragons swirling around inside, tails entwined.

"The Verdanith," she whispered, and had to restrain herself from reaching out to touch it. This page might contain the clues they were seeking, and after three weeks of looking, she almost regretted that her part in the search might soon be over. She began reading and painstakingly transcribing every word into English, reworking the structure into coherent sentences. A piece of the missing fragment's story came to life with every stroke of her pencil on the pages of her notebook. Still, it was only a piece, an incomplete map leading to another dead end. The lack of a complete story seemed suspicious to Camille, almost as though the Council wanted the fragment to stay lost.

A WARM, water-saturated piece of meat was all Eben felt like when Erika and Geva finally arrived for their regular nightly bath. The pair glowed, literally, and he eyed them as though he were a little offended that they'd flaunt it. Of course, this might be the only place in the world where it would be overlooked as natural.

He'd been introduced to the Unbound who lived here and knew one of the major functions of the place was to service dragons. The human men who lived here were all bonded to Kris and Issa, but not in the manner of mates. They were all on a spiritual quest and had the option of celibacy or service. Eben had been surprised at first how many of them actually chose celibacy. After one brief conversation with one of them it all made sense. Choosing to live in a place where your chief temptation was readily available, yet choosing to abstain, was the ultimate challenge to self-discipline. He almost envied those men for their restraint. On the other hand, he also felt a little sorry for them, particularly because he had spent the last few weeks as celibate as many of them.

Geva shed his linen drawstring pants and slipped into the water. He slid a wet hand through his short, red hair and eyed Eben with vivid green eyes. It was a different look for the large Red, but it suited him. Geva turned to watch Erika, lips parted and breath growing shallow.

Eben smiled at the man's reaction to his lovely friend. She could do that to a man, effortlessly. She'd done it to him, in a time that felt like ancient history. Why he hadn't fallen head over heels in love with her, he had no clue. There had been some fundamental connection they had missed. He didn't regret the other connections they had made, though. If anything their relationship was sweeter for its lack of complication and its overabundance of honesty. So it amused him to no end to see what it looked like to be a man who was enraptured with his best friend.

And, God, if Erika didn't work it. She took her time taking off her clothes to join them. First she shrugged out of the loose robe, then shed the linen top. She wore no bra underneath, and her dark brown waves cascaded down her back in a messy sprawl when she took the shirt off. She hung it on a nearby hook then bent down, back facing the hot pool, and tugged her pants over her hips.

Geva let out an exaggerated sigh at the sight of her bare, luminescent ass.

Jesus, the man was already sporting a huge erection just from looking at her. The sight aroused Eben just a little, but mostly he was still amused at the dragon's reaction. Then he just fervently hoped they wouldn't succumb to fucking right in front of him. They were glowing enough from the last round as it was.

When Erika turned to face them, Eben turned away, not wanting to see yet again the reminder of how much Erika had changed since becoming the red dragon's mate. The steady, pulsing glow of the red mark that graced her lower abdomen was as telling as his own dormant one. The sense of betrayal had surprised him with its intensity when he first saw it weeks earlier, but now it just lingered like a persistent itch he couldn't scratch so had given up trying. His half-aroused cock grew limp, and his conflicted interest in perhaps joining them in some fun for once disappeared from his mind completely.

Erika wanted it, too. There was no lying where the magic was concerned. The mark told all.

He sat silent while she climbed into the pool with a satisfied groan that made his balls clench at the familiarity of the sound. He tilted his head back as if he were enjoying the water, and kept his eyes fixed outside one of the windows. He tried to ignore the pummeling thoughts that invaded his mind every night. The worry that he was being an ass to Camille for not giving her what she wanted. Erika was supposed to be his ally, but how could she be if she was already primed for mating?

Mating. Jesus, he was already thinking like them, too. He'd heard Roka say the word a thousand times in his explanations of a dragon's imperative to reproduce. It always perplexed Eben why their political bullshit had forced them to throttle back when that seemed to be their sole purpose. It hadn't been until Roka showed him historical accounts of mass murder that were the result of dragon politics and their lack of control over breeding. "We did this to ourselves, but we'd like to undo it because the world is different now. Dragons have evolved."

Eben wasn't so sure, but he went along with it. If anything it was because of Camille. He wanted more than anything to make her happy, and she wanted more than anything to have his baby.

He tilted his head back against the cold stone of the bath and sighed.

"Eben, what the hell is wrong with you? You've been a mess for weeks."

His head jerked up and he stared at Erika.

Her dark brows lowered suspiciously.

"Nothing."

"Bullshit." She glowered at him and he reflexively glanced at Geva for support, but the Red only seemed amused by Erika's persistence.

She sat forward, resting her elbows on her knees,

completely nonchalant about her heavy breasts hanging between her arms. "I know you better than I know myself. You're beat up over something and judging from Camille's lack of appearance yet again, I have a good idea what's wrong. You just need to confirm it."

"Nothing's…" He only started to get out the word "wrong" when she dove across the pool and gripped his cock in her hand. Her other hand went to his balls and squeezed. The pressure was more arousing than threatening, but her voice against his ear told a different story.

"You tell me the truth. So help me God or I will rip your balls off. If you've hurt her, you better believe me, you deserve it."

The venom in her voice took him completely off guard. He had no idea she was so protective of Camille. Maybe they had talked? But Jesus…

"Holy fuck, Erika, no! I love her. It's this fucking Verdanith that's gotten into her head. She's baby crazy. Like you, I guess. I have no idea what the fuck I'm supposed to do with that."

The grip on his balls loosened and drifted away, leaving him more aroused than he'd been before, particularly since Erika's luscious breasts had been pretty much cradling his chin during the ordeal.

"The Verdanith is our best chance if we don't want to be raising kids in our fifties, or later," Erika said. She shared a glance with Geva that seemed oddly conspiratorial and raised alarm bells. Eben was sure he caught a subtle shake of Geva's head. It wasn't like Erika to hide something from him, but they weren't as close as they once were.

"You don't want a baby?" Geva's deep and slightly accented voice startled him, but the Red's scrutiny made him even more uncomfortable.

"No. I want her. At least for now. I'm just not ready for a

kid. Fuck, I love her more than life and I'm not ready to share even more of her." He took a breath and in a pathetic tone that disgusted even him, he added. "I just want more time with her before it all goes away."

The Red's eyes narrowed as he looked Eben over. Eben hated the look, but knew beyond a doubt he deserved it. He was an immature pussy. A self-centered manwhore. Unable to admit even to himself that he had lucked out with this arrangement. He didn't deserve them.

But he needed them. He needed Roka for his unwavering understanding of their shared masculine plight in the presence of the perfectly unassuming sexual presence Camille possessed. She had no idea how she affected them both. She could do the most benign things and Eben would hear Roka respond at the same time he felt his own heart thud in his chest. She had no idea how beautiful she was and her innocence astounded them both. It was one of the things that he shared with the dragon that had brought them closer in those dark moments when Camille was asleep and he worried that he'd never be enough for her as long as Roka was around. But the dragon had sensed it and drawn him out, eliciting his darkest secrets in the quiet corners of their apartment or their yacht while Camille slept. Whispers and white breath convincing Eben that there could have been no other choice to make that night but to let Roka mark them. Camille still didn't know the things he'd shared with their dragon. His little proprietary quirk of thought surprised him. Roka was theirs, true, but mostly they were his, body and soul.

He and Camille were Roka's just like Erika was Geva's, as evidenced by the glowing red mark beneath her navel.

Erika sat down beside him, tactfully avoiding any more intimate contact. "Is that why you've been a broody mess since you got here? I know you, sweetie. You're the light of the world in my mind. You don't brood."

Eben gave in finally. Confession would be good, he decided. He scrubbed his face with wet hands and combed his fingers back through his long hair.

"She wants a baby. Is it a dragon thing?" He shot a pleading look at Geva who sat on the edge of the bath beside him, elbows casually resting on his knees.

"Maybe," Geva said. "Maybe our influence just brings that aspect out in women?" Geva winked at Erika.

Erika patted Geva in a slightly condescending fashion that still smacked of deep love. "Sweetie, my decision had nothing to do with you. I just remembered how great my dad was and wanted to be that to my own flesh and blood. But bottom line, I had a reason."

"You guys aren't helping," Eben said.

"Sorry," Erika said, shifting to focus directly on Eben. "Have you actually told her this?"

"Would it matter? She wants a baby. I don't. How the fuck do I tell the woman I love that I don't want what she wants?"

He glanced at Geva, who was looking at him with a peculiar expression.

"How do you not want a baby?"

Eben was dumbstruck. He stuttered out a reply. "Because I like my life without distraction?" He felt like a total shit as a result. Jesus, if he'd known dragons were so baby crazy he'd have never signed on.

Erika's nudge turned him back to her. "Talk to her, dumbass. Now go. Go, go, go!" She smacked his ass as he raised himself out of the pool, resolute in his mission. Talk to her and hope she still loved him afterward. She already knew how he felt about kids though. She'd said as much. So why should he bother?

He glanced back at Erika and hustled. It didn't matter,

he'd talk to her. Talking was the goal here, regardless of the outcome. No pressure.

~

CAMILLE WAS TOO peaceful to disturb when he found her in the vaults, her blonde head resting on a pile of ancient tomes and her hand still holding her automatic pencil pressed against her notebook. He remembered nights like that when he was too wrapped up in the research to care about anything else. Except he knew tonight and every night for the past few weeks were as much an escape for her as his nights sitting in the bath. She might have been focused on the work, but if they hadn't pushed each other away that first night, she might have spared more time to talk to him.

Eben pulled a heavy wooden chair closer, making an effort not to make a sound. She still wore the ridiculous robes they'd given them, but the drapes of dyed linen had slid down her bare shoulder, leaving her bosom almost bare. She hadn't bothered with the thin undergarments today.

She had a tendency to pass out when she was faced with intense emotion. He knew this about her, yet it still amazed him when he witnessed it. Maybe she was just tired now. He couldn't imagine her work eliciting a panic attack. And she did just appear to be sleeping.

It was all he could do to avoid touching her, so he just watched for a time, settling back and enjoying her amusing little sounds. Soft snores that shifted in tone as the frequency of movement under her eyelids changed. What he wouldn't give to be in her head right now, to see what she dreamed. Would he find himself there? Or some fantastic universe he couldn't even imagine.

He was chuckling to himself over the idea when she sat up abruptly. "Eben? What are you doing here?"

"Watching you sleep, dummy." He couldn't help but smile a little at her bewildered, sleepy expression.

"Oh." She fidgeted with her pencil and notebook, making a show of reading. Her eyelids blinked rapidly. She was still avoiding him.

"Camille, we need to talk. We should've talked a hundred times already, but I guess I was too stubborn to make the first move."

Her expression drew in at that and she hunched over her notebook.

Eben placed a hand on her shoulder, letting his thumb caress the bare skin of her neck.

"I love you," he whispered.

Her eyes clenched shut, and that subtle barrier between them broke his heart.

"Do you, really?" she whispered back, her voice barely audible even in the near dead silence of the place they were in. Before he could answer she said, "Because you seem pretty intent on making me miserable lately."

He blanched at that. She didn't understand, but it was his fault. He decided to lay it all out.

"I don't want kids. Never did. We never got a chance to talk that detail out, so there it is."

"So you hate children"

"I never said that."

"You just did!"

He grimaced and hung his head. "I don't hate kids... I just...Jesus, Camille, I know you want them so I want to make you happy, and I will gladly do that, but I fucking *hate* the idea of losing you to more needy souls. I still need you. Christ, I hate to admit it, too."

She reached up and caressed his cheek, the touch almost reflexive. He gripped her hand and leaned into it.

"I don't even know you, Eben. I never realized it until

now, though. I mean, I *know* you intimately, but you've held back, haven't you?

He could only nod against the soft brush of her hand.

"Tell me."

So he did. He told her everything. He told her about his early life, the child of a single mother in a small town. One he did everything to get out of as quickly as possible. He told her about his experiences afterward, his failures in college before he'd met Erika and she'd inspired him to turn things around. It all seemed completely natural and somehow cathartic to let it all out. So much that he wondered why he hadn't already. None of his past had seemed remotely relevant to what he shared with Roka and Camille now. But it felt so good in the telling that he knew he had to sit down with Roka when they were reunited and talk.

His chest tightened with a pang of longing when he thought of Roka. As private as this exchange had been with Camille, it still felt like an element was missing. The big white dragon was the missing piece of their puzzle. He had no idea how his conflict with Camille would resolve, but he knew without a doubt that Roka's presence would have made a difference.

"You don't want kids because you had a crappy child-hood?" Camille asked, tentatively.

Eben thought about it, but the true answer was obvious.

"I don't want kids because I want you more. The laws of physics say that two bodies can't occupy the same space simultaneously. You two fill my heart. That doesn't leave enough room for anyone else. You and Roka are my world right now. Maybe it's selfish of me, but I'm just not ready to give that up."

Surprisingly, she smiled and leaned in to kiss him. "You have room, trust me," she said. "But we can wait."

CHAPTER SIX

*E*ben collapsed to his knees and buried his face in Camille's linen-covered lap. His arms snaked around her hips and gripped her tightly. The warm weight of his embrace sent a surge of tenderness through her. She brushed her palm over the silky blond hair on his head, still damp from the bath. Her fingertips were sore from writing and the cool softness of his hair felt good against the abused skin. He held her a little tighter and inhaled sharply when she dug her fingernails into the back of his neck and scratched along the contours of his skull the way she knew he liked.

"I love you so much," he murmured into her belly, then turned his head to rest his cheek on her thigh.

She gazed down at the dark blond shape of his head, the beautiful profile with clenched brows, sharp cheekbones and long, straight nose. He was just like a child, seeking comfort from whatever tiny yet insurmountable turmoil he had encountered. For him it had been her desire to replace him. At least that's what she realized he had seen it as. It had never occurred to her that either of her lovers might see a child as competition for her love. They were partners, the three of them. On the same side in all decisions. Or so she had believed. Now she saw a different angle. This did change things. Roka might be disappointed, but he would understand. And they had time.

Eben sighed and arched his shoulders up into the steady, soft scratch of her nails down over his bare skin. His head pressed tighter against her belly and she reflexively spread her legs. Her previously dormant sex drive resurged in full force. And hadn't she fantasized about the two of them in precisely this position countless times before? They had never been in this particular situation before, however. Not outside of her dreams.

Without even opening his eyes, Eben pressed his face into the folds of soft linen that concealed her from him. He inhaled deeply, then opened his mouth and bit at the cloth that bunched between her thighs. The increased pressure against her core shouldn't have been enough to even register with her—it was no more intense than the tightest jeans she'd worn, digging into her flesh. Yet it made her gasp and shift her hips toward him.

His hands gripped her hips with deliberate force and pulled her even closer. He burrowed through the folds of her voluminous robes, panting in frustration at not finding what he sought.

Finally he gave in and reached up to her neckline, tugged at the drapes of linen until they fell away, exposing her breasts.

Eben gazed with feverish longing at her breasts. He latched onto one pink tip and sucked, drawing her into him as though she were his sole source of sustenance. He took her other breast a moment later with as much zeal, until her nipple began to ache from his desperate attention. He switched back to the other breast, kneading both in time with his sucking, and his hands tore at her clothing, finally pulling the robes apart and pulling her hips closer.

Her pussy ached almost as painfully in the absence of his touch as her nipples tingled from his constant abuse. God, if he would only transfer that intensity a little lower…

That sweet dream came back to her as he pushed her thighs apart, bent his head, and slid his tongue between her slick and ready lips. The heat of his mouth was just as startling as it had been in her fantasies. Even though she'd had him like this before, this time the experience was so profound as to be transcendent. She rested her hands atop his head, one foot draped across the pile of books on the table beside her, the other foot resting on Eben's bare shoulder. Her head tilted back against the chair and she sighed with pleasure.

We can wait, she thought, and was about to say out loud again when the steady swirls of his tongue over her clit sent her spinning. Every thought that had been in her head became a cyclonic mess as she cried out and clutched his head against her throbbing flesh. The only thought left in her head was that first one. She would wait for centuries, if that's what it took, as long as she had him.

Roka leaned against the stone wall of the corridor, listening while Camille came to pieces under Eben's expert tongue. His own arousal was almost unbearable. He had missed them, but as much as he wanted to be with them now, their ordeal was only just being resolved, even after weeks away from him.

He had considered leaving again, letting the pair bask in their reunion without his interference, but after so long apart he craved them the way a dormant seedling craves the sun. Instead he climbed back to the moonlit breezeway above and waited.

Rafe's silent, shadowy presence became gradually apparent, though there had been no signal that he had arrived. Without looking away from the glow of the silvery disc in the sky, Roka greeted him wordlessly. His friend broke the silence first.

"Rowan was here," Rafe said. "Barely two days past. Darius confirmed it, though it was tricky enough to get the details out of him. He's sure none of the others saw her was and she only interacted with him and Zak long enough to replenish enough to fly again. Darius said he believed she was a Court dragon at first, based on her size and remaining reserves of energy. She'd been flying for more than a week and only just stopped to rest."

"Kris and Issa didn't see her?"

"None of the other dragons did. Darius believed she was Geva out for a flyabout at first, until he greeted her and learned the truth. He wouldn't have let her stay any longer than absolutely necessary, which I am grateful for. She had no idea how close she came to discovery."

"That is fortunate, particularly to know we have an ally here. Kris and Issa would be, if they could, but they are too close to the Council to risk it. I haven't even seen Issa yet, have you?"

Roka shook his head. The violet dragon's absence had seemed odd to him, and Kris's excuse unusually cagey. Then when he had greeted Geva and Erika, the pair had been more closed off and secretive than usual as well.

"Something isn't right," he said.

"You've sensed it, too?" Rafe asked. "Sometimes I think your intuition is as keen as Kol's."

"With all that I have shared with the other members of the Court and their mates, I would expect more honesty.

Perhaps it's only anxiety over finding the Verdanith that has affected them, too, but I get the feeling there are deeper secrets at play."

"They can keep their secrets as long as they don't interfere with me finding Rowan. Or with you getting what you desire…"

Roka smiled at his friend's not-so-subtle insinuation. He was at least relieved that Eben and Camille seemed to have finally broken through their own barriers. Even now, he could sense their relief at getting their differences out in the open. Roka was only a little disappointed at the decision they had come to. Time was one thing they had in abundance, and if everything worked out with the plan Rafe and Kol had hatched, their entire race would have infinite freedom soon enough. Seeing that mission through to the end was far more important now than planning to have a child, no matter how much he wanted to produce such a treasure. Patience was something he was adept at.

A delighted yelp pierced the shadows behind them and he turned to the sound of running footsteps coming toward him. His heart leapt at the same instant Camille launched herself into his outstretched arms and began peppering his face with those sweet kisses he had missed so much. She embraced him so tightly he nearly lost his breath.

Eben seemed only slightly more subdued when he approached and placed a hand on Camille's back and one on Roka's shoulder. Roka gazed into his eyes, looking for that troubled uncertainty that had been there weeks ago when they parted. Relieved to find nothing but calm satisfaction, he gripped the back of Eben's neck and pulled him close, kissing him fiercely.

Rafe cleared his throat and moved to leave.

"Wait," Camille said, slipping out of Roka's embrace and

grabbing Rafe's hand. Rafe gave Roka a startled look and moved to pull away while stammering out an objection.

"I'm not trying to suck you into our little trio again. There's just something you need to know. I found it."

Her statement stopped Rafe in his tracks and both Eben and Roka let out startled exclamations.

Camille waved them off. "Don't worry, I haven't told anyone else yet, and I didn't literally *find* the missing piece, just a solid trail picking up from where the Council lost track. There's still about three centuries of lost time to find where it is now, though, so you still have time to catch up with her."

"Where is it," Roka said, tugging at her arm insistently.

She gave him an exasperated look. "It *was* in Paris during the seventeenth century. I found a name linked to one of the bonded families of the dragon who it used to belong to—the one that died."

"It'll take time for you to get there," Rafe said. "So that gives me a head start."

Roka grimaced. "No, friend. We have to tell Erika the news."

Eben interjected. "And knowing her, she'll want to have Dimitri pick up the trail right away. She's even keener on finding this thing than the rest of us, I think. Completely blew my mind."

"We can tell Dimitri the issue," Camille said. "He'd understand."

"No!" Roka and Rafe both spoke in unison.

"No one else can know, especially not him," Roka said.

"But the Twins... don't you trust Kol's brother and sister?"

Rafe groaned and Roka chuckled. "Two people more unlike their brother you couldn't even imagine. They are terrible at keeping secrets."

Camille pursed her lips. Roka could see the scheming in her creased brow and lowered lashes.

"Then I'll just give Dimitri one less clue to slow him down."

Rafe startled them all by pulling Camille into his arms and kissing her deeply. "If I weren't already smitten with a certain Red, I might steal you away. Roka is one lucky dragon."

"I'm pretty sure he's aware," Camille said, her bright smile dazzling enough to rival the moon.

BREATH OF DESIRE

Watching the sun rise behind the Eiffel Tower made Aurik itch to fly again. Even though he and his sister had just ended a night-long outing over the darker countryside outside Paris, the desire to stretch his wings and feel the wind caressing his scales lingered. He longed to fly into the bright warmth of the sun, but it was too risky in the changed world the dragons had awoken to.

The balm to his itch moved up beside him on their building's rooftop and he glanced over at Dimitri, whose clean profile was cast in a golden glow from the emerging sun on the horizon. He looked tired, having likely waited up for the Twins to return from their nightly flight. Impulsively, Aurik threaded his fingers through Dimitri's and tightened his grip. Dimitri smiled without taking his eyes off the vista and squeezed back. Aurik's twin sister stepped to the other side of their lover and slipped her arm around Dimitri's waist, leaning her head against his shoulder.

The trio stood that way for what seemed an eternity of boundless, beautiful seconds. Nothing existed but the three of them and the gilded city that surrounded them.

Too soon the peace of their communion was shattered by the sound of the world coming to life. A different kind of excitement filled Aurik at the growing familiarity of the new sights and sounds he lived with. The life this changed world was filled with gave him hope that his own race would soon catch up to new ways of thinking.

Hands tugged at him and he reluctantly tore himself away from the view. It wasn't only excitement but a kind of dread that filled him now.

"Come on," Dimitri said. "Let's get today over with and move on with our lives. The last five are scheduled throughout the day. One of them will be *the one*, I guarantee it."

Aurik forced himself to resist grumbling. "*You* are the only one."

"Right, and I'm not going anywhere. She'll be the one if she's open to our arrangement and willing to stay mum about it in mixed company. I'm sure she exists and I'm sure you'll charm her pants off, whoever she is."

"The only reason I'm doing this is to stay near you. If the Council wasn't threatening to make me leave, I'd be just fine never reproducing. Once the Verdanith is assembled, you and Aurin can have a dozen children. I'll be the happy, corrupting uncle to all of them."

"I've always wanted a sister," Aurin interjected, shoving Aurik's outfit at him. "Find one I would like, too, alright brother?"

Aurik raised an eyebrow at his twin. "I don't think you want a *sister*, sister. You want your own plaything because Camille doesn't visit often enough."

Aurin's gaze grew distant and she flushed. Not from embarrassment, he was sure of it, but from arousal. She gathered herself and looked him in the eyes. "Camille needs a break from Eben and Roka just as much as I need a break from the two of you. We enjoy each other, and yes, I'd love to have someone like her who didn't live halfway around the world."

With that, she turned and walked toward the door. "I'm sure the two of you can handle the appointments today. I'll be around," Aurin said, batting her eyelashes demurely at Dimitri.

Dimitri's look of avid interest followed her out the door. Aurik couldn't read his lover's mind but was dead certain Dimitri was remembering Camille's last visit and the fun she and Aurin had had—and Dimitri's all too eager participation in said fun. Aurik's laugh made Dimitri snap back to focus on the task at hand.

"Hurry up and get dressed," Dimitri said irritably.

THE SERIES of blind dates that day were no more productive than any of the previous ones had been. Dimitri had painstakingly assembled a roster of the most beautiful, if slightly deviant, women from a collection of dating services. He had emphasized discretion as well as a desire for a long-term relationship at all of them. This was not about sex, especially not for Aurik who had very little interest in women as it was.

"You told me you'd been with women before," Dimitri said. "So what was wrong with these women?" He picked at his dinner in frustration, exhausted after another pointless day struggling to find the one woman who would ensure Aurik didn't get sent to the Monastery to live in servitude for breaking the Council's laws. When the trio had stated their case months earlier, the Council hadn't been happy that the twins had taken matters into their own hands. Both Twins had marked Dimitri during the ritual. He'd awakened them both, which was the first unprecedented action. He was supposed to choose one or the other, but couldn't bring himself to. He needed them both. And both had marked him as their mate.

The Dragon Council had given an ultimatum. Since Aurin had marked Dimitri first, they decreed that Dimitri's other lover find a human mate and nullify his dragon mark on Dimitri, or have his magic bound and his wealth revoked and split between his siblings.

The looming threat of losing one of his lovers had been eating at Dimitri ever since, and time was quickly running out. He raked his fingers through his hair and sighed. Aurik stared back at him with a pained expression.

"Nothing is wrong with the women. I just can't bring myself to want them, in any way, as long as I have you. You fulfill me."

"Well, was there something special, *anything*, about the women you have been with that you loved most?"

Aurik refilled his wine glass from the nearly empty bottle nearby. He appeared to contemplate the answer in the burgundy liquid. "My parents were thieves," he said, and Dimitri came close to reaching out and strangling him with the collar of his shirt, but restrained himself. Aurik liked telling stories, so Dimitri downed his drink, refilled it, and sat back to listen.

"I thought your mother was First Shadow," he said.

Aurik nodded. "Yes, but that wasn't how she amassed the bulk of the wealth that belongs to the three of us now. She mated a Sultan when she awakened, but he feared her too much to breed. So she mated others. Kol's father was a spy for a nobleman. But my father was a cat burglar, a pastime he didn't give up after meeting our mother. She caught him stealing from her and his skills impressed her so much she decided to employ him to steal from her enemies."

"How did her mate feel about her interest in this thief?"

"Amused, mostly, but soon he got involved, too. I think he grew bored with intrigue and saw the fun Mother and her new pet were having together. He would do the reconnaissance for a heist, and Mother and Father would ghost in and take the spoils. And because of Mother's influence, no one was ever the wiser. They took from so many, but they also gave infinitely more. Love to each other and their children. Protection to the citizens, even to the subjects of their enemies during the various wars. The women I was most drawn to were givers, nurturers, protectors. They always deeply cared about those close to them, without expecting anything in return."

"But any one of those women might be like that. You can't know until you get to know them better."

"Not one of the women you have introduced me to gave any indication that she thought about more than herself. That she had any desire beyond her own desire for a mate. Even your trick questions only produced superficial answers. Perhaps they just weren't the right questions, but they were all pretty telling."

If you had a life span of centuries and wealth beyond imagining, how would you spend your time? Dimitri thought it had been a clever question. The million-dollar question, as it were. He had cataloged all the answers himself and Aurik was right. Not one of the women had answered in more than the most frivolous way. Some may have had more down to earth answers than others, but they were all very self-centered. He'd been a fool trying to appeal to Aurik's more hedonistic nature. But there were depths to his lovers he was still discovering. As much as the Twins relished physical pleasures—food, sex, music—they were acutely aware of both the suffering and rejoicing that was ever more prevalent among the human race than it was when they were young.

"I'll try again," Dimitri said. "I'll rework the questionnaire and we'll find her for you. She is out there."

Aurik's expression darkened. "No. If I can't have you then I'm better off alone, I think. It would be a disservice to any woman I did choose to bring her into such a permanent prison with a man who didn't truly love her."

"Goddamnit! I don't want to lose you any more than you want to leave. We still have a few months."

"I would rather not waste these months searching for something that may not even exist, my love. Let us enjoy what we have until we must part. Please."

Dimitri hated the utter resignation on Aurik's face and in his bearing. They left the restaurant, both quiet and subdued.

Aurin greeted them at their shared penthouse apartment, her face eager for happy news, then abruptly resolute. Dimitri was sure a brief message passed silently between the Twins, but had given up objecting to their covert volleys. They would share if they meant him to know. Besides, he was fairly certain what the exchange entailed and didn't mind not having to talk about it any more than absolutely necessary.

Dimitri took Aurin desperately in his arms, her embrace only a slight comfort in the face of the looming threat of losing one half of the pair that had brought him back from the brink of self-destruction after the death of his brother. The parallel wasn't lost on him, and he wasn't sure if he could survive another relationship crumbling to pieces when one crucial facet of it disappeared.

Would he and Aurin be able to survive her brother's absence? His relationship with Thea had crashed and burned after Alex's death. No matter how much he loved her, it wasn't enough.

Aurik would live, at least, but what kinds of empty lives would they have without each other?

Dimitri reached for Aurik and pulled him close, found the sweet lips Dimitri had kissed so many times, relishing the brush of goatee against his own shaved chin. Two pairs of hands tugged at his clothing, pushing his suit jacket off, pulling at his buttons until he stood naked. Somehow he always managed to lose track of them at the beginning of lovemaking, the pair of blond heads seeming interchangeable the way they kissed and touched. They were two halves of a whole to Dimitri, and to remove one of them from his life might well cleave his heart in two.

He regained the awareness of which was which when Aurin's warm mouth slid down his hard cock. He groaned at the skillful pull of her tongue against his flesh, but it was too soon. With a solid grip on her chin he pushed her back. She stood and pressed herself close, his chest tickled by her small, pert breasts and their hard, dark peaks. Aurik's larger presence embraced him from behind, erection pressed solidly against Dimitri's ass, but in spite of their intense arousal, the embrace only meant comfort to all of them.

The trio stumbled naked the few steps to the sofa and fell in a tangle of limbs into the deep cushions. Aurin's smooth body weighed Dimitri down from behind and Aurik caught him, embracing him.

Aurik clutched his face as his slick, velvety tongue wrapped itself around Dimitri's tongue. Dimitri moaned at the stroking pull of the one dragon appendage he still viewed with novelty. Their tongues were the things that differentiated them the most from his past human lovers, and that gave him the most pleasure. God, he thought he could come just from this kiss. He threaded his fingers through the silken lengths of Aurik's hair and pressed his hips tighter. Their erections throbbed in tandem, surging and brushing against each other between them. A glimmer of hot wetness slid across Dimitri's belly, cooling in the air. He wasn't sure whether it was evidence of his own need or Aurik's, but it didn't matter.

Aurin's smooth caresses persisted, her kisses beginning at his shoulders and moving downward. Her soft breasts a luxurious brush against his heated skin. She worked her way down his back, each touch a perfect tingling counterpoint to Aurik's more persistent contact against the front side of him.

She lingered at the top of the cleft of his ass, her tongue a torturous distance above where he wanted it to be. Goddamn did they love to torture him sometimes. He shifted his hips, hoping to get her moving lower, but she laughed softly and sank her teeth into his right ass cheek instead.

"Sister, don't torture him too much."

The vocal admonition was unusual between the twins, but welcomed, particularly when Aurik gripped his ass and pulled him even tighter, spreading his cheeks for his sister to work her magic in between.

"Oh, God," Dimitri groaned against Aurik's mouth, nearly certain he would come this time, but Aurin slowed down to a steady tease, her tongue switching between a slow caress of his balls and a tease of his ass. She delved in so intently he lost himself, until she withdrew her tongue from his ass so abruptly he nearly cried out an objection.

Aurik pushed Dimitri up, raising them into a sitting position, never leaving off with his urgent kisses. Dimitri followed his lead, accustomed now to the Twins' telepathic link and their wordless choreographic direction of their lovemaking. They always managed to surprise and please him in different ways.

Aurik shifted to sit upright against the back of the sofa. He slid one hand down Dimitri's side to his hip, urging him to turn and straddle his legs.

To Dimitri, the only thing better than fucking either of the Twins alone was being fucked by Aurik at the same time

Aurin worked his cock. He slid one leg across Aurik's lap and settled back with his ass resting on Aurik's thighs, careful not to sit too snuggly. Aurin knelt between his spread legs and raised her face to him in supplication.

With a pang of despair he leaned forward and kissed her upturned face, sinking his tongue between her lips. He rejoiced silently when Aurik's fingers invaded, delicately prodding before sliding deep into the tight, sensitive channel. The token bit of foreplay was far from necessary after Aurin's attention with her talented tongue, but Dimitri would never object. He leaned farther forward, bracing his weight on Aurin's shoulders while Aurik positioned his cock.

A silent, gentle nudge from Aurin let him know to lean back, and he did. The thick, solid heat of Aurik's cock slid in to the hilt. Dimitri's cock kicked violently in response to the intense pleasure of the friction and pressure.

He spread his thighs wider and braced his feet on the floor, reached both hands behind him to grip the back of the sofa for leverage as he raised and lowered himself, slowly.

Aurin's lovely mouth kept tempo, her tongue and lips teasing and sliding along the length of his cock, circling and sucking at his balls. She might bring him off this way easily and he would happily give in to her, but what he really wanted was to be infused with both their magic at once when they came. He needed to be inside her, but was loath to change positions to accomplish the deed.

He looked down at her, hoping his desperation showed in his gaze because he was too far gone to speak. Her honey-colored eyes gazed back across the tip of his engorged cock. She lowered her gaze, gave his cock one more long, slow lick, then stood. Straddling her brother's knees, she carefully climbed up and lowered herself onto Dimitri's pulsing shaft.

The sweet, slick sheathe clenched him tightly. Slammed down onto Aurik's cock, pulling her with him, he elicited a sharp groan from the man beneath him. Aurik's hips began to rise up and meet Dimitri's undulations. Soon the three found their ideal rhythm, Aurin sliding her sweet pussy up and down Dimitri's cock with slow, rocking swirls of her hips and Aurik plunging into Dimitri's ass with ever greater ferocity.

Aurin's eyelids fluttered in ecstasy, her mouth descending onto his, lips parting and tongue demanding entrance. Dimitri clutched at her hip with one hand, his other entwined with Aurik's hand where it wrapped around his chest. The familiar surge of energy began, a tingling that was simultaneously around him and inside him. Aurin's eyes flashed with brilliant yellow light and she tilted her head back to let out a harsh, high cry. Her muscles clenched around him, urging his own climax forth, and he didn't have far to go. Aurik sank his cock deep in a final thrust, his voice rough in Dimitri's ear, a promise of eternal devotion.

The warm comfort of their energy flowed through him, his own mingling with theirs as it flowed the opposite direction. The steady, pulsing glow of their tangled bodies reflected strangely in the windows, superimposed over the twinkling yellow lights of the city and the golden spire of the Eiffel tower in the distance. The sight of the glowing architectural wonder seemed to mimic the brilliant sensations tingling up and down his cock as his orgasm persisted.

Finally the delicious spasms subsided and the three crumpled into a giddy mess.

Aurik groaned. "I can handle quite a lot of weight, but seem to have lost sensation in my legs."

Aurin shifted over, pulling Dimitri down into a heap beside her. They sank into the downy cushions of the sofa, legs entwined while Aurik stood and shook the feeling back into his legs. He wandered away and Dimitri closed his eyes, reveling in the sweet scent of Aurin filling his nose, eagerly waiting for Aurik to return and complete their perfect unit that would too soon be dashed to pieces.

Aurin's fingertips traced light patterns up and down his back until Aurik returned, tucked himself behind Dimitri and covered the three with a throw.

Dimitri wished he had a solution to their dilemma—was sure there had to be something he could do, but was too exhausted to broach the subject again. Aurik didn't need him to keep worrying over it. He would let it go for now and keep hoping.

AURIN LAY QUIETLY, her limbs entwined with Dimitri's, enjoying the steady, even gusts of his breath against her skin as he slept. Her brother's slow breathing from the other side of their lover signaled his slumber but she found she couldn't sleep, in spite of her own weariness. It was a mental exhaustion more than physical, however. The worry over Aurik's issue had them all on edge lately. Even the flight the night before hadn't calmed him the way it normally did.

Her brother had been less forthcoming about his feelings lately, less communicative than usual. His distance worried her and she had hoped that he and Dimitri would find him a female mate so he could stay. It seemed he had all but given up hope, and the understanding broke her heart.

Dimitri's breathing changed and she looked up to see his eyes open and filled with sadness.

"He's going to leave, isn't he?" she whispered.

Dimitri nodded and wrapped his arms tightly around her, burying his face in her hair. He sniffled and let out a soft, mournful sound against her skin. The wet warmth of tears became evident, along with the salty scent.

"It's my fault," she said. "I marked you first. If only I'd let him mark you first—the Council would let him stay, and I'd be the one forced to find a second mate. Maybe I'd have better luck."

"We'd still be in the same bind, though," he whispered. "He said they expect all Court dragons to produce offspring. He needs to mate a human woman one way or the other. If only he would just choose."

"He loves you so much," she said. "As do I. It's no wonder that he wants only you."

"But I need you both. If only he could see how much I need him as much as you. Losing him would be like losing Alex all over again. Aurin, I don't know if I can survive that. It destroyed me and Thea. I'm terrified that I'll lose you both if he goes."

She held him tighter and pressed her lips to his. "I'll never leave you."

Dimitri responded with raw hunger, his kiss a desperate invasion that she accepted. The air around him pulsed with the nearly visible surge of magic seeping into him, and his arousal pressed insistently at her hip.

Aurin responded, the warm, tingling between her thighs an automatic reaction to that rising accumulation of energy Dimitri always seemed to attract when they made love. She needed more than just the energy, however. Feeling him buried deep inside her would provide more comfort than a fresh taste of his Nirvana. Seeing his twin marks alight as they did and knowing he desired to fill her womb with his seed made her ache with joy, but at what cost if her brother couldn't share it with her?

He pushed her onto her back and mounted her with an urgent thrust that startled her. The slick friction of his cock sliding in and stretching her made her gasp and cling tighter to him. Roused by their movements, Aurik shifted closer. Dimitri's mouth left Aurin's breast long enough to kiss her brother deeply. Dimitri and Aurik clung to each other, hands clutching each other's napes and foreheads touching while Dimitri shuddered and cried out in climax. The sweet Nirvana rushed through her, its shimmering reflection coursing over Aurik's skin. She felt his larger hand cling to hers where she clutched at Dimitri's shoulder.

"Please don't leave, brother." She sent the thought hoping for a response but he only clenched his eyes shut and wrapped his arms around them both, burying his face against Dimitri's shoulder the way Dimitri had to her only moments ago.

She fell asleep with fingers linked to the hands of both her brother and her lover, but dreamed of both of them slipping away in the darkness.

THE OBNOXIOUS, insistent buzz of Dimitri's cell phone drilled into his dreams. He sat up with a start, blinking and trying to catch his bearings. Aurin's beautiful, otherworldly image filled his field of vision from the other end of the sofa, an amused smile on her face framed by tousled golden hair. In one hand she held a mug of steaming coffee. In another, his phone with its screen flashing *Erika* along with a photo he'd captured of Erika's red dragon mark from a still of their adventures in the Temple months earlier.

"You can choose," Aurin said, waggling the phone at him next to the coffee mug. "It's the third time she's called. I told her to call back because I didn't want to wake you, but she might be pissed by now."

Dimitri snatched his phone and swiped his thumb to answer.

"Good day, Mistress Erika," he said in a deep, scratchy

voice while groping for the mug that Aurin kept pulling slightly farther from his reach.

"None of that today, smartass," Erika replied through his earpiece. "I need your expertise."

Her businesslike tone made him sit up a little straighter. His glower at Aurin caused her to give in and she handed his coffee to him with a sheepish grin.

"What is it?" he asked, taking a tentative sip of the hot liquid and groaning softly as the life-giving substance swept down his throat.

"Camille's tracked the missing fragment to seventeenth-century Europe. France, to be exact. We need you to pick up the trail. You have historian friends, don't you? If there's someone you trust implicitly, you have my permission to bring them in."

Dimitri raised an eyebrow at how she'd tactfully avoided mentioning Hallie, their friend who had touted her skills as an historian to Erika in order to be included on their expedition. Hallie had other skills that had been invaluable on their trek, but *history* hadn't been on the list. He only knew one person who fit the criteria, but cringed at the idea of making that particular call.

"Just send me the research you have so far. I'll see what I can do."

"I mean it, Dimitri. You might be thinking you can follow up on this yourself, but we can't spend a year hunting for this thing. It isn't about our careers. It's about our lives."

Dimitri glanced at Aurin whose eyes had widened at overhearing that dire statement.

"Um, aren't you overreacting just a little, Erika? Having kids is an accomplishment, but there's no need to rush it, especially now that…you know." *Now that we will probably live for centuries.*

The other end of the line was silent for a long moment.

Dimitri pulled the phone away from his ear to look at the screen, worried that the call might have dropped, but the call timer still ticked steadily away over the image of Erika's dragon mark.

"Erika?"

A heavy sigh sounded through the earpiece. "There's more to the Verdanith than the fertility thing. It's a kind of focus for their magic. When it's assembled and placed in its sacred location, it can be used for other purposes. I can't tell you more than that right now. There's more information in the data I'm sending you, but we can't waste time. I need you to lead this part of the search, but we need an expert to get this done. As good as you are with what you do, this is not your field of expertise."

Dimitri repressed the urge to say, "Yes, ma'am." Erika was right. He was decent enough when it came to historical research, but he preferred the hands-on work of studying bones and artifacts. He had to feel them in his hands to find a connection with the past. Women like Camille were better with the words on the page, or the characters carved into the stone slabs, but even Camille was limited to her own area of study.

He knew one person who could intuit deeper meanings and somehow read between the lines of those translations and historical accounts to finding the truth and sort it into a logical chronology. But she was across an ocean right now and he hadn't spoken to her in more than a year.

The thought of Thea made the coffee he'd just swallowed seem to turn instantly to ice in his belly. His memories of her were what he'd managed to subdue in his relationship with the Twins. He hadn't just lost his brother the year before. He'd lost her, too. The Twins were his redemption in so many ways.

His brother was gone, at least. But Thea was still there. To have to confront that old loss might just destroy him again. It scared the shit out of him.

He glanced at Aurin, her wide golden eyes beseeching. They'd had the talk about what her purpose was. What she wanted. She'd been subtle about it, as was her way. She wanted kids. With him. Half of her urging of Aurik was to get him to want the same thing and find a mate he'd want to accomplish that with. Ideally one they could share, of course.

Finishing this damn quest would be the biggest step to at least fulfilling her desire, which he wanted more than anything.

"Fine, I know who to call. It might take some convincing for me to get her here, but I'll give it my best shot. We didn't exactly part on the best terms.""Do what you have to. Money is no object."

"Don't worry, I'll take care of it."

When he ended the call he stared beseechingly at Aurin. "What the fuck am I gonna do? She'll never come."

Aurik had appeared again and now sat on the coffee table resting his elbows on his knees. The twins glanced at each other, then at Dimitri.

In unison, they said, "Make the call."

CHAPTER TWO

The worst thing about loneliness were the dreams of not being alone. Thea had gotten to the point where she'd prefer not to sleep because she would inevitably have to wake up. To go from the happy escape of dreams of Alex and Dimitri, both alive and warm beside her, to the dark solitude of an empty bed, was the worst kind of hell. Except she was running out of excuses to stay awake. Her latest research project was long done, but she'd given the Foundation a three-month timeframe and they had already paid her paltry stipend for those three months. The fact that she had managed to complete three months-worth of research in half that amount of time wouldn't matter to them. They would only think she'd miscalculated the difficulty of the project, not that she'd been working double-time on it just so she could avoid having to sleep.

She re-read her research paper for the third time, scouring it for some detail she might have missed, a date she might have gotten wrong, a name, a lineal connection out of place—anything that would mean more work. She glanced at the clock that was nearly buried under her stacks of books and notes. Three AM was too early to sleep. If she exhausted herself enough, she could fall into dreamless slumber for an hour, then wake up and start again.

The pile of papers in front of her began to vibrate and for a second she worried she'd gone off the deep end and succumbed to hallucinations. She blinked at the rhythmic rattling buzz for a couple seconds before it finally registered. Quickly, she dug through the pile to find her phone somewhere buried under a cataloging of the lineages of twelfth-century French monarchs. Incestuous bastards, royalty.

The number was marked "Private" which she would generally ignore, but tonight she was grateful for the distraction. Any excuse to avoid sleep.

The sound of his voice caused that surreal sense of vertigo to return with a vengeance. The room spun around her and she grabbed the edge of her desk to steady herself, even though she was still sitting.

"Thea, are you there? Oh, shit, I just did the math. I'm sorry. I probably woke you up, but I need your help. And… well… it really can't wait."

Alex? No, that wasn't right. Alex was dead. Her knowledge of that fact didn't stop her mind from taking the leap and almost believing it *was* Alex and he was somehow contacting her from beyond the grave. No, there was a logical alternative, but not much less disconcerting.

"D-Dimitri?"

The voice on the other end hesitated, the tension in it mirroring the tightness in her throat at hearing that voice again after so long dreaming about him. "Yeah. Listen, I'm sorry for calling out of the blue like this…It's just that I have… Ah, fuck, it *can* wait. It's good to hear your voice, Thea."

"How are you?" Her voice sounded a little too high-pitched due to the emotions surging inside her. The roiling morass of grief she had buried for so long bubbled up, but when he spoke again his words made those feelings evaporate. She only felt pure relief at hearing his voice again after merely dreaming about it and waking up to a world without either him or his brother in it.

"Good. I'm living in Paris now."

"Oh? Lucky bastard." She smiled and tears trickled off her upper lip leaving a salty tang against her tongue.

"I regret how we left things."

"Me too." Regret was an understatement. It had been all her doing, though. Alex dead and Dimitri reeling from both guilt and shock. He'd been driving the car that night, but he couldn't have known how drunk the other driver was. Thea had been safe at home in their bed, but in the end she'd been the one who deserted him, pushed him away in her own grief. Understandably, he had left.

He let out a heavy sigh, filling the silence. "I need your help with a research project. Remember Erika?"

Thea wiped her eyes and sniffled, hoping her voice didn't sound too emotional. "How could I forget. She was a force of nature among the faculty until she left on that crazy expedition. And took you with her."

"It was something Alex and I had been planning to do for a while, actually. We were going to bring you with us, too. It would have been an adventure we'd never forget."

"So you didn't go?"

"Oh, no, I absolutely went. Alex would have wanted me to. I wish I'd made you come with us. It was the best thing I could've done to get past his death and move on."

"I'm getting by."

She was grateful that he didn't call her on the lie, though she thought he might for a second.

He only paused for a second, but it was long enough for her to read into the gap the scrutiny of her entire life since they'd parted. True to Dimitri, he never judged. He just gave.

"Come to Paris. I have a research project for you that I think you'll love. It's related to the expedition we just finished. Erika's expedition.'"

Not *"Come to Paris because I miss you and want you back."* She supposed that might be too much to hope for. *"Come to Paris and work for me."* He just said he'd moved on.

"I don't know, Dimitri. I have a lot of work to do in Boston. The Massachusetts Antiquities Foundation just hired me a few weeks ago for a project. I can't just drop it."

"I know you can do that stuff in your sleep, Thea. I'll pay you ten times what they are, too. And you'll get to visit all the old archives you always wished you would have time to dig into. I'm talking 17th century French history. The pieces you'll be working from go back even farther."

Thea laughed weakly. "You don't have that kind of money. How the hell can you promise me that?"

"There are interested parties who have very, very deep pockets. Erika is just one – she's the one providing the research. We'd like you here starting on this within the next 48 hours if you'll agree. First class airfare paid. You're welcome to stay with us—with me."

Welcome to stay with us. She wanted so much to say no, for so many reasons, but to what end? To go back to sleepless nights trying to fake her way through a life that had ceased to have any meaning for her? At least he was offering her something worthwhile. Once she was there and focusing on the new project, it was very likely she'd become so engrossed in it she would even manage to forget about him.

"Alright, but I have two conditions. I'm staying in a hotel and once you give me the details you have, you let me run with it. I work better without distractions."

"Anything you want."

~

DIMITRI WAS STRUCK by how withdrawn Thea looked when he met her at the airport the next evening. She'd insisted that she would come right away, surprising him with her decisiveness after her initial objections. He pasted on a bright smile to cover up his concern. She had an almost hunted look about her, like she hadn't slept in a week. He was familiar with the look, having seen it in the mirror for the first few months after Alex's death, until he'd joined Erika's expedition and trekked off to a part of the globe where mirrors didn't exist. The visual reminders may have faded, but the memories had always remained—of Thea and of Alex.

Before the false front could falter, he pulled Thea into a tight embrace. Her petite frame shuddered against him, so solid yet so delicate. Everything he remembered of her came crashing back. Her sweet, subtle jasmine scent, how unbelievably small she was in spite of her overwhelming presence in his life.

He held her quietly, letting her clutch at him until the tremors subsided. It had been more than a year, and Dimitri had finally found a way to heal. He had taken for granted that Thea would have managed to find her own way to a similar peace since his brother's death. How wrong he had been. After a moment, she relaxed and pulled away. Her eyes were bright with emotion and moisture when she looked up at him.

"You look good," she said, forcing a smile. Her pixieish haircut was a little mussed, the short glossy black of her hair curling around her cheeks and framing her pale, wide-eyed face. Her lips were still the same delicate shade of peach he remembered finding himself so fascinated with the first day he'd met her, when Alex had introduced them. He'd fallen for her then and spent the next couple months simultaneously hating himself for wanting his brother's girlfriend and craving her presence regardless of her accessibility. Her acceptance of him into the bed she shared with Alex had surprised him, but the subsequent months of pure bliss had surprised him even more. Until it all fell apart.

Dimitri resisted the urge to pull her back into his arms and kiss her, but the look in her eyes told him she wasn't seeing only him. The pain and longing apparent in her expression made it evident she was seeing past him to the image of Alex alive.

A loud bell rang suddenly, redirecting their focus toward the baggage carousel that had just lurched into motion.

They stayed silent during the half-hour drive to the hotel. He'd made a point of choosing one of the nicest hotels near the luxury apartment he shared with the Twins, and insisted that the room he reserved for her had a view of the Eiffel Tower. Before his brother had died, the pair had been making plans to surprise her, first with the expedition, then following it up with trips to all the cities Thea had expressed the desire to visit, either for historical research or just to enjoy the sights. This was one of her dreams, and one he had once hoped to share with her and his brother.

She was still subdued when he checked her in.

"Are you hungry?" he asked when he'd dropped her bags off in her room.

"No. I'd just like to get to work. You brought Erika's research with you, right?" The strain in her voice sounded more like exhaustion than any kind of anxiety, but Dimitri couldn't be entirely sure. Either way, it was painfully apparent that she needed rest.

"Actually, no. She's sent it by a… um… private courier. I'm not expecting it until tomorrow sometime. You should rest up. Order room service—I hear the food here is great. I'll come pick you up for dinner tomorrow at my place and we can talk about the project. How does that sound?"

She closed her eyes as though bracing herself to tell him something unpleasant. "Listen, Dimitri. I appreciate the work, but I'd prefer to keep this visit professional. You don't need to hide your life from me. I know you've moved on with someone new, so don't pretend on my account, alright? I'm glad you're happy, but please don't turn this visit into anything more than it is—a job."

He pursed his lips, frustrated at her response. "All right, let me be a little clearer then. Remember those interested parties I mentioned on the phone—the ones who are funding this project? Two of them want to meet you. Please come to dinner tomorrow night. I at least owe them an introduction." With any luck, her strong desire for a professional front would push her to accept. It was a slightly underhanded tactic to get her in front of the Twins, but he hadn't been lying, and from her appearance, being in a room with the Twins for an evening would do her good. He'd seen them work their magic with others. Joy was their modus operandi and if anyone needed an infusion of joy, Thea did.

With a weary sigh, Thea nodded. "Fine. Just dinner. After that I'm working."

Dimitri gave her a bright smile and a quick peck on the mouth. "I'll pick you up at six."

THEA STOOD DAZED FOR A MOMENT. The kiss had startled her both with its abruptness and its utter lack of innuendo. Just a peck on the lips. He'd kissed his brother that way—chaste, familial—it was just something he did without even thinking. It had taken her long enough to understand Alex and Dimitri's dynamic at first. Seeing two such beautiful men so casual about such a relatively benign signal of affection had taken some getting used to. When you grew up in as conservative a home as Thea had, public displays of affection even between close family members were almost unheard of except on very special occasions. The twins had behaved like it was nothing, which it was, really. Their behavior when in bed with her was more telling of their level of intimacy. If they touched each other it was only accidental, or by sheer necessity. Their focus had always been purely on co-facilitating her pleasure, which they accomplished masterfully and without even a hint that they held any shame in the act of doing so in each other's presence. Two halves of a whole.

But that kiss had never been bestowed on her before. Was it a signal of his acceptance of her, or of his lack of desire?

The room suddenly felt too closed in. She walked around, turning on all the lamps, then threw the drapes across the wide windows open.

The view beyond made her heart skip a beat and a startled gasp erupted from her lips. A pair of French doors opened up onto a narrow, wrought-iron balcony. Beyond the balcony the Seine snaked through the city, and beyond that, the Eiffel Tower stood, sparkling in gilded glory.

Perhaps she was a fool to have hope. He hadn't denied her accusation that he had moved on with someone new, however. And yet, he hadn't confirmed it, either—merely deflecting the comment to request she meet her latest employers.

Professional, she had said she wanted to keep it professional. She could almost believe, based on the kiss, that Dimitri was honoring her wishes.

The view out her window somehow told her otherwise.

CHAPTER THREE

*D*imitri was as prompt as any date. He'd had a haircut since the day before, which disappointed Thea a little. She preferred the shaggy, unkempt version of him. This version looked too much like Alex. Her stomach lurched at the sight of the living replica that stood in her doorway just now and she forced herself to find the subtle differences she knew existed, features that were wholly Dimitri. She'd loved discovering their differences and learning how few there were. Identical in so many ways, she finally gave up. But there was always one method to figure who was who, and she could do it with her eyes closed.

She swallowed hard and pulled her door closed, trying to ignore the look Dimitri gave her. Would he still make love that way? So different from his brother. So much more present. She always felt like she had been given all of him. Not just his body, but his soul, too. His brother had always kept something in reserve for some reason she had never discovered.

Those blue eyes seemed to know her too well still, so she stared at the floor.

"What's for dinner?" she asked, lamely.

"Whatever they make. It's always a surprise."

"Who are 'they' anyway?"

"My friends. They enjoy entertaining. You'll be the high-light of their year, I bet."

"Fuck. No pressure."

Dimitri laughed as he steered her toward the lift.

"You'll love them. Nobody doesn't, after meeting them."

He remained quiet during much of the drive, but slightly tense, his eyes flicking away from the road to look at her every few minutes as though he had something to say but couldn't find the words. Thea knew how that felt. She'd had the urge to ask him about the kiss the night before, but was at a loss as to how she should frame the question without it sounding lonely and desperate. She finally forced herself to ignore him and gazed out the window at the passing scenery. It was full summer and the city bustled with life. In spite of her anxiety over seeing Dimitri, she began to feel a sense of eager anticipation. This could be a good trip for her if she could just let herself get past those old wounds. If the project was of the scope Dimitri had hinted at, it could be just the thing she needed.

"I honored his memory on this trip," Dimitri said, star-tling her out of her fantasies.

"Oh?"

"You know how much he loved dragons. The idea of them."

"He said the dragons were your dream." His flustered look entertained her. "You never knew?" she asked.

"Knew what?"

"He hunted for signs of them to please you. Everything Alex did was to please you."

That shut him up for a long moment. Eventually he replied, slowly and carefully, "Everything *we* did was to please *you*. The expedition would have been for all three of us. We had a spot on the team for you already guaranteed. It was strange going without you, at first, but by then I didn't know where else to go. I couldn't stay."

She watched him in silence for a moment, then gazed back out the window, seeking that bright hope she'd grasped at earlier. A cloud must have crossed in front of the sun, because the day somehow seemed dark again.

"It was better that you left, I think. You seem happier now."

"If you had come with me, maybe…"

"Dimitri, no," she said, cutting him off. "It wouldn't have mattered where we were. We were spinning our wheels at that point. Staying together would have only made things worse."

He nodded and sighed, cutting the wheel of his small car hard to the left to descend into the shadows of an underground parking garage. She glanced up in time to view the pale walls of a stately and meticulously maintained apartment building before the shadows overtook them.

His subsequent brooding silence made her regret snapping at him. But she couldn't exactly tell him everything was okay, because that would have been a lie. She was far from okay, though if she could manage to not think about Alex for more than a ten minute stretch, she might at least pretend.

Soon enough his dark demeanor dissipated into one of agitated eagerness. He fidgeted with his keys on their way to the lift at the far end of the garage. A few paces from the shiny doors he clenched them tightly in his fist and stopped short.

"Fuck! Aurin wanted me to stop at the market on the way back." He dug into his pants pocket for a second and produced a folded piece of steno paper. He held it up sheepishly. "She gave me a list."

Thea quirked her mouth. "You forgot. That is so..." *So Dimitri.*

"So, we're here..." He hesitated, glancing between the lift and his car. "You can come with me and we can collectively avoid her wrath, or you can go on up and run interference for me?"

"You go. Just tell me which apartment and I'll introduce myself."

"You can't miss it. It's the penthouse."

When he kissed her goodbye that time, she just smiled after him. His excitement had always been infectious, and to see that certain things about him hadn't changed a bit was more a comfort than a worry. Perhaps the casual kiss was really just his way of showing she fit in his life regardless of their relative level of intimacy.

The elevator opened a few moments later into an airy foyer with a bright skylight. Another set of closed double doors were before her. She rang the bell.

A lilting laugh greeted her through the opening door, followed by a teasing voice, "Did you forget your key, love? Oh!"

The young woman couldn't have been any older than Thea. She was petite, with striking golden eyes almost too big for her face. Haphazard tendrils of blond hair fell around her bare, tan shoulders, mingling with the artfully crinkled silk of a sheer summer dress. The dress itself was cinched high, just beneath the girl's small breasts, and the skirt just brushed the tops of her thighs.

Thea stammered a greeting, suddenly self-conscious about her own darker appearance in the presence of this golden beauty. She had almost forgotten the undenied suggestion that Dimitri had a new lover. Somehow she'd developed the impression that today was merely about meeting her new employers. It had never occurred to her that they might be one and the same.

Or two, come to that.

A wave of dizziness came over her when a much larger, male figure came into view. He could have been the woman's twin, with his identical golden eyes and mane of thick, almost unkempt hair. She caught herself staring between the pair, with an odd sense of puzzle pieces clicking into place.

He greeted her warmly, gave her a quick peck on the cheek, then dashed toward the elevator with a sense of purpose as though propelled by some unspoken command. Thea was left with the oddest impression of being blessed by the sun. Her cheek tingled from the warmth of his lips and the soft brush of his golden goatee. Her heart raced as she watched him go. She only had a moment to recover before the pretty blonde woman pulled her into a fierce embrace. For the first time in more than a year she entirely forgot what it meant to grieve.

Aurik's heart pounded so fast he felt a little lightheaded on the way down the lift to catch up with Dimitri. The image of the petite, dark, and strikingly beautiful Thea had seared itself onto his eyelids. This was the lover Dimitri had told them so much about. The woman who had been Dimitri and his brother's balance—their fulcrum—the same as Dimitri had become for Aurik and his sister.

Aurik had known about Thea for months, including many of the details of her relationship with Dimitri and Alex, even some more intimate details. He felt like he knew her as well as Dimitri did, but it had always been in an abstract way, like how he now knew about many of humanity's most popular celebrities. He hadn't expected to be so affected by her—or by any woman, for that matter. Only Dimitri had ever truly made him feel that way. Not even the women he'd known prior to hibernation came close, though there were a handful he may have claimed to love in some fashion.

He'd only had a moment to greet Thea. Just long enough to catch her sweet jasmine aroma and the underlying lush, fertile scent of her sex that lingered in his nostrils now.

He cursed himself for not taking a few seconds longer to test whether he was imagining things or not. The softness of her cheek beneath his lips had left tingling warmth behind. Her beautiful, dark-fringed eyes had widened in surprise followed by instant understanding. How much had Dimitri told *her* about Aurik and his sister? Not much, he would wager, but Thea was likely intelligent enough to work out most of the details.

Dimitri had just started the engine when Aurik caught up and slid quickly into the passenger's seat. He shrugged at Dimitri's raised eyebrow. "Aurin was worried you'd get lost and forget where you lived." Aurik turned his gaze forward again, afraid that if he met Dimitri's eyes, he would see the conflict that had risen inside him.

"Did you meet her?" Dimitri asked, steering his way around the narrow streets.

"She seems lovely," Aurik said, hoping his tone didn't carry anything telling along with it. *So lovely I may be hard pressed not to have her for dinner.* The thought emerged unbidden and he clenched his eyes shut to suppress it, but his mind chose that moment to display an image of Thea naked and spread open beneath him, her delicious scent inundating him, her milky skin supple and silken under his touch, her breathy moans music to his ears.

"I can see that…" Dimitri said. He glanced at Aurik's lap, then chuckled. "I had a feeling you would like her."

Aurik snapped back to reality, realizing belatedly that the

front of his trousers seemed painfully snug, and for good reason. He grimaced and attempted to readjust himself.

"I can't even bring myself to be jealous," Dimitri said. "Do you suppose Aurin likes her as much?"

Aurik sent a mental thread to his sister but only felt a slightly playful push back. He kept trying.

"Aurin and I are usually of like minds, this is likely no different."

"I should remind you both that she is here for work. And Thea is pretty single minded when it comes to her work, too. Alex and I used to have to take drastic measures to pull her away sometimes."

"You'll have to remind Aurin when we get back. She's shut me out. Something about *girl talk*, she says."

"Girl talk? I think she's been watching too much television lately."

"I'm sure it's more than that. She's up to something."

CHAPTER FOUR

Thea wandered through the large, open, loft-style apartment, marveling at the decor and the view. It was situated to take maximum advantage of the sunlight throughout the day, with a multitude of skylights and high windows. She paused in front of one east-facing window while she absently fielded question after eager question from Aurin. The view of the city beyond rivaled the view from her hotel balcony. Finally she had a question of her own, having had just enough wine to gain the courage to ask it.

"Dimitri lives here, doesn't he?" She turned and wandered back to the bar counter and perched on a stool to watch Aurin cook.

The pretty blonde smiled suggestively and popped a fresh piece of mango in her mouth before setting a plate of succulent slices in front of Thea.

"Yes. You know what it's like living with him, I'm sure."

There was something purely sensuous about the young woman that Thea would have considered blatant if it hadn't been for how comfortably Aurin carried herself. Aurin's brother, Aurik, had given a similar impression. His golden eyes had taken Thea in with an oddly penetrating intensity before he left to catch up with Dimitri. The juxtaposition of the two in that brief whirlwind of a moment had made Thea just a little dizzy, and the impression still lingered of being on the verge of the kind of experience so rare few people could claim it.

Twins, Thea kept repeating to herself, marveling at the serendipitous nature of this trip. Where the hell had Dimitri found these two? She was curious beyond reason to see the three of them together. She didn't want to assume he was with them both, but somehow she absolutely *wanted* that to be the case. It would have been a kind of validation to learn he'd given in to a need so similar to her own. So much so that she didn't even feel a scrap of envy that he had found something so amazing in her absence.

"I do know, very well. I practically lived with *two* of him." She smiled conspiratorially. God, it was liberating to be able to share even that small detail about her relationship with Dimitri and Alex. One she had been compelled to keep secret while it had existed, but she threw caution to the wind and divulged that small detail to Aurin, believing—hoping—that her new friend already knew at least that much.

Aurin raised an eyebrow as she refilled Thea's wine glass. She leaned her elbows on the counter. "Two Dimitris might be too many. Better to have to share him, I think. Or I might overdose." She took a sip of her own wine. "But I would die happy." She grinned, the bright glow of her smile infusing Thea with warmth.

Thea laughed in response. "They were never too much for me. He and his brother were different in just the right ways." She speared a chunk of mango with a small fork and savored the slick, sweet juiciness while she pondered those particular differences in more detail than she had in ages. How she'd missed that part of their relationship sometimes above all else. She'd avoided sex at all costs since Dimitri had left, knowing in her heart that nothing could ever compare to the two brothers.

"You want to know what I like most?" Aurin asked, moving around the long, polished granite of the kitchen island. She stopped next to Thea and leaned casually against the counter. "It's how slow he starts. Like he's…hmm… savoring every moment. When we met it was like that. A touch…"

Thea sat still as Aurin ran a fingertip lightly along Thea's jaw, across her lower lip, and back, following along the curved outline of her upper lip. The touch left Thea's mouth tingling and she involuntarily licked her lips, tasting a remnant of the mango juice.

"Yes, he always did take his time," Thea said, her words coming out as only a whisper. Her chest seemed too full of anticipation, her heart beating wildly. She swallowed hard, watching Aurin's head tilt and the pretty blonde's odd eyes drift lower.

"I don't think I've ever been touched quite like he did. So slow. So perfect."

Thea was enthralled by Aurin's rapt expression, the way her gaze fixed on Thea's chest. Thea didn't look down, but her breathing quickened when she felt the gentle tug of Aurin's fingertips at the top button of her dress. It must be the wine going to her head, a subtle euphoria that grew more pronounced with each second. It couldn't be Aurin's touch, though the light caress down the center of Thea's sternum made her inhale sharply. More buttons popped open. The built-in support the dress provided disappeared, her heavy breasts released, their weight pushing the sides of her dress further apart.

She could almost see herself in Aurin's eyes. Her pleased

half-smile, the lovely tilt of her head, the gaze tracing over every inch of her skin reminded her of how *her* twins had looked at her.

With a small, delicate palm, Aurin cupped one of Thea's breasts, the touch so gentle, deliberate, and so slow Thea almost believed she was dreaming.

"He touched me like this at first," Aurin said, finally raising her gaze. Their eyes met at the same instant Aurin's thumb brushed over Thea's taut nipple. The startling rush of sensation made Thea gasp out loud.

Her gasp turned into a muffled moan against Aurin's lips when she shifted closer and pressed her mouth against Thea's. The sweet taste of mangoes hit Thea's tongue, mingling with the fresh scent of citrus. Her mind reeled at the newness of Aurin's touch. It had been so long since she'd been touched so intimately. Dimitri had been the last, so long ago, during an encounter she later wished she could forget. He hadn't been his deliberate, gentle self. He'd been angry, hurt, and full of so much despair. They had hurt each other that night—both physically and emotionally.

Aurin's touch reminded Thea what tenderness felt like, and how much she had missed it. The novelty of kissing another woman barely registered aside from a glimmer of curiosity that rose in Thea with each new caress of Aurin's hands on her body.

Thea's dress spread farther apart, her breasts fully exposed to Aurin's gentle cupping and squeezing. Thea hazarded a reciprocal touch, placing her hands on Aurin's shoulders. She threaded fingers into the silken gold strands at the back of Aurin's neck, and pulled her into a deeper kiss. Aurin responded eagerly, a light moan vibrating from her throat, so resonant it almost sounded inhuman.

Thea's palms tingled with each incremental pass over Aurin's warm, silky skin. Thea pushed the thin straps of

Aurin's dress off her shoulders, exposing small breasts with a luminous and pale tan, so perfect they seemed to shimmer as if gilded. She pressed her palm against one erect nipple, then flattened her hand, letting the hard nub rub in a circle against the center of her palm. Some foreign urge overtook her, and she tugged harder at Aurin's dress. Thea needed to see Aurin entirely naked, to see what Dimitri saw, to find a sense of communion with her old lover in her experience of this woman. The need to share this kind of abstract intimacy with Dimitri overwhelmed Thea. What would he have done?

The question propelled Thea into action, and she urged Aurin back a step so she could stand. Thea felt awash in a glow of certainty mixed with desire as she let her gaze trail down over Aurin's lithe body. Aurin's dress draped precariously off her round hips. With one light tug, Thea sent it billowing to the floor. The lack of any undergarments excited her and made her wish she'd been so confident in herself. She also wished she'd had even a scrap of forethought to shave or get waxed before coming, aside from the basic necessity of her legs and the most cursory trim between her thighs.

Aurin's bare pussy glistened with wetness already. The instinct to touch drove Thea on. Dimitri would have touched lightly, so that's what she did. He would have taken her nipple in his mouth, so she bent and lightly sucked Aurin's in between her lips, relishing the young woman's quiver of ecstasy as she rolled her tongue against the hard nub. The rest came naturally. She sucked a little harder, switched sides, sucked again. With a slight nudge from Thea, Aurin moved to sit on the nearby barstool.

Thea's sight seemed to narrow, her entire world seeming nearly lost in the pair of golden eyes that watched her as she lowered to her haunches between Aurin's spread thighs.

The shock of noise that interrupted their heavy breathing

when the front door opened only barely penetrated her rapt focus she had for the dewy pink folds that beckoned before her.

THE FAMILIAR, pungent aroma of sex hit Aurik's nose before he opened the door to the apartment. He paused, inhaling deeply, then handed Dimitri the bag of groceries he carried.

"What is it?" Dimitri asked.

Aurik was too buzzed from the scent of Thea's arousal to answer. It presented itself as a steady flow of magic in the air around him, that familiar, invisible web he'd tried and failed to explain to Dimitri. The energy seemed drawn to a sexually primed human as to a magnet, sucked in during sex, then released again at the moment of climax.

The magic seemed even denser the closer he got to Thea's scent. Even through the door it nearly overwhelmed him, mingling slightly with his sister's familiar scent, so like his own he rarely even registered it. But Thea's was bold, earthy, and potent. A tentative whiff of Dimitri's arousal emerged and Aurik turned his head in response.

Dimitri's eyes were wide. "Dude, you're hard again. You know what it does to me when I see you like this, right? It was all I could do not to pull the car over a little while ago and suck you off."

"It's her. Why didn't you tell me she had so much pull? Sweet Mother, she's even more potent than you."

Dimitri blinked at him. "Who, Thea? I told you she was irresistible. I didn't expect her to affect you this way, though."

"It never occurred to me before. There was a reason she was able to keep a pair of twins sated. Humans that open to the magic are rare." In truth, Dimitri was the first Aurik had encountered who had such a strong pull, and he had believed

Dimitri was unique. To have two at once would be a magical feast beyond Aurik's dreams. More than that, he believed she might be the answer to his worries. Once he was gone, she could easily fill the void in his absence.

The dizzying draw of the magic flowed around him as he stepped through the door, Dimitri close on his heels. When they rounded the wall that separated the entry from the living space, Dimitri let out a low curse. They both paused to watch, the bags of groceries forgotten on the floor at Dimitri's feet.

Aurin rested on a bar stool, entirely naked, chest arched forward and head tilted back in ecstasy. Thea's dark, short-cropped head was between Aurin's thighs and one hand covered her breast, thumb and forefinger teasing at her nipple. A brief impression of Aurin's pleasure hit Aurik when she opened her eyes and smiled smugly.

Thea was only naked to the waist, but her dress had ridden up to display the twin creamy arcs of her ass framed by pale lace. Even without a touch, her arousal was so intense Aurik could almost taste her from where he stood. He craved the surge of magic he was sure would be present if he *were* touching her.

Suddenly, Dimitri's face obscured Aurik's view, his lover's own need a harmonious addition to the web of magic that surrounded Thea. Dimitri's blue eyes were bright with lust and excitement, his kiss urgent, though a little clumsy and rushed. Aurik quickly came back to himself, responding to Dimitri's kiss and the tug of his fingers on Aurik's clothes. They made quick work of each other's clothes, their kisses deepening and the sweet warmth of Dimitri's cock brushing against Aurik's hip arousing him further and reminding him there were two very potent attractors to the magic that sustained him, and he meant to have them both at once.

"Go to her," he whispered to Dimitri, who kept glancing back at Aurin between caresses and kisses.

His lover went, and Aurin's eyes brightened at his approach. Aurik watched and waited, holding his hard cock loosely in his hand, stroking it in time with the light tilts of Thea's head between his sister's thighs. Aurin seemed content to receive the pleasure without responding in kind, and eagerly accepted Dimitri's kiss when he reached her. Dimitri bent to tease Aurin's nipple with his tongue, gently grasping Thea's hand and clasping it atop Aurin's thigh.

Thea seemed to shudder slightly at the touch, her shoulders rising and falling, but she didn't halt her rhythm.

Dimitri whispered something in Aurin's ear, the breath of words too faint for Aurik's keen hearing to pick up. To his amazement, Aurin nodded and urged Thea to stop.

Thea's flushed profile came into view when she turned her head to look at Aurik. Her lips glistened with Aurin's juices and she darted out a pink tongue. Her eyelids fluttered as though the flavor had her mesmerized. The sight caused a burning craving inside Aurik for Thea's flavor on his own lips.

He moved as though pulled by her gaze, every movement of his body seeming to register by the shift of her eyes from his head to his toes. Then another graze of her tongue over her lips when her avid glances rested briefly on his erection before moving back to meet his eyes.

She smiled and looked up at him when he reached her, but didn't rise, so he lowered himself to her level, resting on his knees just behind her.

The magic vibrated in the air around her. Aurik raised a hand and tentatively brushed it down the curve of her spine, enjoying the warm tingle of the power that enveloped her like a cloud of static electricity. She turned back to Aurin, let out a soft sigh, and bent to her previous task again, but this time she reached one hand behind her to brush it along his bare thigh.

Wordlessly he urged her to stand, shifting back slightly to make room. She released her mouth from Aurin's pussy just long enough to rise up, then bend at the hips. Dimitri had spoken of her eager willingness to accommodate her lovers, but her reactions were akin to mindreading. She glanced over her shoulder again and spread her legs slightly. Aurik tugged her dress and panties over her hips, enjoying the silken fire of her skin beneath his palms as he slid the garments down over her naked thighs.

He realized abstractly that he hadn't touched a woman this way in centuries, and never one so vibrant and alive with energy. The dark fringe of curls perfectly framed her glistening pink folds. With both hands he cupped the full, round swell of her ass cheeks, grazing his thumbs between along the edge of her rosy puckered opening in the center and along the juncture of her thighs. Aromatic moisture had gathered and felt slick beneath his thumbs. He teased her delicate folds apart, enjoying the slight clench and opening of her before his eyes and the stronger surge of magic that coalesced around her in response to her rising pleasure.

Hot, clinging velvet wrapped around his thumbs as he sank them into her eager opening and spread her apart. He spared the slightest glance up at Aurin, but her face was obscured by Dimitri. They kissed deeply and steadily while Aurin stroked Dimitri's cock and undulated her hips in time with Thea's tongue.

Aurik barely caught himself before he darted his dragon tongue out to taste. He wanted to pleasure her as fully as possible, but she didn't know his true nature. For the time being he contented himself by tasting her with his human tongue.

Thea responded enthusiastically, a muffled moan reaching his ears from between Aurin's thighs. Her sweet juices coated his tongue and he lapped them up. He tilted his head to reach further between her thighs, seeking out the center of her pleasure and finding the thick, throbbing bundle easily. The hot pulse of it against his tongue elicited a similar reaction from his cock. He'd have her that way, too, but wanted to taste her Nirvana first, to feel the rush of all that magic surging into him.

Aurin's familiar breathy gasps grew louder and Thea's movements more hurried. She was nothing if not a diligent, attentive lover. One long, drawn out and quavering cry announced Aurin's peak. He paused, waiting for the feedback of energy to flow through Thea before remembering she wasn't marked and so couldn't take in their power directly. And Sweet Mother what a shame that was.

Thea's shoulders sagged as she dropped her forehead against Aurin's thigh. Thea's ass pressed harder against his mouth and he eagerly accommodated her, lapping and teasing at her pussy. She shifted her stance at the same time Aurin finally saw fit to communicate with him.

"Take her, Brother. I will have Dimitri now, he is ready."

His protest back to her was nearly incoherent even in his head. Her responding laugh hit his ears followed by the words in his head. *"You can have them both later. She needs you more right now. Focus."*

Thea stood a little unsteadily, but upright when Aurin murmured a soft command. "Let my brother finish you, love."

Aurik gazed up from his kneeling position, enthralled by the glowing pale skin as it caught the dwindling rays of sunlight streaming through their windows. He slid his hands up Thea's sides again, gripped her gently at the hips and urged her to turn. Just as she began to shift in his arms, she darted an uncertain glance at Dimitri that Aurik was sure held the slightest hint of longing.

Dimitri stepped close and clutched the back of her neck, pulled her into a deep kiss, then whispered into her ear. "Please let me share them with you this once."

Aurik smiled at his lover's assessment of what was happening. He had no argument, however. They belonged to Dimitri as much as he belonged to them. They were his to share in that sense.

Thea looked down at Aurik, her lips parted and her breasts rose and fell with the cadence of her breath. He rose up enough to capture one pink nipple between his lips and flick it gently with his tongue. She sighed and threaded her fingers through his hair, holding him closer. He slipped one hand up her inner thigh, longing to return to the luscious center of her. Thea tilted her hips, inviting him in, and he went, stroking her again until her slick, hot fluid coated his fingers.

Her nails dug into his scalp when he slid two fingers deeper, testing slowly as he went, seeking the spot that would make her crumble in his arms and let loose that swirling mass of power that clung to her like iron shavings to a magnet.

A harsh whimper escaped her and her knees gave, signaling that he'd found her sweet spot. He held her up with his free arm wrapped tightly around her waist and stroked the tender patch of her inner wall a moment longer, wishing he could use his tongue on her there—his *real* tongue—and feel her flying to pieces against his mouth. He would drink the power like a baby at its mother's tit, soaking in every last drop.

"Fuck me, please," she said harshly. "God, I need to be fucked."

Desperation was as clear as day in her voice, making him

wonder if the swirling eddies of magic that clung to her were palpable to her somehow, were what had weighed her down so much she couldn't hold herself upright. Aurik urged her down to him and she went. A stuttering sigh rushed out of her when she straddled his cock and sank slowly down, her hot pussy seeming to devour his entire length. Her slick muscles clenched tightly making him shiver at the intensity of the pleasure. He could almost taste the power now, pushing at her barriers—barriers she had no control over, but were impossible to breach until he'd brought her to the edge and let her plunge over.

In his periphery he was aware of Dimitri and Aurin fucking. Their coupling seemed to happen in a series of still frames, like dancers caught in the strobe of one of the night clubs Dimitri had taken them to. All the while, his own little world had slowed down to a crawl, every nuance of Thea in hyper focus. Her hot breath gusting into his ear was accompanied every few seconds by a rough affirmative as she gained purchase with her legs around his hips and found her rhythm on his cock. He let her set the pace and gradually moved his hips to meet her movements.

Aurik closed his eyes and let himself become attuned to her and her alone. Her lips sought his and he opened to her, kissing back with fervor, matching her hungry bites with nips of his own. He reveled in her climbing lust, holding her hips and thrusting deeper when she whispered *harder* in his ear.

As with the first time with Dimitri, he wished for the moment to never end. The buildup to the climax was only half the pleasure, however. The power seemed to crackle around them both to the point that he was sure if he opened his eyes, the world around him would only be a disorienting blur.

"Oh, Sweet Mother, Thea," he groaned. "Never leave." He

buried his face in her neck as the tight clench of her pussy pulled him to the brink. Her orgasm burst from her with a roar of magic, flooding him with power so strong his ears rang from the force of it. He tipped across the edge, falling into his own abyss but unwilling to stop the steady plunge into her.

CHAPTER FIVE

hea floated back to earth an eternity later. At least that's what coming down from the most intense orgasm of her life felt like. She may as well have been the downy kernel of a dandelion tuft finally letting gravity take its toll in the absence of the winds that had been blowing her to the ends of the earth and back.

Her world had tilted somewhere in the middle of it all. Literally tilted, she realized, opening her eyes to see a skylight high above her and feel the cool wood floor beneath her naked back.

Aurik was still poised above her, resting on his elbows just close enough to still touch but far enough so as not to crush her beneath his weight. Tangled tendrils of his long, golden hair fell on either side of their faces. His eyes were identical to his sister's, their golden depths seemed to understand her deepest longings with a glance. He understood this half of it at least—this need for a deep connection. Something else in those eyes told her he longed for something, too, something he had lost, perhaps?

His whispered plea from their moment of climax came back to her just then.

"But I just got here," she said.

His brows drew together in confusion. "What?"

"You said, 'Never leave.' I only just got here. And then there was wine and Aurin and, oh… oh fuck, you're wearing a condom, aren't you? Please tell me you are!"

Aurik shook his head minutely and pulled back farther. "No need."

"What, you're fixed?"

"Was never broken."

Dimitri's amused voice broke in from somewhere behind them. "She's asking if you've been surgically altered to prevent you knocking her up. He hasn't, Thea, but he can't get you pregnant."

She tilted her head back toward the sound, but only saw the smooth wooden base of the kitchen island. Finally getting her bearings completely, she realized they were on the floor between two of the bar stools. Jesus all that really *had* just happened. She could still taste Aurin on her tongue, could still feel the woman's velvet softness against her lips. Her pussy clenched in response to the memory.

Aurik's eyes fluttered closed and he groaned. He shifted his hips, sliding out of her a touch, then slowly easing the rest of the way back until he rested on his heels again. His flushed skin and tangled gold locks made him look about as thoroughly fucked as she felt. Holy Christ was he sexy.

A flutter of cloth materialized from above, one hand towel coming to rest on Aurik's head. He caught the second deftly.

"Get cleaned up. Dinner will be ready in a little bit." Dimitri's disembodied voice reached her ears again. The sound brought back all the best memories of living with him and Alex, of being in this pleasantly buzzed and disoriented state right after sex and having one or the other of them already thinking of her needs.

Thea's stomach rumbled in response to the scent of sautéing onions. She accepted Aurik's proffered hand and stood, grateful for his supportive arm around her waist. She was still a little spinny from the intensity of her orgasm. She glanced up at Aurik, about to make a comment to that effect, but the words halted in her throat at the troubled expression on his face when he watched Dimitri. After a moment, he tore his eyes away and smiled down at her.

"We have time for a quick shower. Join me?"

She nodded and gathered her clothing from the floor, then took his hand and let him lead her up a wrought iron spiral staircase to the loft above.

"Is something wrong?" she ventured when they were alone in one of the most luxurious bathrooms she'd ever seen. The Twins must be loaded if they could afford all she'd seen so far. It wasn't even the decor that impressed her the most. While that was nice, the most impressive things were the priceless antiquities that littered every spare surface and corner in the place. Dimitri had struck gold with these two, assuming their relationship was as close as her first impression told her. *Let me share them with you, this once.* But would once even be enough?

"It's complicated," Aurik murmured, testing the heat, then stepping in and gesturing for her to follow.

"Ow! Shit!" she yelped when the stream of scalding water hit her skin. He abruptly blocked the flow from her and adjusted the knobs until she gave the nod that the temperature would do. She sank beneath the warm stream, marveling at how comfortable she felt with this near perfect stranger. Like they'd known each other forever already. She remembered feeling the same way about Dimitri the day Alex had introduced her to him, but that may have merely been by virtue of her familiarity with Alex.

"Trust me, I know complicated. Dimitri explained our relationship… er… former relationship, right?"

He nodded, stepping under the water when she moved to make room. "I fear I must leave soon, and he isn't happy about it. Neither of them are."

"Leave… Why?"

He hesitated as though trying to find the words. "Legal reasons is the best way I can explain it."

She let that percolate while she soaped up, then turned to watch him from beneath the water while he did the same. He eyed her breasts in an amusing way for a second, but made no move to touch her again. She was a little disappointed, but hungry enough to keep the shower businesslike.

"Are you screwing your sister?" she asked abruptly.

Aurik blinked at her, then broke out into a ringing laugh that filled the room. "Sweet Mother, no. She's fine, yes, but that would be even more pointless than masturbating when we have Dimitri. We don't enjoy each other that way."

"Oh…" Thea trailed off, confused. "What legal reason could you possibly have for leaving *him*, then? I saw the way you looked at each other, so I know you're together. I'm not a stranger to precisely that kind of arrangement and there was nothing that could take either of those brothers away from me." She caught herself too late. In a quieter tone she amended, "Well, almost nothing."

"My life is different. I have… obligations. Neither of my choices are easy, particularly because both preclude my being with him."

"You do know gay marriage is a thing now, right? Not everywhere in the world yet, but it's definitely legal in this country. Nobody's going to care who you love."

"I wish it were that easy, but I don't have a choice."

"So you're just giving up and leaving when Dimitri still loves you? That's a fucking shitty choice. You'll break his heart." She grabbed a towel and dried off, then proceeded to glare at him while putting her dress back on. She grimaced at her panties, which were still damp.

"Let me," Aurik said softly, reaching out for the bit of lace. "I'll put them in the wash with our clothes, you can pick them up tomorrow."

Thea gaped at the comment, completely flummoxed by it. By Aurik in general. By far the best single-partner sex she'd had in her life, which she was damn certain he would agree with, and here he was insinuating that they wouldn't be spending the night together.

"Fine with me," she said, shutting the door in his face before heading back downstairs.

Dimitri's bright smile at her reappearance faded quickly when he caught sight of her expression.

"Thea?"

"I need a drink or three, and then you're going to explain what the fuck that *jerk* up there thinks he's doing." Pissed didn't begin to describe how she felt. Confused was part of it, of course. She *hated* men who only told half-truths. And where did he get off with a comment like *"Never Leave"* if that's precisely what *he* was planning on doing? Forget that he'd said it in the heat of passion, she had felt that need of his deep down.

To his credit, Dimitri didn't waste time before pouring her more wine. At least he still knew her that well. Aurik might have an excuse since they'd just met. *And then had earth-shattering, universe-tilting, black-hole inducing sex.* The alcohol calmed her after a few minutes and she got lost in watching Dimitri and Aurin cook. They shared a couple somber looks that weren't lost on Thea, though, along with one sad glance on Aurin's part to the upper floor when she heard her brother start to come back down.

"Dimitri…" Thea began in an impatient tone. She wanted it out before Aurik was back in the room.

Dimitri shook his head. "We'll talk when I take you back to the hotel, alright? Besides, the research data arrived while you were in the shower. I'd like to go over it after dinner."

That news let her relax. If nothing else she could finally get to work on her real reason for coming all this way.

Except for the rest of the evening, her mind kept replaying those moments with either of the twins, spinning endlessly over the way Aurik had made love to her, then slamming to a halt again at his confession.

AURIK LINGERED under the shower until the stream of water grew ice-cold. He was still, acutely attuned to Thea's words coming up clearly from below. Her voice was as mesmerizing as her scent, drawing him back down to her.

He should have told her the truth. All of it, but believed she was still in Dimitri's domain so Dimitri was the one responsible for imparting the necessary knowledge to her. Aurik wondered if Dimitri had any intention of doing it. Their secret was sacred and unless one of them had a good enough reason, they couldn't share it without consulting with the others first.

Part of Aurik hoped Dimitri would tell her. Another part of him dreaded it.

He had to prepare for the worst. He had already resigned himself to giving in to the Council's decree. None of the potential mates Dimitri had gathered had borne any fruit. Aurik felt nothing for them.

But Thea. She wasn't on that list. She belonged to Dimitri

as far as Aurik was concerned. It didn't matter that he'd tasted her Nirvana already—she wasn't marked by him. She belonged to another. That she was a human who had given herself to him didn't matter. He still saw her as belonging to his friend in spite of her lack of magical link.

She was Dimitri's. The kiss she had shared with Dimitri had conveyed that much. Dimitri still loved her. Aurin seemed smitten with her, too. Aurik had worried for months about what he would leave behind. A hole for them to fill. But Thea could fill it. That day had told him as much. She was the perfect replacement. She commanded the energy even better than Dimitri, whether she knew it or not. She'd feed Aurin's magic and Aurin could use that infusion to fulfill every wish of their mates.

Our mates? Do you mean to mate her before you abandon her? No, Aurik didn't, but Aurin should. And that meant divulging their secret first.

It was always the first step after establishing a connection. He and his sister had been taught it this way, at least. Taught to learn the distinct difference between a potential source of energy for one night, and a long-term mate. The taste was very different. Thea was a perfect mate, as Dimitri had been. So she would be a perfect replacement for Aurik. Aurin could mark Thea without any backlash. But was Thea ready?

The scowl on Thea's face made him cringe inwardly when he went down to join them for dinner. Dimitri was being solicitous of her mood in that special way he had that calmed and distracted so expertly. Soon, Thea relaxed, buzzed from the wine, happy from Dimitri's attention, and pointedly ignoring Aurik.

The shift in attention away from him made it clear his decision was right. Thea fit that role so perfectly, the way Aurin and Dimitri's steady banter seemed to hinge on Thea's responses. They talked mostly about the Twins' collection of ancient artifacts passed down from their parents.

"Your family must have been collecting for generations to have such an impressive variety. I've always loved wondering what the stories were behind pieces like these," Thea said as they wandered away from the dinner table. Aurin and Dimitri followed while Aurik stayed behind to clean up.

A strange calm came over him while her words continued, pondering the history of each piece she admired. She was amazingly astute in her speculation about each piece, too, judging the age and circumstances around them to an impressive degree of accuracy. So impressive it even worried him a little that she'd suss out their secrets without even having to be told. That deep understanding would make it easier for her, and the idea calmed him further as he pondered what his life would be like afterward. It was as good a time as any to begin cutting ties. Perhaps he should go already, if he could convince Dimitri sooner was better, now that Thea had arrived. And Aurik's leaving would mean he could leave Dimitri marked, which would be preferable to nullifying it and staying, shifting his mark to a stranger he didn't love.

Soon Aurik went back to them, feeling Dimitri's pull with a glance filled with love and sadness. This was a tether Aurik would have to break. Perhaps he should nullify the mark, after all, even though the thought of it left a cold pit in his stomach.

The fascination of the data Erika had sent them managed to distract him from the feelings. The tiny piece of technology containing all of Camille's research fit perfectly into the USB slot of Dimitri's laptop. Of the many things Aurik would miss once exiled to the Monastery, technology might be near the top of the list. Magic without the need for any effort expended on his part. He tried not to think of the other things he would miss. But perhaps he could find peace at the Monastery, too.

Needing a bit of that peace sooner than that, he excused himself and headed toward the roof.

"Where are you going, Brother?" Aurin's lilting voice filled his head.

"I need some time to think away from distractions."

"Please think about what you're doing. There must be another way."

"I won't give him up to take another mate. I'd rather have no one and know he is at least happy with you and her."

She didn't say more, but he could sense her displeasure as though it were a prickly presence in his mind.

He shifted in the shadows of the roof and took flight, stretching his wings as wide as they would go, soaring high to catch the thermal eddies above the city. He could taste the faint trails of magic he and Aurin left behind each time they flew, subtle markers to signify to other dragons who passed through that this territory was under the protection of a pair of Court dragons.

He caught the fainter trail of the courier who had delivered the data while he and Thea were showering. The pale coldness of the dragon's essence told him it had been a Blue, but not one with a large reserve of power. The trail stopped at their building so the dragon had probably remained in human form and gone into the city for the evening to replenish his energy.

Aurik flew for hours, hoping to exhaust himself enough that he could have a dreamless sleep, and hoping Thea would be gone when he returned so he wouldn't have to endure her disappointed glances. He began to distract himself by flying slightly lower, breathing an extra cloak of obscuring magic around himself, and skimming along above the streets, low enough to catch the ebb and flow of sustaining magic that existed as a web around the city, connecting all the living creatures to each other, particularly the humans. He enjoyed catching the pull of lust that was so prevalent, finding the threads that tugged hardest, catching a little taste of each one and enjoying the different impressions he got of the interaction transpiring between the individuals involved. If humans only knew how vibrant those threads were. How strong and undeniable the connections. He wondered if there would be so much despair.

A brighter thread than the others appeared, the shimmering filament of it like a dazzling line of fire. He followed it, curious if there could be others like Thea and Dimitri in this city. The thread didn't seem to have a strong connection, however, the end of it trailing in the air as though caught in a strong breeze. The loose end of it tickled, causing a quiver of energy to race over his scales.

He followed it to its origin—the high balcony of a hotel not far from his home. The doors were open, the summer breeze catching the drapes and causing them to billow into the dark room. The thread grew even brighter, seeming to fan out into a knotted mesh as it reached its source. He reached the balcony and shifted silently, watching the shadows of the interior and listening, curious about the person who alone could have a thread of energy that reached so far.

Her scent hit him a second later and he went rigid. Thea's lovely jasmine aroma lingered in the doorway, evidence that she had stood on this balcony not more than an hour ago. It was no wonder he'd been drawn to her. Thea's pull was the strongest he'd experienced, but he'd first felt it while she was in a state of high arousal.

Aurik listened from the shadows outside her doors, but could only hear her deep, steady breathing. He shouldn't intrude on her sleep, but the draw of her was too strong. He took a step past the threshold, paused, and walked into the room. Thea appeared peaceful as she slept, but the web of magic around her tingled against his skin, arousing him. He wondered if she were dreaming, and if so, of what?

She had kicked the downy covers off in her sleep, her creamy skin caught the light that filtered in from her open balcony doors. She slept nude, which somehow surprised him. As uninhibited as she had been earlier that night, she struck him as more practical and a little reserved. His palm itched with the urge to touch her and his groin throbbed with arousal. He could wake her with a breath, use his magic to seduce her. But the euphoria his breath induced would be an artificial emotion. And if he ever made love to her again, it would be to experience the dual pull of her and Dimitri together so he could drown himself in the depths of the magic they produced.

He turned to leave, but stopped short at the sound of a soft sigh from behind him. Thea had shifted and rolled onto her back. Her eyes were still closed, her face turned away from him, but her body seemed more awake. The pull of the magic grew stronger, the web of it flickering around him as her hands moved. Aurik stood mesmerized in place, unable to take his eyes off her while she touched herself.

His palms ached even more at the sight of her hands clutching both her breasts, tugging at her tight nipples until she sighed again at the pleasure. Her thighs rubbed together, then parted. Her fertile aroma reached him with the force of a bolt.

Aurik inhaled sharply, the scent of her rocking him back.

Thea abruptly opened her eyes wide and sat up. "Who's there?" Her words hit his ears as he launched himself through the balcony doors and shifted in mid-air, cloaking himself with magic in the process.

CHAPTER SIX

Thea stared out into the darkness beyond her balcony, confused as hell. She clenched her eyes shut and opened them again. The disorienting pleasure of her dream still lingered, making her think the sense of being watched had to have been part of the dream, too. And she *had* been watched in the dream. Aurik's honey-tinted gaze had been all over her while Dimitri and Aurin shared her. Dimitri had been fucking her from behind while Aurin attended her from the front, reciprocating what Thea had done to her earlier that day. Only the Twins' eyes had begun to glow partway through. Aurin's gaze grew brighter when Dimitri removed his cock and let Aurin slip an impossibly long and agile tongue deep into Thea's pussy.

She had the sense that they were preparing her for Aurik. Working her up so that her climax was even more powerful once he took her. The dream had faded when she was on the precipice and she'd begun touching herself to chase it, easily imagining Aurik taking over, replacing his sister's acrobatic tongue with his own, thicker, stronger and more insistent one. She longed to have him like this, and to have Dimitri once again after all this time. She had always loved for him to take her from behind with Alex inside her from the front, but there was something wholly exotic about Aurik that compelled her even more than Dimitri or his brother had. As though Aurik's mere touch could set her off.

Thea fell back into her pillows with a frustrated huff. What was the point? The fool said he was leaving and it didn't take a genius to see neither his sister nor Dimitri were particularly happy about it. Thea just wished she knew exactly why. Splitting up with Dimitri after his brother's death had left them both at the end of their ropes. That she had ultimately been the one to push him away still ate at her. Now he had finally worked his way back to something good —something phenomenal, if she were being honest—and that knowledge had somehow let her feel absolved of her own part in his despair when they had parted.

She could see the sadness and uncertainty in Dimitri's eyes that night when he'd looked at Aurik. Dimitri and Aurin had shared similar glances that Thea knew well the meaning of. Would they survive together without Aurik?

Knowing it was a futile task to try to fix their relationship without knowing all the details, Thea shifted her thinking to the project she'd been hired for. She'd been tasked to track down a bloodline more than five centuries old with multiple gaps in the documentation of the lineage. The process of it excited her more than anything. More interesting, however, was how excited Dimitri and Aurin seemed to be when they'd skimmed through Erika's data the night before and watched Thea point out the obvious details she could anchor her research on. Family names were one thing, but locales were another, particularly if they were small towns that had an active church, or at least a library of archives.

She'd decided to begin the next day, and stick to her guns when it came to her insistence that Dimitri let her run with it. His eagerness to be involved amused her, but she couldn't deal with the distraction of him if she were going to get this done in a timely fashion.

His attentiveness the night before had affected her nearly as much as Aurik's lovemaking. That old longing had returned and with it the constant stream of memories of how happy they had been at the beginning. A reflection of that happiness must have existed between Dimitri and these Twins, and it made her heart ache for him to be a witness to it crumbling. Maybe when she returned from Rouen in a week or so, she would have it out with Aurik. Make him tell her everything and point out to him what a fool he was being. Dimitri deserved to be happy, even if she couldn't be a part of it. She didn't know Aurik well enough to know whether she ought to blame him. She definitely couldn't bring herself to hate a man she knew so little about, but if he didn't come to his senses and broke Dimitri's heart she most definitely could hate him then.

She dozed off again filled with self-righteous anger at the man she'd earlier been in the midst of a luscious fantasy about fucking. The anger was almost as satisfying a feeling.

AURIK HELD the bit of lace to his nose, enjoying the soft texture. Even after going through a wash and dry cycle, Thea's scent still lingered.

"Where did you get those?" Dimitri asked, pushing past to start a fresh load. "Don't tell me you've discovered the joys of cross dressing. I can't quite picture you in a bra and panties, but if it gets you off…"

Aurik crumpled the panties in his fist and shoved them

into his pocket. "Thea left them. I was going to give them back to her today."

"Well, that'll be a challenge seeing as she's in Rouen for the next week, following up on a lead." Dimitri eyed him curiously. "She's gotten under your skin somehow, hasn't she?" He seemed almost excited about the prospect.

"No." Aurik lied. "It's just fascinating to meet another human with as strong a draw to the magic as you have. I can't help but wonder what's so special about the two of you. Why aren't more humans like that?"

Dimitri turned on the washer cycle and looked him over. "It might have something to do with you. With dragons, I mean. In the temple I remember Kris talking about how it was our destiny to be there. Thea and my brother were supposed to go, but it all changed after Alex died. Maybe she was meant to meet you. I mean, there *were* two of you, and only one of me."

Aurik shook his head. "By that logic, all the others should be like you, too. I didn't get that impression from Camille or Erika or any of the others. They don't have any more draw than a normal human. As for it being your destiny, I'd like to point out that Kris didn't obey the laws any more than we did, choosing to mate with a Court dragon without Council approval. The pairings never added up to begin with."

"They might have if Thea and Alex had gone. They didn't, so their spot was taken by Hallie. One person. I have no doubt she was meant to be there, too." Dimitri patted the front pocket of Aurik's pants. "Listen, we can argue destiny until we're blue in the face, but you're lousy at keeping secrets. If you're into her, just say so. It would solve all our problems, you know."

"If I did, it would introduce new ones. I don't want to fight with my sister over either of you."

Dimitri's face hardened. "Giving up is a lousy fucking

alternative, and I know Aurin agrees even though she hasn't said as much out loud," he said as he stalked out of the small room.

Aurik wanted to tell him that he had a better alternative in mind already, but couldn't say so without ensuring Thea would agree to it. And he couldn't stand the idea of the argument that would come if he had them all in the room at the same time when that happened. He regretted having to break their own unspoken rules, as well as the pact he had made with his sister when they were awakened, but he saw no other way.

HE AGONIZED over it for the rest of the week, finally concluding that he had to leave before Dimitri and his sister knew and had a chance to object to the idea. He just hoped Thea would be too surprised by his confession to do anything but accept. The shock of such knowledge tended to render humans either entirely terrified and in denial, or eager to know more. He had a strong feeling Thea was the type who preferred knowledge over ignorance.

In his true form and at full size, Aurik could fly faster than the average car could drive. It was a straight shot between Paris and Rouen, though he would normally prefer the scenic route along the winding turns of the river. Getting there quickly would serve him best. He would leave that night, then hopefully be beyond his sister's reach by the time she and Dimitri found out he had gone.

The flight took even less time than he expected. Halfway through the valley, the unmistakable pull of Thea's energy reached him, as though even from more than a hundred kilometres she reached out to them. Was it Dimitri she wished for? Knowing their history, that had to be the case. Dimitri's suggestion that she was fated for him somehow seemed absurd. Thea, Dimitri, and Alex had been a unit, and Aurik couldn't imagine how any of the dragons of the Court could have asserted themselves in the middle of a trio that tight. He assumed Dimitri's brother must have been like him as well. Three such potent wells of energy would have been able to command the dragons. Perhaps Geva could have absorbed their energy easily, but it would have taken more than one dragon to avoid wasting any of it. The thought crossed his mind that one of them could easily have awakened a Queen. Speculation was pointless now, however. The team had awakened them all, regardless of the lack of a perfectly equitable match, at least on his part.

He disagreed with the Council on that point, but there was nothing to be gained by arguing. When such an ephemeral ruling body made its decree, they tended not to invite further discussion. Either he followed their laws or they would come back later with an even heavier hand, and he couldn't risk either his sister or Dimitri being caught in the crossfire.

Aurik found himself growing eager the closer he got to Thea. To have this weight lifted would be a relief. He was more and more certain with each stretch and pull of his wings through the air that his sister and Dimitri would understand and agree with him. He did feel some regret that he hadn't told them first, but it was too late to turn back.

It was near midnight when he followed Thea's trail through the cobbled streets of the village. He landed in a darkened churchyard and shifted, clothing himself in modern garments before approaching the small hotel where she must be lodging for the week. Her energy was less potent than it had been before, but still easy enough for Aurik's attuned senses to follow.

He wished he could reach out to her mentally like he

could with his sister. Being able to assess her mood before approaching her would have eased his anxiety over what he was about to do. Telling a human his secrets without the intention of marking them was against dragon law, but he would explain that detail to her and make sure she knew Aurin would have to handle that detail quickly.

He entered the small, but luxuriously appointed lobby of the hotel with purpose. The desk clerk smiled amiably as he walked past, giving the illusion that he belonged.

The web of human energy was strong in this small hotel. A murmuring couple walked through the lobby to the elevator, their own threads intermingled and tangled to the point he couldn't differentiate. The man pushed the woman against the wall and whispered into her ear, his words eliciting a throaty laugh from her, and their energy pulsed brighter with the subsequent arousal.

Aurik felt himself becoming aroused merely by their proximity and waited to let them have the privacy of their own lift before pushing the button for himself. He could sense them as they traveled upward, the allure of the magic growing dimmer the further away they got. There were no threads seeking their way outward from that pair, either, so engrossed were they in each other, cocooned in their own desire.

Rather than hit the button for the floor of the room he'd been assigned, he hit the button for the sixth floor, the level he'd sensed Thea on. He had no plans to stay the night.

THEA SMACKED her hand down on her notes, frustrated. Something was missing. Some crucial detail left out of the information Dimitri had given her. She scoured through the files again. There were hundreds of subfolders on the small drive. Some contained scanned pages of illuminated texts. How Camille had managed to get those, she had no clue, but Thea was impressed with the woman's translation skills. All except for one particular passage. It was almost as though it had been overlooked, and the poor attention to detail in that particular spot was inconsistent with how thorough all the other translations had been.

She'd managed to trace the family's lineage backward at first, to ensure she was following the right paths going forward from the point in time Camille had left off. The focus of names shifted every few generations, when a female descendant would marry and take her husband's name. She'd followed the family from Germany to France and was now stuck, trying to figure out what this impossibly obscure language meant. All she had to go on were the images in the margins of the scanned page on the thumb drive. Roses. Red roses coiled around the edges of the page and around some circular emblem at the top, a medallion with six dragons entwined within, that she'd seen repeated on many of the other images. She wasn't after that image, but couldn't shake the feeling it was significant to her search somehow.

She cursed, the feeling that she'd been deliberately left in the dark over this whole project returning even stronger than before.

"What the fuck are you keeping from me, Dimitri?" she muttered, her words almost obscuring the knock at her door. She checked her watch trying to remember if she'd ordered room service. She had forgotten to eat but couldn't remember if that detail had already crossed her mind. Work tended to take precedence over all else when she had her teeth sunk deep enough in such a meaty project as this one was.

When she opened the door, it took her a moment to register what she was seeing. His hair hung in shining waves to his shoulders, framing the too-perfect golden features of his face. His trimmed goatee caught the hallway light, making it seem to glow against the darker tan of his skin. And those eyes, God, she still couldn't get them out of her mind.

She was simultaneously more frustrated at the sight of him and aroused at the memory of their lovemaking. She stood gaping at him, torn between punching him and kissing him. His bearing and serious expression suggested neither option would be the right one, however, so she merely stood back wordlessly and let him enter.

"Aurik. What are you doing here?" She checked the hallway, but he appeared to be alone.

"I need a favor," he said. "It's about what I told you last week."

She raised a brow. "You mean about you leaving?"

Aurik nodded and swiped a hand nervously through his hair. The utter desperation on his face struck a chord deep inside her. Her ire settled slightly, her previous urge to wring his neck subsiding into mere agitated curiosity. She'd probably had a touch too much coffee to listen patiently to whatever he needed to talk to her about, so she went to the mini fridge and pulled out the bottle of wine she'd been saving for a moment when she chose to relax, something she'd promised herself she would do while she was there.

Aurik accepted the glass she poured for him and sat at the edge of her bed, resting his elbows on his knees. His gaze traveled over her slowly, seeming to take her in with as much thirst as he showed his drink. He swallowed the wine in three long gulps and held out the glass for her to refill it with chilled golden liquid.

"You're still leaving, aren't you," she whispered, and her

heart seemed to clench at the realization. "Please tell me why?"

He glanced away, focusing on her stacks of notes. His eyes fixed on the image of the illuminated manuscript that was still displayed on her screen. "Who's Rosenkrantz?" he asked, suddenly seeming to forget why he was there.

"Nobody, just stay focused here. You were saying something about leaving, and I want you to come out with it already. Tell me the truth. Tell me why you think you have to go!"

Aurik tore his eyes away from her screen and seemed to struggle for a moment to focus. "Thea, I'm not human. I'm a dragon," he began, and took a deep breath. She stared at him blankly for a moment, waiting for the punch line. What he shared after that caused the world to slide out from beneath her.

Her hand shook as she poured another glassful of wine and drank it down quickly, willing the alcohol to hurry and obliterate what she'd just heard. But her body wouldn't cooperate. Her mind raced over all the research she'd done that week, and all the out of place details suddenly fit. The oddly anachronistic names of some of the linked families made sense. Not the families in direct lineage to the one she was searching for, but employers. Until about five centuries before when the last line of names of an employer that had seemingly gone back for generations was eventually severed.

She hurried to her desk and began rifling through her notes, hunting for that name.

"Did you hear me, Thea? I need your answer."

"Not a fucking chance," she said, still irritated at his proposal but too distracted by what she'd learned to give him the courtesy of a full response. "Why the fuck didn't you guys tell me this to begin with?" She shot a glare at him and went back to flipping through her piles of notes. *Third century, come on, come on. Yes!*

She snatched the dog-eared piece of paper out of the stack and peeled off the small Post-It note with her question on it. *"Saint George?"* the note asked. She'd dismissed it as unrelated considering most accounts of the historical figure were likely fabricated. Turning to her laptop, she clicked her mouse on the image files one at a time, going back several centuries from the date on the paper until she found it.

"Does this image mean anything to you?" she asked.

Aurik stared at her, mouth agape. Thea tapped the screen impatiently. He nodded. "Yeah, that's a dragon named Sutylutha. He was killed long before my time, though. He was one of the reasons we have such strict laws in the first place, and why the Verdanith was dismantled. He was a brutal killer."

"Yet he had a mate and offspring. Do you know what happened to them?"

"It was his son who killed him. I believe the son attained Court status at the beginning of his generation's hibernation as a result. Sutylutha supposedly murdered the son's mate, so he retaliated. Suty's mate had her magic bound and lived in servitude to the Council after that. That would have been the first Hibernation, actually."

"Has something like this happened since? A dragon execution, I mean. More like third century." Her mind spun with the understanding. The structure of the research she had been sent had the sense that it paralleled human history, only intertwining with it in key spots, though there were many names that seemed to correspond precisely with ancient legends and mythology.

"It's happened a few times," he said, looking put on the spot as though he were being administered a college quiz. His bafflement at her insistence would have been amusing in any other circumstance, but once she caught the thread of truth during her research she felt compelled to keep tugging and tugging until the entire story was unraveled.

"Just the most recent one. About sixteen centuries ago, or thereabout." She almost rejoiced when he creased his brows and nodded slowly. The excitement of the discovery had her blood flowing hot. She felt flushed, but perhaps it was more from the wine than anything. She reached out and unlatched a window, pulling it open to let the breeze blow in and cool her off before turning back to Aurik to hear the story.

"It was a similar situation. A dragon named Silene went mad and was put down by her son. This time he was in human form, however. Of course the Council and the other dragons knew the son's identity, but it was a strategic execution, meant to protect our secrets since most of dragonkind were attempting to assimilate with humans by then. Not to mention no human alive could have stood up to her."

"And the son? Did he live to sire offspring?"

"The fight rendered him impotent. It's said he passed his wealth down to the servants bonded to him, elevating them to noble status, but I have no idea who they were. Why, did you find something?"

Thea sat down at her desk and pulled up the image that had been displayed when Aurik arrived. "This is the key, I believe. It's taken me centuries' worth of checking through the local archives to find the connection, but I believe this is it. Whoever these *Rosenkrantz* people are, were the last known family name in this line we're hunting down."

"They have the Verdanith?"

Thea jerked slightly at the warmth of his hand on her shoulder. His touch was light, but sent an unexpected zing through her bare skin that made her lose focus for a moment when her nipples pricked against the soft fabric of her tank top.

"I don't know what that is, but if that's why you guys want to know where this family ended up, that's possible."

Aurik squeezed her shoulder, the touch a subtle reminder that she'd succeeded in cutting him off entirely after his confession. Work had always been her diversion of choice when there were other things in life she just didn't want to deal with. She'd spent the last year or so since Dimitri had left avoiding the issue of her grief. It hadn't been until that evening with the Twins that she'd final begun to feel human again. She took a deep breath, bracing herself for the confrontation that she knew needed to happen, especially now that she'd had that breakthrough on her search.

"So…Dragons, huh?"

She swiveled her chair and looked up at him. Those impossible eyes gazed back, their golden depths resolute and tinged with sadness. She could divert the conversation just a little longer. He owed her a little more of an explanation, at any rate. Not to mention an opportunity for her to talk the damn fool out of his ridiculous plan.

Aurik nodded.

"Prove it," she said. Not that she didn't believe him. Even as mind-bending an assertion as it was—she'd seen pieces of Alex's research before he'd died that made it easier to accept —but tangible evidence was always preferable.

Aurik squatted down in front of her, holding her gaze. The jeans he wore stretched tight over his toned thighs and his simple black cotton t-shirt was just snug enough to high-light the outlines of his muscles. The scent of tropical fruit reached her nose, bringing back with a vengeance the flavor of the mangoes she'd shared with Aurin and the way that fruity taste had mingled so perfectly with the flavor of Aurin's own juices.

"I can see your arousal like an aura around you, Thea. It just got a little brighter. What are you thinking?"

"I'm thinking I need to see what you look like, as a dragon."

He glanced around and shook his head. "I can't here. Not enough room. I can show you these, however." He lowered his head slightly and she watched in fascination as a pair of shimmering gold horns coiled back from his temples.

"Can I touch them?" she breathed.

"Please do," he said. He rested his hands gently on her thighs and held his head a little lower for her. They were warm to the touch—almost hot—and as hard and smooth as they appeared. They weren't quite like the bonelike protrusions she normally associated with horns, however. These were semi-translucent and seemed to shimmer with inner light. Her fingertips tingled when she touched them.

"Does that feel good to you?" she asked.

His hands gripped her bare thighs a little tighter and a low rumble emerged from low in his chest. "Yes."

She gave both horns another gentle, suggestive stroke, noticing he quivered slightly, then gripped them tightly in both hands and forced him to tilt his head back.

"I will absolutely *not* let you leave Dimitri, do you hear me? He's lost too much in his life to lose you, too. You leaving would destroy him. Not to mention what I'm sure it would do to your sister."

"You can fill the void for them, Thea. He's told me you've done as much before, and Aurin is adaptable."

She leaned in a little closer, growing more pissed by the second at how stubborn he was being. For some reason just then the horns seemed entirely appropriate. Bullheaded was one way she'd describe the man, but what he didn't realize was how adept she was at getting what she wanted. She clutched his horns and shook his head. "They won't survive it, and asking me to step in would be like putting a band-aid over a gaping chest wound. It isn't fair of you to ask *any* of us to go through that, and you're a selfish bastard if you think you're doing us any favors."

"I'm out of choices. If I stay, I have to find a new mate, and nullify my mark on Dimitri. I would rather die than lose that connection to him."

"And if you exile yourself, he can keep it?"

"If I agree to leave him, yes. The Council only cares about punishing me. If I leave, he gets the benefit of both marks, while I get none."

"Please tell me you've at least *tried* to find a new mate."

"We all tried. It's rare for me to find a woman I connect with on that level and impossible for me to fake it in any event."

Thea bit her lip, mulling over the questions she wanted to ask, but hesitating. She'd misread men before, but sex as good as she'd had with him *never* happened the first time she was with a man. It hadn't even been that good with Alex their first time. It *had* been that good her first time with Dimitri, but then she'd had both brothers and he'd merely seemed like an extension of Alex at the time.

"Did you connect with me?" she whispered, searching Aurik's eyes. She hadn't come looking for any kind of emotional validation or even a relationship, plus she'd almost entirely discounted his interest after his dismissal that first night. Having more insight into his motivations changed her perception of that night quite a bit now, however.

His eyebrows twitched and he glanced down at his hands. Thea released his horns and sighed, taking his failure to answer as a negative.

Aurik's voice sounded rough with tension when he answered. "You belong to him first. I could see it in your eyes that night, and in his when he kissed you. The depth of your feelings was so strong you may as well have been dragon marked. I could never interfere with that." His anguish sank into Thea so deep her heart ached for him.

"That's not an answer. Aurik, did you or didn't you feel a connection with me? Because I sure as *fuck* felt one with you. As for Dimitri, let me remind you that *he* came to my bed second. He would understand if you told him how you felt. Assuming you do feel that way."

*A*urik shook his head, baffled at her reaction to his proposal. "I'm offering them to you. You can have again what you had once before. Why are you fighting me?"

Thea gave him an exasperated look. "Because what we *all* want is for you to stay. To never leave. Why did you say that to me that night? I had only just gotten there and we'd only just met, yet something made you say that. You were honest with me about why you think you need to go, so come out with it. Why did you tell me that?"

He opened his mouth to speak, but found the truth difficult, as contrary as it was to everything else he'd said to her tonight. He would sound like a capricious idiot if he confessed it. Yet all she asked for was honesty.

He swallowed thickly and cleared his throat. "You affect me like Dimitri does. The magic—the energy we subsist on is drawn to you more than it is to other humans. Dimitri is the same. It makes it difficult to keep my distance, even though I must, because of how deep my need is to pull that magic from you."

Thea looked down to where his hands still gripped her

thighs. They'd moved higher without him being entirely conscious of it and now his thumbs idly teased at the edge of her cotton shorts. The magic that surrounded her shifted, became less a steady swirl and more a winding coil, the thread of it reaching toward him. Was she even aware of what she was doing? It was a wonder no other dragons had found her yet, but she may not have been so potent living alone and in grief. If he left, would Dimitri's own well shrink as a result?

"What would it take to make you stay?" she asked. Her hips shifted toward him and the heat of her sank into his fingertips.

The magic teased at his skin, promising fulfillment but he had to draw it from her completely to have it. His answer was instinctual, pulled from his lips before he could think. "To have you both every day. To mark you, too. To fill you with my seed and have it mingle with his in your womb."

"What about Aurin, does she get to mark me?" Thea's breath quavered with the slow strokes of his fingers against the moist, hot velvet between her thighs.

Aurik shifted to kneel between her legs. He was eye-level with her and close enough that the warmth of her breath caressed his face. The question took him a second to process. Of course Aurin should mark Thea, too. Thea should have every privilege offered to Dimitri. The Council be damned. If that's what it took to keep Thea here, that's what should be done.

Aurik shook his head trying to clear it of the magic seeping its way in, confusing him. No, she had asked what would make *him* stay. He forced himself to pull back from her, aware of the fullness of her heaving breasts and the tight peaks of her nipples pressing against the fabric. Thea's eyes were low lidded and glazed, but fluttered and opened wider when he moved away. He shook his head to clear it of her magic, her lush scent. She really was the perfect mate for him, all this time. The Council's decree had been to find a new mate and nullify the mark on Dimitri, but what if he didn't? What if he and Aurin both marked Thea to provide the balance the Council asked for? The entire point of the ultimatum was to ensure he found a mate he could breed with.

Thea sat forward, her expression troubled. "Don't go, please," she said.

Her need inundated him with full clarity. The magic was the answer, as was her potent, fertile scent. All of it combined woke him up to the truth. He could have them both if he proved to the Council his intention to give Thea his offspring, and for Dimitri to do the same for his sister. There would be no loose ends. Once they understood how special she was, there was no way they would object. Or so he hoped.

"Call them," he said in a rough voice.

"What? Why?"

"Because I mean to mark you in a moment and we won't have the breath for calls afterward."

He didn't hear what she said on the phone a moment later, too single-minded in his mission to consummate the plan. She graciously lifted her hips to let him pull off her shorts and panties and nearly fumbled the phone when he sank his tongue between her slick lips to taste her. He had to mark her now to know if she was primed for mating. Maybe they wouldn't need the aid of the Verdanith like the others, as strong as the magic was drawn to her already.

He lifted his head and aimed his tongue at the nearest patch of bare, creamy skin over her hip. With hurried strokes and a breath of his magic the pattern grew visible, the circle growing brighter with each pass of the tip of his tongue.

The phone thunked to her desk and she moaned when he

bent back to her luscious folds. Her fingers threaded through his hair, pulling him tighter against her. The fresh mark pulsed brightly at the edge of his vision, the same way Dimitri's did.

Thea's orgasm surged forth like a tidal wave, the rush of magic through him leaving him breathless and gasping for air. Her thighs quivered on either side of his face. Aurik lifted his head to look at her.

"Will you take my seed? Mate with me for a child?"

"I thought you couldn't…"

"Not if you say no. Please tell me you want this, Thea."

Her mark gleamed brightly, almost blindingly between them and she gasped when she saw it for the first time. She glanced back up at him and nodded.

"Yes. Oh God, yes."

He stood and stripped quickly, helped her out of her top and carried her the short distance to her bed. The magic was already coalescing around her in a tight knot when he slid into her to the hilt. He arched his back while he fucked her, bending his head to pull at her nipples with his tongue, enjoying her rough cries in response to each tug. Then he bent and captured her mouth again, letting her feel the texture of his tongue, hoping she enjoyed it the way Dimitri did. Her hips surged beneath him, her heels digging into his ass, urging him deeper.

The room glowed from the shimmer of magic coursing over his skin. Thea seemed bottomless, each time her orgasm burst forth from her, he soaked up the power and more seemed to replace it. The tingling pull in his balls made it clear he had plenty to give back, and give he would, now that she was his. He slammed his hips against hers, shuddering within the clutch of her thighs and moaning against her lips as the hot pulse of his semen shot from him into her waiting depths. He urged as much of his own magic to follow the life-giving fluid, wishing for it to take so they could have tangible evidence of their union, should the Council feel any skepticism about how they felt. To have that evidence for himself was an even greater need and he would try again and again until it happened.

He slipped out of her slowly and fell to the side, pulling her into a tight embrace. They drifted into a contented doze. The worry of separation disappeared and his dread at losing everything was replaced by the satisfying hum of the magic she'd given him.

Sometime later a knock at the door woke them both. When Aurik opened it, Dimitri's angry face greeted him, followed by instant relief and soft lips pressed against his own, tongue invading insistently. Aurik was conscious of his sister slipping past them and giving him an admonishing smack on his bare ass.

"Thought you could get away so easily? You're a fool, Brother."

"I was afraid you had gone without saying goodbye," Dimitri said. "I need to go thank Thea for figuring out how to make you stay."

Aurik quashed his own apprehension. Choosing this path may have been another mistake to add to their growing pile of demerits, but he hoped to at least have canceled some out. He closed the door and turned back to the room.

Dimitri had climbed onto the bed and held Thea desperately, thanking her profusely until she laughed and silenced him with her kiss. Aurin was doing the same from Thea's other side. It was a large bed, but there was only just enough room for Aurik to slip in behind Dimitri.

His lover's need pulled at him the same as Thea's had. Aurik tugged at Dimitri's pants, soon joined by Thea pulling at Dimitri's shirt.

Still half-dressed a moment later, Dimitri sat up. "We want you between us."

Aurik went, sliding against Thea and wrapping his arms around her from behind while Aurin embraced Thea from the other side. Dimitri's smooth, hard body pressed against Aurik's back. The pulse of Dimitri's cock against his ass made Aurik push back. He pulled Thea's lush, round cheeks against his own cock. Wordlessly she shifted back, lifting her leg to slide it along the top of his thigh and give him access to her. Aurik could sense his sister's movements on the other side of Thea and only knew they were finding pleasure in each other as he was finding pleasure with both their human lovers.

The four moved in tandem, Aurik losing himself amid the tangle of limbs and the brighter tangle of the magic that clung to them like the sustaining light of the sun that began seeping through the window. Thea's cries of pleasure set off a chain reaction. Dimitri's hard length pulsed deep in Aurik's ass, his final thrust pushing Aurik over the edge. He gripped Thea's hip tightly, holding her against him while his orgasm jetted into her.

Aurik opened his eyes just long enough to watch his sister give in. Heat throbbed beneath the hand that gripped Thea's hip. He looked down at the twin to the mark he'd given her, glowing brightly enough to rival the sunrise.

Another perfect mate for them both, and never again would he entertain the thought of giving either of them up.

BREATH OF LOVE

CHAPTER ONE

*H*allie woke up in the middle of the night, disconcerted. Kol's voice reached her ears from another room in their house, yet she was certain he was still lying in bed beside her. His large, strong arms still held her close, his breath soft against her skin. When she stirred, the impression faltered, then grew more solid, warmer.

His shadow. She smiled to herself and settled again, comforted by the muted sounds of his voice—the one-sided tones of a phone call from the direction of his study. Comforted even more by the half-solid presence he'd left behind with her. She liked this part of him because it reminded her of the night they'd met, when his shadow was all he could give her at first. His shadow had awakened her need for him.

While Hallie loved the hot, hard solidity of his body in all its physical forms, his shadow form was always a tantalizing presence when he used it. He could make love to her with it in a much more subtle way than with his body, and it had become his favorite method of foreplay once he learned how she loved it.

She shifted slightly back against the warm presence and it responded. An invisible hand slid softly over her naked skin, down her side, grazing delicately back up her stomach as soft as a summer breeze, the touch more deliberate when it cupped her breast. The fingertips grew more solid when it teased, the hand spanning her breasts to caress both nipples into hard peaks.

Hallie strained to hear Kol's voice, but his words had dipped to a low murmur she couldn't make out beyond the understanding that he was still physically in the other room. She longed to touch him in return, but the shadow hadn't been entirely solid since the ritual—if she tried to grasp it, her fingers would sink through it like it wasn't even there. So she always contented herself to enjoy it instead.

She enjoyed this gift he loved to give her. Lips brushed across her neck, beneath her ear, and along her earlobe to whisper, "You feel so good in my arms."

"Come back to me," she whispered. "I need you."

"Soon."

His erection pressed against her from behind, almost as hot and hard as the true version of it. Fingertips teased between her thighs, followed by a low murmur of appreciation when he drifted a feather-light touch along her moist folds. Her core heated and tingled even more, knowing he was standing down the hall enduring this while doing business over the phone. Or perhaps enjoying it. He was a true master at multi-tasking.

The shadowy hand cupped her breast a little harder, squeezed her nipple until she gasped. The fingertips teased deeper between her thighs. She parted her legs and turned onto her back. The dark caress of him moved down her body, hands parting her thighs wider and urging her to bend her knees. The shadow that was Kol's breath brushed along her sensitive flesh. She sighed when the invisible tongue dipped into the wetness between her swollen lips.

Her mind went blank with the pleasure and she raised her hands above her head to grip the whorled carvings of their headboard. A pair of fingers pressed into her, as thick as if they were real, his other hand slid back up her torso to tease at her nipples again.

She would come like this if he wasn't careful, and her Nirvana would be wasted. He had to be physically with her to soak it up. Oh, God she was close.

"Kol! Oh fuck!" She tried to hold it back. The rising well of energy that he'd taught her to feel spread through her, nearly overwhelming her. She would lose it if he didn't join her *now*.

He was there like he'd materialized out of thin air. His pale, naked heat above her, dark eyes glowing with need. His lips descended on hers, tongue sweeping between her lips as his glorious thickness penetrated her, slamming in deep and hard where his shadow's tongue had been only a second before.

Hallie's orgasm ripped through her, her body convulsing with the pleasure of being filled with him, stretched nearly to the point of discomfort. In spite of the nearly overwhelming possession, it was all delicious sensation. Her climax persisted, its ebb and flow rising and falling in time with the undulating thrust of his cock. He'd opened her floodgate so wide there was no stopping until he let it close again.

He released her lips and cried her name, the word coming out on a gust of his magic breath and lingering in the air like an echo as his hot semen pulsed into her. She let it overtake her, let the energy inundate them both, just hoping that this time his seed would take root.

God, she wanted that to happen so much she ached for it

daily. She dreamed nightly of being filled with his essence to the point of bursting, her belly ripe and round with the evidence of her love for him. She felt it now, her mark pulsing hotly on her skin, signaling her readiness to conceive.

She suppressed a whimper, a small sound of frustration over wanting something so much and being unable to attain it. She knew it was still a remote possibility they would conceive, Kol had told her the odds. Slim though they were, it was possible, though unlikely. It took most dragons nearly a decade of trying before they conceived their first, and dragons didn't want for opportunities to try once they found their chosen mates. It was one of the reasons they took several. Only Kol had insisted she was the only woman he ever intended to mate.

"Did I hurt you?" Kol asked, his worry causing his voice to quaver.

Hallie reached a hand to his cheek where he poised above her still. "No. You could never hurt me. I was just wishing extra hard—I think I pulled a muscle."

He smiled and shifted to the side, rolling her with him as he liked to do, letting her rest on her belly on top of him. He engulfed her in his embrace, burying his nose in her hair. The sheer size of him surprised her regularly, but when they were together like this, everything seemed to fit.

Hallie sighed contentedly, forcing the fervent, futile wish to the back of her mind. What they had was already beyond her wildest dreams. Though one piece was missing, they would have that in time, too. She was happy to enjoy this part as much as she could in the meantime.

"Who was on the phone?" she asked tentatively. She knew he couldn't always tell her, given his business, but he hated keeping secrets from her.

Kol's expression darkened and he groaned. "The Twins. They've found it."

"Found what?" She read a combination of displeasure and excitement in his features that confused her.

"The missing fragment of the Verdanith."

A rush of elation made Hallie's eyes grow wide and her heartbeat speed up. She shot up, pressing her palms against his chest. "Get out! You're fucking kidding me. When?"

Kol chuckled and shook his head, his lips quirked in an ironic smirk. "Yesterday. I guess Dimitri's historian friend tracked down a family name."

"Well, this is good, right? Why do you look so pissed?"

"Two reasons, love. First, that the Twins know of its location first doesn't bode well for Rafe. Second, the family name is Rosencrans."

"Rosencrans… as in Erika?"

Kol's single raised eyebrow was all the confirmation she needed.

She sat up abruptly, shifting when Kol grunted at the unexpected pressure of her backside against his spent nethers.

"No shit," she said. "All this time it's been right under our noses. There's no fucking way she knew about it or she'd have told us. You know that, right?"

His lips pressed together in a tight line. "I know you two are close. It isn't her I mistrust. It's *him*. He's never been a team player. I mean, the crazy Red got himself chained to a bed for five hundred years in a fit of pique over having to hibernate in the first place."

Hallie rolled her eyes at him. "I've heard the stories of the orgies Geva was responsible for. Not the best way to earn the respect of your elders, but you have to realize he wants the same thing you do. Why would he jeopardize that?"

"He may not do it intentionally, but he's developed a

reputation for being a reckless fool who doesn't respect our hierarchy. I already talked to Erika. She says they're on their way to her estate in Massachusetts to finally locate the missing fragment. She swears she never knew about it."

Hallie felt a pang of sympathy for her friend. They had become close during the course of their expedition to find the Dragon Temple. Hallie knew enough about the young archaeologist to imagine how she must feel right now. Confused and betrayed most likely, and by her own father, if he'd been the one to keep this from her for her entire life.

"I'd give them the benefit of the doubt," Hallie said. "I'm just happy this is almost over." Her realization of what this meant hit her and her mirth bubbled over. She laughed out loud. "Baby, we're so close now. When can we leave?"

Kol closed his eyes briefly, as though bracing himself. "I need to leave soon. Tonight or tomorrow to get to Boston in time to meet them."

"Oh no you don't. We're going together."

"But you would be miserable flying." The excuse was weak for him. She looked into his eyes for a second, sure there was some other thing he wasn't saying. It couldn't have been the thing she was trying to avoid thinking about—Boston was the last place she thought she'd ever want to visit again after her abrupt departure when she'd joined the expedition. Even the idea of being in the same city as her ex caused her belly to writhe a little in anxiety, but she'd never told Kol all the details.

She shoved the anxiety deep and leaned closer, affecting a teasing tone. "Not if we flew like normal people fly. Your company has a *jet* for Christ's sake! Use it for once!"

Kol's grimace at the suggestion knocked Hallie back a step. The expression he gave her was definitely not faked. She found it exceedingly endearing. "Do you really hate that idea so much? Humans do it all the time, every day. Don't tell me you are actually afraid of flying. You—a *dragon?*"

He gave her a slight shrug. "Not afraid. The thought of being carried in a tube when I could carry myself just…"

"Scares you." Hallie suppressed a giggle that threatened to burst from her throat.

"No! It just makes me itch. Makes me feel like a weakling to be carried when I can fly."

"Come on. I'll be with you. Just the two of us and a pilot and one or two crew. Maybe he'll let you into the cockpit so you don't get so agitated. Or…I can let you into *my* cockpit." She smirked and shifted her hips back down, brushing her flesh against the sleeping beast between his legs. "We need to warm up for all the baby making we'll be doing after."

Kol gripped her hips and sat up. He slid his hands up her back, spanning the entire width of her body easily as he held her against his chest and pressed his lips to hers. The softness of his mouth contrasted with the steel-hard pressure growing between his thighs, nudging up against her tender pussy.

"Do you promise?" he breathed. He slid his hands down to grip her ass and raise her up. The kneading pressure of his fingertips spread her apart enough for the heat of his shaft to rub against her clit.

"Absolutely," she murmured with a shudder of pleasure. "I'd let you fuck me all the way to Boston if that's what I need to do. Hell, I'd let you fuck me around the entire world. I wonder how much mileage I've got on this beauty already." She reached between them and gave his cock a long, slow stroke, enjoying the pleased sigh he emitted.

"Yes," he said. The word drifted out in a slow gasp when Hallie pressed his tip at her entrance and sank down.

"Yes?" she pressed the question against his ear, raising up

along his length and pausing with just his tip poised inside her, throbbing hotly in time with her own slick flesh.

"Yes, I'll fly in the fucking jet with you."

Hallie cried out in surprise when he pushed her back down hard onto his cock and took control of her movements. All she could do was hang on and enjoy the ride.

CHAPTER TWO

Kol had to duck to enter the cabin of the jet. In spite of a spacious interior that he'd been told rivaled the largest private jets, his skin began to crawl inside his tailored dress shirt and his stomach cramped from the confinement. He calmed a little at the feel of Hallie's hand when it came to rest gently against his shoulder. He turned his head to glance down at her, giving her a sheepish smile.

She smiled back. "You know it is equipped with a bed, but I think the captain would rather we stay in our seats. It's only a six hour flight."

"I won't be able to sleep anyway, so no point."

Hallie punched him in the arm and he stumbled forward exaggeratedly. He laughed and glanced around, trying to redirect his mindset to the logistics of bending Hallie over every piece of bolted down furniture in the cabin once the plane took off. He supposed seated he might feel a little less claustrophobic. The black leather sofa that lined one side of the cabin looked like a comfortable venue to begin letting her distract him. The reclining seats might work, too, if the armrests were adjustable. He chose one large, black leather seat midway down the cabin and sat, testing it with a little bounce. He fiddled with the buttons on it, heard a click and discovered that the seat could swivel freely. *That* could have potential.

Hallie paused to watch him, a cute smirk playing across her face. "What are you thinking?" she asked.

Kol gave her a playful look. "Just wondering if this can fit the two of us." He tested the armrests, which did indeed move up and down. Leaving them in the raised position, he grabbed her hand and tugged. He wrapped his arm around her waist and looked in her eyes when she straddled his lap.

"Ready for practice?" he asked, sneaking his hands under her skirt and sliding them back beneath the drape of fabric to cup both round buttocks. He ventured a little farther after failing to contact any undergarment. A low rumble of appreciation rose up from his chest as he traced his fingertips down the cleft of her spread ass cheeks until they grazed the slick opening of her pussy.

Hallie gasped and twitched her hips. She braced her hands on his shoulders and slid back, coming to rest on his knees. "We should wait until we're in the air." Her cheeks had flushed a pretty shade of pink and it was all Kol could do not to push her back into the opposite seat and bury his face between her silken thighs.

The agitation of being trapped in a metal can kept threatening to invade his mind, but her arousal was extremely calming to him. In spite of her pulling away, the pleasant tickle of the magic surrounded her, growing stronger as he caressed her thighs. He closed his eyes and attuned himself to the flow of it, a smooth coolness like a breeze as it bled past, seeking Hallie's ever deepening well. He took a deep breath, imagining the moment a little later when he'd get to soak it up and forget where they were entirely. But until then he'd be enduring a painfully aching hard-on.

"Sweet Mother, no panties?" Kol opened his eyes and gave her a desperate look, then chuckled at her wry smile. "I suppose torture's as good a method as any to get me to forget I can't spread my wings."

A throat cleared faintly behind him. "Mr. Magnus? The captain asks that you take your seats and buckle in now, please."

Hallie immediately slid off his lap and settled in the facing seat. Kol shifted, trying to ignore the swelling in his pants, and looked up at the flight attendant with a friendly smile. "Tell Jerry we're ready when he is, Melody."

The pretty blonde's gaze shot briefly to his crotch. She flushed and blinked at him. "Yes sir." She stepped back through the doorway to the front of the plane, her fingers absently toying with the shiny medallion that hung at her throat. Kol watched her for a second, smiling warmly when she glanced back at him and flushed even brighter, her eyes blinking rapidly.

"You have no idea how sexy you are, do you?"

Kol turned back to look at Hallie, his brows creased in confusion. "What do you mean?"

Hallie laughed, a bold, throaty sound that made him smile almost as much as the alluring way her breasts jiggled when she did it. "You look like a fucking sex god. And with that..." She gestured at the prominent bulge in his pants. "I'm surprised she didn't climb on and try to rip your clothes off."

"She is a bonded employee. She wouldn't unless I invited her to."

"Yes, I know the rules," Hallie said as she settled back in her seat and clicked her seatbelt together. "The little pieces of charmed jewelry they all wear that keeps them loyal and just a little bit oblivious to your nature while they're employed, but doesn't bond them for life. I'm curious, has anyone ever left a dragon's employment once they start working for you?"

"The benefits are too good," Kol said. "They sometimes request transfers, but usually end up in another dragon's employ. Some become mates eventually. Most have entire families in our employ for generations. They're loyal and happy to avoid knowing too much—an odd trait most humans seem to have, but it works in our favor."

She laughed darkly. "Sounds a lot like the mafia if you ask me." Her gaze shifted distractedly out the window as the plane began taxiing toward the runway.

Kol watched her, concerned about the shift in her normally positive mood. The mention of mafia set his alarm bells ringing. When they'd first moved to Los Angeles, he spent time learning who the big players were within the city, because they would all be potential clients of his security firm. He had both humans and dragons in his employ and hired them out to various parties.

His family name, and the name that the company shared —Magnus—already had a strong reputation for effectiveness and discretion, which clients preferred. Leading it was a role he was good at and enjoyed, though he preferred to delegate as much as possible to subordinates he trusted, like Rafe. In the last eight months since becoming a permanent resident of the city, he'd also become closely acquainted with its darker side, and made a point to learn all those ties in particular. Then in the interest of being thorough to protect the interests of his race, he'd enlisted his subordinates to do the same in every other major city in the world.

That's when Kol had found him.

David "Rocky" La Pietra was the man's name, though Hallie had only ever mentioned his first name and only on one occasion shortly after the ritual, but Kol had never forgotten. He'd only learned the man's full identity when he found mention of Hallie in the information sent from his subordinate, a lesser Shadow assigned to the East Coast. It was only a brief connection, but the details were enough for him to be sure. He'd discovered evidence of a six-month relationship that had begun in New York City, followed by Hallie's departure and David ultimately chasing her to Boston. She couldn't have known the ties he had in that city, but she must have believed there was no safe place to run from him when she left the country entirely. A brave move for anyone, cutting ties the way she had.

Braver still to accompany Kol back to a place where she'd never felt safe.

"I will keep you safe," he said softly.

Hallie closed her eyes, the dark fringe of her lashes casting a shadow on her cheeks from the glow of sunset through the window. A sad smile tugged at her lips. "Thank you. I wasn't thinking about David, though."

Only one other thing could cause her to look at him the way she did just then, and the look broke his heart. He swallowed thickly, understanding well enough that need she felt, though possibly not as keenly as she. To have lost a child, even one unborn, must have destroyed her. He realized in that moment that the father of that child hadn't been the only thing she had run from, and his gut clenched with regret over feeling so fortunate that it had been his arms she had found, that had made her stop running.

"Oh, baby, don't look at me like that," she said gently. "I know we've been trying so long, but you gave me hope, and I haven't lost it."

At that moment the plane tilted as it parted ways with the runway and Kol clutched at the seat. He closed his eyes and took a deep breath, trying to will away the itchiness rippling over his skin. Worse than that was the urge to summon and unfurl his wings to catch the air his instincts told him he was soaring through already. Even though he was flush with energy from their lovemaking that morning, he found it tricky to control the urge. It always began with his skin erupting into obsidian scales. Their rigidity was apparent now, and his horns threatened to follow suit.

Hallie's voice broke through the struggle, grounding him. "I think about her every day. Or him. Which would you prefer?"

Kol sighed, accepting her diversion, and relishing the sound of her voice. "What do you mean?"

"Do you want a boy or a girl?"

He opened his eyes and smiled at her. "Yes."

She laughed. "Fair enough. I didn't want just one either."

"There's a bigger question for us," he said. In a lower voice, "What color do you hope for?"

"I didn't think we had a choice. Isn't it genetic?"

"The personality traits that help determine color are, but that's only part of what gives us our color. My mother was a Shadow, like me, but you've met my siblings."

Hallie nodded, smiling. "Polar opposites to you, those two. How did that happen?"

"The Twins had a different human father than I. Mine was a political spy. My mother and he had their fingers in all the royal intrigue in Europe at the time. But the Twins' father was different. No less devious—the man was a thief by trade, and a smuggler—but what he did, he did for fun as much as money. His personality was infectious, joyous, even. Where Father taught me the things I know to run this business, Audun taught me how to enjoy life and love. I think Mother loved him for that as much as the gifts he would bring her."

"So you're saying it was his personality that made them golden?"

Kol had vivid memories of his mother's second mate. Technically third, but he'd never met the first one, as the man who had awakened Astrid Magnus had promptly gone insane and been sent to the Monastery to live out his days under the care of the monks there. Audun had changed his mother in subtle ways. Infectious was no understatement, because he'd affected Kol's father almost as much, as well as the employees bonded to his mother. The days when Audun would return from his latest adventure had always been the highlights of Kol's youth. It had been Audun who had encouraged Kol to love whom he wanted and damn the consequences.

"It's more complicated than that. His joy was shared by Mother. Where she was calculating and devious with Father, she was bright and joyous with Audun. The Twins were a product of that shared joy in life."

Hallie listened raptly and he wondered why the subject had never come up before. Until now, the subject of children had been so abstract—something they strove for but dared not truly hope for until the Verdanith was finally assembled.

"What about Reds?" Hallie asked.

"Fierce passion, in love, or war. Geva's mother was our Queen before, but she had an affinity for men who were battle hardened, as his father was." Before Hallie could ask, Kol continued down the list, enjoying telling her more about his race. "Greens are born from mates who value both life and wealth. There are only female Greens. Blues are the most spiritual-minded dragons. They say that they are the closest to the Mother. Their colors are the most varied, too—like Issa—she's not precisely blue, you may have noticed. I never knew her parents, but her father was a Guardian and her mother was a virgin who had been cloistered for the sole purpose of sacrificing her to the brood. I heard she fell in love with her Guardian afterward and they had a passionate relationship, but she took up worship of the Mother once she learned our ways."

"What about Guardians? Are they always male?"

"Yes. Guardians are most often born to a couple who are together out of convenience or necessity. They may love each other but their relationship is founded more on goodness, justice, and purity of life."

Hallie screwed up her face. "Sounds boring as hell. Poor Roka."

Kol chuckled. "We tend to develop our own personalities, in spite of our parents. Roka was a determined guardian when we were young. The strongest and most competitive Guardian and passionate about his role. No doubt he's been a valuable help to Rafe in their search for Rafe's Red. I wouldn't be surprised if Roka's first child is a Red."

"What…what color would you like?" she asked tentatively, as though the concept was still alien to her. Sometimes Kol had to remind himself that this was all still very new to her. Her eager acceptance of him at the beginning still astounded him.

"I haven't given it much thought. I'd like a healthy child more than anything. Ours may be Red or Gold, but we may have a Shadow considering how prone we both are to dark moods."

"I'd like that," she said, eyeing him thoughtfully. Her gaze grew distinctly focused in a manner he knew well, as much a signal of her intentions as the scent of her arousal. He had quick enough reflexes to get his seatbelt unfastened before she launched herself into his lap again, her luscious lips against his own, tongue demanding entrance to his mouth.

He gripped her ass tight in his hands, hurriedly rucked up her dress to get underneath and feel her skin. This time he didn't hesitate to press his fingers deeper into the wet heat of her he'd only barely touched earlier.

Hallie moaned a plea into his mouth and pushed backwards against his probing touch. Her hands groped at his waist, fumbled his trousers open and tugged his cock free.

The hot stroke of her palms against his shaft caused his hips to buck involuntarily and Hallie laughed.

"God, baby, you're so hard. You should've seen the look on Melody's face when she got an eyeful of you earlier. I wonder if she's watching now. I would be if I were her."

Kol opened his eyes long enough to glance in the direction of the staircase down to the galley where he'd seen Melody disappear earlier. The scent of the other woman was closer than that, now that he searched for it. A flow of magic similar to Hallie's, though less potent, was converging just on the other side of the open doorway.

"She's there," he said. Hallie's pussy clenched around his fingers, her slick juices flowing wetter and hotter. "Does that turn you on?" he asked, surprised by her reaction. He remembered Hallie's heightened state of arousal during the end of the ritual, particularly when both he and Kris were fucking her, but she'd never ventured a suggestion to invite anyone else to their bed since, and he only ever wanted her.

"Yes." She moaned her answer against his neck as she undulated her hips, riding his thrusting fingers.

"Do you want her?"

"I want to watch you make her come. To watch your tongue do to her what it does to me."

"I can't use my real tongue on her," he whispered. "She's an employee—that doesn't mean she knows what we are. She only knows we're different, that working for us is a privilege. I'd have to mark her if I showed her the truth."

"So don't use that tongue. I don't think she'll complain."

Sweet Mother, she was testing him, but in a good way. The thought of being filled with two women's energy at once made his cock throb painfully.

"And where will you be while I'm pleasuring her?" he murmured.

"Right here," she said, giving his cock a squeeze that nearly made him explode.

It took a moment after he hit the call button for Melody to appear again. She was even more flushed than before, her face and chest a bright pink that offset the smattering of freckles on her previously fair skin. Her up-swept red-blonde hair looked a little mussed, a wisp of it clinging to one cheek. Her lips parted in a soft O when she processed the haphazard state of their clothing, Hallie straddling him and his fingers still sunk deep in her pussy.

Melody licked her lips and faltered in her steps toward them. "Y-yes?" she asked.

Hallie was the one to answer, turning her head to look over her shoulder at the flight attendant. "Mr. Magnus has a fear of flying, Melody. Come help me distract him until we're ready to land, will you?"

Kol's eyes narrowed and he almost objected to Hallie's assessment of his constitution where flying was concerned, but Melody's sweet arousal grew even stronger at the invitation. The pretty flight attendant smiled and stepped closer, her eyes drifting to his cock where it was being thoroughly double-fisted by Hallie.

"Anything you'd like, sir?"

Her submissiveness was such a strong contrast to Hallie's demanding persona he was uncertain how to react, but it came to him quickly. Being in command was second nature to him everywhere but in the bedroom, but he could adapt.

"Are you wearing panties, Melody?" he asked. His voice came out gruffer than he intended, but that was only a side effect of Hallie's relentless stroking of him. She subsided just slightly, and began to tease soft caresses along the underside of his cock with one knuckle waiting to see what he would do.

He didn't think Melody could have gone redder, but she did. "No sir."

Kol's eyebrows shot up and his mouth began to water. "No? What, pray tell, has happened to them?"

Melody took a deep breath, seeming to gather her courage. The rise and fall of her chest caused her full breasts to press tighter against her blouse and he noted the top two buttons had come undone since he'd first seen her. With the inhalation, Kol could sense the rising swirl of magic around both her and Hallie. The tease of it drove him on.

"I took them off a few minutes ago, sir. They were too wet and uncomfortable."

Hallie leaned in and whispered in his ear a question he almost couldn't bring himself to ask out loud, but did, just to see if Hallie's pussy would clench around his fingers like it had earlier.

"Were you rubbing your clit thinking about my dick, Melody?"

Hallie shivered against him, her muscles clamping down hard on his fingers.

"Yes sir."

"Why don't you show me what you were doing?" he asked, catching the rhythm of the game after Hallie's prompting. His mind spun with the introduction to this side of his mate. Adventurous, curious. He'd known that about Hallie but hadn't truly explored the possibilities.

Melody nodded and leaned over to tug the hem of her snug skirt up her thighs.

"Why not just take that off for now. It'll just get in your way."

"Yes sir," Melody breathed. She reached behind and unzipped the skirt, then let it fall to the floor. Beneath, she still wore a sheer silk slip that clung to her round hips. "Should I take off the rest, Mr. Magnus?"

The sound of his name said in that perfectly deferential and entirely sensual way seemed to awaken something deep inside. He'd never lorded over his employees and had it on good authority that they thought he was a fair employer, though the members of the company's board considered him too soft. Hallie owned him, body and soul, in and out of their bedroom. He'd never felt weak or impotent in his life, except for the day he was sent into hibernation. But this moment felt different. Now he realized he'd had no idea what true power really meant. Now that he understood, he loved it.

Kol closed his eyes and took a deep breath, held it in and exhaled. He removed his fingers from Hallie's pussy and rested his hand atop her thigh. She'd apparently become so enthralled with what was transpiring with Melody that she didn't object to his lack of attention to her. She released him and slid forward on his lap, adjusting herself so her slick heat rested just at the base of his shaft. The tiny nub of her clit throbbed against him, a delicious reminder that she was definitely still engaged in the encounter. His gaze was on Melody, but he was still acutely aware of every single movement of Hallie's. She began unbuttoning his shirt, undressing him, and he complied silently while deciding what he would do with the lovely Melody.

"Take it all off," he said.

She unbuttoned and shed her blouse, then pulled the slip off over her head and let it flutter to the floor. Her bra followed. Kol took her in, letting his gaze drift over her lush curves, the dark pink of her erect nipples, the narrow trimmed golden triangle between her thighs that pointed to a peek of her glistening clit he was sure must be throbbing and ready for his tongue. She stood still, waiting and expectant.

"Now show me," he said. "Show me how you touched yourself."

Melody swiveled the seat across the narrow aisle to face

him and sat gingerly. One hand went to her breast, fingers tugging at her nipple. Her eyelids fluttered closed as her other hand slid up her inner thigh and she spread her knees, giving him a view of her glistening snatch. The swirl of magic strengthened around her, tangling with Hallie's familiar energy in the air between them. He was dimly aware of Hallie leaving his lap and kneeling before him, urging him to lift his hips so she could tug his pants off. Once he was naked, he swiveled his seat to face the aisle and hit the button that would lock it in place.

Melody leaned back in her seat, thighs wide apart, her toes the only parts of her feet touching the floor. Two fingers swirled in tiny circles over her clit, the engorged folds of her pussy glistened wetly with the flow of her juices.

"Stop before you come," Kol said in a commanding voice.

Melody jerked, startled out of her rapturous state. She drew her fingers away abruptly and nodded, sitting forward again. "What would you like, sir?"

"I'd like to taste you when you come. To have my tongue on that pretty clit of yours."

Hallie had moved out of his line of vision, but he was aware of her just behind him. He heard the zipper of her dress descend, then her lips were at his ear whispering again, this time to let him know the chair could recline flat. The genius of modern technology, he thought, and nodded to her. He sat forward and let her lower the seat. He glanced back at her and their eyes met briefly. The eager look in her eyes urged him on. She bent and kissed him once, letting their tongues tangle languorously for just a moment before pulling away.

Kol lay back. "Come let me taste you now," he said, raising his head enough to look at Melody. She rose, and walked the few steps to him. Her knee pressed against the top of his shoulder, warm and soft, as she climbed onto the seat, delicately positioning herself over his face. The scent of her inundated him, her juicy center poised above his lips. He wrapped his arms around her thighs and lifted his head enough to dart his tongue out for a taste, targeting the tip of her clit with precision.

Melody gasped and shifted her weight, leaning forward to brace her hands on his stomach and lower herself at his urging. The sweet tang of her flooded his mouth when he slipped his tongue deeper. Her soft moans were drowned out by his own rough groan when he felt Hallie resume her attention on his cock, first with her mouth, then only her hands.

His feet still rested flat against the floor so Hallie had to be kneeling between his thighs. Her masterful tongue slid up his length then back down, up again to swirl around his throbbing tip and suck it into her mouth. The soft swell of her breasts pressed against his inner thighs, hard nipples tickling his balls. The tickling rose higher, the length of his cock embraced by both silken orbs as she slid up along his hard length where it rested against his belly. Sweet Mother, he'd never felt anything quite so exquisite as her breasts embracing him that way. She kept sliding higher, then her warm touch left him.

Melody paused her undulations over his mouth and he looked through the gap between her thighs down his torso, trying to catch a glimpse of what he was missing beyond his limited field of vision. All he could see were Hallie's thighs spread and her dripping pussy about an inch too far away from his cock while she leaned in and slid her hands along Melody's sides. He'd never wished to have a mental link with her as much as he did now, but abandoned the fruitless thought in favor of returning to the task at hand. Melody's clit pulsed against his tongue and she whimpered. He heard a sigh and the sudden, familiar heat of Hallie's sweet sheathe finally engulfed him in one long, excruciating stroke. He bucked against her, nearly coming right there from the long needed attention, but succeeded in holding back. The denser swirl of the women's energy signaled that it wouldn't be long now.

He found a rhythm between his tongue on Melody's pussy and fingers deep inside her, and his hips steadily rising in sharp thrusts to meet Hallie's fucking. Hallie's cries began to grow harsher and louder, her clenching muscles tighter until he couldn't stand it. He gripped Melody's ass with both hands and urged her down, burying his tongue deep in her clenching channel and moving his fingers to her clit. He threw caution to the wind and unfurled his true tongue, just hoping she was as far gone with pleasure as he was.

Melody's hips bucked and she let out a long, breathy cry that was joined a second later by Hallie's slightly rougher voice. The rush of their simultaneous releases burst through him like a torrent. He clutched at Melody's ass and groaned loudly against her pulsing flesh as the hot streams of his seed shot into Hallie's spasming core.

Their urgent undulations slowed. Melody quivered above him, raising her hips and leaning forward. He raised his head to look past her thigh. Hallie's arms were wrapped around Melody in a tender embrace. Melody clutched at Hallie, her head resting on Hallie's shoulder, Hallie's cheek resting against the top. It was a sweet gesture that made him smile.

Hallie saw him looking and smiled back, a twinkle in her eyes.

He let his head fall back and sighed in sated contentment. For once, Kol had no breath to spare for words, but there were no words for what had just happened. All he knew was it definitely wouldn't be the last time.

CHAPTER THREE

The change in Kol's bearing was subtle yet evident to Hallie. Since she'd awakened him, he'd always had a slight air of uncertainty, as though worried about making wrong decisions. He was an excellent leader, but in spite of every effort he took to run his company well, to oversee his obligations to his race, she got the impression he believed he could do better.

When they stepped off the plane in Boston, after cleaning up and taking a brief nap, she was certain that last vestige of self-doubt had disappeared. The tiny crease between his eyebrows had smoothed for the first time. The look in his eyes had grown a little more calculating and confident. The set of his shoulders straighter. He was already an imposing man at his size, but now he fairly exuded the raw power and intellect she knew he possessed but had tried to hide to avoid overly intimidating people. This new version of him excited her, but there was an underlying sense of rage that she began to sense and wondered where it had originated.

They walked across the tarmac to the waiting car and he rested one hand possessively at her hip. It wasn't an uncommon gesture for him, but her mark tingled in an unusual way, the heat of it a persistent reminder that she belonged to him and he to her. She shifted closer to him, an almost imperceptible force pulling her.

"You feel different," she commented, once they were seated and the car began moving, its driver taking them out of the city to the Rosencrans estate.

"I do," he agreed. "Why do you think that is?" He gave her a sly look accompanied by a knowing smirk.

Hallie laughed. "I think you learned how much you love bossing people around. It actually turns you on, but you felt guilty about it before. How close am I?"

The smirk only grew wider and he leaned in to kiss her. The kiss was as sensuous as always, but the soft bite he gave her lower lip at the end sent a jolt straight between her legs and answered her question unequivocally.

The drive was long and scenic, and Hallie let herself relax and enjoy the passing landscape out her window. Kol's hand never left hers, holding gently and stroking the center of her palm with his thumb.

It had been an entirely impulsive action, suggesting they invite the flight attendant into their fun. It had only partly been about distracting Kol from his predicament. Absolving her own guilt over making him fly that way was the bigger motivation. She'd talked to Erika and Camille about their experiences since returning to the real world with their mates, and both her friends had extolled the pleasure of opening up their beds to other willing partners. The diversity of energy their mates absorbed had a more rejuvenating effect on all of them as a result. She had to admit she did feel rejuvenated. Even though they'd exhausted themselves during the flight, she still buzzed with the energy of the magic Kol had shared with her.

The change in Kol had been an unexpected yet pleasant

surprise. The most surprising was that his attitude toward her hadn't changed at all. But to the outside world, he was definitely more attuned and alert, less apprehensive. She wondered if it merely had to do with how he acclimated to the new world he'd awoken to, and what they'd done on the plane was the necessary push he had needed all along. His fresh demeanor was so subtle she doubted most would notice it, but she certainly had. In the process of seeking to please her, he seemed to have discovered an unexplored well of power.

The closer they got to their destination, the more intense he seemed, until Hallie began to worry that she might have created a monster during the last six hours. His expression grew tightly focused, his jaw clenching.

"Baby, what is it?" Hallie asked, alarmed by the shift in his mood.

Kol's voice was dangerously low when he responded. "If Geva has compromised our chances at controlling the Verdanith…"

"You don't even know that he's done anything, Kol."

"I've known him longer than you have. He always liked to manipulate the rest of the Court. Thinks of it as some grand game for his own amusement. I refuse to let him control this meeting. It's crucial that he knows he has to answer to me."

The determination in his eyes made it clear there was no arguing with him, and perhaps he was right. She'd spent enough time with the Red during and immediately after the ritual. Geva had a volatile personality when it came to interacting with any of the other dragons. It was almost as if he were inviting one of them to challenge him. If Kol believed he needed to be taken down a notch, she had to trust him.

The car pulled around the circular driveway of a massive, sprawling, Tudor-style mansion a little later and Kol jumped out before the driver could come around and open the door for him.

"Slow down!" she called after him, but he kept going, his long strides far out-pacing her until she had to run to catch up.

He didn't knock before barreling through the front door of the house.

"Geva!" he bellowed.

Hallie stumbled through the door in time to see Erika walk in with Geva close on her heels.

"Well, just come right in, you two," Erika said with a sardonic expression.

The massive Shadow loomed over Hallie's friend, but Erika stood her ground. "You want to get out of my face, Magnus."

"No," Kol said, casting daggered looks between both Erika and Geva. "What you *want* is to explain how this slipped under your radar. In your own damned collection the entire time, and how did you not know about it? I want to see it. *Now.*"

Geva stepped forward fists clenched, a dangerous expression on his face. "Back up, Brother," he said.

Kol shoved a pointed finger at him. "Her family's been the keeper of the fragment the entire time. I hold you responsible, too."

"Jesus Christ," Erika said, shaking her head. "It's safe, I promise. But I'm not taking you to it until you calm the fuck down." She turned to Hallie, her expression immediately shifting to warm welcome. "Glad you guys could make it, sweetie. It's so, so good to see you."

Hallie gave her friend an apologetic expression and stepped in to accept Erika's embrace. "Sorry about him," she whispered. "He's not quite himself today."

"I'll say," Erika murmured back before they parted. In a

louder voice, she beckoned them to a large, comfortable living room with a massive stone fireplace. Kol stalked in and began pacing. Geva leaned against the mantle with his arms crossed, scowling at Kol.

"I know I owe you all an explanation," Erika began, rubbing her palms together. "Until Dimitri called with the results of Thea's search, I honestly had no clue the thing had been under the care of my family this entire time. You see… my dad had secrets." She gave Kol and Hallie an apologetic look. "I knew he kept things from me, but I was sure I'd discovered them all when I found his research notes on… well, on you guys. So, that's all I cared about. Finding you." She gave Geva a loving smile that made the large Red relax just a touch, but his tense posture went even more rigid when Kol stopped pacing to stand in front of Erika again.

"Who else knows you have it? You know the Twins can't be trusted to keep the information to themselves. We need to do damage control before it gets back to the Council."

"What the bloody hell are you talking about?" Geva interjected, finally getting involved. "Why the fuck do you care if it gets back to the Council? I thought that was the general idea!"

Kol stared hard at Geva, his jaw muscles clenching in a way Hallie had never seen. She'd never seen him even remotely angry before, his darker moods never close to as violent as he had seemed since just before exiting the car.

"It's more complicated than that, *Brother*. If you cared one whit about the rest of the race, you might have an inkling what we're trying to do."

Geva stalked to Kol. He stuck his nose in the Shadow's face. Even at well over six feet, Geva had to tilt his head up to look into Kol's eyes. Through clenched teeth, Geva said, "Why don't you tell me how lacking I am, *Shadow*. Which one of us broke the bigger law, eh?"

"You're a fucking fool if you think all this boils down to is who broke which law. There are laws that should not even *exist* now. We can't even *fuck* without worrying about breaking a law. Having that fragment in our control gives us the upper hand, but if the Council knows about it, we lose that advantage."

"And what the fuck do you think the answer to all our fertility issues is going to do to make them change that?" Geva asked. He shot a sidelong look to Erika and Hallie's hackles went up at the tiny shake of her friend's head.

"You know it's more powerful than that. Don't you think the Council knows that, too? They're only appeasing us so they can regain control of it in its entirety. Once that happens, our cause might as well be lost. We can't let them have the last fragment until they agree to our terms."

Geva laughed harshly. "And how do you propose to convince them? They control our entire lives. If we don't kowtow to their laws, they exile us, enslave us, lock us away for centuries. We've been at their fucking mercy for thousands of years and you think *now* you have the solution to it all? Please, *please* tell me why you think *you're* so special that you can convince them. Don't you think our parents tried? I know my mother did, and failed."

"I can't convince them," Kol said, his voice low and resolute, "but I have a free purebred—an Unbound—who can. Her very existence proves the laws are useless. We also have allies among the shackled Unbound at the Monastery, who will help."

Geva's reaction was so quick and fierce, Hallie almost didn't see him move. She and Erika both cried out in alarm when he surged forward, slamming Kol against the fireplace. Geva's horns glowed blood red on his head, his eyes flashing.

"Where is she! If you know where she is I demand you tell me, now!"

The women moved as a unit, Hallie reaching them first. "Just tell him, Kol. We should have already."

"No," Kol gritted out. "Her safety is too important. I couldn't risk anyone else knowing she exists. Why the fuck this imbecile cares so much, I have no idea." He gripped Geva's hands and forcefully pried them off him. The large red wasn't strong enough to resist.

"Tell me *where she is!*" Geva yelled as he was pushed back, the force of Kol's breath as strong as his grip on Geva's arms.

It was Erika's turn to press the issue. She calmly rested a hand on Kol's shoulder. "Kol, if you know something about this Unbound, please tell us. We have information that might be relevant, too, but not until you share."

Without looking away from Geva's enraged expression, Kol answered slowly and carefully. "Rafe found her a few months ago in San Diego. A Red named Rowan. But she ran. He and Roka have been tracking her ever since. They're close to finding her, and once they do, we will have all the ammunition we need to force a change."

Geva's eyes blazed, the light in them casting Kol's fair features in an orange glow. He roared incoherently at Kol, struggling against the Shadow's grasp. Invisible hands seemed to hold the large Red in the places Kol's hands weren't holding, in spite of his struggling. The sight startled Hallie, and made her realize exactly how powerful her mate really was if he could hold a molten ball of anger in place so solidly with only his breath.

"Oh, Jesus," Erika gasped. "Kol. That Unbound dragon... Are you sure that's her name?"

"Positive. Rafe is in love with her. He will find her or die trying."

"Kol..." Erika said cautiously. "Rowan is Geva's sister. We planned to use the Verdanith to find her."

Kol's eyes blazed with fury aimed at Geva. "You have a

sister? Is she Unbound, too? You fucking fool! Your duty is to come to me with this information! I can't do my fucking job when idiots like you keep secrets!"

The two males degenerated into yelling then, mostly Geva spitting epithets in a not entirely recognizable language and Kol responding with cool ferocity. Hallie felt a nudge at her elbow and turned to Erika.

"Let's get out of here, let these two burn out their rage. Hopefully in a few hours they'll have figured things out."

Hallie took a deep breath and nodded, grateful for an excuse to avoid the argument. She glanced over her shoulder once before they walked out the door, but Kol was too involved in defending his argument and spitting back accusations at Geva for not telling him the truth about his sister.

They took Erika's Jeep back toward the City and Hallie relaxed, enjoying the wind blowing around her and the beautiful scenery sliding past yet again.

"So, a sister, huh?" she ventured, hoping Erika would be more level headed and trust her enough to share the details.

Erika let out an exaggerated sigh. "Yes. I considered trying to convince him to tell at least Kol, but you know Geva…believes everyone hates him except for Issa and he sure as hell wasn't going to tell her considering who she's mated to. We were hoping once the artifact is put together we could find some way to secretly use it to find out where she was. I had no idea there was so much controversy surrounding the damn thing."

"Did he have any idea where she was? Rafe's been chasing her down for months now. You should have seen him after he fell for her and she left. He was beside himself."

"Not a clue, but Geva didn't think she was in danger, considering his mother and Rowan's father gave their lives to hide her."

"Oh, God. No, I guess I might have trusted the magic, too. He couldn't have known."

"Well, now he knows," Erika said. "Hopefully Kol can talk him down. I've always liked Kol, by the way." She glanced in Hallie's direction with a smile. "You seem happy."

"Very." Hallie grinned.

"Good. You'll have to tell me everything. I'm kind of over talking about dragon politics for a little while."

"Where are we going?" Hallie asked.

"You'll see," Erika said, smiling.

A few minutes later they turned down a busy Cambridge Street and Erika pulled into a spot at the curb outside a cafe. Hallie laughed out loud when she recognized the place where she'd convinced Erika to hire her for the expedition the year before.

"Wow, this brings back memories. I was so full of shit when I met you, you know that, right?"

"I knew it then, but it took both balls and skill to pull it off the way you did. I tend to go with my gut when it comes to the people I work with. I've never been steered wrong so far. Plus, I had the feeling you needed the job a lot more than any of the other applicants did. I admit, I kind of hoped you and Corey would hit it off. You both seemed like you needed each other."

Hallie smiled at the memory. "I thought we might, too, but I wasn't the woman for him, as it turned out. Figures it would take two women to satisfy the guy in the end, huh?"

Erika laughed. "Not surprising at all."

They found a small table on the open-air patio. Hallie breathed in the familiar air of the place, enjoying the sunlight that dappled the sidewalk through trees lining the street.

Hallie hesitated to gossip about their friends, but Erika had no such compunctions. After their drink orders were taken by an attractive young college student, Erika leaned in. "He told me Jill is pregnant."

Hallie blinked. "That was fast. It's only been a few weeks hasn't it? How does Racha feel about it?"

Erika began shaking her head before Hallie finished speaking, her eyes twinkling with an obvious secret. "It's not *his*. Jill was mated to Racha's dad. That's what all that drama was a few months back when we started the search for this damn fragment."

The events of the last few months were still clear in Hallie's mind, ever since the call late that night that Kol had received from Rafe that resulted in her mate leaving their bed for several hours, then returning in a foul mood for the first time since they'd moved to Los Angeles. Rafe's dilemma had had only one resolution in Rafe's mind: Find Rowan. But Kol was more pragmatic and sent his friend and Second on a detour first. "He's taking care of some business for the Queen first. It'll make this whole thing a lot easier."

"Was Racha in on the Rafe thing? Does she know?"

Erika shook her head and expelled a breath. "You'd have to ask your tall, dark, and yummy man. But she *is* the Queen and he's loyal to her. I bet she knows. In fact, I'd bet my life on it, especially if that baby Jill's carrying matters to her. God, you should see Corey now. He's in hog heaven with those women." She let out a snort. "You and I together could've snagged him, if we'd tried. Can you imagine how fun that would have been? I watched you with Kris and Kol during the ritual. Damn."

"I have no regrets," Hallie said, sipping her wine.

Erika's gaze grew soft as she stared into her glass. "No. Neither do I."

"I watched, you, too," Hallie said, unable to avoid the images that invaded her mind of the night of the ritual. "I think you and I probably know more about each other than most women do about their friends." In a lower voice, she said, "It's too bad Geva and Kol hate each other."

Their meals arrived, distracting them from conversation, but she caught the raised eyebrow Erika gave her and the more appraising look.

In spite of how invigorated Hallie had felt all afternoon, she was ravenous and dug into her food without thinking more about the topic. It might have been a side effect of how intimately she knew her friends, but she felt more comfortable with them and their mates than with anyone she'd ever known, even her own family.

She was polishing off her hamburger when the hairs on the back of her neck stood on end. She took a quick sip of her drink and turned to look behind her, but saw nothing odd.

"Dude was checking you out a second ago," Erika said. Hallie turned back and raised her eyebrows. "Oh? I missed it."

"He was just leaning on the rail over there, talking on his cell phone, but his eyes were all over you. He was hot, too, but he wasn't your type. I mean, if you were looking for a third wheel…" Erika's smile grew suggestive and she lifted her gaze from her lunch to meet Hallie's eyes.

"Oh? And what do you think my *type* is?"

"Not him. He looked…" Erika wrinkled her nose. "For lack of a better term, he looked like he belonged in the mafia, all slick and slinky. Our boys are more diverse, at least. I mean, Kol looks like a teddy bear in spite of being a fucking monolith on legs. And Geva's filled with Viking blood. He's *too* red. And don't even get me started on the others…"

Erika prattled on about the dragons and the other men in their tight-knit group, but Hallie's skin had grown ice-cold. She'd never told anyone but Kol any significant details about David. She'd only mentioned an abusive ex from New York to Erika once they'd established a habit of honesty after the ritual. She knew there was a possibility he was still in Boston, and she hoped like crazy that she was only imagining things, but she'd only ever gotten *that* feeling when he'd been around.

"Can we get the check?" she asked the waiter when he came back.

Hallie blessed Erika for not asking questions or making comments after that. They paid their bill and left. It wasn't until they were on the road again that her friend said anything.

"You want to tell me what that was about? You don't strike me as the kind of girl who gets nervous when a hot guy checks her out."

"I had a bad experience in Boston before I met you."

"The baby, yeah, you told me that."

Hallie shook her head, leaning hard against her seat and staring up into the cloudy sky beyond the Jeep's roll bars. "No, that wasn't the only thing. The father of the baby was mafia. He followed me from New York to Boston. Turns out his family has ties here, too. He might still be here."

"It probably wasn't even him," Erika said. "You didn't see the guy, right? Let it go, sweetie. You've got nothing to worry about, I promise you." She paused for a second, then added, "Well, depending on what we have to look forward to when we get back, you might have nothing to worry about. Now I'm second guessing leaving those two alone together in the state they were in."

"They won't hurt each other," Hallie said, grateful for the distraction. "Kol said dragons are more likely to fuck than fight if they're upset."

"Yeah…" Erika drew the word out. "That's what I'm worried about walking in on."

CHAPTER FOUR

The room had grown small around Kol, even though he managed to maintain his human form. He couldn't quite say the same for Geva, who he still held subdued in an invisible binding. Only the Red was far from subdued.

"You *knew* where my sister was and you didn't say anything?" Geva yelled.

"You red fuck, I told you I didn't know she was your sister. Your duty was to *tell me the fucking truth.*"

Geva snorted. "And for what? So you can *use* her to satisfy your own agenda?"

"Sweet Mother, are you daft? My agenda is no different from yours."

"And yet you lord it over me."

Kol's head spun with the idiocy of the dragon before him. He had the oddest sense of energy swirling around them, but it wasn't quite like the pleasant yet powerful swells that surrounded Hallie when she was aroused. This stuff just made him hot with rage. Rage he'd like to ride to its logical conclusion, but he'd been trained for this as a Shadow and knew how to channel it. The alternative was always preferable.

"Is that all this is for you?" he shot at Geva. "Is it a test of my power versus your own? Because I assure you, keeping this information from me does *nothing* to give you the upper hand or even to redeem yourself."

"From the atrocities I inflicted, right? Because giving humans a taste of pleasure is so much worse than leaving a human woman you love to a fate worse than death. I am *still* better than you, Shadow."

The taunt shouldn't have affected Kol. He'd left those ghosts behind. But he reacted just the same. With invisible hands conjured from his breath, he flung Geva to the floor before the large fireplace.

"You're a weakling, always have been," Geva taunted, his voice muffled by the carpet beneath his face. "You couldn't even fucking *mark* the woman you loved."

Kol's rage became a pinpoint, focused entirely on the bastard Red who dared to question his honor. The event Geva referred to had been an impossible decision, and a choice Kol ultimately didn't have. The brood was on the verge of their hibernation. Marked, Eveline would have died the moment he entered hibernation. The Council refused to let him bring her, so the mark was nothing more than a death sentence. This taunting Red had no right to question his decisions.

"My fucking past isn't in question here," Kol gritted out. "I'm your superior, *Brother*, and you will answer to me." It had only been a few hours since the events inside the plane with Melody and Hallie, and his blood still sang with the power both women had given him. More than that, he was alive with the clarity of what it meant to hold the position he held among the Court.

Geva laughed into the rug, but he'd given up struggling,

seeming content to use verbal abuse instead. "As superior as your mother was, letting a man compromise her the way she did? Their father. Your fucking loudmouth siblings. I'm actually sad they won't get away with their little threesome, but it pays to keep your secrets."

First his mother, then his stepfather and brother and sister being lambasted by the ass on the floor below him. He wanted to smash the fucker's face into the floor, but his cock raged hard, pushing him to an alternate course of discipline.

It was less a decision than instinct when he knelt and straddled Geva's prone form. He manifested a sharp talon and ripped clean through Geva's clothes from collar to ass. Smooth, pale skin stretched over taut back muscles and round buttocks that clenched when the cool air hit them. He gripped the sides of Geva's torn pants and ripped them off in a violent pull then tore his shirt the same, flinging the scraps aside. Geva quivered slightly in the aftermath, then grew still again, only his head turning and craning over his shoulder to try to see Kol. The invisible bindings of Kol's breath held the other man solidly to the floor. Kol stood up, panting and gazing down at the pale, muscular body beneath him.

"Anything else to say before I teach you a long deserved lesson?"

"Fuck you."

Kol took his time, slipped off his shoes and socks, stepped barefoot around to Geva's head as he unbuttoned his shirt and pulled it off, draped it neatly over the back of a chair near the fireplace. He braced his palms on his knees and bent down to look into Geva's eyes. "That's precisely what I'm going to do, because clearly you won't be convinced to obey me any other way."

The light in Geva's eyes flickered with uncertainty, but the bastard had the audacity to smirk. "You won't do it. Of all the Court, you and your brother were the only males who never showed an interest in *branching out*. Too wrapped up in love, the others said."

"My brother's come to his senses, and so have I. But don't confuse this with love. Fucking your virgin ass is the burden I have to bear to get you to accept me as your superior."

Kol stood up and shed his trousers and briefs. He gazed down at Geva thoughtfully, trying to decide the best way to begin. He'd never have taken this course if it hadn't been for the tryst on the plane. At best he'd have blustered at Geva, then ended the argument feeling even more of a failure at his role.

The effect of Melody's sweet submission had done more than arouse him. It had made him understand that he'd been a poor excuse for a First Shadow since he'd awakened. If he were to maintain the safety and security of his race, he had to be ruthless and direct. He had to command respect. The skills were innate in him, yet he'd kept them at bay all along, believing they compromised his ideals too much. The encounter with Hallie and Melody made him realize that he could give generously at the same time as commanding that respect and keeping his subordinates in line.

What he was about to do was one of his race's most ancient practices. Mated dragons avoided sharing their energy outside their mated bond, but in certain situations, such as this one, it was required to reassert the hierarchy. They weren't truly a violent race at all, preferring to channel every emotion to the singular purpose of procreation, or at least mimicking the process. He'd considered the practice of asserting dominance this way barbaric when he learned about it during his training, even knowing it would ultimately be enjoyable for both parties. He'd always been an idealist, believing he should hold his love sacred and only share himself with his chosen mate. Hallie's enthusiasm for sharing him with Melody had changed his outlook. This was who he was. A dragon. And when a dragon misbehaved, it was the Shadow's duty to bring him in line.

The Red's gaze rested solidly on Kol's erection, a pink flush spreading over his skin from forehead to shoulders. Geva's horns and scales had subsided during their conversation, so the contrast with his fair skin was striking. His muscles tightened in an effort to free himself from his invisible bindings, but Kol was the best at what he did. Once someone was caught in his grip, it was nearly impossible to get free without disabling Kol entirely. Kol stroked his cock once for emphasis of what was about to transpire and quirked his lips into a smile.

Geva swallowed thickly and blinked up at him. "Is this really necessary? Let me up and we can have some fun when the girls return."

Kol shook his head and took a step to stand midway down Geva's prone form, then knelt to straddle Geva's backside. Leaning down, he let his cock brush against Geva's back and pressed his lips against the Red's ear. He recited the words in their native tongue. Words that would leave no room for misinterpretation. *You will submit to me.* Geva bucked beneath him, letting out a curse in the same language. Along with the words he emitted a gust of swirling red breath that hit Kol's nostrils. The power held in that breath was enough to daze him and he nearly lost control.

"Let me go," Geva's voice resonated, the power in it taking hold of the breath that seeped into Kol's mind.

Kol's will was stronger. He responded by sinking his teeth into the back of Geva's neck, targeting the pressure points that would induce compliance. Geva went limp. Kol lingered with his mouth on Geva's neck, tickling the center of his bite marks with his tongue, aware of the effect it was intended to have on his victim—an effect not unlike what Geva had intended with that breath—to confuse and incapacitate with a driving sexual need.

"It will take more than a breath to deter me," Kol said. "But by the time we get started, you'll be begging me for more."

He stood again and stepped backward, then knelt between Geva's legs, pushing them both gently apart. As much as it was a disciplinary situation, it didn't need to be torture, and with Geva relaxed now, it would go much smoother.

Geva's sac rested heavily on the carpet, his ass cheeks spread just above it. He shifted just enough to display the uncomfortable erection that pressed into the floor beneath his hips. Kol brushed his palms down both ass cheeks, pushing them apart to graze his thumbs along the sensitive, puckered flesh between. Geva groaned.

Kol chuckled. "You have a reputation, you know. You fuck, but you've never *been* fucked. It's time, Brother. Time for you to accept your role among us, to fall in line and serve the Court. If you want to be accepted, this is a necessary step. I blame myself for not doing it sooner." He slid one hand between Geva's thighs and cupped his balls, grazing the pad of his thumb up and down the sensitive patch of flesh between testicles and asshole. Geva's hips twitched.

Kol drew in a breath, loosening the invisible bindings that held Geva. The Red lurched up as though to escape, but Kol tightened the snakes of breath around wrists and ankles, holding Geva in place on his hands and knees. Geva glared over his shoulder at Kol.

"You're enjoying this too much, I think," Geva said. "Since when have you ever shown an interest in taking control? This isn't like you."

"I'll be honest, I didn't expect to enjoy it. But seeing you incapacitated like this makes my blood hot. You can't hide that you're enjoying it on some level, either." Kol gave Geva's balls a gentle squeeze and slid his hand farther to stroke the Red's hard cock. The nearly scorching heat of it surprised Kol and he gave the cock another slow stroke, enjoying the silken texture against his palm. A few droplets leaked from the tip and he slicked his fingertips along the small slit, spreading the moisture down the underside of Geva's shaft. Kol's own cock spasmed in sympathy.

His head buzzed with power even stronger than he'd felt having Melody comply with his small commands. Having the powerful Red tied down and nearly ready to give into him gave him a greater rush than he could have imagined. He had to tease Geva enough that the Red begged to be fucked if he wanted to leave an impression, however. It would be more pleasurable for both of them that way.

With one hand still gripping Geva, stroking him, he bent his head to swirl his tongue around the smooth, pliant skin of his balls. Geva's thighs quivered in response when Kol sucked one orb gently into his mouth, toying with it on his tongue. He released it with a slight "pop" and took the other in his mouth.

Geva's hips tilted back when Kol pulled away. The Shadow leaned back with his palms resting idle on his thighs, enjoying the way the Red had begun to sweat, his chest heaving from Kol's attention. He met Geva's pleading gaze over the Red's shoulder.

"Do you want more?" Kol asked. He slid a palm up the inside of Geva's thigh, brushed it against the back of his balls and slid higher. He pressed his thumb at the center of Geva's asshole. "Maybe you're ready to get fucked now, or maybe I need to tease you a bit more until you beg me for it."

Kol leaned in, replacing his thumb with his tongue, twisting the thick, agile appendage just a little deeper before withdrawing and teasing around the opening until it was slick with his saliva. The Red was uncommonly tight, but he supposed it was largely nerves. Kol had never allowed anyone but Hallie beyond his own barrier, not that he'd had many opportunities to since the ritual. The pair had withdrawn from the final step of the ritual as soon as they'd made their contributions.

He gripped Geva again in his fist, stroking harder than before. Geva's cock was slick from escaping fluid, but Kol had no intention of letting Geva reach Nirvana until Kol was ready himself. He pressed his middle finger against Geva's slickened opening and pushed. Geva groaned at the invasion, his cock jerking in Kol's hand.

"You need to submit, Brother. Admit that you're under my power, that you accept my dominion over you and I'll let you finish, but not until then." He released Geva's cock again, drawing back to caress the back of his balls while pressing a second finger into Geva's ass.

In a harsh voice Geva asked, "Are you going to share with me or just take?"

The desperate tone of the Red's voice caused a surge of sympathy to well up. Kol smiled to himself. "That depends on how badly you need it. There's only one way you'll be getting it, though." He pressed his fingers deeper in emphasis, leaned in to swirl his tongue around, ensuring Geva was lubricated enough to accept more. He pushed a third finger in to join the other two, fucking slowly into Geva and beginning to stroke the Red's cock again. Kol's own cock thrummed between his thighs, alive with the need for attention he was presently giving the other dragon. He'd be ready for Geva once the Red finally gave in.

The swirling eddies of magic that had been steadily building around the two of them shifted at the same time Kol sensed the crumbling of Geva's will. The magic tasted like hunger, the Red's bone-deep need to be fucked hitting Kol hard enough that he had to pause for breath.

Geva's voice lowered and he craned his neck to look back at Kol. "Shadow, I am yours to command and will answer to you. My every secret is yours to do with as you see fit. I submit. Fuck me, please." As he said it, red smoke curled out from his nostrils and his skin shimmered with a reddish glow. Kol inhaled what Geva had offered, wary at first, but grateful the Red was honest for once. The power in the breath was the true promise to Kol, more so than Geva's words had been. The message this time was not an effort to counter Kol's control, but was in fact an oath of obedience.

To ensure Geva's total compliance, Kol released the Red from his bindings. Geva remained on hands and knees, his fingernails digging into the carpet. Kol slipped his fingers out of Geva and repositioned with one knee on the carpet and his other foot flat on the floor beside Geva's knees. He gave Geva's cock another stroke while he pressed the tip of his cock between Geva's ass cheeks. The Red moaned a curse in their native tongue and hissed as Kol pushed deep.

"Sweet Mother, you're tight."

"Mmm...you would be too, around a cock that size. Bloody fucking hell, don't stop moving."

"...don't want to hurt you..." Kol muttered half breathless. The friction of fucking into Geva's ass made it difficult to retain the control he needed to follow through with what had begun as simple punishment. Now Kol started to wonder if he wasn't punishing himself just as much.

"Oh, fuck, don't tell me this is your first time."

"It's yours, too, from that end. Stop wiggling or I'm gonna come."

Geva laughed, the sound throwing Kol off. Trying to regain his focus, Kol gripped Geva's hips tightly and pulled out nearly all the way, then thrust hard back into Geva's ass.

"Is that how it's done?" Kol asked, gasping at the rush of pleasure the tight friction caused.

"Sweet Mother. Yes! Like that...only slower?" Geva laughed a little. "That's how I do it, anyway. And maybe... unh..."

Geva's words fell short with another thrust of Kol's cock, slower this time. Kol managed to catch the gist of Geva's thoughts, however, and reached down to slide his fist along Geva's cock again.

He found a steady rhythm and was nearly blind with pleasure when he heard a faint curse from across the room, but it was far too late to stop even if he'd had any intention of it.

CHAPTER FIVE

"You must be psychic," Hallie said, her eyes wide at the view that greeted them in the center of Erika's front room when they entered.

"Not at all. I was only joking," Erika answered in a near whisper. "And I'll be honest, *this* wasn't quite what I imagined would happen."

Kol's dark-haired magnificence, naked and single-mindedly immersed in fucking Geva, had been the last thing Hallie imagined she'd ever see, either. But the sight of it was even more arousing than watching her lover bury his face between Melody's thighs, tonguing her with such abandon that the girl fell into tears of utter joy at the end of it.

Geva's eyes rested on Erika, then Hallie, the red glow evidence enough of his enjoyment.

"It is quite a twist," Hallie agreed, smiling approvingly at Kol. His eyes were half-lidded with pleasure. She had the strongest urge to go to him, but knew she shouldn't interfere directly. "I'm afraid it might go to Kol's head just a little. It'll be good for him, of course, but Geva might be a little sore afterward—and I don't mean physically."

"What are you suggesting?" Erika asked, one eyebrow raised.

"Just a little balance. You've always been the superior woman among us, you know."

Erika seemed about to object, then caught the subtle suggestion Hallie had given her. Hallie's skin tingled when Erika moved behind her and took both Hallie's hands, pulling them and clasping them behind her back.

"Like this, maybe?" Erika asked. Hallie glanced over her shoulder at her friend's mischievous smile.

"Yes," she said with a grin.

She felt something soft wrap around her wrists and tighten. Erika's bandanna, most likely, being used to bind her. It was unexpected but would lend credence to their little game. What Kol was in the middle of was far more than a game where dragon hierarchy was concerned, but that didn't mean she and Erika couldn't add some spice to the proceedings.

Erika's lips brushed against Hallie's ear. "Let's move a little closer—make sure they have a good view."

Hallie let Erika direct her several paces to the middle of the room. The men's eyes followed them both. Kol's eyes met Hallie's and his expression grew more intense, his steady thrusts into Geva slowing while watching the pair of them move.

Erika left Hallie's wrists bound when she stopped them to stand before Geva's bent form. He craned his head to look up at Hallie. He didn't quite look pathetic—no dragon as gorgeous and irreverent as he was could even fake a look like that—but he was definitely subdued, which she was sure had been Kol's intention.

"I'm going to give them a show now," Erika whispered. "Just go along."

Hallie nodded and stood still. Her skin tingled when

Erika tugged the straps of Hallie's dress down. They slid along her arms, resting at the crooks of her bent elbows. The front clasp of her bra unhooked with a deft flick of Erika's fingers, the straps slid off Hallie's shoulders and dangled around her elbows as well. Erika cupped Hallie's breasts and squeezed her nipples while grazing lips along the side of her throat.

Hallie's eyes shifted from Kol to Geva and back. Both of them were coated in a sheen of sweat, their eyes flashing with desire when they took her in. They had to be close to climax but had evidently silently agreed to draw out the experience now that she and Erika were getting involved. She knew from Kol's explanation of the magic that drawing it out would result in a more intense climax once they came.

Erika's touch was gentle but insistent, and incredibly arousing when the eyes of both men followed her every action. Kol had never taken control of their intimate moments like this, and she wasn't sure she would enjoy it if he did—they were equal partners when it came to their sex lives. The dynamic hadn't changed with this particular encounter, but shifting her mindset to that of someone's subordinate was exciting.

She felt the other woman kneel behind her, sliding hands delicately down her torso and up her thighs under the skirt of her dress. A soft chuckle reached her ears when her friend discovered her lack of undergarments—she hadn't bothered to put any on after the encounter on the plane.

"Adventurous, like me," Erika said. "I like that, but I guess I knew that about you." Her palms slid around Hallie's hips to the front, one set of fingertips grazing down the center and finding her clit, already wet and slick, no doubt. She tugged the hem of Hallie's skirt up, tucking the fabric up and under the waist of the dress so that Hallie was entirely exposed from the hips down. "Turn around."

Hallie turned and was met with a pair of hands cupping the sides of her head, fingers threading through her thick hair. Smooth, cool lips pressed against hers, still carrying a hint of the wine they'd shared at lunch. A tongue a little more demanding and forceful than she'd expected invaded her mouth. She gave in kind and Erika moaned slightly at Hallie's eager response.

From behind her she heard Kol's rough, deep voice. "Yes, touch her."

But she's already touching me, Hallie thought before the heavier brush of a hand slid up her thigh and cupped one ass cheek. Geva's thicker fingertips teased between her slick lips, making her gasp and spread her legs farther apart. He found her clit and began deftly rubbing it while Erika stepped back to undress.

"Down," Erika said when she was naked. She placed both hands on Hallie's shoulders and Hallie obliged, sinking to her knees. A pair of growls sounded behind her, a harmonious appreciation of her change in position. Geva gripped her hip with one large hand and pulled her back.

She nearly lost balance and fell, unable to catch herself with her hands still bound. Erika caught and righted her, pausing with her hand cupping Hallie's chin. Erika's smooth pussy was poised in front of Hallie. Experimentally she leaned in far enough to place a kiss against the peak of Erika's cleft. Glancing up, she met Erika's bright-eyed approval and leaned in again, this time letting her tongue slip out and probe between the smooth folds to the top of Erika's clit, then further, hooking her tongue deeper to tease at the tip of Erika's throbbing nub. Erika moaned and tilted her head back, then gently pushed Hallie back.

"Slow down, sweetie, let's do this right."

Hallie let out a yelp when Geva's tongue invaded her pussy from behind and a heavy sigh escaped him.

"That's right, Baby. You like the taste of her, don't you?" Erika said.

Hallie was dimly aware that her friend seemed entirely in her element and she really shouldn't have been surprised. Erika moved around the room for a moment, then returned, piling up several oversized throw pillows on the floor in front of Hallie. She lowered herself to the floor, reclining on the pillows, and spread her thighs, placing one foot on either side of Hallie.

"I think you know what to do," Erika said softly.

The memory of Melody's desperate kiss in the midst of her climax returned, followed by the taste of the girl on Kol's lips when he'd followed suit a moment later. Hallie wondered if Erika would taste the same. She brushed her lips along the inside of Erika's left thigh, teasing her tongue along the smooth skin as she went. The glowing red of Erika's mark shimmered in Hallie's gaze, yet another reminder of all the pair had in common.

She pressed her lips against Erika's swollen folds again in a deep, languid kiss. Geva's attention from the other side made it difficult to maintain her balance. He seemed to sense it and a second later Hallie felt his hand hastily removing the tie from her wrists.

Her fingers stroked gently along Erika's outer lips, which were already shining wetly with her arousal. Hallie spread them apart and bent her head again to the pink-petaled bud that beckoned from between. Erika sighed and shifted her hips up when Hallie sucked Erika's clit between her lips, teasing at it in small circles with her tongue. Hallie released it and slicked the tip of her tongue down lower, sinking into Erika's wet opening, immersing herself into the experience of feminine flavors and textures that were at the same time familiar and alien to her.

Had Kol been as eager as she to do what he did? The

thought of him behind Geva now, fucking the other dragon like he enjoyed it, was enough of an indication that he'd at least been eager by the time he sealed the deal.

She could hear him now, murmuring commands to Geva, who was eagerly following them. "Fuck her tasty cunt with your tongue. Yes, slowly." Geva tongue fucked her so skillfully she almost lost her sense of direction. She'd been with men who weren't even that impressive with their cocks, and knowing her lover was the one choreographing it made it increasingly difficult to concentrate on her own task.

She tried to shove her tongue deeper into Erika's pussy, but lacked the agility of a dragon's tongue to go very far, so Hallie returned to teasing just the clit with flicks of her tongue. She slipped a pair of fingers deep inside instead, beginning to fuck her friend slowly.

"Oh, God, yes, fuck me like that," Erika gasped. "Harder."

The reaction encouraged Hallie, so she pressed two more fingers deep into her friend. Erika's hands went to Hallie's head, fingernails digging in. She cried out again for *more, deeper, harder*. Hallie swept her tongue in quicker circles around Erika's clit and pressed her fingers deeper.

Erika's hips bucked and she moaned and pleaded still for more. Hallie twisted her fingers and slipped her thumb in, pushing her fist even deeper, letting her knuckles rub along Erika's inner walls. Wet heat flooded down to her wrist, the grip on her hair almost painful, but a sweet signal that she was doing something right. Geva's tongue plunged distractingly into her own pussy, his thumb rubbing steadily at her clit.

Erika let out a harsh yell and bucked her hips up against Hallie's mouth. Erika's muscles clenched and pulled at Hallie's hand, seeming to want to pull her in deeper. Hallie kept fucking her, quicker now, but entirely lost the sense of where she was when the rhythmic noises from behind her escalated. She heard Kol's familiar sonorous groan as he came, and the cascade of energy surged forth from Geva almost simultaneously. The rush of it hit her deep, like the euphoric warmth of a strong drug taking effect. It spread through her pussy, inciting her own spasming climax and she reached back, clutching hard at Geva's head with her free hand to hold him in place while she rode it out on his tongue that still thrust rhythmically deep inside her.

They extracted themselves from each other slowly. Geva murmured something incoherent before collapsing sideways onto the floor. Hallie rested back on her heels, then turned to see Kol looking dazed and just a little sheepish. She smiled at him.

"I hope the two of you worked out your differences," she said.

The men shared a glance. Kol's eyebrow tilted up inquiringly at Geva. Geva dropped his gaze in response, looking suitably chastised, but the reaction was minute and less than a second later he gave her a cocky grin.

"We'll always have differences, I'm sure, but Kol will never question my loyalties again, I can assure you of that. Now who's hungry? I could eat a horse."

CHAPTER SIX

The Verdanith fragment itself was unimpressive. When Erika finally revealed it after dinner that evening, Hallie somehow expected something fantastic to happen. Both men sported instant erections after admiring and touching it, however, so clearly it had an effect on them. The artifact did have a slight translucent glow that seemed to Hallie more a trick of light but made her want to touch it, too, just to see.

"Go ahead," Erika said, handing the heavy jade wedge to her. Hallie took it, hefting the hand-sized carving. She ran her fingertips over the raised surface, tracing the outline of a dragon that undulated across the smooth stone. Her eyes met Kol's, and they shared a silent understanding of what it would mean. What she hoped it would mean soon, anyway. Her mark heated in response to the darkening look in Kol's eyes and she handed the fragment back to Erika. She only barely caught the gist of the rest of the conversation regarding their obligation to deliver the fragment to the Council and holding back at least until Geva's sister was located.

Her vision tunneled in response to Kol's gaze and the brush of an invisible touch beneath the curve of her breast. He broke the trance after a second, responding to a question Geva had asked.

"We can put them off for a week, but no more. As soon as I hear from Rafe and Roka that they have located your sister, you will be the first person I call."

"I have a better idea," Erika said. "Stay here until they find her, then we'll all travel together. If we're that close I'd prefer to stick together until we see this through finally. I'm ready to get on with my life." Her eyes met Geva's. "With *our* lives," she amended. She looked at Geva with an expression that reflected the need Hallie felt—that deep longing to have tangible evidence of her union with Kol.

Erika replaced the stone fragment in the safety of the velvet-lined box it had resided in for centuries, and stowed the box behind the heavy iron door of her safe. The four headed out of Erika's study.

"To think that thing's been here the entire time," Hallie said. "Your dad never told you about it?"

Erika laughed ruefully. "Technically he did. He wrote me a letter before he died, but I never bothered reading it. I didn't look at until two days ago when I got back here. I was too laser focused on all the research he'd left behind. I didn't want any more reminders of losing him. I just wanted to find out if they were real."

Hallie's stomach fluttered at the sensation of Kol's fingertips tracing the length of her spine. "I can't say I'm particularly upset on that count."

"No regrets here, either," Erika replied.

They parted ways on the landing at the second floor, heading to doors at the opposite ends of the hall. Hallie and Erika parted with a goodnight and a peck on the lips. Hallie watched, amused, when Geva hesitated with a meaningful look at Kol.

"I'm not kissing you goodnight," Kol said. "As a matter of fact, unless you're utterly depleted of power, I'm not likely to touch you again, if that's alright with you."

Geva gave him a wide grin. "Suit yourself. You don't know what you're missing."

A few moments later Hallie relaxed naked on their bed, watching Kol undress. "After all that's happened today, you don't have at least a small urge to find another mate to mark? Someone to share?"

Kol's brows drew together and he slowed his movements, deliberately meeting her gaze while he shed his trousers and boxers. He was ready for her again, and not shy about it. He was never shy about it, but seemed almost irritatingly over-confident now.

"You are more than enough for me. Am I enough for you?" He slid into bed beside her, bending his head to capture one nipple and suck it between his lips.

"Oh, yes. Absolutely," she sighed. She sank back against her pillows, letting him pleasure her, and enjoying the hum of energy that passed between them when they climaxed together. She needed nothing more in her life but him and the promise of what they would share in the future.

THE NECESSARY DELAY in delivery of the Verdanith resulted in a welcome interlude for Hallie and Kol. She enjoyed the relaxing solitude of Erika's estate, so peaceful compared to the busy day-to-day their lives in Los Angeles had become. In spite of his assurance that she didn't need to work, she'd insisted on it, taking on the role of vetting new employees.

Now, Kol was more relaxed than she'd ever seen him, which only amplified the sense that she should enjoy their brief rest while she could because it would end as soon as they got the call that Geva's sister had been found. As much as she hoped for the reunion of the lost dragon with Rafe and Geva, she didn't look forward to the end of their idyllic vacation.

It ended prematurely when Kol received a call from the local Shadow and left the estate to deal with some unspoken business. He only said it was a potential client before kissing her goodbye, straightening his suit, and climbing into the hired car to drive into the city.

"We're heading to lunch," Erika called out the French doors to the pool where Hallie had been dozing on a chaise lounge, half dreaming, half fantasizing about holding a soft, warm bundle in her arms. One with dark, silver-flecked eyes and a shock of downy black hair. She blinked dazedly at her friend.

"Come with us?" Erika said.

Hallie nodded, relishing the idea of friendly company for the afternoon. She'd begun feeling a lonely longing for Kol that the baby dreams weren't helping alleviate. She looked forward to the distraction.

After a sunny drive they ended up back at Erika's favorite cafe, sipping wine and munching on bread.

"How much do you know about your sister?" Hallie ventured to Geva during a lull in their conversation.

The red dragon's expression shadowed briefly, before breaking into a wan smile. "Not much, I'm afraid. My parents —and her father—gave their lives to hide her. All I know is her first name and her bloodline."

"So, she's..." she paused, wary of speaking the word in public.

"Purebred. Yes," Geva said in a low voice. "Which means she would be very powerful." His chest seemed to puff a little with pride. "Not surprising it's taken this long to find her."

"I'm surprised you're not out looking along with the others. I know if I hadn't checked in with my brothers after I left, they'd have come after me."

A grimace that signaled his regret crossed his face. "I would have, had I known at the start. It's too late for me to begin wandering aimlessly now, but you can be sure once they've located her, that's where I will be going." He turned to look at Erika. "You'll come with me, won't you?"

"I wouldn't miss it for the world," Erika said.

Hallie observed the pair's exchange, yet again amazed at the constantly shifting dynamic between the dragons and their environment. Whether it was their mates or each other they interacted with, they were so changeable. She thought about Kol and the command he so easily took with anyone but her. She'd asked him about it the day before. His reply was simply, "You will be the mother of my children. As such, I am yours to command."

That was when it had occurred to her what the role of mother meant to them. Mothers were sacred to his race, and for good reason if it was such an ordeal for them to even conceive a child. The Verdanith would make it easier to conceive, Kol had explained, but what followed might not be an ideal pregnancy by human standards. Most human women had few issues—no more than they would if they carried a human child. But he explained that the female dragons frequently had difficult pregnancies. Yet Hallie knew how much the dragon females of the Court desired to conceive as much as she did. At least Racha and Aurin had expressed as much to her. Halie hadn't spoken to Issa since the ritual. Nobody had.

Hallie finished her wine, emptied the last of the bottle into her glass, and sat back to enjoy the waning afternoon.

Feeling just a little like a third wheel in the face of Geva's whispers to Erika that were causing her friend to actually blush, Hallie excused herself from the table to visit the restroom. She was pleasantly buzzed and happy, her mind flitting back and forth between memories of the past week and hopes for the future once the dragons got their politics sorted out and she and Kol could start trying to get pregnant in earnest.

A large figure stood in the dim walk-through hallway outside the restroom when she exited. He was silhouetted before the open back door of the restaurant that led to a second dining patio, his features cast in shadow. All Hallie registered at first was another patron waiting for the restroom. Just a second too late, a whiff of cologne hit her nose and made her gut clench with recognition. She hurried to keep walking, hoping he hadn't seen her but knowing full well she was the sole reason for his presence.

"Welcome home, lover," a familiar deep voice said, so close that the cologne became a cloying unpleasant miasma. She remembered a time when she'd loved that scent, but that had been a long time ago.

Hallie tensed and stopped in her tracks. Her skin grew ice-cold, goose flesh rising up instantly. A rush of sick fear seeped into her belly, causing her vision to pinch and grow dark with panic. She was abstractly grateful that she'd just emptied her bladder.

"David," she said in a small voice, hating herself for how meek she sounded. She'd survived the bastard and escaped. He couldn't touch her now. She was protected.

Except Kol wasn't here. Hallie stared helplessly through the cafe to where Geva and Erika were sitting, nuzzling each other at their table.

"I missed you," he said, his voice now close enough that

she could feel his breath against her ear. The touch of his fingertip on her skin caused her to flinch.

Hallie shivered and blinked, finally regaining her bearings enough to move. She managed only a step before his unforgiving grip clamped like a vise around her upper arm, forcing her to swing around to face him.

"Don't think you're going to get away from me again, Hallie. You are *mine* and you are coming home."

"No." She tried to force the word out but it only came as a hoarse whimper. She tried harder, tried to think. Erika and Geva could help if she could just get to them. The clutch on her arm tightened, his fingertips digging in brutally. She made a fist with her free hand and swung it around to punch him, but he dodged in time and her knuckles only glanced off the side of his neck. He caught her fist in his free hand and held her tight.

"Let me go!" she yelled, finally finding her voice. She turned and yelled toward the dining room of the restaurant, just hoping her voice would carry to the patio beyond where the others sat. "Erika! Geva!" But the pair were too absorbed in their own little world to hear.

David wrapped an arm around her waist, still holding her arm tightly with one hand. She dug her feet in, raising one heel to smash the top of his foot, but he dodged again. Her brothers had taught her to fight early on, but no amount of fore-knowledge could counter a man who knew how to fight as well as David did, and who had the muscular bulk and a killer's instinct to back up that knowledge. What David wanted, David had always gotten. Except for her.

There was no use struggling. She just had to hope Kol knew where to find the asshole once Erika realized she was missing. She walked slowly, trying not to stumble when he pushed her forward toward the alley around the side of the restaurant where a sleek town car waited.

She slid into the confines of David's car, silent and grim.

"That's my girl," David said. "How about a kiss hello?'

"You touch me, I will bite your fucking tongue off," she gritted through her teeth.

"I've been *fantastic*," he said, not missing a beat. "How have you been, baby? Had a few little adventures, I take it? You are a clever one. Put on a good chase—so good I was sure I'd lost you. But here you are, right back where you belong. It's fate, I think. *Destiny*. Destiny brought you back to me, baby. And destiny will make you stay."

She turned to glare at him then, meeting his shrewd, pale blue eyes with a withering stare. "You have no fucking idea what that word even means."

David shook his perfectly groomed head with its close-cropped dark hair. He'd grown a narrow goatee since she'd last seen him and it only served to make him look more sinister than she remembered, offsetting the cruel set to his jaw even more. "I know it means you belong to me," he said.

He leaned back slightly in the seat, letting his eyes rove over her. She'd worn one of Kol's favorite dresses, a strappy summer number that was white with smatterings of black flowers printed on it. He'd always said it offset her blue eyes and sleek brunette hair perfectly. David seemed to appreciate it, as well, his eyebrows arching and his lips quirking in overt appreciation. His eyes narrowed when they rested on the mark that peeked out just above the cleft between her breasts.

"Did sweet little Hallie go and mess up her perfect skin with a tattoo? What the fuck is this?" He reached a hand out, extending fingertips to touch the mark. Hallie avoided looking down but hoped like hell the thing wasn't glowing like it did whenever she was within about fifty feet of her lover. Just before David's fingers came into contact with her skin, his eyes widened, then a million things seemed to happen at once.

The car lurched to a stop, throwing Hallie and David against the seat backs in front of them. The driver and David both cursed loudly.

"What the—" David began, glaring at the back of the driver's head, but he didn't get the words out before his door was wrenched open and a large hand reached in, grabbed him by the collar, and dragged him out, kicking in protest. Hallie barely managed to avoid getting knocked in the face with one stray Italian-leather loafer.

Her heart pounded at an unreal pace, but began to slow the second she saw the pair of large men staring down at her old lover, daring the bastard to speak.

"Oh, thank God, Kol."

Geva grabbed David by both arms, restraining him. Kol met David's defiant gaze with one even more menacing.

Hallie's door opened behind her and Erika startled her with a squeeze of a hand on Hallie's shoulder.

"C'mon sweetie. Jesus you scared the crap out of us. Are you all right?"

Halie stumbled out of the car and embraced her friend. "Thank you. How the hell did you guys find me so fast?"

Erika smirked and tapped Hallie's mark gently. "I guess it's a little bit of a beacon for them. As soon as we figured out you were missing, we called him."

They wandered around the rear of the car and paused. Hallie kept expecting Kol to pull back and swing at David— kept hoping that's what he would do—but all Kol did was stare at the man wordlessly. He glanced once at Geva and a smile stretched across his lips, letting her know the pair were likely having a private conversation about what to do with David. The second she took another step toward Kol, his attention shifted entirely and she was in his arms before either could speak. The desperate kiss he gave her took her breath away, leaving her dazed and her heart pounding harder than it had a moment earlier.

"Are you alright?" he asked. "Did he hurt you?"

Hallie shook her head, "Not really, no. What are you going to do with him?"

"Geva and I were just debating it, but the little shit won't shut up."

Hallie would have hardly referred to David as "little" but next to the two dragons, he definitely didn't measure up. The bastard had always been a talker, though, and didn't seem to register how doomed he probably was at the moment. He directed his attention to her, in spite of the grip Geva had on his arms.

"You've settled for this uptight pussy, Hallie? What happened? You were always a wild girl. That's what I loved about you. A survivor. That sense of adventure is so goddamn sexy." He turned his eyes to Kol's, grinning as though he had a secret. "Did you know she wasn't a city girl her whole life? Born in the wilderness, she told me. Out in the middle of BFE in Canada. Had to kill her own meat. But she decided she liked the finer things better." Kol remained stoic, watching David. He already knew all of Hallie's darkest secrets. There were no surprises. David's agitation rose. He looked back at Hallie. "I can still give you that, baby. My family's got ties—anything you want, you tell me and I'll get it for you. This son-of-a-bitch is small potatoes compared to me."

Hallie had an answer on the tip of her tongue but before she could get it out, both dragons reacted to something the man had said. Geva jerked the man's head back sharply, growling a harsh epithet into his ear while Kol stepped swiftly toward him, nailing him in the gut with a fist the size of a sledgehammer.

David doubled over and collapsed to his knees, struggling to catch his breath. Kol squatted and gripped him by the hair, forcing his eyes up.

"I'm watching you, La Pietra. I will know your every single *fucking* move for the rest of your natural life, and trust me, I will outlive you. If you come near Hallie or our family again, you will wish I had killed you today."

As he stood, he slipped a small, black card into the breast pocket of David's jacket. Hallie knew what the card said. It was only a simple monogram on one side—the letter "M"—and on the backside simply "Magnus" followed by a phone number. She'd called the number once after Kol had the cards printed, curious where it led. It was the entry point to contact Kol himself, but was manned by a battleaxe of a receptionist. A female blue dragon who knew everything and wasn't afraid to rip a caller a new asshole if they said the wrong thing. If a man like David couldn't figure out who Kol was based on a single call to that number, he was a bigger idiot than she thought.

They left him there, wheezing on the median, and climbed into Erika's Jeep to drive home.

"WHAT THE HELL made you punch him?" Hallie asked at a stop light a few moments later. "I was sure you guys were making some other devious plan between you. Then all of a sudden it was fists."

Kol had barely had a chance to calm down after the ordeal. His senses had been heightened since before he'd received Erika's frantic call. Sitting in the meeting with the East Coast Shadow and the new client had been a waste of time. Two hours into the meeting he'd had an itch in his gut. The same feeling he'd had when Erika's team had breached the temple. An invasion of his domain. Except this feeling was decidedly unwelcome.

Then the call had come, Erika's voice frantic on the other end. Hallie had disappeared. The smirk of the human across the table had spurred him into action. With a quick instruction to his lower Shadow to deal with the human, he left to find her.

"He played me, at first," Kol admitted. "I'm sorry for that. Had I been prepared I'd have been there for you quicker."

"Baby, you *were* there. I just want to know what was going through your head back there. Not that I don't appreciate everything. Call it morbid curiosity."

Kol cleared his throat. Geva glanced back over the passenger seat he rode in, giving him a grin of solidarity.

"He called me a son-of-a-bitch," Kol said. "Which is a gross insult to The Mother. We couldn't let it stand without punishment. Painful punishment."

Hallie opened her mouth once, then closed it and burst out laughing. "He insulted… oh the poor, poor bastard. I hope he doesn't meet any other dragons. That's pretty much his favorite term. I'm curious, though… if he hadn't said that, what would the punishment have been?"

In unison the two dragons said. "We'd have fucked him."

"Oh, please don't tell me that," Hallie said, she looked up into Kol's face, searching. He didn't feel nearly as mirthful as Geva seemed to, however.

He gave her a resigned look. "Geva would have done the honors, and the man would have enjoyed it more than getting punched in the gut. He deserved the humiliation either way."

When she began to nod slowly, Kol finally relaxed, then bent to kiss the livid bruises on her arm. He should have killed the man, but that would have complicated their visit more than he needed.

That evening they received the call. Roka's voice was on the other end of Kol's line, calm and to the point. "We found her. Get to Tokyo as soon as you can…" He seemed to hesitate, then blurted out. "Can you take a commercial flight? There won't be time to replenish your magic once you get here."

Kol reassured him. "My jet's fueled up. I'm sure we'll be fine. We'll be there tomorrow."

"I think you mean today, my friend. I'll see you soon."

BREATH OF FLAME AND SHADOW

CHAPTER ONE

Knowledge can be an unwieldy burden without the benefit of understanding. Rowan had only scratched the surface of what her life had become in those first two glorious nights spent with Rafe.

Then the man she fell in love with yanked the rug out from under her.

Learning she belonged to a race of ancient creatures previously thought to be mythical was hard enough to process. But add to that the onus of being considered a political pawn, and then to be faced with the knowledge that everything she'd experienced in Rafe's arms over the last few days was a lie—it was all too much. Overhearing their conversation about her destroyed her desire to stay.

"You don't understand, Kol. I have to have her. Not a human."

"You're in love with her."

"What? No... she's just... she's pure. Tell me why we shouldn't be able to breed?"

She knew precious little about the race as it was, but those few words she overheard reverberated through her mind over and over. He wasn't in love with her. He just wanted to breed. *Breed.* As though she were livestock? Every ounce of her soul rejected that idea.

So she ran.

Or, rather, she *flew.*

That first leap was uncertain. She might fall to her death out of the third story window of Rafe's mansion. She took that jump knowing as much.

But once in the air something changed. In a split second of wind rushing past her skin, it happened. The confines of her own familiar body became too tight, just the way she felt when Rafe made love to her. Her body couldn't contain the need, and reacted almost without effort. She burst out of her false skin, became buoyant, the Pacific breeze suddenly a tangible force raising her up. She drifted higher and sailed out over the ocean before she became aware of the new shape of her body for the second time, the muscles and bones that lived beneath her human façade reacting instinctively to the need to fly. The tightening push of the wind against the membranes of her wings felt as good as a massage.

She closed her eyes and soared, mindless, letting her other senses reach out to the world so she could feel the wind around her, the vast, cool darkness of the ocean beneath her. In the distance she could sense the whirling chaos of humanity, and slightly more acute were the impressions of the two men she'd run from.

Dragons, she thought. Not men. Dragons like her.

Yet the look of shock and despair in Rafe's eyes as she turned and launched herself out the window haunted her. Had she made a mistake? Somehow woefully misunderstood his true feelings? He had never *said* that he loved her. All he'd shared was the fact that their union was against dragon law. That he hoped to breed with her if they succeeded in changing that law. She hadn't stayed long enough to work out why, or what the hell her presence had to do with changing anything this "Council" thought.

All Rowan wanted was *him*. And if he didn't want her, all she wanted was oblivion, especially from the vivid memories of the last few days, but she couldn't stop herself from replaying those days over and over as she flew.

The previous morning had dawned with an otherworldly brightness, the sun streaming in through the high windows of Rafe's bedroom. The warm bulk of him groaned behind Rowan, the vibration sending a pleasant thrill through her, as close as it was to the sounds he made during sex. Rather than touch her, he left the bed, grumbling something about it being too damn bright. He glanced back at the bed just as he reached for the drapes and stopped, his hand still poised in midair.

The flick of those dark eyes over her naked body left her tingling from head to toe, as though he'd added fuel to the already bright sunlight on her skin and she'd somehow managed to catch fire. At least something red-hot seemed to ignite in Rafe's eyes. He lowered his hand from the drape and turned slowly, taking her in more thoroughly.

It wasn't particularly warm in the room, but heat grew deep inside her, beginning in her core and spreading outward.

"Sweet Mother, you're beautiful. The sun suits you."

She eyed him with as much open admiration. He stood in a bright sunbeam, haloed by the light on his olive skin. The lines of his large, sculpted body were cast in stark relief from the angle of the sun and Rowan could make out every glorious plane and indentation, even down to the lovely upraised line of a violet vein that stood out along the shaft of his erect cock. She licked her lips, remembering the salty flavor of him when she'd taken him into her mouth the night before, testing out the use of her new tongue to the near detriment of Rafe's sanity.

His skin shimmered slightly, the light of the sun high-lighting the underlying texture of scales on his skin, but they faded as quickly as they became visible. The image reminded her that he wasn't quite human, but neither was she. The knowledge of their shared origin made her smile wider.

He's mine. All mine.

"Why are you smiling?" he asked, his voice husky. He began to slink back toward the bed, his movements even more measured and calculating than they'd been the night before. His eyes narrowed in suspicion, but his lips betrayed his amusement.

"Just thinking about the things your tongue can do. I think I need another lesson." It was almost the truth.

She wanted him desperately, and she'd never considered herself a desperate person, even when she was young and starving because her foster parents chose to feed their own kids before her and she got the leftovers. She found other avenues to sustain herself even then. She'd been the little shaved-head waif convincing poor people to buy pretty found items they didn't even need. She brushed a hand over her head in remembrance of the hate her foster parents had of her vibrant red hair. "Satan's child," they called her as they clipped the red threads and she watched them fall around her like maple leaves in autumn.

It was summer now, and her tresses bloomed as red as the hibiscus that flanked the front doors of Rafe's mansion. There were no maples outside Rafe's window. Only a wide expanse of the Pacific, with the green tufts of a few palms in her field of vision. His beautiful presence closed in, ready to give her that lesson she'd suggested she needed, but in spite of her suggestion, all she really wanted was to feel him inside her again.

He paused to stand at the side of the bed, gazing down at her. The caress of his dark eyes was followed by his hand when he reached out to brush the line of her jaw with one knuckle. His expression was filled with wonder that perplexed her. He looked as though he'd just discovered one of the rarest, most priceless artifacts and was afraid his touch might mar its surface.

Rowan lay still, letting him touch her. He swept the pad of his thumb across her lower lip then let his hand drift lower, tracing the line of her neck and shoulder, brushing fingertips along the harder edge of her collarbone, down her sternum. His touch followed the contour of her breast and she gasped when he passed one fingertip so softly across the underside of her nipple.

Rafe seemed to grow more alert at her reaction, his stance tightening, eyes narrowing in determination. Rowan's own body thrummed with desire, the sensation of ethereal fire growing hotter on her skin until she realized she was doing it again. Her skin had erupted into red scales, her hands elongating into razor-tipped talons that punctured the mattress.

"Shit! I'm sorry," she shook her hands in the air as though trying to shake off the change.

Rafe grabbed her wrists and smiled at her confusion. "Let it happen this time, love. I can show you what it's like to make love in our true forms. Turn over. Let me guide you through the shift."

She did as he asked and he gripped her by the hips, pulling her toward the edge of the bed. With a nudge of his hand she rose up on hands and knees. She didn't need to look to know he was right behind her, bigger than life. The searing heat of his cock brushed against her inner thigh and she moaned, tilting her hips back in invitation, but he just kept up with the almost idle caresses.

She caught a glimpse of herself in a dressing mirror on the other side of the room. The red coils of her horns had reappeared, even heavier on her head now than they'd seemed the night before.

In daylight, Rafe looked magnificent. The sun caught his obsidian horns and the jewel-like sheen of his scales. His chest rippled behind her when he changed his stance and pulled her hips closer. Somehow he seemed even larger than before and appeared to be growing, changing shape in the reflection. Soon his hands were the only things that remained smooth, the gentle brush of his fingertips slipping between her thighs into the wet heat of her.

He rumbled his appreciation, then gripped both her hips, his fingertips growing dark and pointed. She could feel the pointed tips digging into her flesh, but they were only a sharp pressure that sent zings of pleasure to her core. Rafe pressed the shaft of his cock along the crease of her ass and tilted his hips, letting the thick length slide between her cheeks and along the slick opening of her pussy.

His chest rose and fell quickly with panting breaths.

"I'm going to change while I fuck you. Change with me, Rowan. Feel it with me."

He didn't give her a chance to answer, and the sudden smooth thrust of his cock into her tight, wet heat made her cry out, the delicious stretching fullness of him sending a sudden jolt of pleasure straight to the tips of her horns. He seemed even bigger than he had the night before, and Goddamn if he wasn't growing.

"Oh fuck!" she cried out at the nearly painful stretch of his cock inside her. She plunged backward and rose up onto her knees, arching her back and shifting her hips to take him even deeper.

She was mesmerized by the sight in the mirror, his black skin shimmering in the sunlight.

His massive shape engulfed her smaller one. Thick arms the size of tree trunks held her against a solid chest that felt nothing like the soft human version she'd fallen asleep against. He was both molten heat and churning void at the same time. His cock pressed ever deeper, pushing at her boundaries so far she felt she might split in half, but she kept pushing back, meeting his thrusts with equal fervor.

He grew still larger until she had to rise up higher on her knees to accommodate the changing height. She found it increasingly difficult to move, and to even think with the relentless push of his massive shaft into her.

"*Change*," came the rumbling, resonant voice, so deep and intense she nearly orgasmed from the vibration that sunk through her body. A dark, sleek tail whipped around, the smooth tip of it brushing down between her breasts, swirling around her nipples and dipping lower, past her navel, to the place between her legs where she could clearly see the shining wet gloss of her juices coating the length of his cock that she was only barely able to accommodate. An expanse of his length still remained outside her, however. If she wanted all of him, she would have to become like him. And sweet Jesus did she want all of him.

The teasing flick of the tip of his tail across her sensitive clit was too much. She cried out, her voice emerging in the most beautiful, sonorous roar as the room began to shrink. He pulled her backward, wrapped his arms and tail around her, and lifted her up while he continued pumping his beast of a cock deep into her. The sensation of his thrusts changed as she changed.

With a low rumbling growl he sank even deeper, the thick head of his erection pressed at a part of her anatomy that hadn't existed a moment earlier, but that drove her insane with pleasure. She thrashed and clawed at the bed, bucking her hips back against him. The long, red whip of her shimmering tail swept around to her front, twining and tangling with his. Her long neck twisted around, her tongue lashing out to coil around his tongue. Still he thrust into her, with deeper, harder pumps of his scaled hips.

The eyes that looked back into hers were coal black with flecks of shining silver, the pupils nothing but bottomless vertical slits. She groaned and panted, her breath gusting out in a cloud of red that swirled around their heads before being inhaled with a sharp intake of Rafe's breath.

He bellowed out a deafening roar into the high ceiling of his bedroom, his cock grew hotter and swelled inside her. The sudden, violent blast of his hot semen hit that secret inner bundle and sent her spinning and crashing to her own climax. She pushed back hard against him, urging him even deeper while the molten stream of his seed shot into her eager depths and the rush of his power filled her to over-flowing yet again.

She barely had the presence of mind to glance at their reflection once more before collapsing, spent, to the bed. In that brief second what she saw was beyond beautiful. Their entwined bodies resembled something mythical and god-like. A two-headed being that nearly filled the room and gleamed like red and black statues in the morning sunlight.

The bed creaked and splintered beneath the weight of their bodies, but Rowan didn't care, and Rafe didn't seem to, either. They lay panting and tangled, the sensation of being utterly replete extending to every part of her being. She let her eyes drift closed, wishing again for the familiar comfort of his human body and the feel of his hands entwined with hers. The thought itself was enough, and she felt rather than saw the world, and her lover, grow to a familiar size again, the broken bed beneath them big enough to accommodate them both again.

Rowan dozed, more comfortable than she'd ever been in

her life. After a little while she woke to the pleasant swell of Rafe's erection still solidly ensconced inside her. Without moving, she clenched her muscles around him.

"Mmm," he rumbled against the back of her neck. He pushed into her once, then withdrew and moved to hover over her. Wordlessly she rolled onto her back and let him between her thighs, sighing when he sank into her again. His eyes never once left hers during that second, slow, languid, and very human, session. The look of wonder had returned and he made love to her as though he worshiped her, kissing her reverently and nuzzling her breasts with lips and tongue until she cried out his name and clutched her legs tightly around his hips.

"You have no idea what an amazing creature you are," Rafe said afterward, while he held her in his arms.

"Amazing enough that we're fucking on the wreckage of your bed," she said with a hint of humor in her voice. She glanced around at the shredded sheets and mattress that hung beneath the tilted wooden headboard. It was comfortable enough, with the mattress dipping in the center so that they had a nice, soft incline to lie back against. Downy feathers drifted across her skin from the demolished comforter.

She craned her head back to look at the headboard. The master-crafted carvings were gouged with claw marks. Hers or his she had no idea.

"It was only a few hundred years old. I think it's time to commission some new work anyway. Perhaps in welded steel?"

The grin he gave her was more than she could bear. Their first night together had been enough of a revelation to leave her reeling. She had fallen for him and was so certain he felt the same way.

But that certainty had been an illusion.

The mournful looks she caught him giving her from time to time hadn't worried her at first. It was only now that she was flying and had nothing better to do than replay their entire time together that they all came back to her with a vengeance. She'd just believed he had old baggage that she'd draw out of him in time. Heaven knew she had her own baggage she intended to share with him at the right time. There was no sense weighing down the early days of something so potentially wonderful with something as ugly as her own past. If only she'd known how volatile his secrets really were.

He hadn't loved her, in the end. All he'd wanted was a vessel for his fucking sperm.

CHAPTER TWO

*R*owan had a greater appreciation for meteorologists after discovering the joy of flying. Wind was moody. Weather was, too. She found she had an affinity for the changeability of the weather after a week of flying through Central American summer thunderstorms. The streaming wetness of the rain represented the tears she wouldn't let herself shed over her heartbreak. Eventually, she learned she could just increase her altitude and escape it all. Too bad she couldn't do the same for the turmoil that roiled inside her.

The wind became her friend up high, the steady currents shifting in ways that she was able to sense instinctively based on the temperature. It was colder. Much colder, but she found she enjoyed the crisp brush of the currents along her scales, much like she'd enjoyed the wind from the interior of Rafe's car not long after they had met.

The wind did nothing to drown out his touch or his words still vivid in her memory. She grew weary of the images that refused to leave her mind. In an effort to purge the thoughts, she pushed herself to her absolute limits before stopping to rest. She soon discovered she could fly for thousands of miles without stopping, but the hunger that would overcome her when she finally did rest made it more and more difficult to regain her human shape and conjure the clothing she needed to blend into whichever human community she chose to land nearby.

The magic Rafe had shared with her during their lovemaking had left a ghost of sensation deep inside her that she wished she could shake. It was like she'd let herself get drunk on some delicious cocktail and was now waking up to the unpleasant aftereffects and she couldn't shed the ache that didn't seem to want to subside. Replacing the magic was the only method she knew to combat that feeling. She could drown her sorrows at the same time as replenishing her energy.

She found it too easy to return to her old habits when she chose an attractive man in a bar in Costa Rica. She'd chosen him because of how different he'd seemed from Rafe. He was dressed casually, in loose linen pants and a similarly comfortable shirt, open at the neck to display a suntanned chest lightly dusted with gold curls. His hair was disheveled and he looked like he hadn't shaved in a day.

She had the man wrapped around her finger in the span of ten minutes. Within twenty they were alone together in his rented hillside cabana, standing on a wide deck that seemed to overlook the entire world, including the dormant volcano that loomed against the horizon.

"Wine?" he asked. "Or something stronger? I have tequila, too."

Rowan shook her head, keeping her eyes on the volcano in the distance and pondering the shimmering threads of magic that led to its peak. The trails felt familiar to her, and she believed they must be linked to other dragons somehow.

It seemed to make sense to follow them once she had her fill with this man.

"Wine works," she answered distractedly. The thought of tequila turned her stomach. The very scent of it brought back memories of the first night with Rafe.

"It's a gorgeous view, isn't it? One of the benefits of living in a place like this. Money goes a long way."

The man rambled on about living as an ex-pat for a few moments while he poured drinks for them, but Rowan tuned out the sound, instead choosing to focus on the intriguing flow of energy that surrounded him, so different from the magic that made up the paths she'd been following.

She'd learned enough during her time with Rafe to know that magic was attracted to a person's well of desire. It clung to them like iron filings to a magnet until their orgasm released the power that a dragon could absorb. Rafe had also taught her that dragons had their own similar wells, but the magic they absorbed was transformed, taking on special qualities that were unique to the dragon. "Like a fingerprint," Rafe had said. A human's magic was just as unique, of course, but less tied to their essences. It must be that essence of Rafe that she'd been unable to shake. She hoped to dilute it with this man's energy.

Rowan glanced at the man. She smiled politely while sipping her wine and pretended to listen to him. His energy was average, and seemed a little bit uncertain at the moment. She shifted closer to him, let her arm brush against his. Her skin tingled in response to the tickle of the hairs on his arm. The rise in his arousal was subtle, yet almost painfully apparent to Rowan amid his hesitance to make the next move. She desperately needed what he had to give.

"Do the other women like the view as much as I do?" Rowan turned to look directly at him and sized him up with a sweep of her gaze over his body. He really was a fine looking man, broad-shouldered and square jawed. Just self-possessed enough that she enjoyed the way she'd shaken him with the question. She loved that she could do that to even the most controlled men. *Like Rafe.*

He tensed and cleared his throat. "Do you mean the mountain, or…?" He left the question hanging, shot a look out at the view of Irazu, then back to her.

"I do enjoy mountains quite a bit, yes," she said. She set her empty wine glass down and moved closer to him. His warmth seeped through the thin, soft linen of his shirt as she slid her palms down over thick pectorals letting herself explore the shapes of him through the fabric. He stood as though hypnotized by her touch, his lips slightly parted and eyes steadily watching her face. The slow, even rhythm of his breath increased when Rowan unbuttoned his shirt and slipped both hands inside to rake fingernails gently through the coarse blond hair. She held his gaze, watched his lids lower in response to her touch. He bared his teeth slightly and hissed when she pinched one nipple.

"Is it like that, then?" he asked, opening his eyes to look at her more intently.

"Like what?" she asked, digging her nails a little deeper into the curve of thick muscle over his hip. She'd intended to provoke some kind of reaction, to get him to come out of his shell, and it seemed to be working.

He grabbed her wrist suddenly, just as she began toying with the button of his trousers. His erection was plain as day inside the loose-fitting pants that hung low on his waist. He wasn't wearing briefs and his cock hung low and thick along one thigh. Rowan suddenly ached in some deep place she'd only recently understood. In a way, it was an ache to be fucked, but more than that was the hungry need to absorb that rising swell of energy that had begun to swirl with greater intensity around him since she'd pinched his nipple.

"Believe it or not, I didn't just bring you here to fuck you, but I'm happy to oblige if that's why *you're* here."

"Why did you bring me here?" Rowan asked, struggling to restrain her frustration. She didn't want to interact with people any more than absolutely necessary.

"Because you're a beautiful, intelligent woman, and I imagine I would enjoy a lot more than just your body."

His expression was so sincere and direct. Precisely the kind of directness she'd appreciated about Rafe when she'd first met him. The rush of memory only made her angry, however. She raised her free hand and deftly unfastened his pants, smirking at him defiantly. Before she could go further he cursed and gripped her other wrist, tugging her abruptly closer so that his mouth pressed against her ear.

"Is that all you want?" His breath blew hot across her skin, the tickle making her shiver.

Rowan shook her head, pulling back to sneer at him. "I want too much. I want things you can't even fucking fathom. But there's only one thing you can actually give me so don't even fucking bother trying with the rest, alright?"

He looked briefly confused and maybe even a little hurt. She very nearly regretted being so mean. In a past life she would have likely enjoyed his company as much as he seemed to believe he would enjoy hers. But she didn't have the patience for that kind of intimacy now.

His hands clutched her wrists bruisingly tight, his eyes blazing with anger that reflected her own inner turmoil perfectly. It didn't even surprise her when he shoved her down to her knees and released her hands.

"You got it, babe. If this is what you want, have at it." He tugged his cock free and stroked it once in front of her.

Rowan didn't wait. She gripped the base of his cock, took him into her mouth, and sucked once, long and hard along his shaft. Salty, smooth skin and musk inundated her senses.

He tasted and smelled like sex, and for a brief moment she was taken back to the trysts she'd had before Rafe. The enjoyable yet mostly empty couplings. Pleasure was all she'd been after then, lacking the true understanding of precisely why she needed those encounters.

His energy shifted violently, becoming a hurricane of magic brought on by the lust she'd incited with her mouth on him. That power would feel so, so good once it was hers. She could bring him off fast like this, too. Then maybe again after she was finished.

"Holy fucking Christ!" he said, threading his fingers into her hair. His legs nearly buckled when she began bobbing her head, taking him deep enough that she could feel his tip at the back of her throat. She was relentless, sucking and teasing with her tongue. It was tempting to shift, but she restrained herself. He was already far beyond the point that she needed to get creative with her mouth. He came with a buck of his hips and a harsh, incoherent yell. Hot semen pulsed onto her tongue, almost as sweet as the magic that flowed into her.

He collapsed to his knees when she finally released him and laughed a little shakily. "Well, I did always say embrace your strengths. But I have a feeling you're an expert at a lot more than just the perfect blow job."

Rowan smiled back, buzzed and happy from the fresh infusion of magic. It left her content enough to accept his hand when he offered to help her up. It even seemed to make perfect sense when he led her inside and kissed her a few moments later, his lips tender and soft as though in apology for the crude way he'd behaved. He made love to her with deliberate care, as though he hoped to prove to her that he was skilled enough to be worthy, looking at her every so often to gauge her reactions to the things he did.

She came close to believing she'd been wrong about

running away again. Lying in his arms in the dark later, she thought that perhaps this lovely human man could help her purge the memories of Rafe. Perhaps he could love her the way she craved.

Except the very words her subconscious mind had chosen told her otherwise. *Human.* That's what he was. That's what she wasn't. And the itch grew more intense again—the clawing need to not be earthbound, to feel the wind carrying her higher, to get even farther away from the hurt she'd left behind.

She left him sleeping soundly, his deep, slow breaths evidence of his exhaustion. She'd had her fill of him and it was time to move on.

Rowan left her clothes in a heap on the floor, not even certain whether the conjured garments would remain behind once she'd gone. Dawn was just breaking over the horizon when she leapt off the edge of his deck, taking flight over the twilit jungle and heading in the direction of the volcano, following a path of magic that grew clearer the longer she flew.

CHAPTER THREE

From Irazu, the path led on. She didn't bother with hopeful dreams of comfort in the arms of a human man again. Wherever necessary, she chose another man to seduce, but made a point not to let her intentions be misinterpreted. The magic trails sometimes led her to wild places where she didn't speak the language and the people were primitive, but they were somehow even more attuned to her intentions when she arrived. They rejoiced in her presence and treated her like a goddess, sometimes celebrating in ritualistic fashion, catering to her specific needs without even having to be seduced by her breath.

She spent one glorious night in the jungles near Kilimanjaro, serviced extensively by a well-endowed villager who kept referring to her as "sunshine" in his own language.

The longer she flew, the more she understood what it meant to be what she was. Perhaps it was a long dormant instinct that awakened in her and grew stronger with each infusion of magic. She didn't know precisely why, but Rafe's friend's words came back to her time and again. *Leave and*

*live as a human if you wish, but you can have no further contact
with other dragons.*

She'd run from the choice, yet now she understood there
was no going back to her old life—her human life. She
considered returning to find that dragon—Kol—and confess
that she wanted to be a part of their world, but only if she
never had to see or speak to Rafe again.

But Rowan gradually began to doubt that any other
dragons even existed. She'd been following what she was
sure was their secret path through the upper reaches of the
atmosphere for weeks, and had yet to encounter a single
dragon. At least she believed it had been weeks. She
neglected to check the date the last time she paused to
replenish her energy.

Somewhere over Southern Asia she encountered a trail of
magic that was far more potent than the other fading paths
she'd followed so far. This one made a vast swath across the
clouds, as though dozens upon dozens of others had traveled
it, and recently. Unable to contain her curiosity she followed
it. It wasn't until she reached the end of the path that she felt
a sense of uneasy excitement.

Unlike the other convergences of trails that led to deso-
late mountain peaks and dormant volcanoes, this one led to a
very lively and populated mountain. Like her other stops, she
approached it in the middle of the night after flying for days.
The path of magic led through the air to a concentrated swirl
above a well-lit clearing, paved with flagstones and
surrounded by stone lanterns. Human figures wandered
about in loose robes and for the second time in her life she
saw another dragon in its full, native shape. The winged
figure took flight from the center of the clearing and quickly
dwindled into the distance, a pale blue speck soon blending
into the dark indigo of the sky. A shimmering contrail of
magic stretched behind it and gradually faded into the air.

Rowan was sure that if she flew across the clearing she'd be able to sense that trail and follow it.

This might be a place like those wild villages she'd found where she had been received so eagerly. Still, she wasn't comfortable approaching from the air even knowing a dragon in its true form wouldn't cause alarm.

She found a shadowed rocky ledge, the far side of which was concealed by dense greenery, and descended in the darkness. Once shifted, she conjured herself a robe similar to the garb she'd seen on the humans and made her way down the slope.

"Gone on flyabout have you?" a deep voice said from somewhere just above and to one side. Rowan stopped cold in her tracks and turned toward the sound.

The voice cursed softly when she looked up, letting her hood fall away.

"You shouldn't be here," the man said.

Rowan could see two figures resting above on the smooth, flat surface of the large rock she'd landed behind. She hadn't seen them in the dark when she landed.

"Why not?" she asked. She could make out one reclining nude man with inquisitive eyes. An older man stood above him, arms crossed as he stared down at her. Though "older" wasn't precisely the word. He looked wiser, with sad eyes, and was slightly bulkier than his lithe, silent companion. Both men were stark naked with shaved heads.

It was their eyes that caused her heart to pound harder in her chest. The older man's eyes blazed with orange light, not unlike how her own had appeared in the mirror when Rafe had urged her into a passionate frenzy. The other man's eyes smoldered with a pale, yellow glow reminding her of the gas lamps in the historic district of San Diego.

"Because it isn't safe for you. If you belonged here, you'd have landed in the field like the others."

"You know what I am?" Rowan immediately felt like a fool for asking the question.

The man only smiled gently and dropped his arms. "Yes. And more than that, we can help you, but not if you take another step down this mountain."

"Where am I, exactly?" Rowan said. She moved toward the direction he indicated and found worn footholds in the side of the rock that allowed her to climb up. The man who had spoken reached out a hand to her and hoisted her up effortlessly. She stumbled at the top and he wrapped strong arms around her, steadying her.

The second man spoke. "This is the Monastery. The Council lives here, along with a few free dragons, but mostly it's either bonded humans or dragons like us. Unbound dragons shackled by the Council. We'd die if we lived anywhere else."

"I remember hearing about you. A dragon named Kol told me—do you know who he is?"

The two men grinned at each other. "Yes. Kol is a good dragon. He's on our side."

"I don't even know what most of all this means, to be honest," Rowan said, giving them an apologetic look.

The older of the two men pursed his lips and nodded. "Sit and we can talk. First, tell me your name."

She shared her name, and the pair introduced themselves as Darius and Zak.

"We're what dragons call 'Unbound.' Our parents broke dragon law by breeding within the race," Darius explained. "So we were taken from them as infants, our magic shackled. There's no end to our indenture here. If you were to be found, you would end up like us."

"Was that what Kol meant when he said that freedom was all you wanted? That I can help make a stand against the Council?"

"Yes. But it seems like you have other ideas."

Rowan grimaced. Her gut roiled with guilt over the urge to run yet again even knowing she might be the key to these two men finding freedom. Rafe's lack of conviction still stung, but if she kept running she may be condemning other dragons to slavery, and would likely have to keep running, herself.

"It isn't about that," she said quietly. "I fell for someone who it turned out didn't return the feelings. I just need more time to decide what to do."

Darius shifted closer to her, his eyes cutting through the darkness. He rested a hand on her cheek. His touch was gentle and lingered for a moment. "You're depleted, aren't you?"

"Yes. It seems like it takes more effort for me to get full each time I stop. I keep adding more and more to...to my plate but it never feels like enough." She laughed softly at the analogy, but it truly did feel like she was going hungry and no amount of food could fill her empty belly.

"This is what it's like for us daily," Darius said. "We have access to just enough magic to sustain each other, to maintain these human forms we're bound in. We're allowed no more than that."

"What would happen if you didn't have that?"

Zack snorted derisively, earning him an admonishing look from Darius. He shrugged. "We'd die."

"Oh God."

"We will give you what we can, but you'll have to find another source soon. There are coastal resorts only a few islands away—the kind that cater to particular human tastes."

"What Darius means to say is that you can find some pretty eager humans down there if you know where to look. Just be careful because those resorts are a favorite spot for unmated dragons to visit, too."

"If you two were free, is that where you would go?"

Zak and Darius shared a look. With a slow smile, Darius shook his head. "If we were truly free, there's a female dragon we'd mate. She's a lot like you, as a matter of fact. She visits here sometimes."

"Why is it so wrong for two dragons to be together out there? You two are together here, aren't you?"

Zak replied, "We're males, and forbidden to mate or breed unless the Council sanctions it. They do use us as breeding stock if it suits them, but the law is the way it is to prevent inbreeding. Except we both know there's a growing population of hidden purebreds like yourself who are clearly not inbred. Which just proves that we are capable of policing ourselves, keeping our bloodlines varied enough to prevent mutations. No, in here we just use each other for sex."

Rowan decided she liked the easy honesty of the two men, and regretted her own conflict over helping them. She decided that once she replenished she would fly back to San Diego and find Kol and offer to help. She'd have to face her issues with Rafe at some point anyway.

"The female you love, she isn't a purebred, I take it?"

"No, if she were she'd be in here with us."

"Jesus. 'In here' makes it sound like a prison. This place is beautiful."

"A gilded cage. At least we get conjugal visits."

"Does she visit often?" Rowan suddenly had a slew of questions she'd never even considered that popped into her head all at once. When the men both burst out into uncontrollable laughter she stared at them. "What is it?"

"We can hear your thoughts clear as day. Who was the fool who released your binding?"

"He was a…a dragon named Rafe." Darius's brows drew together and Zak grunted, but Rowan plowed on. She needed this. She needed to let go of these awful feelings if she intended to go back and actually try to help them. "He was sweet, really. But he lied to me. That's really all there is to it."

"He's a Shadow. Their MO is subterfuge. I doubt he kept the details from you to hurt you."

"Then why? Why can he be so perfect one minute and then lie? I mean, we broke his *bed.* Two dragons screwing are too much for a piece of furniture that old. And he didn't care. He just..." She couldn't help but smile at the memory. "He just made love to me again."

"You're a dragon." The pair of them said it in unison, like it was supposed to clear everything up.

"So what?" she yelled back. "I fell in love with the bastard. I *don't fall in love.* And then he...said he only wanted me because I'm pure. Because he wants to *breed* with me."

The worst part, that she couldn't even bring herself to say out loud, was the stark denial that had erupted from Rafe's mouth when Kol asked him, point blank, if he was in love with her. He'd said no. There she'd been in the dark, listening, after two days of falling in love for the first time in her life and on the verge of telling him as much. But when confronted with the question, *he had said no.*

She didn't mean to cry, and it was entirely unlike her. The overwhelming flood of emotions was just too strong to hold back. She abstractly wished she'd spent more time crying when she was younger. She'd at least have been prepared for this. But her childhood hadn't had room for crying. She collapsed even further into a blubbering mess at that thought, unable to contain it after all the running she'd done from precisely this reaction, and not just her reaction to Rafe, but her reaction to her entire fucked up life. Oh, God, it was all the same, wasn't it? He *was* her life. He represented every little rejection she'd ever felt, every endeavor she'd tried and been shot down from. She'd risen stronger from all of them but had always wondered if there was one she wouldn't recover from.

The strong arms that encircled her from behind did nothing to comfort her until the words hit her ears. "You're more precious than you know, Rowan. Shush."

Darius nuzzled the words into her ear at the same time as he swept a deft thumb across her cheek, smoothing the tears away. His lips pressed soft and comforting kisses against her temple, almost paternal, but a little too lingering to avoid hinting at his attraction.

The kiss brought her back abruptly to her current situation. She let out a stuttering breath and let her fingers twine through his where they still clutched her tight against him. His hand was warm and soft and he felt too good pressed against her, holding her with virtually all his limbs wrapped around her after moving close to comfort her. His long legs bracketed both of hers where she sat, and his large arms encompassed her. She felt protected, for perhaps the first time in her life.

"Are you all this big?" she asked in a nasally tone, then sniffed and wiped her eyes. "I mean, I've only seen two of you close up before. Kol was huge." She raised an eyebrow at Zak who moved into her field of vision and squatted down with a concerned look. He was less bulky than Darius but still had the look of an Olympic swimmer, all tall and lanky and with muscles in places she didn't think muscles should exist.

Darius laughed. "We're as big as we want to be. This is just the size I'm comfortable with. Once we make a habit out of our human appearance it becomes very hard to change, however. All young dragons start off with a pleasing form. You clearly did, too. You just added to it."

"Are you telling me I didn't really need to go to the gym? Well, fuck."

Darius's laugh rumbled behind her and his grip on her

loosened. His hands slipped down to rest at her hips, but she let herself lean back against his chest, taking comfort in his solid presence. Zak sat cross legged across from them, the moonlight above casting his skin in silver. He watched placidly, but after his few comments Rowan knew he could be opinionated and direct.

"What are you waiting for, Zak?" She asked the question innocently before realizing how it might sound. She'd only thought he seemed like he was waiting for something and she wanted to know what it was. She'd had no illusions that it might be something related to her.

"I've spent my entire life waiting," he said. "For you, perhaps, if you agree to help us." His gaze slipped over her, seeming to see right through the bulky robe she wore. "And to address your alternate meaning, I think you need to get rid of that ridiculous garment so we can get to the business of helping you in what limited manner we can."

"I interrupted you two, didn't I?" Rowan asked, making a move to get up. Darius dug his fingers into her hips, preventing her from moving.

"You're still in need," Zak said. "Take what we can give you. You will be giving back so much more by doing so."

"I don't want to come between you…what you have…"

"Rowan, what we have is yours, but we'll never take what you won't give willingly." Darius lifted a hand to brush along the edge of her jaw from behind. He hooked one finger in the neck of her robe and tugged at the ties of her robe. Zak's eyes drifted over her bare skin as the fabric parted. Darius let a fingertip skim down the center of her chest and he slipped his large hand beneath the fabric to cup one breast. His breathing came shallow and quick in her ear. "I can already feel the magic clinging to you. You would be fulfilling us even more. Trust me, having you would be a rare treat. One we don't commonly get up here."

Rowan shrugged her upper body free of the robe and reached to place her hands at either side of Zak's head. The blaze in his eyes had subsided, but there was still a deep amber glow. His eyebrows drew together. She got the sense that he was on the verge of begging and it only endeared him to her further.

"Yes," she said, and pulled him down into a kiss. He groaned against her lips, letting her slip her dragon tongue into the warmth of his mouth and tease against his tongue. The hand at her breast squeezed gently and Darius's fingertips plucked at her nipple, making her gasp at the sudden burst of pleasure. While she and Zak kissed, the soft sensation of his hands became apparent. Zak pushed at the folds of her robe until the fabric fell away and pooled beneath her, leaving her utterly bare. Zak moved lower, his lips found her inner thigh and he kissed his way along its length, pushing her legs apart to gain access. The wet, velvet heat of his tongue startled her when he found her already throbbing core and pressed his lips against her.

Delicious zings of sensation tingled between her thighs with each stroke of his tongue against her clit. Sweet Jesus, dragon lovers were so much more adept than humans at this. She rested one hand atop Zak's smooth head and reached behind herself with the other to find Darius's thick, hard cock where it pressed against her backside. When she gripped his length, he dropped his forehead to her shoulder, murmuring an incoherent sound of pleasure.

With a nudge of her hand, Zak rose and Rowan turned to face Darius. She stroked Darius's cock more deliberately and scooted backward on her knees to gain better access. He leaned back on his elbows, watching her with bright eyes gazing down his torso as she took him into her mouth and sucked. The eager, probing tongue returned between her legs from behind this time, but was soon replaced with the welcome thickness of Zak's cock pressing into her wet heat and sliding deep. She moaned around Darius, becoming lost in the slick, stretching friction of Zak as he moved inside her.

Their hunger for her was the headiest influence. She realized when Darius threaded his fingers through her hair and began thrusting his hips up against her lips that she could sate these two men easily and have more to spare. Perhaps she was spurred on by the memory of being hungry herself as a child and being forced to find creative ways to sustain herself. This didn't quite resemble the charity work she imagined she might do once she found herself able to give back. This was far more enjoyable an experience because they were just as intent on her pleasure as she was on theirs and she could offer them something even greater. It wasn't only her power she intended to give, however.

Once she left here, she resolved to make her way back home and pledge her support to their cause. Rafe could go to hell, but the rest of their race needed her. She just wished she could find the conviction to believe that she could ever get over Rafe.

Her heart ached at the sudden thought of giving up even the memory of their few days together. She released Darius from her mouth and looked into his eyes, hoping for reassurance. His response surprised her, the voice ringing clearly through her mind.

"Love doesn't care about loyalties or betrayals. If he loves you, he'll find you and it will have nothing to do with his other agenda."

"Is it terrible of me if I don't intend to wait?"

Darius smiled and stroked the side of her head. "No. The chase will be good for him, no doubt. It might do Zak a little good, too." He sat up with a wicked look on his face that was directed over her shoulder. He pulled her close, dislodging her other lover from her rear. She was forced to straddle his hips or else lose balance.

"You shit," Zak said with a laugh.

"We share everything," Darius murmured into her ear, the humor in his tone evident and emphasized by the lovely rumble that erupted from his chest when he sank his cock into the space recently vacated by Zak.

"Does he know that?" Rowan asked. She only had a second to glance over her shoulder at Zak's perturbed face before Darius lay back, pulling her with him.

Zak's laugh from behind her was her only answer. A second later she heard in her head, *"He left me the best part."* The words were coupled with the feel of a tongue probing between her ass and a slick fingertip swirling around the sensitive opening.

Her eyes widened and she stared down at Darius whose grin only widened. "We don't often have the pleasure of a female. Indulge us?"

"Oh God, you two are so fucking evil."

She braced her hands on Darius's wide shoulders, her entire world focused on the thrust of his cock inside her. His mouth latched onto her nipple and sucked, then switched to the other. In between, he looked up at her with raised eyebrows, waiting for her response. He flicked a pointed and very human-looking tongue against the tip of her breast and she realized he had no way to manifest his dragon. She was fortunate to have the freedom she had.

"Yes, okay. Fuck my ass, too. Just… just fuck me."

The hot tip of Zak's cock pressed between her ass cheeks. The very slight pressure against her sensitive opening made her clench her pussy around Darius and she moaned at the converging threads of pleasure that raced through her lower body.

"Like this?" Zak rumbled into her ear. His smooth chest was flush against her back but he held his hips back. She could sense his need to penetrate her, and God she wanted him to, but wasn't quite prepared.

"Yeah, just go slow," she breathed.

She held still, her heart pounding. Her nails dug into Darius's chest and she looked down at him. He had one hand on her hip and the other behind his head, watching her as though waiting to see her reaction to having Zak's cock slide into her ass. He'd slowed down his fucking and his erection throbbed inside her while he waited

Zak nuzzled at the side of her neck, murmuring hungry words. "You have the most beautiful ass. If we had a week, I'd spend every day with my tongue down there, making you come a thousand times." The slick tip of his shaft finally found its way past her barrier, the tight friction making her gasp. She leaned into Darius, who shifted his hips with a tiny thrust up into her as though he couldn't avoid moving them. The sensation his small movement caused nearly made her come, and the tentative invasion of Zak's cock was too much.

"Just do it, Christ! Fuck me!"

Zak gripped her hips tightly in both hands and pushed. Darius threw his head back and let out an otherworldly groan then looked back up at her with fevered eyes as he began fucking her again in earnest.

Rowan couldn't move and just clutched at Darius's chest, digging her nails in until she drew blood. They kept her poised on the edge of orgasm while they fucked her, both glorious cocks filling her to bursting. When Darius shifted a hand between her thighs it took a mere caress of her clit and she was flying.

She was sure she'd partially shifted when it happened, and the trumpeting yell she let out was enough evidence of that. She was only half aware of the hot pulses of their orgasms shooting into her and the brief and anemic bursts of energy that came along with it.

Her own well still felt hungry, but the look on Darius's face told her he'd received a much larger helping of the magic through her than she had through them.

She collapsed against his chest and Zak followed, reluctant to retreat from her just yet. Zak pulled them both to the side and pressed against her, sighing into her shoulder.

"When you find your lover, bring him back here so we can thank him for sending you running."

CHAPTER FOUR

*R*owan left the mountain with just enough energy to make it to a resort village in Bali. Before she said farewell to the two men, Darius shared some dragon wisdom that Rowan intended to make use of once she found the appropriate targets.

"Find a group and use your breath to work them up. You'll replenish your energy much faster once they begin to feed off each other's need. They don't even need to participate at first. Just get them to watch long enough that they are pliant. Humans in that state of arousal are highly susceptible to suggestion."

The craving hit her hard as soon as she shifted back to her human form. Her stomach cramped like she'd starved herself, and her head spun. She turned and braced herself on a palm tree. Nausea overwhelmed her for a moment.

She avoided throwing up, at least, and stood on shaky legs staring down the slope toward the ocean.

"Jesus, this should be easier," she whispered to herself. She expelled a deep breath, concentrated, feeling every molecule of her own breath settle around her at her command. She pictured what she wanted in her head—a short, green summer dress, with a wraparound bodice that pushed her breasts up just so.

The constriction of the fabric ceased just on the edge of discomfort, the silky fabric flowed against her naked skin.

She walked through the foliage and tall palms toward the sounds of revelry that had attracted her. The verdant noises of the coastal jungle bombarded her, its moist warmth a cocoon. The fecund scent of all that life around her filled her nostrils, soon replaced by the salty breeze coming off the ocean. She'd always been unusually attuned to her surroundings but never so much as she was since being with Rafe—since learning what she was and then learning the man she had fallen for was noncommittal about being with her.

Weary of the ache of rejection and hungry for energy, she shoved the thoughts as far back as she could and focused on the task at hand. Soon she came across a smooth flagstone path with glowing globes of solar lights illuminating it in the darkness. She stood in the shadows beside the path for a moment to get her bearings. The path led through the foliage to a wide teak deck illuminated by the windows of a large beach cabana and by strings of twinkling lanterns that crisscrossed above milling partiers. A breeze blew through, setting the palms above her swaying. The current cooled her hot skin but did nothing to shift the steady pull of magic she could feel from the bodies below. Sometimes it was even a visual current if she shifted her eyes the right way, a shimmering mesh over the world. When she got close to a person, she could actually sense their level of arousal like a cloud of static around them.

There was a potent pull here. Multiple pulls, which set her craving on edge. It was akin to walking into a bakery and being surrounded by the aroma of fresh-baked confections when she was starving.

She hovered at the edge of the party for a moment, catching her bearings. It was full of young, beautiful people, all in casual dress suitable for a tropical vacation.

"You look like you need a drink." The deep voice surprised her, but the shimmer of arousal around the bare-chested man who approached captured her interest.

She turned to gaze into deep, sultry eyes framed by black lashes beneath a head of slightly too long hair the color of mahogany. She let her eyes skitter lower, across the loose linen shirt and shorts to his bare feet. He rested easy on his heels waiting for her response and seeming to enjoy her perusal of him.

"I do feel a little thirsty," she said.

"Well, allow me to slake that need." He trotted off and she moved further into the party, skirting the large pool where several men and women cavorted. It was a perfectly hedonistic corner of the world. One couple was on the verge of sex nearby but paused and laughed when they realized how visible they were. Another couple surreptitiously snorted lines of cocaine in the shadows before slinking back to the party.

"I'm Trevor," the pretty man said when he handed her a drink. "Are you one of Meredith's friends?"

"Yes," Rowan lied. "Where is Meredith?"

Trevor chuckled. "Tied up with her man of the week, I guess. Showing off her digs to him and his cronies. We get the perks of her trust fund here and don't question where she ends up in the process. How do you know her?"

"Ah...we met at school." Rowan knew it was a stretch, but vague enough to not raise suspicion. The man's energy pulsed energetically to the point she grew distracted by it. He was being way too polite for a guy as horny as he was. It was almost endearing.

"You went to Dartmouth?" Trevor asked.

"I did, but didn't stay. Transferred to Stanford to be closer to my family." Another lie, but less so, since she had actually graduated from Stanford, but had gone there to get as far away from her upbringing as possible.

"Hah, Meredith didn't stay, either. I don't remember her mentioning a hot redheaded friend though. I'd have remembered you." His dark brows twitched as though he were making a concerted effort not to let his gaze wander lower.

"Meredith and I had a few classes together, but lost touch. We just caught back up online this year and she threw out this invitation…I was planning on being here so I figured why not?" She was reaching, but it wasn't that big a stretch. Trevor's energy pulsed enough to make her want to strip him bare and devour him right there, she was so hungry. But she held back. He was at least a very lovely man. Attentive, considering his eagerness to get her a drink. Attractive, too, with his wayward brown hair and pleasant, straight-toothed smile. He had a pleasing scruff on his chin that contributed to his relaxed, vacation persona. She let her gaze wander over his tanned, toned chest, dusted with dark hair that tapered to a dark line leading into the top of his shorts. He had potential, but wouldn't be nearly enough on his own.

The music pulsed through her, distracting them both. "Hey, you want to get in the hot tub?"

She eyed the pair she'd seen snorting coke a moment earlier. Trevor must've seen her uncertainty. "We don't have to do that if you don't want."

She gave him her sweetest smile and nodded. "The hot tub sounds nice," she said. "I just didn't bring a bathing suit."

"So? Go natural. I will if you will." He grinned widely and waggled his eyebrows suggestively.

His playful glance back at her as he strode toward the hot tub made her laugh. He dropped his shorts and kept walking. She admired his naked backside and followed him, dropping her own dress by his shorts. She slipped into the hot water a moment later, glancing shyly at the other partiers who relaxed around the large tub, some sitting on the edge and others immersed in the steaming water. There were six others—two couples and a pair of men who seemed unattached but who both gave her appraising looks when she slid into the water

"Who's your friend, Trevor?" one of the single men asked. His bright eyes stayed latched onto her face and waves of lust cascaded off him. He was high, she could tell. Most of the partiers were, but the cocaine seemed to be enhancing the pull of the magic to them.

"This is—" Trevor paused, glancing at her.

Rowan filled in the gap deftly. "I'm Rowan. Old friend of Meredith's. And who are you?"

She eyed the man while sweeping her splayed fingers through the bubbling heat of the water.

"I'm Charles."

He was hungry for sex, as was his quiet friend, a blond man who sat patiently watching the exchange. She wondered how best to begin. The men were all focused on her, even the ones with women. They tried to hide it, but she could feel the subtle pulses of their desire like tiny tendrils seeking her out. The women were curious, if slightly threatened. Nothing unusual there. But if she was going to get the most out of this night, she needed them all to love her.

"Nice to meet you, Charles. Are you guys all friends?"

One of the women laughed. Rowan looked at the dark-eyed brunette. The arm of the woman's lover lay limp across her shoulder while his head rested back on the edge of the tub. His low-lidded eyes still watched Rowan surreptitiously.

"I think we all know each other a little *too* well. Charles has already decided he's going to fuck you tonight. Poor

Trevor there will be too nice to stand in his way, even though Trevor's a better lover. You are, sweetie—you should own it."

"I aim to please," Trevor said, but his discomfort was obvious.

Rowan's eyes widened, surprised by the honesty of the woman. "Oh! Well, I see no reason we can't all be friends… and do what friends do."

The brunette grinned and leaned across her man to extend a hand to Rowan. "I'm Paige."

"So, Paige…" Rowan began after releasing Paige's hand. "You seem to have intimate knowledge of most of these guys. Care to share more details?" The man next to Paige let out a derisive grunt of laughter but didn't comment further.

"Jesus," Charles said. "Keep your mouth shut for once, will you, Paige?"

"Forewarned is forearmed," Paige said, giving Charles a wicked look. She turned back to Rowan. "Charles is quick on the draw. No finesse—he thinks he's hot shit because, well, look at him… he's hot shit. His silent partner there, Justin, secretly wants to fuck Charles but goes along with the asshole's ploys for seduction."

The quiet blond man behind Charles turned an even darker shade of red that couldn't have been due to the heat of the tub.

"What the fuck, Paige!" Charles started to surge across the tub. Rowan intervened, rising from her seat to meet him.

Her naked breasts pressed against his chest and she met his wild blue eyes. He really was an attractive man, but devoid of character. He'd be the perfect start. His anger faltered when he met her eyes, an uncertain smile twisting his lips. Jesus, this was too easy.

Rowan took a deep breath, drawing on her remnants of power. She was made for this, after all. As she spoke, she let the breath flow out, seeking her target. "I think Justin deserves a little piece of you, just once, for being such a good friend. Don't you, Charles? Why don't you be a good boy and show us your pretty ass and tell Justin what you'd like him to do to it."

Charles blanched at first, but soon her breath took hold. She could feel it seeping into his blood, making him pliant and willing better than alcohol or even the best drug could. His brows twitched and his mouth spread into a seductive smile. "You want to watch me get fucked?"

"Oh, yes, Charles. I would love nothing more than to watch Justin slide his cock in your ass and fuck it. *Hard.*"

"I brought lube," Charles blurted.

The comment threw Rowan for a second but she absorbed it quickly and nodded. "That's good." She let her hand slide down his muscular arm, down his warm, wet hip, and reach back to grip his ass. Charles closed his eyes and let out a soft gasp. His cock was rock hard and huge pressed against her belly. "Why don't you go get it now?" she said.

Charles nodded and nearly walked on water to get to the edge of the huge tub. He leapt out, splashing water on Paige and the others who watched in fascination.

Rowan turned her attention to Justin, who sat, mouth agape, staring at her. He was an adorable, pretty-faced blond. His hair perfectly trimmed, his face perfectly shaved, his entire body below the neck seemingly waxed to the roots. He looked every bit as spoiled as the rest of the people in the tub, but somehow a little bit sweeter for his shell-shocked longing.

Just another breath and the entire group would be eating from the palm of her hand, but she would draw this out just to see how much she really needed to push them. If she was lucky, it would take very little energy on her part to get things moving. She knew Darius had been right, just incite one or two into the right level of misbehavior and the rest would follow, particularly if it felt good. And what Rowan had in mind would feel very good.

She glanced around at the others. Justin averted his eyes. Paige grinned at her. Trevor made a move to shift closer so she edged her way back to him, the one sane person in the mix.

"Whatever you did to Charles, can you do it to the others?" he asked.

"Why do you think I did something?"

Trevor chuckled softly and spoke in a low tone that only she could hear. "You're not quite human, Rowan. I don't know what you are, but I'm no fool. My family's been working for someone like you for as long as I can remember. We don't talk about it. Ever."

"What do you mean 'like me'?" Rowan asked, cautiously. Her discussions with Rafe had made it clear to her that dragons hid very well among humans, but he'd never mentioned any humans being aware of the presence of dragons without being mated to one.

"I mean someone with a particular knack for bending wills."

"Why are you telling me this?"

"Because I like you. And I really want to see Charles take it in the ass. Mostly the second thing." Trevor grinned at her.

Rowan glanced around at the party. She didn't have the power left for more breath. She needed one infusion. She slipped between Trevor's strong thighs where he sat naked on the lip of the tub, and twined her fingers in the dark, wet threads of hair that clung to the base of his neck. She leaned in and whispered in his ear. "Who do you think is the weakest?"

He stilled to the point that she might have been clinging to a statue. His wide blue eyes met hers, the dark lashes clinging together with wetness. His lips tried to make words, the pink bows of them curling in patterns before her eyes, patterns that should have elicited communication, but didn't. Had she broken him? The swirls of energy around him were evidence enough of his desire, and his cock twitched and swelled just below Rowan's field of vision.

His lips pressed together, then drew apart again. It took her a second to register the barely whispered sound that passed through that changing shape of perfectly sensual flesh.

"Me."

The word and his earlier admission was enough. She reached between them, gripped the shaft of his cock and stroked. Trevor's eyes fluttered closed and he let out a soft moan.

She leaned in to rest her lips against his ear. "You have a beautiful cock. And you have beautiful energy, too. You feel so good."

He shuddered under her touch. "Oh, God. How can you talk like that and not be fucking me?" he murmured back at her. His entire body trembled against her. She rested her cheek on his shoulder. She needed him to come for her soon.

She pressed her lips against his ear. "Your cock feels so hot in my hand. I want to feel your hot come all over my skin." She hated a little that she'd said almost the same thing to Rafe and had to struggle not to imagine that it was his thick shaft she stroked. She closed her eyes stroked Trevor a little harder, leaning into him when his fingers twined through her hair and he murmured words of lusty approval.

"You need this, don't you?" Trevor whispered, not even moved by what she'd said.

"I need you to come, yes."

"Why?"

"Because when you do, it helps me."

"How does it help you?"

"It helps me survive."

His hands fell to her hips, clinging in a weird, hesitant way, but a second later his fingertips sunk in. *"Oh fuck."* Trevor convulsed, his semen spurting in hot streams over her hand. The warmth of his orgasm seeped deep into her, replenishing the empty well with a refreshing infusion of potent energy.

She was too tingly with the fresh energy to even feel when he handed her the towel. She finally opened her eyes and inadvertently gazed into his eyes in that moment. The concerned understanding that met her gaze was more disconcerting than any of the alienated looks she'd gotten so far from the others. She was used to people being confused by her. But knowing her? She wanted more of it. First, she needed to finish what she'd started.

Rowan sensed three pairs of eyes on her. No one had made a sound while she jerked Trevor off, which told her one thing—that they were at least willing observers. The level of magic that had accumulated around the hot tub had reached a steady flow and lingered. It was nowhere near as dense as she needed it to be, but the act of watching her get Trevor off had more than piqued their interest. Trevor's eyes looked glazed and he smiled at her a little drunkenly. She delicately wiped her hand and cleaned off his drooping cock with the towel, then turned to face the others.

Meeting their eyes now made her stomach clench with guilt. She was using them, plain and simple. Like she'd used men before Rafe, only her hunger had grown ten-fold since learning what she was and how to use the power that came along with being a dragon. She needed them and there was no sense denying what she was and how she would go about taking advantage of their desire.

"Well, Charles? Are you ready?" She expelled magic along

with her words, letting it mix with the steam coming off the surface of the water.

"Where do you want me?" Charles asked, slipping back into the steaming tub.

"Hand the lube to Justin and bend over the edge," she commanded with a nod of her head.

Justin looked both excited and terrified when Charles reached out with his offering. Justin's throat convulsed as he swallowed and his mouth opened as if to speak. He finally managed to force out a strangled "Thank you," watching as Charles turned his toned backside to the rest of the party. And it wasn't just the few of them who were taking advantage of the hot tub who could view their activities. The tub itself was at the edge of the deck, and anyone on the deck or just inside the house would have a perfect vantage of Charles' round, pale ass.

A light breeze blew off the ocean, carrying the magic-infused steam from the tub across the deck and the energy of the entire party shifted. The couple in the pool nearby who had restrained themselves before, began going at it again. The flow of hungry desire escalated around Rowan, exciting her along with the others. She forced herself to regain focus.

"He's already hard, Justin, just look at him. He wants you to fuck him, so what are you waiting for?"

Justin stood a little shakily and waded over to Charles. He reached out, resting a palm lightly on Charles' shoulder as though he worried he might get burned and meant to test the heat first. He grew bolder, sliding his hand down, exploring the length of Charles' torso until his hand reached the round swell of one ass cheek. Charles looked over his shoulder and said, "That's right, buddy, my ass is yours tonight. What are you planning to do with it?"

A strangled groan erupted from Justin's throat and he seemed to snap. He bent over, bared his teeth, and bit down hard into the flesh of Charles' left cheek, at the same time as he slipped one hand between Charles' legs and cupped his balls. Charles yelped and flinched, but Justin had a solid grip on Charles' cock and refused to let him go.

After that, Justin's reluctance dissipated quickly and he shifted behind Charles, upending the little bottle of lube and aiming it at the top of Charles' ass crack. Clear liquid squirted out and trickled down. Justin set the bottle down and with both hands spread Charles' cheeks wide, sliding fingers back and forth along his cleft. Charles let out a loud curse when Justin sunk one finger into the opening and began fucking into him.

"You know what I think?" Justin said. "I think he needs something to occupy that smart mouth of his. Like maybe another cock. I'd do it, but I'm a little busy here." He glanced at the two other men. "You two want to take turns?"

Rowan marveled at how eagerly the other men responded, both moving to kneel at the edge of the tub. The two women followed, clearly not wanting to feel left out of the game. Paige sat at the edge of the tub and took over stroking Charles' cock while the other woman settled between Paige's thighs, spread her pussy and gave it a tentative lick.

"Well, fuck me," Trevor murmured beside her. "You really are something else. Are you just going to watch?"

"Just for a little bit," Rowan said. "Until they come. You can join them if you want."

"If it's all the same to you, I think I'll just watch, too. I'm a one woman kind of guy."

"No men?" Rowan asked.

"Not generally, no."

"But watching Charles get fucked turns you on."

Trevor couldn't deny his reaction to the scene. Justin had switched from fingering Charles and was slowly pushing his cock between the cheeks of Charles' ass. Charles feverishly sucked on the cock in front of him.

Trevor tore his eyes away from the scene, glanced at his own raging erection and gave her a sheepish smile. "It's the principle, really, but I don't mind a little ass play sometimes, from the right person."

The scene on the other side of the tub became frenzied. Without responding to Trevor's comment, Rowan stood and went to the group. She paused by Justin and whispered in his ear. *"Wouldn't you like to see the others take a turn?"*

"Fuck, I'm about to come. One of you guys needs to take my place," Justin said, shooting a hurried glance at the two other men.

Charles groaned around the cock that was shoved down his throat. The man who wasn't being serviced moved down to Justin's side to wait his turn.

Justin let out a harsh groan and dug his fingertips into Charles' ass as he slammed in deep once more and quivered through his release. Rowan kept her hand on his arm, eagerly soaking up the energy that flowed through him.

They fell like dominoes after that, and she made the rounds, moving close and whispering words laced with potent wisps of her breath at each of them in turn. It was like standing beneath a fountain of endlessly flowing power and just drinking it in until she was full. Trevor only watched from his spot across the tub. He didn't seem to even notice the thick spike of his hard-on between his thighs.

Rowan was dizzy from the intensity of the magic filling her, leaving her feeling like she'd just downed a very potent drink a little too fast. The group didn't stop after the first round, either. The momentum she'd given them had spurred them on. They only switched places, with Justin eagerly moving in front of Charles, the others coming together in a tangle of limbs around them.

Rowan left the tub, eager to move on now that she was full. She paused, dripping wet a few steps away, shocked to see several other clusters of naked bodies scattered around the deck, tangled in lewd positions, fucking and sucking and generally debauching themselves.

She fled through, navigating them like a mine field, and ran naked up the path into the jungle.

"Rowan, wait!" Trevor called after her. She could have shifted and flown away in the shadows but didn't want to risk him catching a glimpse.

"Fuck," she muttered and stopped. She turned to face him. "I have to go. Just go back to the party and let me go, alright?"

"What are you, some kind of fucked up Cinderella who goes to the ball and leaves an orgy behind? I knew your kind was capable of some crazy shit, but that's beyond what I've ever witnessed."

"What do you think 'my kind' is, exactly?"

"If I had to guess, some kind of succubus, except you don't suck up people's life forces. If anything you left me feeling even better after that hand job. This family my parents work for…they do shit like that, too. Only not quite to that level. I mean…I've been seduced by someone like you before. My dad once told me if they ask, don't say no, and that I'd never once regret it. I wanted her so bad anyway when I was eighteen, so there was no way in hell I'd have turned her down, but she was *nothing* compared to you."

Trevor's confession piqued her curiosity and she took a step back down the path. "Are you telling me you lost your virginity to someone like me? What happened after that?"

"Nothing, really. We fooled around sometimes, but didn't see each other regularly. Then about a year ago they said she died. I don't know how, though. Dad wouldn't say. He just gave me this and said she'd wanted me to have it." He fingered a small round emblem that hung from a leather thong around his throat.

"Can I see that?" she asked, closing in on him and reaching out to his necklace.

"Sure, but I can't take it off without cutting it."

She stood close to him and he lifted his chin for her to inspect the small carving of deep indigo jade that rested in the hollow of his throat. Inspecting it up close, she could see the shape of the tiny dragon etched into it and inlaid with gold. Her fingertips tingled when she touched it.

"What are you?" she asked, meeting his eyes with astonishment. There was definitely something special about him. Something Rafe had left out of their lessons.

"Just Trevor," he said, giving her a sideways smile. "I just take these things in stride—have all my life. I know there are things in the world I have no hope of understanding. But I do understand one thing."

"Oh, and what's that?"

"You're running from something. Or someone. I wish you would stay. Just long enough to put on some clothes and have a conversation over dinner? I'm a great listener."

"Well, then listen, Trevor. You're sweet but I'm not looking for anything long term."

"Not even if I tell you I'm fine with you taking what you need whenever you need it? No questions asked?"

"That sounded an awful lot like a question," she said, amused by his eagerness and intrigued by the offer. Her skin tingled beneath the gentle caress he brushed across the top of her hip, as though he wanted to pull her closer, but was trying very hard to respect her boundaries.

"No *more* questions," he said. "At least let me give you one for the road. Call me dessert."

"You're a little too persistent to be compared to food," she said, shifting closer. Not only persistent, but adorable. She wrapped her arms around his neck and leaned in to whisper in his ear. "One for the road sounds delicious, though." She brushed her lips along his jaw until she found his mouth. She nipped at his lower lip, sucked it into her mouth and then teased her tongue past his teeth. His fingertips clutched her hips, pulling her tighter against him. He succumbed eagerly into the kiss, walking them backward across the path to a bed of lush greenery, then lowering her to the ground.

"Fine, then you'll be *my* dessert." He pushed her legs apart and lowered himself between her thighs, humming appreciatively when his mouth found her already wet and throbbing pussy.

"Oh God, thank you," she sighed. The need to replenish her magic had overridden her own desire. Even as turned on as the experience had made her, she'd been so intent on moving on she hadn't wanted to take the time for this. Now she was immensely grateful to him for making her pause long enough to find this small bit of satisfaction.

When she came, she cried out a pair of names, both leaving a bittersweet sense of loss deep inside her. The familiar rush of magic passed through her, seeking out her partner, but not diminishing the ache of sadness. With human men the magic of her climax had never gone beyond her own boundaries, not as it had with Rafe or with Zak and Darius. Yet the energy easily flowed into Trevor. This signal of how special he was left her regretting even more the need to leave before learning more about him.

Trevor quivered with pent up need when he hovered over her. "I can go now if you want," he said softly in the dark. Without answering, she reached for him, tilted her hips up and urged him back down to her. He kissed her hungrily as he pressed the tip of his cock at her entrance and slid slowly into her tight sheathe.

There was something even sweeter about the magic he

gave her when he reached his peak. It may have been the fact that it was accompanied by the sound of her name falling from his lips when he pulsed inside her, or the last infusion of magic that left her feeling giddy and bubbling with a need for something she hadn't felt since that first night with Rafe. She'd tried to explain the strange, subtly incendiary need to Rafe, but his expression had just darkened and he had told her it was too soon to explain, that he would when the time came.

She curled against Trevor's side with her face buried against his neck and gave into that feeling. Instinct made her act, along with an overwhelming need to hold on to this precious moment, this precious man. He shivered as her tongue teased a small pattern just behind his ear near his hairline, then he turned and kissed her deeply.

"Come back when you stop running," he uttered before drifting off to sleep at her side.

When his breathing slowed, she whispered back, "I think I did just stop running. It's time to go home now. Thank you."

With any luck she was full enough to make it back to California without stopping. Once she took care of dragon business she might come back to find him. And maybe even stay if the lingering memories of Rafe would give her any peace in between.

She made her way up the trail in the dark, regret settling deeper into her bones with each step. She shouldn't have run to begin with, but she'd never had to confront feelings like she had for Rafe. All she could do was get as far away from him as possible. The need was enough, and instinct carried her the rest of the way. Now she wished she could stay, or take the lovely Trevor away with her. But she had something more important to do.

Her race needed her and while she didn't quite understand what she could do, if it meant other dragon children wouldn't be subjected to the solitude of her childhood, it would be worth the effort.

She flew East, her wings taking her high. During the nights she could make out the coastlines of some of the cities of the South Pacific islands she'd visited in her old life. The first one she passed that was recognizable was Singapore, and there were other, smaller cities that twinkled below her like glittering mosaics.

Her wings beat hard, and she made good time, but not quite good enough. She felt her energy lagging just past Taiwan and kept pushing on, determined to make the leg across the Pacific without stopping.

The bright sun glared in her eyes on the fourth morning. A wayward gull screeched at her and she impulsively blasted it out of the air with a gout of flame. Nothing but blue sky and sea stretched before her in every direction, seeming to merge together. The universe tilted and she let out a cry as she lost altitude and tried to regain it.

San Diego was close, she was sure of it. It had to be, as long as she'd been flying. It was home for her. Rafe was there. Rafe would love her if she returned. He would be hers, she knew with certainty, and beat her wings harder against the currents of air, but lost her bearings in the midst of the vast nothingness of sea and sky.

Which way should she fly? The sun was heavy over the horizon, but she suddenly had no idea whether it was morning or evening.

She spun in the air, uncertain, growing more panicked by the second.

Letting herself descend, she saw a cargo ship making good time across the placid ocean. She aimed herself in the same direction, hoping that she could find another trail if she found its destination.

The teasing pull of magic distracted her a few hours later. It tickled at her senses first. Something familiar about it tugged at her, making her turn away from her previous course. The familiarity of the magic intrigued her and she was so delirious from the hunger that followed. She'd already been flying too long. Three days was safe. Four was her limit, and she was at the edge of four days now. Or had it been longer?

The magic she sensed as a rippling ribbon through the air was indescribable. It caught her and beckoned to her like a comforting whisper, drawing forth old images that felt like long lost memories. Memories of being held close, of being loved.

"Mother?" she murmured into the air. Her heart pounded as the whisper answered, *"Come to me, my Rowan."* And she followed.

CHAPTER FIVE

*R*afe was the model of self-restraint when he spoke to the pair of Unbound dragons, Darius and Zak, at the Monastery. They'd found him when he and Roka arrived and urged him apart from the others. Rowan's essence was strong on the pair and Rafe found it difficult to decide whether he wanted to bed them both just to taste her magic once again, or to strangle them for their intimacy with her. The surge of jealousy was unlike him, but once he regained control of his emotions he understood the feelings for what they were—desperation at knowing she had been there only two days earlier.

He had trouble meeting Darius's critical gaze, but the other dragon didn't hesitate to shoot a mental barb at Rafe.

"You should have told her you loved her to begin with. This could all have been avoided."

"I know, brother. I just didn't want to give her false hope before finding out if she could sway the Council in our favor. I was a fool and I'm accepting the consequences. Please just tell me where she went?"

Darius's cheek spasmed from the tension in his jaw and

his eyes blazed red. He clenched his fists at his side, and Rafe prepared himself for a more violent onslaught. But the older dragon only sighed in resignation. The disappointment in his gaze was more potent than any words the man might have given him.

Rafe had only met Darius on his first visit after his Ascension but respected the man. Darius had been trapped here for nearly their entire hibernation, the product of an illicit mating between two dragons from the prior generation. Darius was almost as old as Rafe, but had far more experience, having been awake for all those years. Rafe had always considered hibernation to be a form of purgatory, but now realized purgatory would be much more effective if the victims were required to stay awake the entire time. He also realized that his lack of experience left him at a disadvantage, both in words and action. He needed to say more, he realized. Because if he didn't, Darius might actually resort to violence.

He took a few deep breaths, breaking out in a sweat under Darius's gaze. The effort wasn't in the confession itself, but in admitting that he'd failed the woman he loved. By the time he found the breath for words he had tears in his eyes and his chest felt so tight he wasn't even sure he could get the words out.

"I love her." His voice faltered and he took another unsteady breath, blinking back the wetness in his eyes and trying to begin again. All he could see was Rowan's face, the look of hurt in her eyes when she confronted him and then jumped out his window. That was the last time he'd seen her and he'd wracked his brain ever since trying to figure out what she might have heard to make her run the way she had. Ultimately he just assumed she'd overheard his entire conversation with Kol. He'd been beating himself up over it ever since.

"I've failed her though. She deserves better."

"Yet she still loves you. And hates herself for it."

Rafe swiped a hand over his face and lowered his head. "I just want to make things right. If she doesn't want me, I'll leave, but I want to make sure she's safe. You know what it would mean if she were caught. You sent her away yourself."

"Yes, because I'm no fool. You *are* a failure if you don't find her. I know what she means for us, and so does she. She was planning to go pledge herself to the cause when she left here. Your love be damned. She's a good dragon. Are you as good as she is?"

"She told you this?" Rafe asked.

"Not so much. She needs to learn to shield her thoughts. She was determined to help us when she left, but there were some very unsavory thoughts that involved you. So be careful when you do find her."

"You'll tell me where she went?"

"Yes, but only if you promise to come back. Zak has some unfinished business with the two of you."

"Brother, if everything works out, we will most certainly be back and I will accept whatever punishment you two feel the need to give me."

Darius's broad grin suggested that the dragon would relish every second of it. Rafe scowled at him.

Darius rested a comforting hand on Rafe's arm and his expression slipped back into seriousness. "She's resting in one of the resort villages on another island. I expect she'll be well received there, brother. They're known for harboring dragons, whether the clientele realize it or not. One of the resort owners is bonded to a dragon. His family has been for generations. They may not know what she is, but they will be willing to service her."

"You have an advantage in some ways, you know," Rafe said. "Your kind are not left in the dark for centuries to protect the bloodlines. You can't breed, but you know so much more than we do."

"I do know more," Darius said. "The Council has always had a plan for you. The ones they can control. I don't think they really know what they're getting, though. They let too many slip through their fingers. Their plans are falling apart now."

"What are you talking about?"

"Walk with me and I'll tell you about your lover."

Rafe humored the man, sure he was crazy, but once they'd traveled up a worn, rocky path away from the Monastery, Darius said, "Once the Verdanith is assembled, things will change. The Council will take a step back, but they'll always be watching."

"What if we get Rowan to…"

"It has little to do with her. Her presence will help, but not for the reasons you think."

"You're being very cryptic, you realize this, right?"

Darius laughed, the sound shaking his broad chest and making Rafe wonder what kinds of things the man had done with Rowan, and especially how well she'd enjoyed them.

"There's always more to the Council than they let on. Their tie to the Mother is strong, but not as strong as the Catalyst's. Since the ritual, Kris has learned the answers, but his hands are tied. He can't overtly tell you what he knows."

Darius gripped Rafe's shirt and pulled him hard into a shadowy spot along the path. He pressed his lips against Rafe's ear. "You believe in fate, don't you?"

"Of course I do. I don't know a single dragon who doesn't."

"The Council's been struggling for centuries to hang on to what little control they have. But they are at a loss as to how to change fate. They've been trying for generations to gain some control and have only just discovered that they are as caught in the web as all the rest of us. If they keep strug-gling at this point, they'll only destroy themselves."

"What did Kris tell you?" Rafe asked through clenched teeth. "What does it have to do with Rowan and the Verdanith?"

"I can't even be sure it's her, but several months ago Kris told me he dreamed of a red spider who would arrive in the dark. It would pluck the threads that bind us all, draw us together, and carry us into the sunrise."

"And that's supposed to mean something to me?"

"Zak and I shared a little of her essence when she was here. It was strong enough to leave us drunk, even the small amount we could take. She likely has the blood of a queen. If she's that strong and was raised in this new world her entire life, her presence will be enough to convince the Council the path to her sun is the right one."

"But you and I both know bloodlines have nothing to do with rank. Every dragon has the opportunity to rise to that level."

"Ah, that's the law, yes. But how often do the royal blood-lines shift?"

That made Rafe pause. Aside from the Guardian who was granted a token place on the Court at the time of Ascension, Court families had always been the same bloodlines for as long as he was aware of. There were occasionally other dragons who vied for the positions, and there was always a grand ceremony prior to each hibernation to choose the next Court based on the riches acquired by the families at that point. But the contenders never quite succeeded. Was it truly fate, or was there some kind of conspiracy at work? He could believe either at this point.

"It does pay to be a silent observer for a few centuries," Darius said before Rafe could answer. The other dragon's face grew soft, his expression distant and sentimental. "Kris's mother occasionally spoke of her own dreams to me, just before Kris was born. They were of a similar vein. There are only a few of us who are close enough to the Council to see their gradual surrender. This has been brewing for a lot longer than your generation knows."

"Longer than you've been here?"

"Yes. I think your lovely little linguist might have stumbled across the details, but doesn't know what she found."

"And you think the Council may be ready to surrender?"

"Not surrender, but compromise. I would give them a token of loyalty once your demands have been accepted."

"That isn't my decision to make, but I can find Rowan. How long since she flew from here?"

"She's about two days East," Darius said. "She loves you. I don't think you deserve it, but she does. She's trying very hard not to, but I think that trying might destroy her if you don't find her soon."

"You think she'd be better off without me, don't you?" Rafe asked. He believed it himself as he uttered the words. He never should have approached her in that bar. He never should have shown her what she was. He never should have fallen in love with her.

"Maybe. I suppose it depends on what you do next."

"Where to next, my friend?" Roka asked a couple hours later.

"A few islands to the East... there's a resort village Darius sent her to."

"Are you ready to find her?"

There were so many messages in those words, Rafe hesitated to respond knowing that he might respond to the wrong one. He let the question sit while he shifted, then stretched his wings wide, testing the air.

"I will find her and we will prevail together."

"Well, then let's fly, brother!"

Roka trumpeted into the dusk and took flight. Rafe followed, launching himself into the air and leaving a clattering of pebbles behind.

~

"SHE'S SPREAD ALL over this place," Roka said after they landed. "Sweet Mother, what was she doing here?"

"Replenishing," Rafe said, letting out a breath to clothe him in casual khaki and cotton shirt before walking down the path toward the house that sat silent in the dawn beside the beach. The remnants of a very long party were littered all over the landscape. Half empty cups and bottles caught the rising sun. A couple wayward bodies rested like corpses tangled together. They weren't dead, but they'd fallen asleep or passed out in the middle of fucking each other.

Roka laughed. "Reminds me of Geva's stunts. Remember those?"

Rafe clenched his teeth. He remembered the rogue Red's antics and didn't have any love for the dragon, but looking around now, he knew what had happened had to be an act of desperation. She'd needed energy, and these humans were the best source. The fact that she might not understand her true strength was Rafe's fault.

"Do you think we need to do damage control?" Roka asked. It was a valid concern. Kol might have come in and wiped everyone's memories, but he'd need a Blue to get that job done.

The door of the house opened and a lone male figure stepped out, two steaming mugs held in his hands. Rafe could smell the sweet aroma of fresh coffee from where he stood.

"You're looking for her, aren't you?" the bearer of the mugs said. He shoved the mugs at them and Roka and Rafe both accepted without question. The hot liquid flowed easily down Rafe's throat and he ignored the human's gasp of astonishment when he handed back the still steaming empty mug.

"Do you know where she went?" Rafe asked.

"Dude, I want a little more info from you before I start sharing."

Rafe met he dark-fringed eyes of the human. "What do you want to know?"

"Why are you after her?"

"She's crucial to our—"

Roka's knuckles hit his ribs from behind in the most painful spot and the Guardian whispered in his ear, "Humans, you fuck. This one can lead us to her if you don't fuck it up. Her magic is linked to him already, like she was on the verge of marking him."

"I love her?" Rafe said. He didn't quite intend the inflection he added to the confession, but it came out anyway.

The man laughed a little bitterly. "Yeah… so do I, so I guess we have that in common. She left us both, but I'd really love to know why she was running in the first place. Do you mind telling me that?"

Rafe silently sized up the other man, painfully aware of Rowan's essence lingering around him and the intent look he had on his face, as though he was prepared to battle to the death for the woman he loved. Rafe's eyes caught on the blue medallion resting at the man's throat.

"Who's your boss?" Rafe said, narrowly avoiding blurting out the word "master".

The human didn't miss a beat. "The new guy that took

over is a man named Skye. I liked his mother better. She was…friendlier. This guy is cold as ice, so I don't know how he manages to convince anyone to…well, to fuck him, if I'm being blunt."

"Your family's been with us for a while, I take it?" Rafe let a little of his guard down upon the realization that this man was a bonded employee of another dragon. The man would be honest and wouldn't give away any secrets he discovered during their conversation, except to his own employer.

"Long enough for me to know one of you when I meet you, even if I don't know exactly what you are. Rowan was pretty damn special. But I get the sense you knew that. Why was she running?"

"Because I'm a fool. I just need to find her."

"Tell me what you really are and I'll tell you where she went."

Rafe bristled at the man's reluctance to give up Rowan's location. He was tempted to just fly on, follow the remnants of her trail the way he had so far. But the pull Rowan had on this man was as clear if they were physically tied by a visible thread. Trevor hadn't lied about loving her. Rafe could tell the pair had shared their Nirvana with each other very recently.

The essence of her the man carried tugged at Rafe's desire as strongly as if Rowan were standing in front of him. He longed to have a fresh taste of her. If this human wanted to know what they were, Rafe would show him the same way he had shown Rowan their first night, if only to have that taste he craved.

The man had no idea what he was asking for, yet he held his chin out defiantly as Rafe and Roka both sized him up.

"He'd let you mark him just for her," Roka's voice murmured into his mind.

"Yes, but I need more than to mark him. I need what remnants of her essence are in him."

"Need, or want? How long has it been since you were with her?"

"Want. It's been months. Skye won't be pleased if I take this human from him."

"Skye can be an unforgiving churl of a dragon. But you outrank him, so if he took issue, it's Kol he'd have to answer to."

"Kol can easily handle Skye."

Rafe met the man's steady gaze. His heartbeat sped up at the proximity to Rowan's potent magic that lingered around the human like an aura. He took a deep breath before speaking, hoping to get his emotions under control. "What you're offering requires a bit of sacrifice on your part, Mister..." Rafe raised an eyebrow, inviting the young human to give up his identity.

"Trevor Markham." He held out his hand and Rafe gripped it tightly. Rafe didn't release the hand, instead pulling closer. Trevor reluctantly moved until his chest was against Rafe's and Rafe's mouth was at his ear.

"I'm Rafe. Is there a private place for Roka and I to finish this, or do we have to resort to exhibitionism like the rest of your friends?"

Trevor's eyes widened. "You're Rafe? Oh. Ah, sure. H-how private are we talking?"

"Depends on what you want advertised, buddy," Roka said, clapping a hand on Trevor's shoulder hard enough to make the human flinch a little. Roka's huge, white-haired form loomed threateningly and Trevor glanced back once, his eyes widening.

Trevor nodded and grimaced slightly, darting a look between the two dragons. "I should tell you that I'm not really into...that..." His voice trailed off when Rafe raised an eyebrow, daring him to finish his sentence. So many human men he'd met were rigidly against coupling, so he'd avoided them. He preferred women, but men could be even more potent sources of energy, as long as they were willing. Trevor's physical reaction contradicted his words, however, the rigid line of his erection pressing into Rafe's hip and his pupils dilating in response to Rafe's breath against his skin.

"Are you absolutely sure you're not?" Rafe asked. He lowered his hands to Trevor's hips and pulled him tighter so the man could feel Rafe's arousal, thick and pulsing, growing ever more insistent the longer Rafe spent in contact with the delicious tingle of Rowan's energy that lingered around Trevor.

Trevor averted his eyes, but made no move to escape Rafe's grasp. "Are all of you this insistent about…sex?"

"It's a means for survival as much as enjoyment," Rafe said, releasing Trevor from his grip. "Now lead on, Mr. Markham."

The conflicting flow of energy around Trevor amused Rafe, and he shared a covert look with Roka on their way into the house.

"He's a fucking trooper, we should go easy on him," Roka sent.

Easy was a relative term. The human would enjoy the experience as much as Rafe did. But by "easy" Rafe knew Roka was referring to the depth of feeling they put into the act. And because this was for Rowan, he had no qualms about making it worth it for the human.

"If he's doing this it means he's fallen hard for her. He cares for her. He deserves nothing less for his offer to help."

Trevor led them up a wide flight of stairs to the upper floor of the expensive beach-side house—a house that any dragon might be proud of. Rafe could see a trickle of sweat making its way down the back of Trevor's tanned neck, beneath the short, dark hair, until it was absorbed by the pale cotton collar of his t-shirt. In spite of the obvious scent of clean skin on the young man, Rafe was acutely aware of the smell of Rowan that melded with it and wondered if Trevor had pleasured her as well as Rafe had. Oddly, he didn't feel jealous, but he did look forward to the possibility of sharing Trevor with Rowan when they found her.

"Are you taking him, or am I? I just want to be prepared," Roka asked.

"I'm taking him. You're damn good with your mouth, so use that."

Roka chuckled out loud, the sound causing Trevor to tense and look over his shoulder at them.

The entire scenario reminded Rafe of weekend nights searching out a lover, except Roka's presence made it much more enjoyable. He almost wished he'd had his friend with him before. The pair of them could have pleased so many women to the point of delirium. The fact of his love for Rowan aching in his chest made the need all the greater.

Trevor led them to a door at the end of the hallway. Once inside he diligently locked it behind them and stood with a harsh scowl looking at them both.

"It's just us now. Does this really have to happen?"

Rafe had been expecting the question. He stepped past Trevor into the room, looking like he was admiring the view. A gorgeous vista of the sun rising over the ocean shone through a bank of wide windows. Early sunbeams fell in golden pools onto the king-sized bed in the middle of the room.

"You know something of what we are already, don't you? How much do you know?" Rafe asked.

"I just put it together over the years. Mora never seemed to age. I knew her my entire life. She was just the beautiful philanthropist employer when I was a kid, then when I got older she turned into more. My parents thought I was nuts, but I only mentioned it the one time."

"You were lovers?" Rafe asked, surprised by the man's

confession. It was unusual for dragons to take regular lovers from their staff who they didn't intend to mark. Anonymity was so much easier unless the employee was particularly loyal. Maybe this one was, which raised him exponentially in Rafe's opinion.

"Off and on. We didn't see her that frequently, but when she did visit, I always…delivered. How could I not?" Trevor's eyes shifted down Rafe's torso. He swallowed harshly when his gaze came to rest at the bulge in Rafe's pants, then darted up again to meet Rafe's steady, unmoving look.

"Do you miss her?"

Trevor seemed a little agitated at the question before settling. "Yeah, I mean, there was something about her and how she reacted to my pleasure…how I felt afterward. Rowan felt just like that and it wasn't until I was with her that I put it together. There has to be more with you guys. Is there?"

"There is," Rafe said. "Your employer is Mora's son, Skye?"

"Yes." Trevor shivered. "Not one shred like his mother. He's definitely never tried this with me."

Rafe grinned. "He owns you, you know. But if you're willing, we're about to steal you from him."

Trevor's eyes widened. "No shit, it's like that?"

"You want to know what we are, right?" Rafe said.

Trevor nodded.

"If I show you the truth, you will belong to me."

"What the fuck are you?" Trevor asked, somehow alarmed. "You talk about me like I'm some pawn to be exchanged. I didn't lie when I said I was in love with Rowan. But I can also walk away, because this is some crazy shit."

"You can. Go now if you want to. This is your last chance to learn the truth, though."

He gave Trevor a moment, but the man didn't budge. He

just stood in the patch of sunlight that streamed in, clenching his fists in determination.

"We're dragons," Rafe said, sending a mental message to Roka to shift a tiny bit when he said it.

Horns erupted from both their heads. Scales glimmered along Rafe's hands. As added emphasis he signaled again to Roka and they both blew out their breath. Rafe's transformed into tendrils that became a dark hand cupping Trevor's cheek, brushing fingers through his hair. Roka's smoke was more amorphous, but no less potent, the white cloud hovered before Trevor's face before sliding down the front of his body, making him quiver with pleasure.

"Now, if you've had enough of the revelation, once we're done with you, I am going to mark you. This will make you mine. No other dragon may touch you without my say so. Then you will take me to Rowan."

"I don't honestly know where she is. All I know is that she said she was going home. I'm sorry, I lied."

Roka laughed, but Rafe responded differently. The knowledge was more than enough. If she was on her way back to San Diego, she may be looking for him. He stepped close to Trevor, gripped him by the shoulders, and kissed him.

Trevor remained tense for a long moment, then his lips softened and his mouth moved, clasping at Rafe's in response. He could even taste Rowan on him, but he wanted more. He wanted all of her, not just this brief flavor she'd left behind on this man whom she'd given her particular attention to.

Their bodies seemed to merge halfway into the kiss. Trevor relaxed and tilted in. Rafe dropped one arm and wrapped it around Trevor's shoulders, pulling him close. The man was hard as a rock against Rafe's own erection.

He dropped his lips from Trevor's mouth to his cheek,

then his neck. In his ear he heard Trevor whisper. "Why are you still doing this?"

"You taste of her," Rafe said gruffly. "I need more. I need just a little of what she gave you. Please."

Trevor's body quivered against him and a set of fingertips clutched hard at Rafe's hips. "How badly do you need what I have?" Trevor asked. He pulled away slightly and pressed a palm against the rigid shape straining against Rafe's pants. Trevor gripped him through the fabric and stroked once while holding Rafe's gaze intently as though challenging him to beg.

Rafe dropped to his knees and feverishly unfastened Trevor's pants. He gripped Trevor's hot shaft in one hand and flicked his tongue around the smooth tip. The flavor of Rowan was unmistakable even beyond the clean taste of the man's flesh. Rafe slid his lips down Trevor's length, reveling in Rowan's essence that coated the flesh sliding beneath his tongue.

"Holy fuck," Trevor said.

Roka chuckled and Rafe glanced up. The Guardian slipped his hands under Trevor's shirt from behind and tugged it off. "Might as well get naked," Roka said. "You belong to us for the next few minutes. But I think if you enjoyed Mora, you'll enjoy us, even more."

"But she was…ah…yeah, do that."

Rafe cupped Trevor's balls and stroked, his fingertips meeting the velvet wetness of Roka's tongue as it teased between Trevor's cheeks from the other side.

Roka had shed his own conjured clothing and now knelt with a huge erection just behind Trevor, who seemed to be gradually pushing towards Rafe as if to escape the large Guardian, even though his energy signaled how much he enjoyed what Roka was doing.

Rafe released Trevor's cock and urged Trevor to turn. The man gave him a startled glance but complied.

Rafe stood and disrobed with a breath. "Rowan has beautiful breasts, doesn't she?" Rafe commented, the image of her clear in his mind after the close contact he'd had with her flavor. He pressed himself fully against Trevor from behind, brushing his hands along Trevor's hips. With one hand, he gripped the man's cock again while the other caressed his chest. "Tell me what you did with her breasts." He let his hand slide along Trevor's length, stroking until Trevor's flesh jerked in his fist.

"You want a story? While you're...ungh..."

"Do you like this?" Rafe asked. He eyed Roka over Trevor's shoulder. The massive form of the Guardian knelt watching, his white hair long and loose over his shoulders. Of all of them, Roka was the only one who looked exactly the same as Rafe always remembered, refusing to conform to any modern standard.

He gripped Trevor's cock tighter and stroked quicker.

"I do," Trevor said in a strained tone. "God, you're good at it, too. Hell, I worshiped her even before she let me touch her. I'd have given her everything."

With a look and a thought from Rafe, Roka leaned in and clasped the tip of Trevor's cock between his expert lips. Rafe moved his hand away, making way for his friend.

"Ohhh, oh, Jesus," Trevor said when Roka took him greedily into his mouth, sucking his cock in deep. Rafe watched for a second. He knew firsthand how adept Roka was.

"What did you do first?" Rafe murmured, trying to imagine Rowan landing here, desperate for energy, and what she might do to gain it. He'd only seen the remnants of the party that had occurred, and had been surprised that this man, out of all of the humans, still seemed sane enough to talk to them. He supposed being bonded to a blue might have something to do with it, though. Bonded humans were a supposed to be resistant to the influences of other dragons, but even Rowan's power had been enough for this man to give in. Unless he'd merely fallen in love.

Trevor stared wide-eyed at the shape of Roka's head, bobbing on his cock. He hesitantly let his hands drift down to cling to Roka's head.

"F-first? First she, ah, jacked me off. Just like it was nothing, but it helped her I guess."

Rafe's own cock was painfully hard and worse off for the fact that Trevor kept pushing back against him in response to Roka's steady sucking. The Guardian's hands reached back and clutched at Trevor's ass, pulling him tight against Roka's face so he could control the thrust into his mouth. In the process, Roka spread Trevor's cheeks apart. Roka took a moment to release the human's cock and lash his long, wet tongue between Trevor's thighs. He slicked it between ass cheeks and teased Trevor's balls along his way back to the cock he'd been concentrating on.

Trevor let out moan at the renewed invasion, but went back to surging his hips against Roka's face in spite of the grip the dragon had on him.

"What did you do next?" Rafe asked, bending to lend the wetness of his own tongue to Trevor's puckered asshole.

"We—oh God, yeah. Like that."

"Keep talking," Rafe said. He stood again and brushed his fingertips in a series of light circles around Trevor's sensitive opening, then let one tip push past, experimentally.

"Ahh…Right, we watched my friends fuck. She took what she needed, then left. I followed, and oh God, you really are gonna fuck me, aren't you? I don't know if I can take it if you do that."

"You don't seem to mind having your cock in Roka's mouth."

"No, no…he's amazing at this, but…"

"I'll be gentle," Rafe said, sliding his finger deeper. "Tell me if anything doesn't feel good, and I'll stop. And tell me what you liked about making love to Rowan."

"Oh, fuck, that's why you're doing this, isn't it? To get even?"

"No, I have a very good reason for doing this. I'm just trying to distract you so it feels better for you."

Trevor shuddered again, and Rafe thought the man might come, even though Roka was being very slow and deliberate about the cock sucking.

"She tasted so goddamn sweet. Christ I could've gone down on her for days. Then when she came… I felt like the fucking master. I still remember the moment. She said my name, except she said it after another name—your name, confused the hell out of me at first."

"She said my name?" Rafe asked. He pushed a second finger into Trevor's ass at that moment, making the man cry out in surprise and surge into Roka, who sent an irritated mental curse at Rafe.

"Yeah, she said your name, Jesus, do you have to do that?"

"Do you not like it?" Rafe added another finger and pushed deeper into Trevor's ass. Rafe's body buzzed with elation at the idea that Rowan might not hate him entirely, that she had cried out *his* name in the heat of passion with another man.

"Um…"

"You love it, don't you?" Rafe asked, pushing his slick fingers deeper and curling them in just the right spot.

Trevor only let out a gasp and reached back, clutching at Rafe's naked hip. He let out a deluge of words as Rafe plunged his fingers into him.

"Please fuck me, I'll tell you anything you want to know. Like how Rowan tasted like heaven and her pussy felt like as much when I made love to her. I was the only one she fucked, if you're worried about that. It seemed weird to me because she seemed so goddamn turned on the entire time, but never touched one of the others until they were already coming all over each other. I think that's why I loved her at first. Watching that gorgeous, perfect body of hers enjoy just being next to the sex was mesmerizing. I'm glad I didn't let her leave and it was even better when she let me into that tight, wet pussy of hers. Jesus, she felt so fucking good. Nobody's ever felt as good since Mora. Or…or…"

"Or?"

"Or this."

"Tell me more," Rafe said as he pressed the tip of his cock at Trevor's opening. Trevor didn't resist, but pushed back with a soft moan until Rafe began sinking in even sooner than he'd planned.

Amid pants and moans of pleasure, Trevor kept talking. "That first stroke almost made me come, but then she wrapped her legs around me and I wanted to last longer, for her. She'd come already from my mouth, but I needed to feel her fall apart under me. I needed to know my cock had done it to her."

Trevor's monologue only faltered a couple times while Rafe fucked him, but Trevor kept going. He pushed back, supporting his weight on Roka's large shoulders in a struggle to maintain balance. Trevor seemed to have figured out what Rafe needed. When Rafe wrapped his arms around Trevor's chest, Trevor leaned back and gripped Rafe's hands.

"I fucking love her. The tight clench of her was so amazing, but it was so much more. Oh God. Fuck, I'm coming."

Rafe lost track of events at that moment, beyond ready to finish, but holding back until Trevor did. Trevor shook and buckled, his Nirvana pooling around both Rafe and Roka and seeping into them like a vortex. The cyclone of it hit Rafe and he cried out, the burst of pleasure surprising him enough that he plunged his cock hard into Trevor's ass and held tight to the man's hips while they both rode out their orgasms.

The bit of Rowan's energy that Trevor shared left a warm, familiar glow in Rafe. Roka made a humming sound of approval. He had tasted her before, by proxy, but not to this concentrated extent. Even the diluted remnants of her were dizzying to experience.

Trevor pulled away and collapsed on the floor in front of the bed, eyelids fluttering. He held out his hands, wrists together. "Do what you gotta. I surrender."

Rafe knelt and took one of Trevor's hands, wasting no time in marking him with a few quick lashes of tongue against wrist.

"Oh, right. Fuck, you said you'd do that." The drunken look on Trevor's face amused the two dragons. Roka laughed as he wiped his mouth. Trevor stared at the small circle on the inside of his wrist, dismayed. "You couldn't have put it somewhere Skye won't see it?"

"Skye's the least of our worries."

"You've met that asshole, right?" Trevor said. "Mom kisses his ass worse than she did Mora's. He'll be pissed, which will piss her off worse."

"I don't care about your mother, and neither should you right now. Skye will likely know within hours that one of his bonded employees has been appropriated. He'll go to his boss, who also happens to be *my* boss. But it won't matter by the time he can state his case because you'll belong to both of us if Rowan agrees to it."

Trevor grew silent after that. He left the room briefly to

clean up, then came back looking introspective. "Where to now?"

"You don't have to come with us. We can come back for you once we find her," Rafe said.

With bright eyes and a determined stance, Trevor looked at him. "I'm going, even if it's just so I can make sure she really does want you when it comes down to it. After that I can do whatever the fuck you want me to. I guess I belong to you now, after all, don't I? So if she wants neither of us, we might as well stick together. As much as I've always preferred women, if I can't have her…well…" He gave Rafe a sheepish smile and half-hearted shrug.

Rafe smiled ruefully. "I hope she does, but if our luck is that bad, I appreciate your willingness to join me."

CHAPTER SIX

*I*n spite of only being a couple days behind Rowan, they didn't account for inclement weather and carrying a passenger who would need to stop for breaks.

Trevor climbed off Roka's back a day later, cursing when they finally stopped in a secluded section of woods. He stalked off toward a nearby road, the two dragons hurriedly shifting and clothing themselves before running to catch up.

"Haven't you guys heard of airlines?" Trevor asked a little later when they returned to their secluded landing spot. Rafe and Roka waited while Trevor smeared on more sunscreen and adjusted the odd-looking goggles he'd just bought at a makeshift sporting goods store in a small beach-side town in Indonesia.

"It's unnatural for a dragon to pay someone to fly them places," Roka said, the sneer in his tone reflecting Rafe's feelings on the subject.

"Whatever, dude. It's clear you're not used to having a regular rider. I get that we're in a hurry, but she's not that far ahead of you."

"All you knew was that she said she was going home,"

Rafe said. "At full power, she can fly non-stop for about a week. Even with your link to her leading us like a beacon, we can't afford to keep stopping, and if we don't stick to the open air, we risk flying off course, losing her trail."

"She'll have to stop in a week, though, right? I'll muscle through it, but I've gotta have an hour a day. That's all I ask. Tie me on or knock me out...do what you have to in between."

"It's better if you remain conscious. It's your desire for her that's the strongest path to finding her," Rafe said, ashamed at the bitterness in his tone. He'd been grateful to find someone who'd forged such a strong connection with Rowan, but the idea of her connecting on such an intimate level with any other male occasionally grated on him.

"Listen, Rafe," Trevor said, clenching his jaw and stepping threateningly close, "if you want her so badly, why can't you follow your own fucking *desire?*"

Rafe held Trevor's gaze for a moment, then looked away, trying to hide the hurt and embarrassment he felt over being such a fool as to let her go. "It's been nearly three months since we were together. My link has faded too much. Her trail is still there, but it's nothing more than a series of bread-crumbs. Your link to her is still as strong as if she's marked you. You're drawn to her like a moth to a flame, whether you know it or not. So, I'll follow you, since you're our best chance at catching her sooner, even if we stop for an hour a day. I just hope she stops to rest soon—perhaps we can catch her then."

"Alright," Trevor said. He fiddled with his gear a bit longer. He'd bought a bundle of climbing ropes and a small cargo net so he could ride longer and stop for shorter dura-tions. The excess fidgeting and distinct lack of eye contact worried Rafe. Trevor cursed and grew still while Rafe watched. Finally, Trevor spoke again.

"Do you need—ah—more? Of me, I mean." He cleared his throat, glancing between both Roka and Rafe.

Rafe started to answer, but Roka beat him. The Guardian took two strides to get to Trevor, clutched the back of the human's head with one large hand, and pressed his lips against Trevor's mouth. Trevor went rigid for a second. When Roka refused to release him and continued assaulting his mouth, Trevor moaned and gripped the sides of Roka's head, clutching desperately.

"You're terrifying him," Rafe projected to his friend.

"Is that all I'm doing?"

Rafe chuckled. *"No, he's lit up like the sun right now."*

"Ohh, fuck," Trevor gasped when Roka finally released him. "Was that a yes? I was hoping you'd say no, but it seemed polite to offer."

"No," Rafe said. "But I appreciate your willingness. Expect me to take advantage of it."

"Yes, actually," Roka said. "We know it pays to be cautious on long trips like this. Take a friend, or stop frequently to replenish. I'll wait until you're finished with what you're doing."

Trevor barked out an awkward laugh and bent back to messing with his gear, spreading the ropes and nets out. "This is some road-trip. Except you guys drive all night without rest. How the hell do you do it? How the hell is Rowan doing it? She's alone."

"That's one of my worries," Rafe said. "She doesn't know what her limits are. The magic can sustain us without even food or water for a long time, but it isn't the only thing we need. If she pushes herself too far, it could kill her."

Trevor froze for a split second, then began moving even faster. "Fuck, man, why didn't you tell me that? Get shifted so I can fit this stuff on you." He looked down at the collection of provisions. He'd bought enough for a week, from what

Rafe could tell, but suddenly Trevor was looking at it like it wasn't enough.

"It'll work," Trevor said, mostly to himself. "I can sleep in the air mostly, if I stick to the rations I won't need to take that many breaks. You guys probably still want to stop for me but I can cut it down to ten minutes. I don't give a shit if it's in water, either, just so I'm not turning your back into a toilet."

Rafe and Roka shared a look. "How hardcore are you?" Roka asked.

"Man, I hiked across the Outback when I was nineteen. Rite of passage for myself. I did things I never thought I'd have to do to survive then. I can do this."

"Give me ten minutes with you and you won't need to piss or shit for the next week," Roka said.

TREVOR STARED MUTELY at the white-haired man, the more silent party in the entire ordeal. Roka had said only a few words the entire time, but Trevor had the distinct impression a *lot* of conversations were going on without him even hearing them.

Could they even speak telepathically? His own experiences couldn't answer that question, though he wouldn't have discounted the possibility.

He'd known from an early age that his parents' employers were different in some bizarre yet intriguing way. Mora had never aged, though her husband had.

It wasn't until after the husband had died that Mora approached Trevor at one of his parents' parties. She was always there, at those parties. Trevor was fresh out of high school, enduring the celebration thrown in his honor and ready to leave to go to the *real* party at his friend's house.

Christ, she'd been persistent and then proceeded to blow his mind so hard he forgot to leave his bed and even go to that other party.

These two men had become the same kind of distraction. He felt agitated, on the verge of a hard-on every time he moved the right way. He wasn't gay, God no... he'd never been in love with a man a single moment in his life. But this wasn't love. This was an unbearable itch to get one of them inside him as soon as fucking possible. To feel more of that powerful rush when they came—like Mora had felt, only times a thousand. And fingers were nothing compared to the utter invasion of Rafe's cock.

Rafe's cock...the idea of it loomed behind him as solidly as the man himself. The thick weight of it had been shoved deep inside Trevor's ass for God knew how many minutes the day before. At least as deep as Trevor had penetrated Rowan a few days ago.

And Jesus, if that juxtaposition of images didn't turn him on immensely.

Now the other one with the perfect mouth was offering something and Trevor kind of short circuited.

"H-how does us hanging out prevent my bodily functions?" Trevor asked lamely.

His fingers grew numb around the cords he'd been tying when Roka came close. The man was fucking huge. Both of them were huge enough to intimidate anyone. Trevor wasn't easily intimidated...he was a big guy himself, and he'd taken advantage of that feature on many occasions. But these two put his size to shame.

"Magic, brother," Roka said. "I don't need to take a piece of you to give you this, but it would be a fair exchange if you offered."

"You want to fuck me?" Trevor asked, irritated at the

squeak in his voice when he said it, and particularly at the way his cock twitched in his pants.

"That would be a fair assessment," Roka said. The man closed in and bent close, his smooth lips ghosted along Trevor's cheek, past his ear, and down his neck. A cool, tingly sensation followed and within a few seconds Trevor was sure a light fog had surrounded the two of them.

But fuck. Having a man that massive and intimidating fall to his knees and suck his cock again for the second time in as many days was nothing short of apocalyptic. The world might end at the tip of Trevor's cock. The brief thought passed through his brain, just as the bubbling surge of his orgasm started to well up, but Roka abruptly stopped and leaned back on his heels.

"Christ, man, why did you stop?"

"To give you the choice. I can finish you like this again, or you can have more. You know how much better it will be if we're both sated."

Hell yeah, he wanted that. Trevor turned and stumbled, his pants still wrapped around his ankles. Rafe's thick arms caught him and steadied him, then helped Trevor lower to his knees, Roka behind him.

They were like some perfect drug, these two, and now that he'd seen their true forms, none of it seemed the least bit strange. All he had to do was touch and be touched, accept the deep, passionate kiss Rafe gave him, push back against the delightful pressure of the other dragon's touch behind him.

Rafe held him, not asking for more, only smoothing his fingers over and over through Trevor's hair as though to comfort, and occasionally placing a sensuous kiss against his lips.

He supposed it was instinct that spurred him on—at least he had no other word to describe the urge that led him to unfasten Rafe's pants and take the man's weeping tip into his mouth and suck. The image of Charles in the hot tub days earlier kept flashing through his mind. He'd always envied Charles his seemingly charmed life and his luck with women. But as Trevor sucked on Rafe's cock and rejoiced at the push and stretch of Roka into him from behind, he knew without a doubt that he'd long since trumped his arrogant friend.

Twigs and grass pressed against his knees, but none of those sensations registered in the blaring perfection of the steel-hard flesh that invaded his ass, and the palm that brushed deliberately across his balls and gripped his cock from behind.

He gave in, eyes fluttering, struggling to see through the dense white cloud that surrounded the three of them.

"Give it to me," Roka murmured, and Trevor had trouble processing things beyond the unspeakable pleasure Roka's steady thrusts were inciting in him. Bluntness worked with Trevor. This kind of direct message was appreciated but Jesus. Jesus. He needed more.

He released Rafe's cock only long enough to beg. "Oh, God, harder. Please."

Roka squeezed Trevor's erection almost painfully as though giving Trevor a message, then began to steadily stroke him and fuck him to a point where Trevor lost his mind completely. He only vaguely heard the two men exchange words that sounded something like, "Finish him."

Then he was engulfed in nothing but white. White before his eyes, white pleasure when he came. He tasted the salty sweet heat of Rafe's cum shooting into the back of his throat and a similar sensation in his ass. The feeling accompanied by a harmony of deep cries into the sky and that perfect rush of energy that sped through every cell in his body. The world tilted and all he could see was blue sky framed by the green canopy above. He forgot entirely where he was for who knew how long, until someone began shaking him.

He blinked his eyes into the bright sunlight and Roka's smirking face where it hovered over him.

"I fucked you pretty well, didn't I?"

Trevor had an urge to punch the cocky expression off the man's face, but chose diplomacy and humor instead. He was better at those things than violence, anyway.

"You might as well have knocked me unconscious with that cock."

Roka laughed, an odd sonorous sound that definitely didn't sound human, but that made Trevor's balls quiver.

"What did you do to me with all that smoke?"

"Gave you some momentum. You've got several days of my essence sustaining you. You might still feel the need for water or an occasional snack, but the more you imbibe the more often we'll need to stop anyway. Just know you don't actually need it. Trust me."

"I'm down with that. What if I fall off?"

"I'll catch you if you fall," Rafe said. "If you start to feel dizzy, say so."

"Alright then," Trevor said. He felt invigorated beyond his wildest dreams at the moment. His mind was razor sharp as he directed the pair after they shifted so he could secure their gear to their huge bodies. *His* gear, he corrected. The understanding of his need to be involved lingered as the obvious roadblock to the task at hand. Yet they were being patient. He glanced at Rafe a few times, trying not to hold the black dragon's gaze because the memory of the man's cock in his ass would rise up unbidden, and make him too flustered to get shit done. It helped a little that Rafe wasn't human at the moment, but the looks Rafe gave Trevor with those bottomless black eyes were no different.

Soon, the task distracted him from everything else, and

Roka's drug Trevor had inhaled drove him on as singularly as the best pharmaceuticals he'd tried in his wayward youth. He'd longed to be this focused during all his crazy adventures. Rock climbing, surfing, racing. He'd had the money to risk his life in dozens of locales. Rowan had found him in the middle of one of his trips, but none of them had involved sex. Sex had always been a happy side effect of every thrill seeking adventure.

Now, all he wanted was to fuck. And he'd satisfied that urge tenfold the last two days, but still wanted more, just like he did every time he had jumped out of an airplane, or ridden an epic wave. He wanted more of their secrets. More of their magic, and he didn't give a fuck whether it meant he'd live or die. He just wanted more.

Climbing on Rafe's back and tying himself down felt like an act of thrilling bondage. Trevor would gladly push his limits during this quest.

"It's almost like she's the princess at the end and we need to save her," Trevor said.

Rafe's deep, rumbling voice answered, "She may need saving, but once that happens, we are her slaves."

"I'm okay with that," Trevor said. "Are you?"

"Yes."

CHAPTER SEVEN

The hurricane of energy was unmistakable when they reached Japan, and grew even more intense the closer they got to the mountain. The fading stepping stones of her trail led to the mountain and no further. Trevor's glowing thread that was linked to Rowan had grown gradually brighter over the last few days, and crackled with energy now, but it, too, terminated somewhere beneath the peak of the volcano.

"Get to the city and call the others," Rafe sent to Roka mid-air. *"Get them here soon, we need them all."*

Roka veered off without a word and headed toward the city beyond the mountain. It might be another day before the others could get to them, but Rafe might need at least a day to convince her. He still had Trevor on his back, still conscious, which amazed Rafe.

He flew on, targeting the white peak of Fuji in the distance.

"I'm losing it, brother," Trevor said. "Sleep... food... anything."

"Hold on a little longer. We're almost there."

"Right. Rowan."

Trevor's voice was a wisp of sound, as it had been for the last day. Rafe worried the man might not last, but Trevor had never begged to be let down to go his own way. Rafe hated Trevor a little for his dedication but knew at the same time Rafe would want no other human mated to the woman he loved.

As they drew closer, Rowan's trail converged in a spot in the shadow of the mountain, as plain as day. Mixed with it, however, was an energy even more ancient and therefore immensely powerful for the fact that it lingered so clearly.

Rafe dipped to follow it, sinking through the air without care, as desperate as he was to reach her.

He landed with a shuddering surge, the earth shaking and dust rising up around them at the entrance to a cave. Trevor slid off his back and fell boneless against a rock.

"She's in there," Trevor said, as though he sensed it as much as Rafe did.

Rafe peered into the narrow, dark space. It wasn't a pleasant kind of cave. Wet and craggy. Upon his first look, he didn't see how a full-sized dragon could even fit. But she had, because she was in there now. Maybe in her human form, but his senses only read *dragon*.

"Rowan?" He sent the question out, grasping at anything, but got no answer.

Shame wasn't a common emotion in Rafe's repertoire, but he felt it then. It had been entirely his fault for not giving in and marking her that first night, the very second he knew he could be happy with no other woman. The problem was her, though. He couldn't simply *claim* a dragon like her. It would disrespect her to do so, as majestic as she was. He wished he knew what bloodlines she belonged to, but it had to be Court. He'd sensed that power in her from the beginning, known she was better than him all along. So how could he claim ownership of her when the opposite was more preferable? And the opposite was something she was unlikely to agree to, on simple, human principle.

He should have asked. That was his mistake. He should have told her everything, then gotten down on his knees and begged her to claim him. But there was no precedence for a dragon submitting to another dragon as a mate. They only submitted if they were being disciplined. For thousands of years they'd only been allowed to mate with humans. She couldn't have known that, either. His other mistake was not giving her the details of their political history. But politics kind of put a damper on sex and sex had always been a dragon priority.

It still was, if they were going to save her.

"Rowan, I don't know if you can hear me, but we're coming in."

Trevor handed Rafe a head lamp, which he declined. The human was prepared for anything. He was geared up now with a pack of supplies on his back and stood at the entrance, waiting for Rafe's signal.

"Why are you hard?" Rafe asked, point blank.

Trevor's face flushed and he looked down at the bulge in the front of his snug-fitting pants.

"Proximity? I don't fucking know. All I know is that I want what you want so much I'd fuck that feeling until it came all over me. Do you promise I can still be hers when we're in there?"

"Yes. You first."

The passage wasn't that tight, so they could walk upright, but had to remain single-file.

"Do you wonder if only one of us will survive to save her?" Trevor asked, some ways in.

"We'll both survive."

Trevor laughed. "You don't see the parallel to insemination?"

Rafe paused, considering the comment. "What do you mean?"

"We're the sperm swimming up the vagina. She's the egg. It's a contest, I think... Who will she let impregnate her first?"

"You think too literally," Rafe said.

"Do I?" Trevor asked.

The human was getting impetuous, and was beginning to endear himself to Rafe for it. Trevor reminded him of Rowan in some ways. He believed it possible she might prefer this man over himself, and if she loved Trevor more, Rafe didn't want to have a hand in keeping them apart.

"Move on," Rafe said.

"You can't even answer me. I think you love her. Is that literal enough?"

"You love her, too."

"So you don't deny it."

"I would die for her. Would you?"

Trevor stopped moving.

"Yes. God yes," Trevor said, turning his head slightly to glance back at Rafe.

They stood silent for a moment. Rafe was surprised by the human's response in spite of being able to sense his conviction. Trevor began moving again, quicker now that the floor of the passage had smoothed enough to not impede them as much. Rafe followed, catching the gist of the man's intentions. All Trevor wanted was to get to Rowan.

Rafe wanted nothing more himself.

~

THE STRANGE ANCIENT convergence of energy that swirled around Rowan's trail continued to grow stronger as they went. Soon the passage widened again after a junction of several other passages branching off, but there was no question which way they should continue. The wider passage was less dusty, the floor flat and smooth, the ceiling much higher, and the walls no longer dripping with moisture.

Rafe and Trevor walked abreast, the beam of Trevor's head lamp illuminating their way. The passage seemed to go on for miles. Every so often Rafe would try to communicate with Rowan again, but to no avail.

"What would you have done without me?" Trevor asked. "Wandered blind into a mountain?"

"I don't need the aid of a light. I have her trail, for one thing—"

"Which you need me to follow," Trevor interrupted.

"True, but there's another trail in here and I believe it's the trail *she* followed."

"A trail left by what? Another dragon?"

"Yes, but a very old one. The energy's faded beyond identifying, but it's still powerful. Like an entire brood passed through a thousand years ago."

"How many of you are there?" Trevor asked abruptly. He walked at a quick and steady pace now. He'd tried running once they had reached the wider passage, but after an hour at a non-stop, rigorous pace, had finally given in and paused, panting and sweating, cursing the distance around the serpentine twists and curves the seemingly endless passage took them through. Rafe couldn't be certain but he was sure there was a subtle but steady downward slope to their path.

"I used to know, but now I'm not sure. The brood I was born with is around a thousand in number, but Rowan wasn't part of our brood. There may be many more like her out there—dragons born without the sanction of our Council. We need her to help us change our laws. But all I care about is finding her."

He stopped suddenly when his eye caught a subtle irregularity in the texture on the wall beside him. No, it wasn't an *irregularity*, it was precisely the opposite—if anything, the texture had become *too* regular. He studied both sides for a moment. They were too faint to make out, but if he looked further down the corridor—

"Sweet Mother, this is the path to a temple." Rafe pressed his palms against the wall several paces further on. The pattern was clear here. Carved in a wide band at shoulder-height along the walls of the passage was a single, continuous scaled length. He continued, trailing his fingertips along the upraised shapes. Soon he reached a more detailed section where a head twisted around a tail and the pattern continued, along the body of another dragon.

"Are you going to explain to me what all that means about your Council?" Trevor asked, trailing his own fingers along the carvings on the opposite wall.

Too overwhelmed with awe to object or even to consider his own words much beyond spouting his rote knowledge, Rafe told Trevor his race's history. From the first hibernation enforced by the Council to both curtail dragon violence on humans, and to prevent the increasingly devastating retaliation, to his own hibernation and eventual ascension many centuries later.

"When the youngest in each new generation reaches maturity, that new brood is forced to sleep in human form for five centuries, just to be certain we remember how to maintain this shape. Over the course of our existence, we discovered we preferred it. It's much easier to live among you if you believe we are one of you. Human energy sustains us as well as our own, and mating with you preserves our bloodlines."

"It seems like it would dilute it, if you ask me."

"Our magic overrides your genetics. Each dragon child born to a human and a dragon couple is entirely a dragon. The choice was a matter of survival for our race. Our population had dwindled. We could no longer safely mate with other dragons without risking inbreeding."

"But now you can? She's not your sister or cousin or anything, is she?"

"All I know is that her parents were both dragons and she couldn't be more perfect if she tried. We believe the only reason the Council had to isolate us for centuries was to facilitate our strongest members breeding with humans when the humans came to release us. We're hoping to convince them to let the next generation choose for themselves. Rowan is far stronger than any of the rest of the Court, and pure-blooded. If a dragon like her can be born without the sanction of the Council, then we don't need their laws."

"Alright, alright," Trevor said, pausing beside him, wide-eyed with surprise.

Rafe realized he'd gradually begun speaking more vehemently and took a deep breath to calm down. "But none of that matters more to me than her forgiveness. I won't ask you to help me, but…"

"It's alright man," Trevor said, giving Rafe's shoulder a comforting squeeze. "I have no idea if my opinion matters, but I'll try."

"We're getting close now, I can sense her."

"So can I," Trevor said. "It's like an itch. Thoughts of her keep appearing in my head with insane clarity."

"How—?" Rafe began, when it dawned on him the thing he should have realized days ago. He grabbed Trevor by the arm and spun him around. Rafe blinked when Trevor's headlamp blinded him for a second, reached up and ripped the offending object from the man's head. "Did she mark you?"

"What? No! I—At least I don't think so. I'd remember that, wouldn't I? All I remember is..." Trevor paused, his voice growing faint, "All I remember is her last kiss before I fell asleep. It seemed so sweet." He rubbed a thumb idly behind one ear, his eyes unfocused and sentimental.

Rafe grabbed the headlamp from the floor and clutched Trevor by the neck, aiming the light at the spot he'd just rubbed. There, on the pale skin just beneath Trevor's hairline was the tiny shape of a red dragon. It wasn't a medallion like the others typically were, but a simple red squiggle that matched the dragon from Rowan's necklace—the necklace that Rafe had left resting reverently atop the neatly folded pile of Rowan's things in his bedroom, in the hopes of her return.

"Sweet Mother, she's already done it. She marked you." His voice cracked on the word "marked" and he struggled a moment to tamp down the rising emotions. Too many questions came to mind. Why would she mark him and not take him with her? Was it confirmation that she no longer loved Rafe like he feared? He wouldn't blame her for that. And of course, would she accept him once he found her?

"Hey, man. We'll figure this out once we find her, alright?" Trevor reached a hand out, clasping Rafe by the back of the neck and squeezing gently.

"If she doesn't love me, I'll relinquish you to her and go my own way."

"Well, if she's as generous as she seemed when I met her, I have a feeling she's got love to go around."

"You don't understand, I betrayed her. She said she loved me, but I lied to her."

"You told me when we were flying that she didn't even know what she was when you met her. That's got to be a hard situation to deal with for anyone. So she ran. Every now and then I just leave when I need to clear my head. But the last thing I heard her say was that she was going home. And I admit, I wanted to follow her right away, but something told me she needed her space for a little while. I decided I'd give it to her, then I'd go find her. Somehow I'd find her. Now we've got that chance, together. So what the fuck are you waiting for? If you love her, give her the chance to make her choice."

Rafe took a deep breath and gripped Trevor's shoulder in solidarity. He handed the human back his light and the pair moved on.

THEY TRAVELED for several more hours. Soon it became apparent that Trevor didn't have the energy to continue any farther, away from the bolstering influence of Roka's breath. Rafe relented and they stopped to make camp together. He admired the man's endurance and efficiency. Trevor simply stopped, quickly scarfed down a foil-wrapped energy bar, chugged some water, then lay down and was asleep almost instantly after telling Rafe to wake him in half an hour.

While he waited, Rafe sent his breath ahead. The invisible shadow skimmed down the corridor, following the tendrils of energy. His shadow flowed along the undulating shapes of the dragons carved into the walls until the floor of the corridor dropped away from beneath and he entered a vast chamber.

Rafe paused with his shadow hovering just beyond the ledge. The entire place was huge enough for several dragons to fly across, wing-tip to wing-tip, but the size of it wasn't what made him stop. The temple on the other side of the cavern loomed, seemingly perched on a ledge of crumbling rock the entire long breadth of the cavern. It resembled a traditional Shinto-style temple, but Rafe knew it had to be constructed of dragon stone to have survived this place for more than a thousand years. Beneath him, between the ledge on which he stood and the temple where he was certain Rowan rested, was a treacherous expanse of black rock split with cracks that glowed with molten fire even from his elevation. It resembled the cracked mosaic that he was afraid his relationship with Rowan had become. Soon enough, his love for her might devour his soul entirely, leaving him nothing but a broken mess.

He'd have gone farther, but it was time to wake Trevor and tackle the next leg of their trip as quickly as possible. It had only taken his breath a matter of minutes to reach the chamber, but on foot it would still take them a few more hours.

The human woke as though he'd merely been resting his eyes, though Rafe knew he'd been sleeping soundly from the shift in his energy. Trevor stood, shouldered his pack and donned his headlamp before heading wordlessly down the corridor. They didn't speak until they finally reached the opening Rafe had found earlier.

"Holy fuck," Trevor said, gazing down at the semi-molten landscape that rested between them and the eerily illuminated temple on the other side.

The massive structure was dark except for the glimmer of a few small lava flows that trickled down the edges of the rocks below and around it. There was a single narrow, crumbling path that led down from their ledge into what probably appeared to be certain death to the human, but Trevor set down his pack and began rummaging through it anyway, pulling out coils of densely woven ropes and small, metal latches. After a moment of frantic scrambling and tying and cursing, he finally let the entire tangled mess fall at his feet.

"Fuck! This is never going to work!" Trevor stared at

Rafe, his face tight with despair. He glanced down beneath, then to the walls of the cave, gesturing. "What the fuck do we do? We can't climb around, and we can't simply *walk in.* There's no fucking way to avoid that bullshit down there. And in case you haven't noticed, I'm about to roast right here as it is."

"We're not walking," Rafe said, letting his conjured clothing fade away. "We're flying."

CHAPTER EIGHT

*R*afe flew them across the cavern, aiming at the curled eaves of the roof that reflected the glow of the lava beneath. He'd instructed Trevor to don every item of clothing he had and cover his face, too. He'd also cloaked the human in a cloud of shadowy breath, hoping that would prevent some of the heat reaching him. His breath might help, but had nowhere near the protective qualities that Roka's breath had. Roka would be needed to protect the others if they all agreed to follow.

As he expected, the top tier of the temple had a wide balcony that allowed him access to a chimney-like opening. The shaft itself could have accommodated a larger dragon than he, and it was comfortable enough to descend. The air was comfortably cool at the bottom of the shaft and Trevor swiftly dismounted and yanked off most of his clothing, emerging panting and sweating and taking several thirsty swallows of water.

"No stopping now, brother," he said with a grin.

"I meant what I said before," Rafe said solemnly. "What-ever she decides, I will honor."

"I'm with you, man. I'd be her slave if she asked me to, and gladly."

Rowan's essence grew even stronger the closer they got, to the point that Rafe grew hard with the vivid memories of making love to her. He hadn't bothered conjuring clothing for himself and was oddly touched when Trevor gradually began to shed the rest of his clothes as they traveled the polished jade corridors to reach her.

The place was even decorated on the interior like a Shinto temple, with sliding screens and glowing lanterns hanging at intervals or perched on pedestals. Had this been where Rafe's father's brood had hibernated? He couldn't imagine the constitution required of the humans who had come to awaken that generation if they'd been forced to travel here. But some humans had particularly strong constitutions, as evidenced by the man at his side. Rafe was comforted by that, at least as long as they could convince the Council that she remain free.

Finally they reached a chamber at the very end of a long hallway lined with sliding panels covered in elaborate paintings. Unlike the other rooms along the side, this room had a hinged door built from a single huge slab of green jade, on which was carved a beautiful dragon. A dragon who Rafe recognized.

"It is her," he said with reverence, barely risking a brush of a finger along the edge of a single scale.

"Who?" Trevor asked. "Do you know her?"

"Bren, the queen of my father's brood. This was where she slept for five hundred years."

"Well, what are you waiting for? Fucking open it!"

Rafe pushed, but the door wouldn't budge. "Fuck. If the magic senses her in there asleep, it might have locked it."

"Let me guess, there's no key," Trevor said.

"The way the ritual works, once we're sealed inside the

temple, only a human can open the doors of all but one of the rooms. Only the Queen's fated human mate can open her door. I just hope this doesn't mean the magic has put *her* to sleep, too."

Trevor wasted no time slipping in front of Rafe and placing his hands against the door. He'd barely brushed the surface with his palms when it swung inward on silent hinges. The two men tumbled in, grabbing at each other for support. Once inside they stopped cold.

"She's only asleep," Rafe said with relief.

"Jesus Christ, she's beautiful. I never got to see her look like…like a dragon." Trevor released Rafe and walked into the room to the huge bed Rowan slept on, curled into herself upon the brocade coverlet like some giant, red cat.

"Rowan," Rafe said out loud after repeating it in his mind ever since he'd sensed he was close enough. "She's too depleted of energy. It's exhausted her. We need to give her ours, and soon. If she awakens this depleted, she'll be hungry and too delirious to know how to ask for help."

"Just tell me what to do. I'm ready."

CHAPTER NINE

The rough cadence of the voices tickled at her memory. There were two.

Rafe. Lover. Mate. Betrayer.

The new one was here, too. His mark blazed in her mind, his desperation and desire warring with each other. *Live, please live,* she could hear in her mind. Not in words, but in his need. Rowan's heart softened at his presence. He was worthy. He could live.

If only she could find the energy to open her eyes. Give the Betrayer his due, take the other for her mate. Live here in this temple and hold dominion over the lands outside.

Too tired now to move. When she awoke she would fly. The countryside would bow to her. Soon.

"Rowan."

She struggled to bring her mind back to consciousness. The world was a dark, amorphous place. She floated on a whirling vortex that gradually sucked her in. The voice became her anchor, but she couldn't even find the energy to respond.

Light touches spread over her body. Her breasts tingled

beneath one pair of hands. Another pair slipped down her body, caressed her thighs.

The shape of her felt wrong, though. The hands caressed horns atop her head, not breasts, but the sensation was the same.

A hand at her thigh urged her to move. She needed the touch, so she shifted and was rewarded by a slight caress along her inner thigh, but it paused just at the part where she needed contact the most.

Without thinking she expelled a breath. It was all she had power for, so she let it loose, and commanded it to seek out her companions, to urge them to her will. The red magic wormed deeper into one man's head, teasing at his desires, at his need like a whisper of her words.

Rafe. She recognized him instantly by his thoughts. All regret and desire, combined with a need to submit to her beyond all other things. The revelation invigorated her slightly, but not enough to open her eyes. She still could possess him with her breath, even as weak as she was. And possession was what she was best at.

"You are mine. Your duty is to please me."

A combination of sensations began around her horns and between her thighs at the same time. She moved her hips and her head, encouraging more.

The hot sweep of a tongue slid between her thighs. Hands stroked her horns, the sensations exquisite, especially when the hands reached her tips in delicate caresses.

Trevor. She could smell his familiar scent close to her. She'd never have forgotten him, but how was he here? She struggled harder to rise out of the dark well of semi-consciousness, to make her large body respond to him. All she could move was her tongue, so she lashed it out for a taste. Trevor's naked skin responded, the flavor of him shifting from apprehension to outright arousal. His voice whispered close.

"We're here, baby. Let us wake you up."

Us? Who was us?

"It's me and Rafe. I know you're probably pissed at him, but I couldn't have gotten here without him. Give him another chance, alright?"

Was Rafe the steady teasing lick between her thighs? Yes, it was a dragon's tongue.

The memory of that particular dragon's cock inside her at full size shifted her into yet a more wakeful state. She nudged at Trevor, whispering with a weak voice, "Hold my horns."

At the same time she lifted one thigh to the dragon at her other end, tightening her grip on the red worm of her breath in his mind. *Fuck me.*

Trevor's lovely ass fit perfectly upon her nose. It was a strange sensation, but being a giant was a liberating feeling. And she'd already admired his ass and had ideas about things she'd like to do to it. He obediently gripped her horns, stroking them enough to send a thrum of pleasure through her body to her core, making her pussy even slicker for the thick cock that pressed ever deeper.

Rafe.

She wasn't ready to confront those feelings. She needed their Nirvana first. She'd deal with feelings after.

Trevor's legs spread and he found purchase with his heels on the edges of her lower lip. Her tongue snaked out, teasing along his thighs and tasting every inch of skin between. She was semi-blind, still. Her world was still fuzzy if she opened her eyes, but she was acutely attuned to the feel of the cock in her pussy and the human draped across her head.

Rafe. That's who was fucking her now. She remembered the feel of him from before, and his cock was just as glorious. She tightened the pull on his consciousness now, still too raw to confront him, but in dire need of what he had to offer otherwise.

Trevor, on the other hand…she darted her long tongue out, coiling it gently around his balls. He gasped and twitched his hips. His entire body was surrounded by a giant bubble of energy, just waiting for her to inflate and pop. He'd been building it up for awhile, it seemed.

She went slower the second time, slipping her tongue out and caressing the twin tips of it between his ass cheeks, behind his balls, then coiling her tongue around the base of his cock.

"I love you," he breathed. "Do whatever you want to me."

The hunger screamed in her at his surrender. The cock on the other side of her slipped out and she instinctively swept her tail around and grabbed Rafe, pulling him back into her, her pussy clenching tightly around his thick, filling presence. She missed that so much, but she needed something more from him than that carnal fulfillment. She needed his energy and wouldn't let him go until he gave it to her.

Trevor squirmed and panted at the grip she kept on his cock with her tongue. She pumped him relentlessly, too eager to have his Nirvana, too. He gave in abruptly, writhing and crying out. His Nirvana spilled into her emptiness, as filling as if he'd just plunged into her for the first time. She tasted the salt of his spend on his belly before he collapsed in a heap beside her.

The clarity Trevor's energy brought made the feel of Rafe's cock all too apparent.

Rafe. He was in full dragon, and so was she. The beautiful moment they'd had before was too much to repeat now. She couldn't let him touch that part of her again. Not yet.

She shifted and with a twitch of her control of the breath that still snaked through his mind, she made him shift, too.

With a twist of her hips, she spun them both so that she was astride him.

His eyes glowed violet and gleamed with lust. She withdrew the tendrils of red smoke from his mind and rose up, sliding her tight pussy along his cock and settled back down just as slowly.

Rafe. Lover. Mate. Mine.

"I missed you so much," she said.

"I missed you, too."

"You came for me. That's something. And you brought Trevor. That's something else." She glanced at Trevor who was outside Rafe's field of vision. Her thoughts grew tender when she laid eyes on the man.

"He helped me find you," Rafe said. "He's a worthy mate."

She was poised at the end of his cock and slammed down hard, making him gasp. "You *don't* fucking tell me who's worthy of me. I get to decide that. You get to decide whether you'll say yes or no to me. At least if you want my mark. I am Bren's daughter, yes? You aren't quite worthy yet."

"Yes."

"Good," she said.

Her pussy felt like a live wire sending out jolts with every down-stroke, but she worked him so slowly that he started to look like she was torturing him. The energy was potent enough in this place that she couldn't tell the difference anymore between what already lingered here and what swirled around them from their own activities. And it didn't matter one iota to her, either.

All she wanted was to wrap her power around him, dig it into him until there could be no denying who was superior. To watch the olive-skinned, dark-haired god beneath her submit to her will. To see his eyes roll back in his head and his hands clutch at the bed, his head tilted back. Sweet Mother did she love that. She didn't care if she never came.

She'd hold back just to watch him try for eternity. If that was the vision she was left with, she would accept it.

"I think you're worked up enough to fill me up now," she said. The words seemed to confuse him as much as her shift in position.

She pressed her lips to his and he gasped. She slid her breasts against his chest and rocked her wet pussy against his hips, sucking him in deeper with every thrust.

He met each of her thrusts with equal enthusiasm. For some reason he still held back, so she fucked him even harder, demanding he come with the pull of every muscle.

He came hard, filling her up in every way. His hot seed shot deep inside her and the well of magic he had pooled in him flowed directly into her.

Rowan collapsed to the side, panting before shakily reaching for Trevor. He slid across the bed toward her and wrapped his arm around her, burying his face in her neck.

Rowan remained lying where she was, dazed and drunk. As familiar as Rafe's Nirvana was, it was still a shock to feel that much power surge into her all at once.

When she recovered a moment later, she glanced at Rafe, only to see him hanging his head in apparent defeat.

"You, too," she said, reaching for him.

Rafe jerked his head up at the sound of her voice. He moved to her side, tentatively sliding an arm around her waist alongside Trevor's.

"I forgot to tell you something before you left," he said softly once she'd moved to face him and rested one thigh across his hip.

"I know," she said. "You don't have to say it if it's hard for you."

"It isn't. I love you. Since the moment I met you, I've never wanted another woman. I should have told you the first night we were together."

Rowan frowned, and held his gaze. Rafe's brow drew together, the shame apparent in response to her own pissed expression.

"You should have told me."

She pushed him onto his back and moved astride him, threaded the fingers of both hands into his thick hair and yanked his head back. So many things clamored in her mind to say just then, but his wide-eyes and utter submission disarmed her. He knew precisely what he'd done and would gladly accept every ounce of punishment she chose to give him.

Suddenly the well of emotion she'd only let loose with Darius and Zak rose again. She tamped it down with a vengeance, determined to follow through with Rafe's absolution first. The act of doing so would liberate her as much as him.

"If there's anything I learned during all this it's to *never* give up what I know belongs to me. You are mine. Trevor is, too—I can feel him through his mark."

"No..." Rafe answered in a low, calculated tone. "I'm only halfway there yet. You haven't marked me."

"Roll over," she said with a nod. She slid off him and waited.

Rafe turned and lay placid while she considered how to proceed. This couldn't be the same as the tiny blessing she'd given Trevor already. But at the same time she didn't want to draw out her anger at Rafe any longer than necessary. *Give it to him and be done with it, move on.*

Her words accompanied her talon slicing the pattern into his back, her measured tone a far cry from the turmoil in her belly. She hated the idea of causing him pain, but he bore it with barely a twitch.

"You'll remember how this feels, because this is how I felt when you turned your back on me." She moved as quickly as she could, but still deliberate enough that she could be sure Rafe felt every inch of the cuts she made into his skin. Trevor hissed in sympathy beside her, but thankfully remained otherwise silent.

Finally she stopped and let out an extended exhalation of breath. Rafe let his own held breath release, too, but Rowan wasn't finished yet.

Summoning her magic, she focused it on the pattern she'd etched into his back. The flames shot out with surgical precision, landing like an amber snake coiling around the bright red circle, an intricate medallion of blood that graced Rafe's entire back.

As the magic took hold and the mark's bond began to tie them together, she could feel the prickle of it in her own skin, the pain growing with each inch of flickering fire as it branded him *hers*.

He begged for mercy and forgiveness over and over, then broke down into harsh sobs that wrenched her heart. When the flames finally subsided she expelled the healing breath. The luminescent red smoke seeped into his skin and he relaxed. Finally she lay across his healed back, pressing her own weight on him, her breasts adding soft pressure to the middle of his back. She let her lips brush against his shoulder.

"You didn't have to feel that if you didn't want to. I know that much. I've clawed you just as badly before. Why?"

"I've been in pain since you left, and it's been my own doing. I couldn't let you forgive me without making it hurt."

"Who says I forgive you?" A hint of humor tinged her words and prompted Rafe to turn over. Rowan shifted again, resuming her position astride him. The truth was she had forgiven him the moment she'd felt his power infusing her, but there was no sense making it easy for him. She raised an eyebrow, expectant.

"Name your price," he said.

She turned to Trevor and beckoned.

Trevor sat up straighter, ready to answer.

Rowan bent and kissed Rafe, teasing her tongue against his in tiny, swirling coils that she knew he loved. The act of being marked had already made him painfully hard and she wasted no time rising up and engulfing him again in her slick warmth. She didn't move for a moment, enjoying the thick fullness of him pulsing inside her. Instead, she extended one long, graceful arm to her other mate and Trevor slipped closer. He wrapped an arm around her waist and kissed her, his mouth sweet and soft against her own.

Trevor lowered his mouth to her breast and Rafe's eyes flicked lower, staring in wonder for a second until darting back up to meet Rowan's gaze. She had one more piece of punishment to dole out to him, and wondered how he'd take it.

"I want Trevor to get a full view of your mark whenever we fuck."

Trevor's head shot up in surprise at the sound of his name, but Rafe didn't hesitate to flip her over, baring his back to the other man.

"As you wish." Rafe pushed her hands above her head and smiled down as he pumped his cock into her with one slow stroke.

Trevor didn't move for a second until Rafe looked over his shoulder. "I don't think I need to explain this to you, brother."

"Ah...No." Trevor said. He sat back on his haunches and laughed. "No, man, I got the picture more than a week ago what she likes. I'm just happy to get in on the action finally. Especially since it means I get a little payback." Trevor grinned. "I'll be gentle, I promise."

Rafe laughed and bent closer to Rowan, his face hovering

over hers, eyes feverish. His lids shut tightly and a pleased smile flickered across his face when Trevor moved behind and dipped his head too low for Rowan to see. Trevor appeared again a moment later.

"Are you ready?" he asked, his arm moving in a rhythmic motion, but his hand obscured. Rowan could see both their faces clearly. Trevor's expression was intent and almost business-like, Rafe's mouth open and panting from pleasure.

"Yes," Rafe said, holding Rowan's gaze.

Both men's breathing sped up when Rafe's cock pressed deeper into her in response to the shove against his hips from behind. Rowan lifted her legs to wrap around Rafe's torso, her own body responding to a mind-altering degree, every movement of Rafe's hips making her pussy clench and quiver. She wanted more.

Trevor's hands slid down her thighs and found the place where she and Rafe were joined, caressed them both with his fingertips. The slight touch made her moan in ecstasy.

"God, I would do anything for you. Both of you," Trevor murmured.

"Fuck me harder," Rafe groaned and they moved as a unit, hips rocking in steady rhythm.

Rowan closed her eyes and let herself feel everything. The steady thrust of Rafe, so long missed. His cock's familiar bump against the most sensitive parts of her felt like coming home. When she delved deeper into their union, she sensed the hints of every emotion that passed through both men's hearts, tangible now through her links to them. Their movements soon reached a crescendo and the emotions spilled from them with their Nirvana, flooding her with the comfort of their unspoken devotion.

As she came, Rowan cried their names in one long, smoky breath that settled over them, carrying with it her own promise of forgiveness and love to them both.

Rowan lay quietly between them afterward, not quite sated but almost as close as she'd been a week earlier. Their arousal had siphoned a measure of the lingering magic from the room, that magic that had lured her to this place. Her mother's place.

"Did you know her?" Rowan asked softly.

Rafe leaned up on one elbow and smiled down at her. "Yes. She was our queen once. I'm not surprised it was she who gave birth to a creature as amazing as you."

"Did you know my father, too?"

Rafe frowned and shook his head. "I doubt it. But your brother may know who he was. You're a purebred so it won't be the same father he had."

Rowan's eyes widened and she sat up abruptly. "I have a brother? Who is he? Tell me everything!"

Rafe opened his mouth to speak when a commotion of footsteps and chattering voices echoed down the corridor outside the chamber. Someone cried out excitedly and the footsteps coming toward them sped to a dead run and a deep voice yelled Rowan's name.

"I think you're about to meet him, love. I'll let him tell you the rest."

BREATH OF FATE

CHAPTER ONE

Issa dreamed of flying into an eclipse. The chill of darkness seeped through her scales as the moon covered the sun. The coolness of it soothed her aching need, but only briefly. Soon enough the ache returned as a searing burn. She couldn't backtrack fast enough, though she tried to turn and flee. The dark of the moon kept sucking her energy dry, bit by bit, leaving her longing for the sun to come again. She relented, giving into it. Wind rushed past her folded wings as she plummeted. Gravity took its course. At least she was cool, giving up. The moon could have her as long as she could stop the struggle.

"Issa!"

The voice jolted her into semi-consciousness.

"Issa, wake up!"

"Kris?"

"Yes, love. Wake up, you're okay."

She tried to open her eyes. The world swam in her vision. Distorted shapes merged into his pretty face, his beautiful multi-colored eyes framed by creased brows. Sweet Mother, she loved him.

The world swooped and turned and she clenched her eyes shut again. "I can't. It's too much for me to even move right now."

"I'll give you anything. What do you want?"

What did she want? To not be a ridiculous mess over this pregnancy? To not be forced to beg her mate to replenish her energy every few hours? She loved him for being so willing. But she felt like a needy infant crying for the breast most days. She knew she was close to the end. Only days from her imminent labor, in fact. The twins inside her had told her as much. They weren't particularly eloquent, but they were insistent, and hungry.

"They like your magic more. You know this."

Kris gave her a sly smile. "Then let's give them that."

With that, he kissed her, his lips giving her the same sweet soft pull they always had. She'd always think of him as innocent and inexperienced, and she his first true exploration of love. But when he released her mouth and met her eyes, she knew there was so much more. The feverish glow in his gaze set her alight. Then heat grew exponentially in her core when he bent his head to her breast.

Every part of her was already intensely sensitive. More than she'd ever been in her life. It only took a flick of his tongue over her nipple and she writhed in ecstasy. The barest touch of his hand inside her thigh had her surging against him for more. His fingers moved deeper and she nearly came just from the contact.

"We can give them both of us," he murmured.

"Yes. Let me feel you inside me."

He moved behind her, shifted her thigh up to give himself access. Velvet heat pressed against her too-sensitive flesh, his tip sliding back and forth between her folds.

"Kris, don't tease me, please. I need you to fuck me. Now!"

Kris let out a slew of rough curses that didn't make sense to her, finally ending with, "I love you."

The glorious stretch of his thick cock inside her instantly sent her to climax. She yelled out and clawed at the arms wrapped around her. She rode the wave of pleasure, enjoying each subsequent stroke of him into her hungry depths.

The babies pressed against her womb as if they were dancing. The cock inside her kept moving, and every stroke felt better than the last.

His arms clasped tight around her, his face buried against her neck. "I love you," he murmured again while he plunged ever deeper to the point she lost herself again. All she could feel was the deep, lovely push of his beautiful cock inside her, thrusting harder and harder until it swelled and pulsed with his climax.

They'd already made these babies together. Her only regret was that they couldn't make more right now. But they had time to add to their brood after these were born.

He palmed her thigh and pulled it higher, slipping out of her and moving lower. The sensation between her thighs changed, becoming something wholly more erotic. Sweet Mother, she loved it when he did that. She came again, with his tongue sunk into her.

The babies finally settled.

"Thank you," she said, pushing herself back against her pillows.

Kris looked offended. "I would be a poor mate if I didn't see to your needs."

"Baby, you're a terrible liar."

He broke down. "I hate seeing you suffer. I would give everything to help them but just don't know what more to give."

Issa sighed and pulled herself back up against her pillows. "They can't help, can they?"

Anguish filled Kris's eyes for a split second and he dipped his head, kissing her shoulder to disguise his emotions. Issa was well aware that he couldn't share the things the Council told him. Sometimes there were details he could share and she just had to read between the lines when he did. They'd both become adept at subtlety, even when they shared their silent thoughts.

"They can't share their magic directly." It was the first thing he'd said that hinted at more.

"They're letting you tell me this?"

"They want to do more. They just can't. These twins you carry mean more to them than anything. I can feel it every time I meet with them. They're afraid. I don't know what they have to fear, but their hands are tied to do anything about it."

"But if we had the others here, they could help. Even human energy, if I had enough of it, would be better than sapping your energy every day. Has the Council given any hint why they wish this pregnancy kept secret?"

"No, but I believe it has something to do with two Catalysts being conceived so early in a generation. I was the last child conceived in our generation, only a few decades before your hibernation was over. My mother was at her fullest power when I was born, and sacrificed her remaining life energy to me with her last breath. These twins signal too much change for our race; I believe the Council is afraid knowledge of their existence might be dangerous."

Issa shifted awkwardly onto her side and pressed her palm against Kris's broad, tattooed chest. She traced the glimmering outline of the dragon tattoo that represented the transfer of his mother's power to him in his infancy. The dragon's scales illuminated in multicolored light under her touch. She couldn't imagine having to make the kind of sacrifice his mother had—to give her life simply because their laws required it. Issa would give anything to be able to see her children grow and thrive

The twins inside her shifted in languid recognition of the tiny surge of power that transferred into her from her mate. Kris would give his life for her and their children, of that she had no doubt. He had nearly done so during the worst moments of her pregnancy, but they'd come to an agreement that he hold back. Their race needed him. They would find other ways to sustain their offspring until they were born. The small gifts were just Kris's reminder to her that he was willing, if necessary, to give all of his power to her and their children. Nearly every time they touched, she felt the small surges, even when he believed she was sleeping. He wasn't like the others... he could give without the buildup and release. His touch was sacred for that reason. He could take just as easily, if he chose, as long as she was willing and had energy to give—which had been the case until the pregnancy had taken its toll and the twins absorbed every spare ounce of energy she had. Still, they preferred Kris's over hers and always settled easier when he gave.

Giving to her had been Kris's sole purpose for so long. Issa objected, then forbade him from doing it the first night he collapsed in their bed and began to shift while unconscious. She had panicked, unable to shift herself to meet his dragon and sate him back into his human shape. The babies wouldn't withstand a shift if she tried it. She'd called for the Unbound, but only Zak had come. Frantic, Issa asked where Darius was, but Zak only gave her a dark look. "I'm here. I can help."

It had been quick enough, with Kris as delirious as he was. Zak's human legs and Kris's scaled ones twined together, the pair embracing and writhing in ecstasy. Kris's cock dwarfed Zak's, even in that in-between state. Both glorious columns of hot flesh pressed together, Zak's hand stroking until they both shot pearly liquid on their bellies while Issa watched. Zak's Nirvana flowed into Issa's half-shifted mate and Kris subsided back into his human shape.

Issa felt both exhausted and aroused after Zak gave her a quick kiss and left them alone again. Kris apologized and objected when she climbed atop him, taking his cock into her with a single slow stroke. It didn't take much of her own power to restrain him and fuck him, cursing him for his stupidity the entire time until he took what little she had to give as well.

"Don't ever do that again. I need you. We all need you."

"The babies need me," he said. "There are no human monks at the Monastery free to offer. If only I'd had time to find more human mates to mark and bring to you to see you and the babies through. Darius said my mother practically had her own harem of mates to help her through by the time I was born."

"They were unexpected, but I don't regret this pregnancy. If we fail to make the Council see reason, all our children will have their futures put on hold for five hundred years. We don't want that for them. The babies need you more as their advocate now, than as a source of energy. We'll find another way."

That had been months ago and they had yet to find another way. The Unbound would give what they could to Kris, but it was never enough and the babies always hungrily absorbed his power. Kris's face was drawn and haggard, his skin too pale, his normally healthy prismatic aura woefully weak after seeing to her needs. A light rap sounded outside their door as she was brushing his hair off his sweaty forehead. Issa called out for the visitor to enter.

"Darius. Welcome," she said to the tan-faced dragon who stood in the doorway. The stark look of worry on his face was no different than the others. For a moment she wished for a happy look from someone—anyone.

Kris tensed beside her. Without opening his eyes he said, "Did you finally come to make your own offering for our childrens' sake? Or is it still too great a burden for you?"

Darius's expression pinched from the sting of the words and he cast his eyes to the floor. His shoulders rose and fell with a deep breath as though he were bracing himself for an even greater confrontation. He stepped into the room and closed the heavy wooden door gently behind him.

The babies shifted inside her, somehow sensing the tension in their father's touch where his hand rested on her swollen belly. Issa placed her hand over his and squeezed, holding tight while Darius approached their bed.

"No, it would be no burden to me, if I could bring myself to cross a line I believe is sacred."

The intensity in Darius's gaze made Issa sit up a little straighter. Kris opened his eyes, his expression wary, and watched the man approach.

"What line?"

"That of family. Words are of little comfort, I am aware, but I have merely come to offer a blessing for my grand-children."

Kris surged up from the bed. "What do you mean?" He turned and looked at Issa, brow creased in confusion, his eyes flashing with prismatic energy.

Issa shook her head, understanding dawning with the memories of Darius's affection toward Kris and his stories of Kris's mother, always told with a kind of sweet nostalgia. "He means you are his son. My father was a Guardian—you know this. But Darius, how? Unbound aren't permitted to breed."

The confusion of emotion that washed from Kris caused her heart to clench in sympathy.

"You were with me for my entire life and never told me this? You told me my parents both died! You talked about my father like he was someone else entirely. Was it all a lie, what you told me?"

Darius took a tentative step closer, his hands palm out at his sides. "I never lied to you. I am that Red with no status, so I may as well have been dead to you. It would not have served you to know exactly how little status I had. The fact of our link was merely a matter of convenience to the Council. Your mother was very special to me, and my bloodline was pure enough for the Council to release my shackles just long enough to breed with her. She chose to end her life shortly after you were born, to give you her power so you could fulfill the ritual."

"Why are you telling me this now?" Kris asked. His voice was tense with anger, the back of his neck erupting into shimmering scales. Issa reached up to stroke him, relieved when her touch seemed to calm him.

"Because your lives and my grandchildren's lives depend on you understanding. You already know the Council is aware of their nature. It is as clear to me as your nature was when your mother was pregnant with you. They are twin Catalysts and no Catalyst has yet been born without a parent giving their life force to ensure they survive their birth. Your mother gave the last of her power to give you your mark. I would have given mine to you as well, but the Council shackled me again before I could."

"We would gladly die for them," Kris said. He turned to Issa again, his jaw clenched.

"And leave them at the mercy of the Council?" Darius asked. He shook his head. "No. You and Issa are far too important. There is another way, but we need the rest of the Court and the Verdanith for it to work. We must convince the Council to change Dragon Law before the babies are born. Please try to hold on until the assembly."

"Do they want us dead?" Issa asked. "Is that why they refuse to help?"

The two men turned to look at her in unison and Issa was suddenly struck by similarities she had never noticed before. While Darius was rougher of feature, and Kris had lovely smooth lines to his face, the pair shared the same broad shoulders and solid, confident bearing. Their eyes both blazed with the same intensity and they shared a slight crease between brows that indicated their worry, though Darius's lines were more pronounced due to his age.

"It would solve some problems for them if that were to happen. Kris is more than aware of their motivations. Aren't you?"

Kris's shoulders sagged. "They consider that an acceptable risk, but that doesn't mean they're refusing help. They simply can't focus their magic into the desired potency without the Verdanith. And even once it's here, it will take time for the assembly. Time I'm not sure Issa has."

Darius stepped toward Kris and placed his large hands on his son's shoulders. "We will find a way."

"How?" Kris asked, the desperation clear in his voice. "The babies are at the point where they need an almost constant flow of energy to sustain them. The Unbound don't provide me nearly enough of a supply to sustain both myself and the babies, even if they visited non-stop for the remainder of the pregnancy. I won't leave Issa to find a human village to restore my own power. I'm no Red, it would take me far too long."

"Then we wait," Issa said. "And hope the others arrive soon."

He shook his head and stepped back toward the bed to kiss her. Both his large, gentle hands cupped her face and he gazed into her eyes, his own blazing with fierce determination. "No, I won't sit idle. There must be something they can do."

Kris left her with a glowing sensation from the burst of energy he sent through his palms. She settled back against her pillows with a sigh, rubbing both hands over her covered belly.

"We'll get through this, little ones," she murmured. "Your father will take care of us."

CHAPTER TWO

he novelty of meetings with the Council had long since worn off. Kris now trudged wearily beside Darius up the path to the peak and into the center of the pavilion at its summit, where he regularly communed with the six immortal dragons who had overseen the progress of their race from the beginning of their existence. The slight benefit of the visits was in the trickle of power that infused him in their presence. Unfortunately without the focus of an aroused partner it was too difficult to absorb enough power to sustain him for very long.

Outside the Monastery, only Kris's sister, Racha and the Council knew of Issa's pregnancy and had already given what little help they were capable of. The short trek up the mountain to the meeting place seemed unbearably steep this time, as weighed down as Kris was with the certainty that the Council would have no new alternatives to his dilemma. Yet he had to ask.

The Council itself resided half in this world, half in the ether where their magical aspects existed. They were as much a part of the flow of magic through the world as their beautiful, massive bodies were a part of the corporeal world. The six immortal dragons were slaves to their circumstances, tied to each other via bonds even closer than the bond between mates. Kris didn't feel any more charitable toward them, however, after gaining a sense of the steps they were willing to take to get what they wanted. He just wished he knew what really motivated them.

When he and Darius took their spots in the center of the Pavilion, Kris closed his eyes and calmed himself. Once centered, he sent out the mental call to the Council. The communication always felt like tugging on a collection of threads bound to his core, each one with a distinctly different energy.

The six answered simultaneously, their calls converging in his mind with a vibration of the threads that resulted in a white heat low in his belly. This answering pull was one of the more pleasant parts of communing with them, the way it aroused and briefly invigorated him. He rarely bothered to dress for the meetings, but had conjured a short sarong around his waist for this visit, suddenly irrationally modest now that he was aware of his true relationship to Darius.

Thunder rumbled through the air around the pavilion, signaling their arrival. Kris had the impression the six dragons were flying from somewhere far away, yet they always simply appeared out of thin air between the six columns of the pavilion. They hovered with wings beating in the air, their variety of colored bodies casting glimmering shadows of matching colors on the ground around him. The shadows drew closer and where they met in the center, a white light shone on Kris and Darius like a spotlight where they knelt.

Darius let out a sigh that mirrored the sensation Kris felt deep in his belly, all the way down to his cock. Simply being in their presence was often as satisfying as making love to

Issa, though by the end of his meetings the euphoria rarely lingered. He hoped this meeting would prove to be more productive.

"Greetings, Catalyst. Unbound." The large green female was the first to speak when the six dragons settled onto the ground around the pavilion and walked forward to surround them.

"Numa," Kris said, nodding his head toward the Green and glancing around at the others.

"What prompted this summons?" The black one, Ked, said in a deep, throaty tone.

"The lives of my children are in greater peril even now. They won't survive much longer without aid."

"They will survive if you and their mother give enough of yourselves. Are you giving enough?" The white dragon, Aodh, spoke. Kris glanced at him but immediately away from the blinding brightness of his scales.

"We have given all we can without jeopardizing our own lives. We will not leave them orphans."

"There is only one way we can help." Belah, the blue dragon answered in her delicate, gentle tone. "It is out of our control otherwise. We need the Verdanith assembled and reactivated to weave our magic together for to them to absorb. Be assured we value yours and Issa's lives as much as the children."

Kris looked beseechingly at Gavra and Aurum, the red and the gold. "But you can give to me in the traditional manner, can't you? Surely one dose of Nirvana from one as powerful as you..."

Gavra's eyes flashed red, his deep voice cutting in. "We cannot couple with you, Catalyst, as enticing a prospect as it is." He let out a low, rumbling hum that signaled his appreciation. Aurum hummed back in agreement, her voice harmonizing with Gavra's in a way that vibrated down to the base of Kris's spine and made his already uncomfortable erection throb even harder. The sensation was compounded by the bright look the golden dragon gave him, as though she'd gladly couple with him, if it would do them any good.

"Can't or won't?" Kris said. "You forget I know where we came from. It's been hundreds of thousands of years since the Mother created the six of you, and you found your first mates among the humans." He looked pointedly at Gavra. "It's time the rest of the Brood knew as well. You fathered our oldest ancestor more than a hundred generations ago. I'm not asking to mate with any of you. Only to help sustain my mate and children until the twins are safely born. Our race owes our existence to you already. Isn't that enough?"

"They are right," Numa said, her green eyes glowing. "The Mother was the first Prismatic, and her power only resurfaces once in each generation. As a Prismatic dragon, your power is the embodiment of the Mother in this world. The essence of her that you carry prevents you from absorbing the pure energy the six of us possess. It would be like shining a light at a mirror if we tried. The Verdanith is the only way we can effectively focus the appropriate combination of power to sustain you or any other dragon. Until it is assembled there is nothing we can do."

Kris sensed a murmur of dissent. "Are you hiding something? Please tell me if there is any other way. I refuse to accept that we are out of options entirely."

Numa settled her disconcerting gaze back on him. "There may be one other option. There are humans we call 'Udara' who possess an even greater capacity for absorbing magic and transferring it. But they are exceedingly rare and difficult to find. Even if you could find one, they would require being mated and marked before even being allowed on the mountain. It would be easier to find as many mated dragons as possible who are willing to offer their mates on a regular basis. Most dragons aren't willing to share their mates so readily."

"It's the only option we have at the moment, except you have forbidden me from sharing Issa's pregnancy with others," Kris said.

"This close to the birth, we can make an exception if you promise to only invite those you trust the most."

"Very well," Kris said, relieved that he finally had more than vague guarantees. He would have to give in and call the others, and just hope those who weren't actively trying to locate the lost fragment of the Verdanith would still be willing to help after he confessed the secret he and Issa had kept from them.

"What word from the Court on the missing fragment, Kris?" Numa said, moving on to other business.

"I only know they were close to locating it. I haven't heard from them in several weeks."

The Council didn't respond for several moments. The hum of their private communion irritated Kris. Sometimes he was alert enough to break through and catch a few pieces of what they shared, but today he was too exhausted. While he waited, his mind was free of them, at least. He sent a quick thought to Issa letting her know things were progressing but not in which direction. He'd tell her the full details later, when the Council wasn't around to overhear his thoughts.

The second he'd finished the thought, his mind split with blinding pain, a bombardment of nearly deafening voices clamoring for attention. He cried out, clutching his temples. *What do you want?!* he yelled silently back.

The voices ceased instantly and he sighed in relief. A moment later, a single familiar voice came back through, sure and deep.

It's Kol. We have the fragment. We're all here and on our way to you now.

"*Hurry. And bring your mates, too.*" Kris sent back, then immediately sent a message to the Unbound dragon guards that surrounded the pavilion to give Kol and his retinue full access, regardless of status.

He needed all of them.

CHAPTER THREE

After half a day in a plane flying between Tokyo and Singapore, Rowan relished the chance to stretch her wings again. They'd waited until nightfall before climbing to the top of one of the city's tallest hotels before shifting. From Singapore it was another few hours to the island, which passed quickly now that she wasn't confined to a metal tube.

Rowan landed in a field surrounded by men in robes, allowed Trevor to dismount from her back, and shifted to her human form. The rest of her companions either dismounted or shifted around her. Trevor and Rafe moved to one side of her while her tall, red-haired brother and his beautiful mate flanked her on the other side. With the others at her back, Rowan felt for the first time like she truly belonged. These were her people. Her family. And she would do whatever it took to help them.

A single broad-chested man with a shaved head stepped eagerly toward her, his expression filled with gratitude.

"Zak?" she said. She almost didn't recognize him in full daylight until she caught sight of his yellow eyes and attractive face a second before he gathered her into his embrace.

His strong arms crushed her to his chest. With her cheek mashed against him she gave Rafe an apologetic look, but the Shadow only laughed.

"Your timing couldn't be more perfect," Zak said when he released her. "Darius is with Kris and the Council now. We need to get you to the peak as soon as possible."

Kol and the others walked toward them with determined looks.

"Can we even get up there? I thought there was a restriction," Rafe said.

"Kris has summoned all of us," Kol said. "However, the magic that protects the peak allows only Court dragons to access via the air. Racha will fly ahead as our representative. The rest of us will walk."

The petite Asian woman Rowan had only met a couple days earlier embraced the bear of a human man who had accompanied her. They whispered to each other softly, then kissed tenderly. Racha quickly shifted into a majestic green dragon while her mate looked on. Rowan didn't think she'd ever get used to seeing the transformation, even though she'd accomplished it countless times herself.

Rowan fell into step behind Kol. Her insides churned and she felt on the verge of tears after everything. This had to be the end of it. She clutched tighter to the pair of hands that held hers, and they gave back with as much strength. The crush of Rafe's and Trevor's hands in hers calmed her, gave her courage to face whatever would come.

She looked around at the others climbing the narrow mountain path with her. So many she barely knew, but who she already loved. Her brother smiled encouragingly at her and she smiled back.

As rushed as their journey was, so close to the end, it had still taken them a day and a half to get back to the Monastery from the temple where Rafe and Trevor found her. From there they'd trekked back out and headed to the Tokyo International Airport. She'd laughed at the other dragons who met them there, blustering about being stuck in a tube to fly them places quicker, but grew quiet soon after when the same urge to spread her wings sank into her after Kol's private jet was airborne.

"How the hell do you deal with this?" she asked out of the blue half an hour later. Her skin itched with the need to shift, but there was nowhere near enough room in the small cabin to do so.

"Sex," several of the others replied. There were sixteen, altogether, filling up the cabin.

"We shouldn't," Kol said. His fingertips had turned into sharp talons that pierced the leather armrests. The others were in similar states of tense restraint.

"We don't need to," Roka said. "My Queen, will you join me?"

The large, white-haired dragon took a deep breath and expelled it in a shimmering cloud of white. Racha did the same, their breath mingling and dispersing throughout the cabin. Rowan let herself inhale the pleasant-smelling smoke. A sense of relaxed euphoria came over her within moments and the overwhelming urge to shift and catch the air currents with her wings disappeared. They spent the next several hours in subdued, but happy conversation. She got the sense this meeting was a long needed reunion for many of them. Even more so for herself and the brother she'd never known she had.

Geva had been solicitous of her from the very first moment, anxious to confirm that she was well and that Rafe hadn't harmed her. When Rafe turned to the group to display the mark she'd given him, the subject of his loyalty was dropped. The others treated Trevor with warm interest, but he had refused to leave her side for a single moment.

Even now he walked at her side as they trailed up the mountain. "What exactly are we headed toward?" Trevor asked.

"The confrontation of our lives," she replied. "So cross your fingers."

"We're meeting with the Dragon Council," Rafe clarified. His voice caught and he cleared his throat with a nervous cough. Rowan darted a concerned look at him.

"Are you scared of them?"

Rafe gave her a sheepish smile. "I've never met them before. Only the Court and the loyal slaves that serve them have ever been in their presence until now. But Kris insisted we all go, even the humans."

Their destination came into view far above, a huge pavilion that sparkled in the sunset at the peak of the mountain. There was a collective murmur of awe from those around her and they increased their pace up the winding, cobbled path.

The structure was the size of the Acropolis, only built in a hexagonal shape. Jade columns as thick as redwoods held up a roof that she could barely make out as obscured in the clouds as it was.

Shimmering curtains of multicolored light filled each space between the columns, beyond which Rowan could make out three figures standing in the center looking out at them. The Queen, Racha, stood in between two large men, one bare-chested with shoulder-length black hair and a violet sarong, the other in a robe and sporting a shaved head and familiar eyes that flashed red when they settled on her.

She restrained herself from surging forward, though her heart swelled to see the large Unbound who had helped her when she'd visited last.

"Darius," she whispered.

"Yeah, Darius." Rafe said the name with a distinct lack of

hospitality. He snorted and bent to kiss her on the cheek. "Sorry, love. I know he helped you, but..." He trailed off with a shrug.

"Trevor helped me, too, but you don't seem to hold it against him."

"Trevor isn't a dragon."

His jealousy toward Darius perplexed her at first, but ever since the entire Court had come charging into her chamber a few days earlier, she'd learned they all had peculiar quirks that made no real sense. At least not until she remembered they'd only lived in the modern world for less than a year. Though, one detail that became clear in watching the others was Rafe's resistance to confessing his love to her to begin with. Their race had been forbidden from mating and breeding among themselves for as long as they could remember. Aside from a few extraordinary exceptions, any dragons who mated with one of their own went to great lengths to hide such a union. Her existence was evidence of that. And Darius, Zak and the other Unbound, as offspring of other matings between two dragons, were evidence of the persecution of dragons who broke that law.

"Roka helped you. Can you explain to me the difference?"

"Roka..." Rafe stopped, his mouth half open as though he were searching for the words. "He helped out of necessity, and he is already mated." Under his breath, he murmured, "It's not as if we'd be able to breed."

"So it's only because they're unmated males that you've got your panties in a bunch?"

"You're a beautiful, powerful dragon. I've submitted to as your mate already, against the laws as they stand now. If those laws change, you'll have the right to take others, I imagine. Other dragons *and* humans. Male and female, if you choose. That, and it's not exactly easy to get over centuries of backward thinking. The idea of you breeding with another dragon feels…not right."

"Unless it's you."

Rafe's jaw clenched and his hand tightened around hers. "I used to feel differently," he said quietly. "Two dragons lying together was against our laws, except for the sacred union of the Catalysts and the dragon mates chosen for them by the Council. I believed in our laws and held to them so tightly that I considered such unions among other dragons an abomination. It wasn't until the night I met you that I knew what a fool I'd been. I could sense in your magic how pure your blood is. Yet all I wanted was to awaken your nature and make you mine. But once I did that—I discovered you were even more powerful than I'd dreamed. I couldn't go back without letting you claim me. *This* feels right, now that it's done."

"It's not quite done yet, though, is it? We still have a law to change."

"That we do," Rafe said, bringing her hand to his lips.

CHAPTER FOUR

The escort of Unbound dispersed around the Pavilion and Kris finally caught sight of the retinue of Court dragons and their mates. The group was led by a few unfamiliar faces. He recognized Geva and Erika instantly—but the trio that accompanied them were new to him. The striking female Red in the center exuded power beyond even Geva's vibrant energy.

"There she is," Darius whispered beside him.

"You know this dragon?" Kris asked, jerking his head to look at his father.

Darius cut a sideways glance at Kris and gave him a smug smile. "She's our salvation. I couldn't tell you about her before today, or we'd have lost her assistance."

"Who is she?" Kris asked, turning back to watch as the group approached, still far enough to be out of earshot.

"Bren and Warik's daughter. The newest Unbound. So new, the Council doesn't even know about her. Or they didn't until now, but it's too late for them to do anything."

Darius sounded pleased with himself. Kris glanced at him again and caught the smug smile and twinkle in his eye. Kris braced himself for a reaction from the Council who had faded out of visibility until the others came into the Pavilion. Nothing happened aside from an agitated crackle of energy around him. They were aware, but holding their tongues.

"The lineages say Bren was mated to a human named Bertram…" Kris began, but Darius cut him off.

"Warik the Red was the son of our queen, Freyja, two generations past. Warik mated with Bren, our queen, almost three decades ago, just before Bren died. You and I are both aware that the only dragons allowed to breed pure are Catalysts, from whom every generation of Queen has been born. This beautiful young Red represents multiple generations of the purest breeding in our history."

"Her parents shared a bloodline and still mated?"

"Yes! That's my point. The bloodlines don't matter within a single generation. At least that's my theory. It's the magic in a dragon's essence that the child is conceived from, and two dragon parents produce a much stronger magic in the child. Genetics are such a small part of it. Why else would they have let me mate with your mother? They simply needed my dragon essence, and knew that because both my parents were dragons, it would be strong, though hers was still stronger. Our combined magic made you who you are, but physically you resemble her more than me. The only physical trait you have of mine is that infernal furrow between your eyebrows when you're anxious or upset."

"Are you sure you should be making these speculations *now*?" Kris asked. The Council's agitation had grown to the point that his skin prickled from the energy being cast about within the pavilion. His own gut twisted with his nerves and he was suddenly very conscious of how tense his brow was.

Darius snorted. "Every dragon needs a hobby. Besides, what could they possibly do that's worse than what I've endured for hundreds of years already? If they're upset, that's just proof that I'm at least not far off the mark. They're probably angry that they didn't have a hand in determining her parentage."

Kris turned to look at the pretty young Red again, wondering how two such prominent dragons could have managed to breed, under the Council's nose. Several generations of mostly pure breeding was a lot of time to build up power. How powerful was she? She appeared confident, though bemused at the entire situation. She was flanked by Geva and a Shadow Kris hadn't met. The pair were imposing guards for an Unbound. Erika and another human stood at the outside on either side of the trio of dragons.

"They love her, don't they?" he observed.

"So do I."

"You were with her?" He gave his father a critical stare.

Darius shrugged. "She needed what little energy Zak and I could give. We were more than happy to oblige."

"I'd wager you gave her more than energy... how many secrets did you tell?"

"Enough."

Kris laughed to himself, his chest full of mirth and love for the man beside him. His father...whom he'd known for his entire life, but never truly known due to the ridiculous laws their race had endured forever.

Things would change, if the presence of the beautiful Red with the determined expression really meant what he thought it did—that the Council had less control over the course of events than they believed. The Court, including his own sister, their Queen, had been keeping secrets from him for months. He had to believe Rowan was the biggest one. He regretted that the rest of the Court couldn't tell him everything, sequestered as he was on this mountain.

Her aura hit him first, his cock instantly pulsing and swelling beneath his sarong.

Reds were like that, and this was energy he could take back to Issa if he managed to control himself well enough. The hard-on would have to wait.

"Sweet Mother, she's even more powerful than when I met her," Darius said.

She ascended the steps and stopped in front of Racha before Kris could say another word.

"My Queen," the Red said. "I am your servant and pledge my loyalty to you. Every ounce of my love and power is yours to command."

"Your love?" Racha asked. "Who do you claim as your lover, if you pledge your love? Pledging that requires a strong commitment."

Kris sensed a shift in Rowan's energy but she kept her expression placid. He wondered if their little exchange had been rehearsed considering they had all arrived together. Her greeting definitely sounded too formal to come from one so young, and the question Racha had asked was too leading to be spontaneous.

"These men beside me. My personal commitment is to them, through the marks they bear. My sovereign loyalty goes to you and our race."

She gestured toward the Shadow and the human man on the other side of him.

Racha's eyebrows raised, her face still a mask, but Kris sensed the rising excitement in his sister.

"You have marked another dragon as your mate. This is a grave transgression."

The Red didn't flinch and Kris wondered if she could already sense Racha's acceptance of her. The Queen had no choice in her dialog. The Council were all still there, watching from their ethereal thrones around the pavilion. The others wouldn't be made aware until the Council chose, but Kris and his sister always knew when they were present.

"You are a purebred like me. You and your brother." Rowan's red eyes settled on Kris for a split second and that small bit of glowing magic darted straight to his soul. "We want the same things. The freedom to mate and breed with whom we choose."

Racha's voice sounded brittle when she answered. "You are Unbound, are you not? Your parents broke our laws. Why should I accept your mates along with you?"

The bitterness surprised Kris, even in light of the stress both he and his sister had been under, trying to negotiate with the Council to approve assembly of the Verdanith. Once Issa's pregnancy and the nature of their children became apparent, there had been no more resistance, but getting there had been an ordeal. Of the entire Court, only Racha knew about Issa's pregnancy. Dragons were rarely susceptible to envy, so Kris believed it was merely the idea that Rowan had been so easily conceived by her parents, while Corey and Racha had followed all the laws and were still childless. His and Issa's own good fortune likely didn't help.

"My parents' transgressions are not at issue. All of that happened a generation ago. I only care about what happens now and in the future. My men are *mine*. If you hurt them, I'm pretty sure I can rain down fire on the rest of you. I haven't tried it yet, but I'm not shy."

Kris stepped forward. "Threats aren't necessary, Princess."

Rowan blinked in surprise at the title he'd just given her. He knew well enough it was a demeaning term in this modern world he'd grown up in but remained apart from. In truth, he'd meant it twofold. She was by birthright a member of the Court, being the daughter of their last Queen. If her brother hadn't misbehaved, Geva would have been the highest ranking member of the Court. As it was, Geva stood second to a dragon who had broken their laws out of love, not boredom. None of those details had been lost on the

Council. Now this lovely, illegitimate Red had decided to show her face and assert her dazzling power.

Rowan's existence, however, *had* gone unnoticed by the Council until this moment. Kris's mind buzzed with the Council's background chatter. He had to suppress an urge to rejoice when those immortal bastards began scrambling for purchase over their apparently failed plans.

He wasn't privy to all their secrets, only glimmers here and there. He'd gleaned enough to understand they'd had an ongoing agenda to orchestrate very specific breeding among the race, though to what purpose he wasn't sure. Darius's theory made perfect sense. His and Issa's mating and conception of the Twins, and now Rowan's presence, indicated that the breeding of incredibly powerful dragons could easily occur without the Council's influence. Their restriction on pure breeding must only be so they could maintain control over *who* bred pure or not.

This particular dragon was entirely unexpected, yet the Council seemed as excited at her presence as they were when they'd learned of the Twins. Before Kris told the Council that Issa was pregnant, they hadn't been happy he'd chosen his own mate without their input, and had been on the verge of forcing him and Issa apart. After that, they had been filled with almost desperate regret every time he'd requested their help to sustain her.

"And why not?" Rowan replied. "I lost almost my entire family as a result of our laws. I deserve a little bit of retribution."

Racha sighed and stepped toward Rowan. "Forgive me, Rowan. I didn't mean to threaten you or your mates. We all have a lot resting on this assembly so tensions are understandably high. Please, cousin, let's make peace and move forward, all right?"

She took Rowan's hand and led her to the edge of the

circle etched into the floor of the pavilion, where the inlaid stones depicted a pattern of six serpentine figures entwined. As she moved, the others began to gather in a circle around the pavilion. They finally settled under Darius and Zak's gentle command. When they were finally all silent, Kris spoke.

"Welcome, all. Humans, forgive me for not wasting time with a heartfelt introduction. We are here for business. Court, do you have the Verdanith fragments?"

Several figures moved, converging together, then came forward one by one until they stood equidistant from each other around the circle. The keepers, then. And they weren't all dragons, either. Most were unsurprising. Racha stepped forward first, facing Kris with her fragment held gently in her hands. Kol followed, stepping forward to stand at a spot a few degrees to Racha's left. Rowan stepped forward next, with the large jade wedge held in her palm. "This was my mother's. It is my right to present it, is it not?"

Kris glanced back at Geva and suppressed a smile in response to the smirk that graced the wayward Red's expression. Pushing his sister in the faces of the Council was a bold move and one that would definitely catch their attention.

Roka shifted his tall bulk smoothly around the circle, carrying the fragment he'd been presented upon acknowledgment of his Court status after their ascension. The pale green wedge looked tiny in his hands compared to the females.

The fifth was Erika. For the first time since Kris had known her she looked nervous.

"I guess I belonged to you guys all along," she said with a tiny shrug.

Kris rested a palm on her shoulder. "You will never belong to anyone you don't choose."

"Where is the sixth?" Erika asked.

Kris nearly grimaced at the question. Like a fool, he had forgotten to bring the fragment the Council had enlisted him to protect, not expecting the assembly to occur so soon.

"I have it." Issa's reedy voice carried above the other chatter and everyone grew instantly silent.

Kris turned and the others stilled as they watched Issa step carefully along the path that led from her small temple. He swallowed hard, the desperation of their ordeal rising again. She shouldn't be out of bed, but if she'd chosen to do this, he wouldn't make a fool of her by stopping her.

She was radiant in the sunlight beyond the cover of the Pavilion, her hair flowing in a shimmering dark violet cascade over bare shoulders. Her full bosom and huge belly swelled beneath a simple lavender colored gown, so gauzy and ethereal it could have been made from clouds. The others gasped at the vision, surprised voices murmuring around him. All Kris could still see were the harsh angles and hollows of her face, evidence of the toll the pregnancy had taken.

Issa stepped into the circle, taking her place in the last spot around the center. The heavy stone she gripped in her palm glowed with the energy she'd given it.

"Why did you come? You could have sent an Unbound to carry it," Kris asked.

"I should be here," Issa said. Her cheeks were flushed pink from even the slight exertion of the short walk from their quarters to the Pavilion. He longed to go to her, but sensed the Council's awareness now that the Court was in place.

"I am fine, my love." Issa's thought pressed into his mind, strong and sure in sharp contrast to her voice a moment earlier. He held her gaze, again amazed by her strength, but terrified at the same time of how quickly that strength seemed to fade each day. She nodded her head slightly and fixed her eyes on the edge of the Pavilion past his shoulder.

The Council's power grew incrementally stronger around them. Kris rotated in a slow circle, watching each of the shimmering veils of color grow more substantial and form into the huge shapes of their immortal forebears.

It was time for the Assembly to begin.

CHAPTER FIVE

"Welcome children." Numa's voice resonated through the Pavilion, the immortal green dragon's words sinking into Kris's skin like the warmth of a summer breeze.

The other dragons and their mates all let out tiny exhalations of pleasure in response. The Council's voices had that effect, as though their intention was to prime their audience for sex. Again, Kris regretted that his own nature prevented him from carrying their power to his mate. If their words alone held that much power, he could only imagine how much a single infusion of their Nirvana would hold.

"I am Numa, speaker for the Council. We are gathered to officially hear your petition to reassemble the Verdanith, one of our most valued and powerful artifacts. This is not a decision we take lightly, due to the power this object will possess when it is restored to its full power. Each of my brothers and sisters carry equal weight in the decisions we make, but you will address your concerns to me. First, each Keeper of a piece of the Verdanith must re-state their reasons for requesting the Verdanith be reassembled."

"My mate and I are eager to conceive a child soon," Racha said.

Kris turned to the sound of his sister's voice. She held her fragment up, the jade wedge glowing with her magic.

"When this generation was sent to hibernate, the New World we live in was in its infancy. We need more offspring to fill our ranks to ensure our treasures are well guarded and that we maintain our status among the humans who have grown ever more powerful over the centuries. My father knew a more robust dragon population would be paramount, and in his last written missive to me, asked that I promise to maintain our legacy."

With grave formality Numa said, "Your petition is heard, Queen Racha, daughter of Irisa and Aris." She turned her head just a fraction to aim her gaze at Kol next.

As Racha had done, the large Shadow lifted his wedge of the Verdanith up and spoke. "Hallie and I desire many children and sooner rather than later. With our current laws, we have too short a time to enjoy a family. There are too few dragons to balance the wealth that humans have accumulated and to ensure that our treasures are secure."

Again, Numa replied, "Your petition is heard, Shadow Kol, son of Astrid."

Kris rotated slightly, his eyes coming to rest on Issa who held Numa's gaze proudly. His heart swelled at the sight of her in profile. Wetness seeped into his eyes and he took a deep breath, holding back emotion that threatened to break out. Her voice was strong and sure when she spoke.

"As you are aware, Kris and I are already expecting our first children. The Twins are strong and growing stronger with every bit of power they consume, but what we have to give is not enough. My petition is for the power to sustain them until they are born and come of age. The Verdanith will supply that power."

After Numa acknowledged Issa, it was Roka's turn to face Numa. His shoulders tensed, the Verdanith fragment held so tightly in his grip, Kris feared it might crack.

"Esteemed Council," Roka began with a nod of his head. "While I share the desires of those who petitioned before me, my petition is not for the aid to fertility the Verdanith can provide. My mates and I have agreed that until dragon law is changed, we will not conceive a child. I have seen many sunrises over the months since I was awakened by the sunrise of my heart, Camille. But I have missed *thousands* of sunrises during my lifetime already. My petition is to allow our children to see a sunrise for each day they are alive, and to be able to share in their glory. Assembly of the Verdanith would enable sufficient oversight by yourselves to support multiple generations sharing the world."

The Council's silent deliberation buzzed in Kris's mind for a second. He was as surprised as they were with Roka's bold petition, going against what had earlier been a unanimous Court petition to assemble the Verdanith strictly for fertility purposes. He closed his eyes, hoping to gather enough of an impression of their reaction to decide whether it was positive or negative, but it sounded conflicted. Numa's response was as much a surprise as Roka's request.

"Your petition is unexpected, Roka, son of Ronin. Why have you jeopardized the Court's petition as a whole to state your case?"

"Is it not Dragon Law to hear each petition and consider them on their own merits as well as together? I still wish for the Verdanith to be assembled, but only to facilitate a necessary shift in our antiquated system of laws. Humanity and modern cultural changes have accelerated to a blinding speed relative to our lifetimes. We can only grow stronger by maintaining closer familial ties over the generations. Preserving our genetics through hibernation should be a much lower priority relative to maintaining our competitive edge over the richest humans."

More irritating deliberation followed. Finally Numa said, "You are very much the product of your parents, both loyal and law abiding dragons in spite of their opinionated natures. Your petition is heard, Roka, son of Ronin and Ryoko."

Kris raised his eyebrow at the acknowledgment of Roka's human mother. The mere mention of the legendary female samurai indicated that the Council had more than heard his petition. They were impressed. Kris only hoped he could live up to his own mother's name.

There were only two petitions left. Kris braced himself for the unknown. He'd heard Erika and Geva's original petition but suspected Erika might follow Roka's example and share their true reason for requesting the assembly. He had no idea what the newcomer, Rowan, might request.

Erika nodded, wisps of her chestnut hair drifting across her cheeks in some unseen breeze. Her eyes were bright with excitement as she held up the glowing stone. In a loud, clear voice she spoke.

"When I was a child, I dreamed that my father would discover that your race's existence was not a myth, but a fact. He died before he could prove it, and so I picked up where he left off, following his research like a map to buried treasure. I didn't find his personal journals until after we completed the ritual. It wasn't until I read them that I learned how close the ties were between my family and your race. From his research and the research my team has done, I understand why you split the Verdanith six generations and more than three thousand years ago. The race had too much power over humans and some dragons abused that power. The dragon whose fragment my family kept for generations gave up his life to ensure that power was no longer abused. Splitting the

Verdanith effectively hobbled the race, and allowed the six of you to assert greater control. But even with it split, you still didn't have the control I believe you wished to have."

Erika paused for breath and turned, meeting the gazes of each member of the Council in turn before beginning again. "Do you even know how many were born outside your sanction? Dragon children you had no knowledge of until today. Do you know how many dragons live out their lives with no offspring whatsoever? The dragon who was once the keeper of this fragment I hold had no progeny to pass it on to and so it was lost, passed down through the generations of his bonded humans. Your laws didn't protect him or offer him an alternative that would protect his legacy. We can't change the mistakes of the past—I believe Fate dictated the events that brought me to you—but we can ensure a stronger future for the race with the Verdanith at full strength. I petition for assembly of the Verdanith to ensure that future generations, including the children I wish to bear with my mate, are free to take advantage of the Verdanith's power when in need. Even if those future generations are born without your sanction. Slavery was abolished among humans in the western world more than two centuries ago. It is against our laws now. Don't you think it's time your race caught up?"

Kris forced his face to remain placid, though he grimaced inwardly. Erika had just challenged one of their most contentious laws without overtly stating her objection to it. He glanced at Geva and then Rowan, both of whom wore pleased smirks. Rowan shifted her gaze to him. The red blaze of power in her eyes sank through his defenses in much the same way as the Council's power did.

Then she turned toward Numa and the power increased tenfold. Kris sensed magic converging on the entire pavilion, drawn to the arousal induced by Rowan's magic. She hadn't even breathed and everyone's pulse rates had increased.

The Council itself grew utterly still and silent. Whether their silence was in response to Erika's question or Rowan turning up the power, Kris couldn't be sure. They'd never lashed out before, however, so he had no reason to fear any kind of wrath from them. Reasonable to a fault would be the best description he had for the six.

Numa's calming green aura pressed outward, enveloping the Pavilion in a hazy bubble.

"Your petition is heard, Erika, daughter of Gabriel, bonded servant of Jorian." The normally resonant voice held a faint quaver that was reflected in the agitation of the other Council members.

If Kris didn't know better, he might believe the six of them were actually anxious to hear Rowan's petition. In spite of Numa's breath surrounding them all, Rowan's power persisted, overlapping and entwining with the magic that held the bubble in place. Kris's groin ached with the effects of it, while at the same time Numa's power gave him the strongest sense of euphoria. It was all he could do to avoid touching himself. He conjured forth a memory of when he was younger and that action would only result in discomfort. After the assembly was done, he would deal with his need. Not in the middle of it. The combined arousal and conflicting frustration permeated the area from the others as well. Issa's eyes were wide, her hands clasped across her belly, the wedge of the Verdanith still held tightly in her fingers.

"*What is it, my love?*" he asked.

"*The twins sense the energy. They are hungry.*"

"*Just a few more minutes and we will be done.*"

Issa nodded slightly and gave him a small, worried smile, but stood tall and still.

Rowan spoke, her voice as strong and sure as Erika's, but holding the otherworldly vibration that only dragons could produce. "According to dragon law, I am Unbound. I was born outside your sanction and am therefore not bound by your laws unless you force me to be, as you have forced countless other dragons over the centuries. I am here to petition a change to that law, and also to honor my parents' union and request that you honor it, too. You may have heard of my parents, Bren and Warik. It is their power I carry, which I can use to help our race if you choose. In honoring them, you will also honor my union with the dragon Rafe. I petition you to use the Verdanith to find others like me, not to persecute, but to legitimize, for they were born from love between two dragons, something only your Catalysts have been honored with publicly. An honor which I have no doubt they would happily share."

The briefest glance Kris shared with her was enough acknowledgment of understanding, as though she sensed the need to move things along for the sake of his mate. He hoped the Council would make their decision quickly.

"Your petition is heard, Red Princess, daughter of Bren and Warik. The Keepers have made their petitions. Are there any petitions pertaining to the assembly that others wish to make?"

Kris shifted his gaze around at the outer circle of observers, which included most of the humans along with the four other dragons. Geva and Rafe remained silent, their heads held high. Aurin and Aurik shared a furtive glance but didn't speak. Their predicament was no secret, but this was not the time for them to state their own petition to the Council.

"Very well," Numa said. "Catalyst, proceed."

Kris nodded and gestured toward the six who stood in a circle around him. They approached in order once again, each one handing their respective fragments to him. The first piece pulsed with gentle heat in his hand and an involuntary surge of his own energy flowed into it before he could stop it. The stone was enchanted with the same energy as the altar beneath the Queen's chamber of the temple visited so many months ago. If he wasn't careful, this object would bleed him entirely dry of power. He carefully restrained his power from it as he accepted each successive piece. The first two wedges snapped together like opposing poles of two magnets. One by one, each fragment fit together with its brothers.

Roka was the last to step forward. He held his piece out to Kris, the nearly completed circle of the Verdanith physically beginning to pull Kris toward its last missing piece.

In a split second, there were gasps around the circle. Issa's voice rose faintly in his mind, *"Kris..."*

"Issa!" Kris yelled, seeing his mate sway from the corner of his vision, but he couldn't release the object. He seemed fastened to the center of the Pavilion, the Verdanith adhered to his hands.

Roka moved in a blur. Releasing the final jade wedge, he lunged to the side around Kris. The Verdanith seemed to suck the last remaining piece from the air with a snap into the void left for it. Blinding white light bloomed in Kris's hands, the power of the artifact growing exponentially, the pull of it forcing his hands downward into the center of the Pavilion's floor. He released it and stepped back in one swift movement.

The Verdanith slammed into the floor, its impact shaking the entire mountain and causing everyone but the Council to waver, holding their hands out to steady themselves against each other.

The pattern in the floor of the Pavilion lit with a series of colored lights that quickly faded to black, but Kris was done with the ceremony. He needed to see to his mate. He turned to find Issa cradled against Roka's chest, one arm dangling limply. Aurik stood at Roka's shoulder, his sister and their mates close behind. The four of them and Roka had been standing the closest to Issa. The others moved closer, gathering around with concerned looks.

"Give her to me," Kris said. "She needs my energy. The babies, too."

"We can help," Roka said. "My breath might be able to help."

Kris met his friend's concerned gaze with one of defeat. "I wish you could, brother. Only an Udara can help now, until the Verdanith is charged." He turned and walked toward the edge of the Pavilion. The charging of the Verdanith would have to happen without him. He didn't dare hope they could complete the task before it was too late for his mate and children.

Issa's pulse fluttered weakly beneath his fingertips. *"Hold on, my love. I will keep you safe, or die trying."*

"Wait."

The voice vibrated through the air close to his shoulder, sending a current of wind through his hair. His skin tingled from the slight caress of Aurum's breath, his ears still vibrating with ecstasy in response to the simple address. He'd never heard the immortal Gold speak before, and the fact of that one small word surprised him so much he paused to look up at her, amazed that he could find hope in only a single syllable.

She didn't address him next, however, but the pair who stood behind him. "Are these your mates, my children?"

Aurin and Aurik's worried looks transformed to identical defensive scowls, both dragons bodily moving to protect their mates.

Aurum puffed out an exasperated breath. "Fools, I wish to help the Catalyst. Did you know you were mated to not one but *two* Udara? I sensed them when they stepped foot on the mountain but couldn't be sure who they were until they moved this close. You keep them well primed, I see."

The Twins shared a surprised look. Aurik said, "We knew they were special. But the truth is, they chose us. I don't think Aurin and I ever really had a choice."

"It is the way with Udara. And it is Fate that brought them here. You must let them help."

Dimitri and Thea both moved forward over the objections of the Twins. "Damn right we'll help," Thea said. "Show me the way."

Kris buried his bafflement at their insistence and continued out of the Pavilion, leading them down the path.

"The two of you must stay," Aurum said. The Twins paused a step before exiting the Pavilion and looked back, identical expressions of confusion on their faces.

Rowan was mesmerized by the synchronicity of their movements and their features. They might be the most beautiful dragons she'd ever seen, and their anguish over seeing their mates leave left her heart in a state of intense longing. She looked back at Rafe and Trevor, who stood side by side watching events unfold. They met her gaze and she went to them, gripping the hands they extended in each of hers, the simple touch conveying the depth of their feelings as much as their eyes did.

"What happens now?" Rowan whispered.

"We follow Aurum's lead," Rafe said. "The Verdanith will need to be charged to full power. Only dragons can accomplish that."

The huge golden dragon bowed her head toward Rafe, indicating she had heard. "Yes, child. We will need all of you to join us in the Mother's Glade, but your human mates will need to remain behind. It is a place where only dragons may go."

"What are we supposed to do, just sit on our asses and wait?" Erika asked.

"On the contrary. Your assistance is needed along with the Udara who have followed Kris. The pair of them are ideal sources of energy for Issa, but they can't provide a constant flow. When they pause to rest, Kris will need other sources. Your presence here is quite fortuitous. The six of you should follow Kris while the Court—and our new guests—join us in the Glade. When the Verdanith is at full power, you will know it, but the hours flow differently where we are going, so it may take some time." The dragon's glimmering eyes rested on Rowan and Rafe, her long tongue darting out in a distinctly eager lick of the air between them.

"What the hell is that supposed to mean?" Rowan said to Rafe.

His hand squeezed hers a little tighter. *"Which part? The part where we've been invited to assist the Council in recharging the Verdanith? I'll give you three guesses how it works. And I think she has just staked her claim on having us to herself during the process."*

Rowan glanced around at the others, trying to gauge their various moods. Erika shared a long look with Geva, but neither of them appeared upset about the prospect of being separated. In fact, if Rowan had to guess, the pair looked excited. Her brother gathered his mate in his arms, and gave her a long, sensuous kiss, then urged her to go. Erika strode the few steps over to Rowan, her cheeks still flushed. The aura of her arousal clung to her brightly. Rowan hadn't quite gotten used to the awareness of the magic and the eagerness with which all the human mates seemed to embrace the nature of their lovers. Erika might be one of the most enthusiastic women she'd ever met when it came to sex. She quickly reevaluated that assessment when the petite, blonde Camille walked up to them and nudged Trevor's shoulder.

"Looks like we'll get the chance to get to know you a little better," Camille said, not even trying to hide the suggestive tone. She eyed Trevor up and down, then Rafe. "This one's got a very talented tongue," she said, patting Rafe on the chest, then glancing at Rowan. "You're one lucky girl."

Rowan raised an eyebrow at Rafe. He cleared his throat and gave her a weak smile. "I've been blessed with friends who are happy to share when they have a friend in need. She and her mates saved me much the way Trevor and I saved you."

Erika laughed. "We are nothing if not giving. Come on Trevor. I promise we'll take good care of you and I have no doubt your efforts will be appreciated. Kris and Issa mean a lot to us."

"Um, all right, I guess. You're okay with this, Rowan?"

"I think I have to be, as long as you are. Just make sure you enjoy yourself." She nudged him toward Camille and Erika.

"I don't think that'll be an issue," Trevor murmured, eyeing both beautiful women who were already leading him away to follow the others down the mountain path and away from the Pavilion.

"Where is this Glade? Do we need to fly there?" Rowan asked.

Without answering, Rafe pulled her toward the center where the others were gathered, linking hands in a circle around the glowing shape of the Verdanith that had embedded itself in the floor of the Pavilion. Around them the shapes of the dragons of the Council shimmered as they exhaled deep breaths. Colorful clouds of smoke coiled and swirled around them, the tendrils of each color twining together until it formed a twisting rope. The column of it arched over their heads and flowed into the center of the floor between them, sinking into the round opening at the core of the Verdanith.

As though a key had thrown the tumblers of a lock, the entire floor of the Pavilion shifted beneath Rowan's feet. The world around her wavered and flashed, colorful smoke filling the air so thickly that it obscured her vision of everything around her. All she could see was sparkling, colorful fog, but Rafe's hand still gripped hers tightly on one side and the smooth warmth of the golden dragon's, Aurik's, hand gripped tightly around her other hand. The mist seeped through her clothing, though not with the expected sensation of moisture. The ethereal cloud had the texture of silk sliding between her garments and her skin, whispering across every inch of her flesh like a breath. Before she could control herself she let out a soft moan in response, giving herself up to the pleasure. Her mind buzzed with the power of the magic that surrounded her, infused her with every breath. Vaguely she understood for the first time what the humans might have experienced in response to her own breath.

Her eyes fluttered open when the sensation subsided and she found herself and the others in a sun-dappled glade. In the center was a circular pool filled with crystal clear water. The center of the pool had a stone island roughly the size of the center of the Pavilion where Kris had stood when he assembled the Verdanith. The Verdanith itself was visible in the center here, as well, glowing with rhythmic pulses.

A pair of lips pressed against her bare throat. Another pair against her shoulder. Fingertips tugged at the bindings of her clothing and with barely a thought she dispersed the conjured dress she wore. She heard a splash and the sound of ringing laughter. Movement caught her attention at the periphery of her vision. She pulled her attention away from the teasing hands on her body to marvel at the tableau before her. The familiar faces of her friends had been joined by new faces and it took Rowan a moment to register that the Council had shifted. While human in shape, however, they each retained an otherworldly quality that surpassed even the quality she'd noticed in the dragons she'd met the last two days. Both the men and the women were taller, more muscular, the men imposing in their size. The black dragon, Ked, dwarfed the petite naked form of Racha who teased him from the water. He dove in after her, wrestled with her briefly until they came together beneath the water, Racha's face abruptly transforming from mischievous fun to pure pleasure with the movement of Ked's hips against hers.

The other Council Dragons seemed to have each chosen one or two of her friends. Kol and her brother flanked the beautiful blue Belah. Geva knelt before Belah, pressing urgent kisses down her torso while Kol cupped the woman's breasts from behind.

On a smooth stone ledge across the pool, Roka was already tangled with Numa, her full breasts worshiped by his lips and tongue, her long legs wrapped around his waist as he fucked her.

Lovely, golden Aurin lay sprawled on the grass, the tangled crimson curls of the immortal Red, Gavra, moving between her thighs, while on the other side of them, Aurin's brother was similarly engaged with the white dragon, Aodh, Aurik's fingers twined in Aodh's hair while the Council Dragon's pale tongue and lips worked deftly at Aurik's cock.

A beautiful face obscured Rowan's view, golden eyes set deep. Aurum's sweet breath hit Rowan's nostrils first, and she inhaled. The power infused her with joy like a drug. She exhaled in response, sending out a red gust of her own power.

Aurum hummed her appreciation. "A game then?" the

immortal Gold said. She pressed closer, sliding her hands up over Rowan's bare breasts. Tender palms cupped both breasts, the pads of her thumbs brushing over Rowan's nipples before Aurum moved higher, holding Rowan's chin lightly with both hands. The light contact sent a buzz of pure pleasure through Rowan's body and it lingered hotly at her core.

Aurum's lips parted as she leaned closer, still a hair's breadth from skin on skin. Her warm breath puffed out against Rowan's mouth and Rowan followed her example, opening her mouth slightly and exhaling.

The warm velvet of Aurum's lips made contact, her tongue pressing deeper. Rowan's heartbeat thudded in her ears with every increment of the powerful breath that fused with her own, deep in her lungs. She slung her arm around Aurum's neck and tilted her mouth against the sweet, soft kiss, opening up and exhaling again. The soft length of Aurum's body slid against her, thighs brushing together, hands squeezing breasts, hips, and ass.

They traded breath until Rowan lost track of her surroundings, but through it all she remained acutely conscious of the other pair of lips and hands that kissed and caressed her from behind. Aurum finally pulled away a dizzying moment later. She shifted her lithe golden body around Rowan. Rowan turned and watched while she clutched Rafe by the back of the neck and pressed her lips against his.

Swirls of their mixed red-gold breath expelled from Aurum's mouth, tendrils of it escaping from between their lips. Rafe pulled it into his lungs in a single inhalation, his eyelids fluttering and his lips twitching into a euphoric smile. When they parted, Rowan followed suit, pulling Rafe down to meet her own mouth and sharing with him the lingering combination of her breath mixed with Aurum's.

Rowan had only a vague idea what needed to be done. Recharging the artifact could have meant all kinds of things, but the more understanding she acquired about the nature of her race, the more she realized there was really only one way that would happen. They must have been transported into some kind of magical parallel world, or a tiny pocket of one. The Council's magic swirled thickly around them, arousing her to the point that the other dragons' power seemed like faint background noise by comparison. When the first pair of orgasmic cries resonated through the air, Rowan looked up from the distracting kisses and caresses Rafe and Aurum were sharing with her and watched, mesmerized, as the bright green light sailed through the air from Numa and Roka and sank into the center of the pedestal. The Verdanith remained brightly lit for a moment, before subsiding back to its low, pulsing glow.

With disconcerting synchronicity, the six immortal dragons disengaged from their activities, leaving behind baffled looks of mild frustration among the others.

"It's time," Aurum whispered to Rowan. "Don't fret, my dear. We will be gentle." With strength far beyond what Rowan was capable of resisting, Aurum clutched both her wrists, twisted them behind her back, and urged her to walk forward into the water. Steps led down into the cool, waist-deep pool, then up again to the flat, circular island in the center.

"What the hell?" Rowan looked back at Rafe, alarm bordering on fear.

Rafe's eyes widened briefly, then he seemed to come to some silent understanding. He looked back at her, resigned. "We broke their laws. Therefore they must administer punishment."

"Punishment? For falling in love? Rafe! I didn't even

know it was a law when I fell for you. And I thought you said my presence would make them change it!"

"Darling, the only thing to do now is to accept it bravely. When it's over we will be able to make our arguments."

Belah moved to Rafe's side and Rafe nodded, holding his hands behind him for her to restrain and drive him forward. They weren't the only ones, Rowan soon became aware. They were joined in the center by Aurin and Aurik, who both looked as chastened as Rafe.

"What did you guys do?" Rowan asked under her breath.

In a sardonic tone, Aurik murmured, "Fell in love with the same human. Two dragons aren't allowed to mate and mark a single human at the same time."

"Well, that's news to me, too." She eyed Rafe from across the platform, finding it hard not to be as amused as she was irritated. "Too bad you didn't give me a legal lesson when we met, baby. Is Trevor going to be alright?"

"He'll be fine. No doubt he's enjoying himself more than we are at the moment. Camille is nothing if not attentive."

The fact that Rafe and the others didn't seem worried or even afraid let Rowan relax a little. The four were positioned at the four cardinal points of the platform. She and Aurin faced each other, with Rafe and Aurik to either side of them.

The immortal Shadow, Ked, stood just outside their circle where the water lapped at its edges and gestured for Kol to move to the opposite side. Both exhaled deeply, their dark breath quickly fading to nothing as it left their mouths. Air currents that hadn't existed before moved around Rowan, tickling her skin. A second later, the sensation of invisible silk bindings coiled around Rowan's wrists and tugged her arms up in front of her and over her head. The others' movements mirrored her own. Similar sensations coiled around her ankles, tugging her legs apart so she stood spread-eagled. The magic ties held her snugly enough that she could let her weight hang entirely from her wrists without any give, if she chose to.

Rowan had to crane her head around her arm to see Rafe. His dark beauty took her breath away, particularly with the slight shimmer of his scales appearing along the surface of his skin. She recognized it not as a need for power, but the simple response to intense arousal. The presence of his shining horns as well as of his erection were obvious signs as well. The Twins attracted similar swirls of magic. Rowan wondered if they enjoyed misbehaving for the simple sake of enduring the punishment. In spite of her own humiliation at being disarmed so, she found herself growing just as aroused at the prospect of what might happen next.

"It seems like you're enjoying this, so how the hell does it count as punishment?" she sent to Rafe.

"Most dragons prefer to do the tying rather than be tied. Our pride suffers, and the magic of the dominating dragons will linger like a bad hangover. We will have to submit to the others to satisfy the Council."

"Even to my brother?"

"That is up to the Council. It's possible."

Before she could voice her objection, Ked spoke, his voice so deep it sank into Rowan's gut, leaving her with a pleasant buzz. "Geva shall secure Aurin's submission, Racha will secure Rafe's, Roka will secure Aurik's, and Kol will secure Rowan's. When each of you has submitted to your peers, you will submit to one of us."

"That's it? I can just say I submit to Kol and it's done?"

Rafe didn't answer and before Rowan could turn her head to look at him, a large hand twined in her long hair and yanked her head back severely.

"Ow!" Rowan cried out and jerked her head forward again. The hand slipped around, fingers clasping loosely around her neck. The gesture was only a vague threat, but sufficient enough for Kol to make his point. She was at his mercy now.

Kol's voice seeped into her mind, a cool, languid suggestion that crept like the dark predator she'd learned a Shadow could be. *"I daresay I might enjoy this as much as I enjoyed disciplining your brother, if you are as hot-tempered as he is."*

"What does your mate think of this?" Rowan shot back.

"She would assist me, were she here now. Ask her later—or ask your brother now to confirm the story."

Rowan trained her eyes across the circle to where her brother stood behind Aurin, his large hands sliding down her sides. He met her gaze, then his gaze shifted past her shoulder to Kol and he grinned. So much for family loyalty.

"It's your fault we're in this circle, you know," Rowan said to Kol. *"You should have told me the truth even if Rafe couldn't bring himself to."*

She tried to turn her head but Kol still held tightly to the back of her neck with one hand. She could only catch a glimmer of movement of his dark head and the free hand that reached around and slid up her stomach. When he finally answered, the words were accompanied by his thumb and fingers spanning both breasts and teasing her nipples into achingly hard peaks. The pleasurable distraction made it nearly impossible to focus.

"I should have bound you like this and showed you the truth that night. Instead I was too lenient and let you leave without truly understanding the stakes. I've since learned my lesson."

"The only thing at stake for me was love and honesty," Rowan gritted out through her teeth. "You as much as promised Rafe and I could never be together under current Dragon Law. I will *not* submit until the laws are abolished." She raised her voice, the words hanging in the air as all the others paused, their attention fully on her.

Kol chuckled and pinched her nipples lightly. He nipped

at her neck with his teeth, the light contact causing delicious trickles of pleasure down her spine. *"The longer it takes you to give in, the more fun it will be for them when they take you. However, I did not lie to you Rowan. You are crucial to our cause. You couldn't be doing better if we'd rehearsed beforehand."*

"I could have done better if I'd known this is how things would go."

"If I had known, I would have prepared you."

He released her neck and continued his playful nips over her shoulders and neck. With one hand he pushed her hair up, carefully coiling it on top of her head and binding it with a tiny breath that wove itself into her thick locks.

She shivered at the light brush of his lips over her neck at the base of her skull. Heat flushed through her from that point outward, as though he'd found a sleeping ember and fed it enough fuel to become a blaze. His large bulk of warm muscle and skin pressed against her from behind, his erection searing hot along her spine. Both hands cupped her breasts this time, teasing her nipples relentlessly, the light swirl of his tongue against the top of her spine never letting up.

After a few seconds more of it he paused and whispered in her ear. "Do you submit now, Princess?"

"No."

"Then you shall get to witness how the others give in and take their own punishment."

CHAPTER SEVEN

ol reached up and tugged lightly at Rowan's wrists. The bindings seemed to give but tightened again when he had her arms repositioned so that her elbows were bent at ninety degree angles. It gave her a better vantage to either side, and allowed circulation back into her arms.

"Thank you," she sent to him.

"Don't thank me yet, I'm just taking my time for emphasis. You will submit when I'm ready for you to." He nipped more deliberately at the back of her neck, the sudden contact causing more wet heat to flood between her thighs. His caresses grew idle, almost comforting as she watched the other three endure their own ordeals.

Rafe's entire body was taut from strain against his bindings. Racha rested on her knees before him, her mouth wrapped around his cock, sucking with slow, steady motions. The magic churned around him, and the second Rowan was sure Rafe would come hard in Racha's mouth, the Queen abruptly stopped and stood, leaving Rafe's wet cock standing like a solitary pillar, his tip weeping.

"Submit," Racha whispered in his ear.

"No," Rafe said, the word coming out in a strangled groan.

Racha only nodded and stepped to the side, wrapping one arm around his waist and caressing him in a less arousing fashion but never ceasing contact.

Aurin looked across the space at Rowan with a secretive smile. The pretty blonde shared a glance with her brother as Geva's large hands teased her. Rowan's Red brother followed Kol's example, teasing Aurin's nipples, then nibbling at her neck. Only he went one further and slid a hand between her thighs, dipping his fingertips deep into Aurin's glistening, bare pussy.

Aurin moaned and tilted her hips into his touch. Her eyelids fluttered halfway closed, but her gaze still held Rowan's.

"Submit," Geva said, his lips brushing against her ear.

The bound Gold turned her head, her eyes seeking out her tormentor. Geva clutched her chin with his free hand and captured her mouth hungrily with his own in a tangle of lips and tongues. When they pulled apart a second later, Aurin simply said, "Yes."

She nearly collapsed when her bindings released, but Geva caught her and lowered her to the ground until she rested on hands and knees in front of him. His wicked smile grew broader, his red eyes glowing when they met Rowan's.

Rowan had barely known her brother for two days, but had the distinct impression that he was showing off for her. She'd have been lying if she said she wasn't impressed. He let his thick cock nestle along the cleft of Aurin's ass and leaned over her smaller body whispering in her ear.

"This is only the beginning, love," he said, and sank his teeth into the back of Aurin's neck.

Aurin cried out and pressed her hips back against him in urgent invitation. He chuckled and tilted his hips back far enough to gain entry. Both dragons let out sighs of enjoyment when he plunged to the hilt into her with a smack of hips against her ass.

Rowan's pussy ached in sympathy. The base of Kol's cock still brushed hotly against her own ass, the soft velvet of his balls pressed just close enough for her to make out their pendulous contours. His hands rested at her hips now, holding her tighter against him as they watched their siblings begin to fuck.

Out of the corner of her eye, Rowan sensed movement. The tall bulk of Gavra, the immortal Red, moved past into the center. His massive cock stood thick and nearly perfectly erect in spite of its size. His thighs flexed as he lowered himself to one knee before Aurin.

Aurin's wide golden eyes looked up at him reverently as Gavra caressed her cheek and tilted her chin up with one fingertip.

"Are you ready for more, little one?" he asked.

Aurin's eyelids fluttered closed, and she whispered the word *"yes"* and opened her mouth. She raised both hands to clutch desperately at Gavra's thighs as he slid almost his entire thick length deep into her throat.

Rowan swallowed and breathed deeply, wondering how the delicate, beautiful golden girl could take all that. At the same time, her mouth watered at the very idea of such a glorious cock being shoved into her own mouth. She hazarded a quick look at Rafe and their eyes met. His dark eyes flashed with the same lust she had seen the first time she'd allowed him to fuck her mouth like that. While Rafe watched, Kol's hands slid back up to her breasts and lifted their heavy weight, teasing her hard nipples for her mate's benefit.

"If you submit next, you can let him watch while I shove my cock into you like that. I know Rafe. He would enjoy it."

"I want to hear him tell me he wants it."

"Very well," Kol said.

A split second later, the vivid image of her very memory of the taste and texture of Rafe's cock blazed through her mind, along with the sensations that accompanied that first experience. For a moment she was no longer in the glade, but in Rafe's bedroom, with his palms on either side of her face, his hot length sliding between her lips and along her tongue. When she returned to the present, Rafe was watching her and smiling.

The scene in the center escalated, the threads of magic that permeated the air in the Glade clinging to the three participants like sticky webs. Rowan's ears buzzed with the increasing volume of the men's lusty groans, and Aurin's muffled moans. Her mouth slid off Gavra's cock and she abruptly cried out, bucking back hard against Geva's steadily pistoning cock. Rowan's brother let out a yell and rammed into her, his entire body quivering with his climax.

The glimmering threads of magic sank through them as though seeping into their pores until they both glowed from within. In the span of a breath the floor beneath them where they made contact with it shimmered with red and yellow light that surged toward the center. The Verdanith glowed brightly again for a moment, then subsided, but its pulses remained more luminescent than before, shining along the underside of Gavra's still erect cock and casting a dark shadow against his belly.

Rowan's arousal had her almost too dizzy and distracted from pleasure to follow events after that, but soon enough, the center was filled with writhing bodies again. This time it was Aurik, who obediently submitted to Gavra. Rowan blinked several times before she realized it was no longer Aurin in the center, but Aurik with Roka's cock his throat and the immortal Red, Gavra, sliding his cock deep into Aurik's ass until all three of them came with loud yells.

"It's your turn again. Second chance," Kol said. He drifted a hand down her belly and cupped her cunt, sliding his fingers along the soaked lips and drawing his hand back up to hold it before her. "You need to come so badly you can taste it." He slid one glistening fingertip along her lower lip. Her own heady scent wafted into her nostrils at the same time Rafe's moan hit her ears. His gaze was fixed on her mouth and he licked his lips as though wishing she would do the same. No thoughts reached her from him, but the intensity of his desire nearly overwhelmed her.

She restrained herself from even tasting her own juices, though it took all her willpower.

"No! I want promises before I do."

"What promises?" The immortal Gold, Aurum, appeared before her again, as quietly as before. "I can promise you pleasure beyond your wildest dreams." Aurum bent to her knees and snaked out a forked tongue that tickled at the top of Rowan's pussy. The twin points of it slid further, parting the slick, swollen folds, moving slowly and sensually as though Aurum intended to taste every inch of her. The tongue slipped deeper, pressing into the dark, place Rowan desperately needed to be filled.

The pleasure was maddening. Rowan tried to pull away otherwise she feared she'd lose her mind. She knew from the proceedings so far that she would have no release until she submitted. But she needed guarantees, first.

"Promises..." she gasped. "That Rafe and I can stay together, that the Unbound will be freed, that our children... our families can enjoy a full life the way h-humans do."

The incessant teasing ceased, and Kol loosened his grip on her slightly. His breathing grew silent, his body tense, waiting for the other shoe to drop, she guessed.

Aurum stood. "We heard your petition during the assembly, Princess. Yet you keep restating it. Your submission is not a condition of your request being honored."

"I have no reason to trust that you will follow through, I guess. So, if you want my submission that badly, you'd better honor my request, and all the other ones that were made."

It wasn't precisely anger that flashed through Aurum's eyes, but something like intense frustration. Frustration not unlike what ached deep in Rowan's core at the moment.

"You do need my submission, and badly, don't you?" she asked.

"Yours and your mate's, yes." The Gold's gaze heated when she looked at Rafe. "His love for you is what is keeping him from giving in. If things change the way you hope them to, this generation will need strong guidance from someone familiar with the new world we live in."

Aurum seemed sad when she turned back to Rowan. "We always encouraged bonds of love for all dragons. We knew some would follow out of a sense of obligation, but most would be happy with the humans who woke them. We chose the ascendant teams so carefully. The team that awakened this generation was perfect. Each human an ideal mate for a single dragon among the Court. It's the first time we've been so lucky. We finally had hope that our work would bear fruit. But then the matings didn't go as we intended. The Catalyst wasn't meant to choose a mate from the Court, yet he did. The Guardian was meant to have a single female mate. The Twins were meant to be a choice for the young Dimitri to make, yet he somehow succeeded in waking them both."

"I'm sorry things didn't go your way," Rowan said, "but that's no reason to punish the dragons for the choices the humans made."

"On the contrary. In spite of our carefully made plans going awry, the results were even more amazing than we could have imagined. When the Catalyst's Twins were conceived, we wondered if it was only in the areas where we had no control—where the Brood made their choices against our wishes—that the results we hoped for might finally be achieved. And then when you arrived, we were presented with another sign that in spite of how rigorously we make our plans, fate has a way of asserting itself. You are a miracle, as are the unborn children of the Catalyst. So we have decided to let fate take its course. We are giving up, Rowan. After we finish here, you will have your wish. The Court will take over jurisdiction, and we will simply control the use of the Verdanith as we did before."

Rowan's heart ached for the tall, lovely woman. She involuntarily pressed at her bindings, hoping to comfort Aurum, but the tightening of the coils reminded her there was still no escape.

"What do you think went wrong with your plans?" Rowan asked.

"You did. But it was inevitable anyway. We were fools to think we had full control. Dragons have always been victims of fate and we thought we might stay a step ahead of it for a change. We were wrong."

"Wrong about what? Just me? I'm sure I'm not the only one out there like me."

"No. But you're the only one birthed of multiple generations of Queens. The only one who could be a harbinger of what might come." She lifted a delicate hand to Rowan's cheek. "Your presence here is enough of a sign that we were mistaken all along. We have failed and it is up to your generation to protect our race."

"Protect us from what?" Rowan asked the question even as every other member of the Court in the Glade sent it to her telepathically.

"That I can't yet say," Aurum replied. "But we know we

are in danger without your help."

"You're giving up… allowing the Court to rewrite the laws. Yet you still seem intent on punishing us. Why?"

"Punishment is necessary for more than just censure. It's also a test to determine whether you are a viable conduit to recharge the Verdanith. You couldn't have known, and neither could the others, but one of the other three would have been chosen for the task. Punishment was to encourage your complete submission, which is required to transfer our power into the Verdanith. We'd like you to have the honor for other reasons, however."

"Don't tell me you have more secrets."

"No more secrets. Just this last task if you choose to submit. But before you agree—before we give into fate completely—there is one last thing we must do." She turned and strode to the edge of the platform, took a breath, and turned back to look at Rowan, her expression resolute. "Kris's children are sacred. Right now I hope the Udara are ensuring the children thrive until we can complete this task. The Twins will need protection as they grow. But they are not destined to be our protectors. They are the ones who will power and protect our savior. You are the offspring of Queens. If you are willing, when you submit we all will infuse you with our essence. When you leave the glade, you will be impregnated with the Ashemis. The essence of all our power, combined with yours."

"Ah…so what will my hypothetical baby be saving us all from?"

Aurum didn't answer. The larger form of Ked, stepped in front of her. "You will save us from ourselves."

"Ked, no. It isn't time." Aurum moved back in front of the large dragon with an irritated look.

"When is it time? When Sutylutha's curse is already tearing us down? We failed, Aurum! We've doomed ourselves out of our fear of our own race. The Mother created the six of us to ensure the race's safety and longevity and we failed. Rowan is right to request what she has."

"The curse hasn't come to fruition as far as we know, but the presence of the Twins and Rowan are signs that it will come to pass in spite of our efforts to avoid it. Fragmenting the Verdanith was the only way we could control the bloodlines. And now reassembling it is the only way we can find the source of the curse if it exists. We can't even be sure what form it will take, but once the Verdanith is at full power we will know soon enough. We need Rowan to recharge it and her daughter's power to help us repel the curse."

Kol's gentle nudge was enough of a signal. In spite of her reservations about all the other things they'd just suggested, this was what they were hoping for, and the thing Rowan vowed she'd do anything to secure.

"If that option is on the table, I will at least negotiate."

The pair of dragons turned to stare at her.

"You're at our mercy, yet you suggest negotiation?"

"Are you going to give the Court jurisdiction or not? If not, I will continue to refuse you."

"And if so?" Ked asked, moving close. The dragon seemed much larger right up against her. She pressed back against Kol's solid body and he wrapped both arms around her. Ked's black eyes focused on hers, then slid down her body, leaving every inch of her skin tingling. One large hand cupped her breast, toyed with her nipple with excruciating tenderness, then he bent and flicked his tongue against it.

"You do taste different from the others," he said, humming in appreciation. "Purer. I wonder..." He dropped to his knees. Rowan watched him mutely as he eyed her pussy, then slid two hands up her thighs to spread her open. A second later he had his entire tongue shoved deep inside her and she writhed against his mouth.

Holy fuck, Ked's tongue seemed to vibrate inside her. She clutched at Kol's arms, pressed her ass back against him. That cock of his needed someplace to be…

"Ked!" Aurum yelled.

Abruptly the invasion ended.

"You didn't answer my question," Ked said.

Kol's fingertips sank hard into Rowan's hips.

"Sweetie, if you've got something to share, out with it," Rowan said to him.

"I am not at liberty to speak to the Council now. Only the accused can make arguments. Tell them the Court would gladly continue protection of the race if we also have jurisdiction over the laws."

"Um…What question was that?" Rowan asked out loud.

"If we give the Court jurisdiction, what will you do? Will you refuse our request?"

Rowan closed her eyes tightly. She wondered for a moment if she could request he go back to what he'd just been doing with his tongue.

"No. As long as Rafe submits and is a part of it, I will do it."

"Every dragon here must be a part of it, the males with their essence, the females with their magic. Now that we are all inside the glade, the Verdanith won't accept our sacrifices until they are equally given. To the stone and to its proxy. That would be you. As soon as it's charged, our first task will be to channel energy to the Catalyst's children."

Kol's whisper tickled her ear. "Good work. Let's just hope our loverboy is on board."

A single glance at Rafe spoke volumes. He smiled at her and in a soft voice filled with reverence said, "I submit." The two words he spoke out loud were only half his full message, however. In her mind Rowan heard the rest: *"…to you, for eternity."*

Racha released a relieved sigh and hung back while the others converged. Roka was the first to reach his friend. He led Rafe to the center of their circle and urged him to kneel. Kneeling in front of the Shadow, he made quick work of stroking Rafe to completion with one hand before the others came forward.

Rafe leaned back on his heels and looked at Rowan, his eyes bright and his chest heaving from his orgasm. He smiled and said, "You want to watch?" He gestured and the others came toward him. "Whatever you plan to do to her, you'll do to me, first," he said, fixing his gaze on each of them in turn.

"I will be right back," Kol whispered in her ear.

"You don't have to, do you?"

"I plan to do it to you, love. So yes. I do. This will at least give you an idea what you're in for."

Still tied, Rowan had no choice but to watch while the others took turns coupling with her lover, and through it all she received the vivid impression that he enjoyed every second. They all took their turns, sometimes two or three at a time. Each time Rafe or one of the others climaxed, the Verdanith grew brighter

Rafe lay limp and gasping after they each finished, one by one leaving to plunge into the pool to bathe. The Verdanith pulsed brightly beneath him, lending an unearthly glow to his skin.

"I love you," she whispered.

Rafe's lips twitched in a smile and he lifted his head. Sweat soaked his hair and it clung to his forehead and neck in dark strands. His eyelids drooped low, but he focused intently on her. He said nothing, only the smile on his face and the intense emotion that washed over her indicated his understanding of their shared situation and his acceptance of what they both knew she must do.

CHAPTER EIGHT

"Do you submit?" Kol asked Rowan for the final time after the group had bathed.

"Yes."

The bindings instantly released. Her strength left her, but Kol caught her in strong arms. His beautiful face was before her, kissing her. "You did well," he whispered. "This is the easy part now."

"The part where you fuck me finally?"

He chuckled. "Yeah, the part where we all do."

He held her close and laid her down gently in the center of the platform. Deep warmth seeped into her back. "What is it?" she asked, trying to move to see, but the hands of all the others held her down.

"It's only the Verdanith," Aurum said, kneeling beside Rowan. "Your power will be the final charge. You need to stay in contact with it for it to transmute our essences into the seed that will become the child."

The immortal White, Aodh, knelt at Rowan's other side and exhaled. Her sight became obscured with a solid white mist. She could see no one. She could only feel the hands on her, holding her down, and the deep heat of the Verdanith against the center of her back.

Suddenly the memory of Rafe's anguished objections their first weekend together flooded through her mind. She was pure, like he had said. And here she was, consciously agreeing to being the thing she'd objected to the most. Their entire race needed her to be their broodmare. She wanted it as much as anything, and it seemed a small sacrifice to make to be able to have him.

"Rafe, where are you?"

"I'm here, baby," his voice called to her, and a hand pressed against her hip, warm and comforting. It moved along her contours up to her breast. "I'm here," he said again, the sound moving around above her head. Strong, gentle hands lifted her head just enough for him to move beneath, letting her rest against his crossed calves. His warm lips pressed against hers from above, and she sighed at the welcome contact, letting herself get lost in the familiarity of him even as the others began to touch her. He kept contact with her, caressing her face with soft fingertips and kissing her every so often.

"Ready her," a deep voice said. Was that Ked? Gavra? It had to be one of the immortal dragons. Aodh even. She didn't recognize it as one she knew, though the mist could be transforming the voices, too.

Several hands gripped her legs, spreading her wide and pulling her knees up to her chest. Other hands held her arms down to the warm stone. Still others were on her body, cupping her breasts, teasing between her thighs.

She gasped when a hot tongue unexpectedly hit her clit, the teasing flick of it making her quiver and want more, but it left only to be replaced by another tongue, similar but thicker, more insistent. This tongue wanted her to come. Wanted her essence. It, too departed after only a few brief licks that left Rowan's pussy aching. She was on the verge of begging now. She'd submitted and yet they were only teasing her. She needed more.

And they gave it to her. The hands held her thighs still. Her hearing became acute, every sound making her turn her head in an effort to discern who was moving. She inhaled deeply through her nose, hoping to catch familiar scents of those she had come to know as her family over the last few days. Rafe was easy enough to sense through their shared bond, and his constant contact. Another she was sure of was her brother, whose hand was one of the ones resting firmly behind her knee, keeping her spread open for the others.

"Tell me what you see. I'm blind here," she sent to Rafe.

"You're beautiful, unfurled as you are. An exquisite crimson flower, and we are the bees."

"She is ready," Roka said, his voice coming from between her spread legs. The scent of him was familiar enough from their first meeting. Abruptly his hot, thick cock pressed against her spread cunt. He slid his tip around in a circle against her clit, torturing her for a moment before slamming deep enough to make her cry out. *That* was what she needed, Oh, God.

Their hands continued to hold her thighs while he pounded into her. Mouths found her nipples. A familiar voice or a scent told her who was close, but she decided it didn't matter. They were all giving her what their entire race needed.

Roka's cock slid in and out of her, the thick ridge around the tip rubbing inside with delicious pleasure. The hands and lips that shared her mouth and breasts never let up. She imagined the magic seeping into her, was sure she could feel every tingling thread of it as her pleasure grew. The threads sank deeper into her core with each steady stroke of Roka's cock until the knot of it that filled her womb was too much for her to contain. The blinding ecstasy burst from her and she cried out, arching up against their caresses with her first orgasm. A second later Roka answered, his hips smacking hard against hers with his final thrust as he came.

He withdrew quickly and another took his place. First, with quick, agile fingers that teased at her cunt. She heard the sound of someone licking fingers.

Aurik commented, "She tastes delicious with hot Guardian spunk in her."

Rowan almost made a retort, but before she could, the hot, sweet scent of female sex hit her nostrils. A second later someone's thighs brushed against her cheeks. She darted out her tongue, curious, and encountered exactly what she expected—a slick, swollen pussy. Essence or magic was what she'd been told they would give her. She didn't need to be fucked to get all of it. Rowan tilted her head and darted her forked tongue out, teasing it around and around the thick bundle. The possessor of the clit gasped and rocked her hips lower. Rowan wrapped her lips around the throbbing little nub and sucked, barely aware of the new cock shoving into her from the other side. Sweet juice flooded her mouth, both tangy and salty, with a slight bite of hot spice. The breathy moan the female let out was Rowan's only clue that it was Aurin she serviced. The salty spice that mingled with Aurin's tang must be Geva's seed. Their combined flavors coated her tongue when she sank it into Aurin's slick depths.

Soon, Rowan's pussy wouldn't be denied. Aurik fucked her so expertly she lost track of other things.

"Suck her clit. Don't think about me," Aurik said. Rowan sucked, but it was impossible not to think about him. At least not until the pussy pressed over her mouth spasmed and its owner yelled a few profanities in a language Rowan had never heard and the bright power of Aurin's Nirvana flowed through her.

The cock buried in Rowan's own snatch swelled and pulsed when Aurik came. Then he disappeared, leaving her disappointed.

But only a moment later something massive brushed hot against her inner thigh. Large hands clutched her to spread her wider and a thumb caressed her slick folds, sliding up to rub gently over her swollen clit.

"Stay wet for me," Kol's deep voice said.

"I don't think that will be an issue," she replied with a small chuckle that transformed into a surprised gasp when he plunged into her to the hilt, his path amply lubricated by the semen of the two that preceded him, along with her own juices. His hands slipped beneath her hips to hold her up higher. The angle caused his cock to press with excruciating precision against her inner wall, his strokes becoming more deliberate and focused so that he rubbed maddeningly against the same spot.

"That's it," Rafe said from above her. "He's found your weakness, hasn't he? Give in to him, Rowan. Sweet Mother, I love watching your face when you come." His lips came down on hers again and she surrendered. Her pussy clenched in hard spasms around Kol's cock, relentlessly milking him until he cried out and his hot seed shot into her.

The silken warmth of another pair of thighs slid along the tops of her shoulders. Rowan tilted her chin and opened her mouth, her tongue extended just enough in anticipation of the slick heat of another female. Racha's verdant scent already clung to Rafe, and now Rowan found herself immersed in it. The Queen faced the opposite direction as Aurin had. While she snaked her tongue around Racha's quivering folds, she felt the woman's hands grip Rafe. He shifted slightly beneath her head and sighed.

"She's an attentive leader," he said to Rowan before she could comment.

"Fuck her while I do this. I want to taste you on her."

Rafe murmured her request to Racha, and the Queen moved, turning the other way. Rowan was forced to extend her tongue a little farther when Rafe moved out from under her head. Racha's breathy moan was the first sign of Rafe's penetration and Rowan darted her tongue out to find where her lover's shaft sank into Racha's tight opening. Rowan teased and licked at them both in equal measure, determined to taste Rafe's spend mixed with her Queen's delicious juices. Distracted by her quest, she was only partly aware when another thick cock found its way into her sopping cunt.

Rafe let out a harsh groan and his movements slowed. He pulled out of Racha and sank back in, the motion seeming to mimic the cock that slowly fucked into Rowan from the other side. Rowan had ceased to wonder who was where, losing herself to every sensation below her neck. At least she had some control over what happened above.

At the moment her body was not her own, but belonged to all of them. The realization let her give in completely, every delicious sensation another message that she was only the vessel for their salvation, and that the culmination of their shared essences was the seed. Aurum's words rang in Rowan's ears again as Rafe's cock and balls quivered under her tongue and his salty semen flooded her mouth from Racha's spasming pussy. *"Fate has a way of asserting itself."*

Whichever cock was asserting itself in Rowan's pussy now moved with gentle, deliberate strokes, its velvet heat urging the magic into a knot like a ball of flame in her belly. Above her lips more silken folds of flesh surrounding a pulsing, needy clit descended. Aurum moaned with Rowan's first lick, but the sound wasn't enough to drown out the familiar growling groan of the dragon fucking her.

"Your cunt is as perfect as Erika's, sister." Her brother's delighted words sank into her mind. Far from shocking, they

incited the most explosive release yet. She threw her head back in a harsh cry, her pussy grasping hungrily at the shaft that pierced her, pushing her further and further into oblivion.

The Verdanith seemed burning hot against her back, its pulsing need as urgent as Aurum's clit, so hot it forced her back to awareness. She surrendered to them both, unable to do more than accept her role. The energy from Geva's climax had passed straight through her into the Verdanith, but she was left with the lingering sense of him. She had no time to be confused or even disgusted. And how could she be anything but grateful for his attention and gentle urgency in the midst of everyone's desperate need?

As though sensing her confusion, Rafe returned to her head, caressing her sweat-soaked temples even as she continued to service the immortal Gold with her tongue. There was no time to be confused or worried. She'd known Geva for two days. And he wasn't her brother now, he was only a small part of the seed to her vessel.

Geva departed and another wholly otherworldly cock took his place, the thick, hot length of him stretching her nearly to the point of pain and almost obliterating the feel of her brother's cock with a tingle that seeped into her. She resumed her guessing game, deciding that with the pleasant, refreshing sensation of him, it must be the White immortal, Aodh, who fucked her now.

It took a mere half a dozen strokes of Aodh's tremendous length before she was flying, her tongue lashing with abandon at the presence of a new quivering snatch that pressed against her lips. Both immortals climaxed in unison, their power flooding her with blinding energy that seemed to sear every cell in her body before it was absorbed by the stone talisman beneath her back.

She recognized Gavra by his heat, so similar to her brother's. He fucked her more urgently, as though he sensed the powering of the Verdanith was close to complete. Numa pressed a gentle kiss to Rowan's lips and murmured words of encouragement before moving to spread her nether lips over Rowan's mouth.

The immortals each left Rowan buzzing from head to toe with the intensity of the power their climaxes flooded her with.

Ked was the last of them, and began with an attentive lick, picking up where he left off before it all began. He found her clit with his tongue, swirling around it in tight little circles before he plunged the agile length deep into her. She writhed against the hands that held her, beyond the bounds of sanity from all the orgasms, but in spite of sending her over the brink yet again, Ked wasn't content to leave it at that. While her muscles still clenched, he moved up and slid his thick, hard shaft deep into her. The heat of his huge body hovered over her, closer than the others had been, and she felt the warm exhalation of his breath sweep over her skin with a very deliberate caress. The hands of the others disappeared, replaced with the cooler sensation of Ked's shadowy hold. Rather than coils of inanimate ropes, they became delicate caresses that covered every inch of her skin, sliding and probing to find the points that gave her the most acute pleasure. The caresses moved lower, driving her mad with desire so intense she sent an incoherent plea to Rafe, the only one who could keep her grounded.

"You enjoy what he's doing, don't you? I can do the same for you, if you'd like," he said, and she heard his own exhalation. Soon, Ked's shadowy caresses were joined by another set, but Rafe's were bolder, taking advantage of his intimate knowledge of what pleased her. Rafe's mouth teased her nipples, and one hand slipped between her and Ked to find her abused clit still throbbing and needy. His breath slid down

her thigh and over the curve of her ass, brushed past the steady smack of Ked's balls against her asshole and teased around the tight barrier that as yet had remained unpenetrated today.

Ked grunted in a kind of recognition when Rafe's shadowy touch pressed into her. He held his cock halfway out of her, his hips seeming to press backward more than forward.

"You're a brave one to be so presumptuous, Shadow," Ked's deep voice said.

"Neither brave nor presumptuous," Rafe said. "I'd like to have her back soon, that's all. If I have to fuck one of you to get her, then I will."

Ked laughed, the sound rolling out of him and sinking into her bones like thunder. "I can take more of your Shadow than you're giving her. If you want me to speed things up, you'll have to try harder."

Ked's breath came out in a sharp gasp. At the same time, he slammed hard into her, his strokes suddenly moving quicker and more frantic than before. "Yes, just like that," he panted.

"Oh, God, yes, like that," Rowan sent to Rafe when his shadowy touch penetrated her ass deeper, becoming thicker and more tangible with every slow thrust. *"You're doing the same thing to him, aren't you?"*

"Just a little bit more for him. Or a lot more. He's getting properly fucked while he fucks you."

Ked's swift strokes into her seemed to grow more determined and measured. Rowan wished like hell she could actually see the immortal come undone from Rafe's attention.

Rafe's clever touch never ceased, winding her up in ways only he knew. She let out a plaintive moan when the waves of pleasure grew almost too much for her to bear. Rafe kissed her then, and she devoured his mouth with her own, the contact sending her spinning and gasping for breath when he pulled back.

Ked's cry of climax mingled with her own, both leaving her ears ringing. The Verdanith's ever-present heat increased with the surge of energy that passed through her into it. After the violent flood of Ked's semen ceased, he slid slowly out of her.

"She needs one more, Rafe. Make it good."

The binding grip of Ked's shadowy hands left her and she let her aching legs drop to the ground. The blindfold of white fog dissipated. She blinked into the sky, mesmerized for a moment by the ethereal glowing circle that hovered far above, throbbing with the same heat as the stone beneath her back. From her low vantage point she had the oddest sensation that they were trapped inside a bubble.

Rafe's face came into view, his brow creased with concern. He moved to lie on his side next to her, propped on one elbow, and rested a gentle palm against her belly.

"We should to do this soon, but you can rest for a moment if you need."

"I get to have you all to myself?" Rowan asked, dazed and still buzzed from the almost constant flow of energy that had used her body as a conduit. She struggled to sit, but Rafe placed both hands against her shoulders.

"Not yet. When we're finished you can rise and I will take you home."

Rowan reached up and laid a palm along the side of his scruffy cheek, urging him down to her. The kiss was the sweetest he'd given her yet, more gentle and reverent than their first morning together. He pressed closer, his erection undeniable against her hip. She slid her hand down his chest and belly, enjoying the tightening of his abs beneath her fingertips when she reached lower.

Rafe groaned against her lips when she gripped him, his

velvet length hot and hard in her palm. She stroked him once, eliciting a sharp gasp from his lips. His arousal was all she needed for her own well of desire to crave him.

"I need you," she whispered. "Make love to me, please."

"I submit," he murmured back as he moved above her.

Rowan spread her legs one last time and raised her hips to meet his thrust. She wrapped her legs around his waist and held him tight against her, gazing up into his eyes. He stared back with those bottomless black eyes that always seemed to draw her in. His expression was somehow amazed. "I submit to you, too," she said with a smile.

Rafe laughed and kissed her. "Sweet Mother, I need to fuck you. Holding me hostage isn't getting us anywhere."

She released her tight hold on him just enough to let him slide out, then lifted her hips to meet him as he plunged back in. Every sensation she'd experienced over the last day came flooding back under his touch. They moved together in the only way that made sense after everything, and his voice seeped into her mind with each thrust, each word a promise. *"I love you. What you did today was beyond my wildest dreams. You are my heart."*

"You shadow-fucked an immortal," she said.

"He liked it."

"Do it to me again," she whispered. With his breath, her pleasure grew exponentially. He watched her raptly, his face tight with the need to let go, yet he didn't. She loved him for his need to see her fall apart beneath him, but she loved seeing him do it, too. She let go then, let the pleasure take her. Every muscle tensed and she arched into him. He held perfectly still, holding her caged between his arms just as his hips were trapped between her thighs, her heels pressed hard into his ass holding him deep inside her.

"Fuck me hard, so I can watch you, now," she said.

At first his brows drew together, then he smiled. He

braced both hands beside her head, his elbows locked, and bent to kiss her.

"Hold on."

The first stroke was a test, but after that Rafe's jaw clenched and he slammed into her relentlessly. Every emotion seemed to pass through his eyes and Rowan caught pieces of all of them through their bond. Some were heartbreaking for their intensity. His love for her, and the torture she'd put him through after running. She felt his anger toward her, which he took out on her with a vengeance now, but mostly she simply felt his love and desperation, and finally relief that they were together again.

Through it all, her own responses welled up, blasting back at him in full force until his eyes grew wet with understanding. They kept hold of each other's gazes, their bodies moving more frantically as the pleasure built up, until neither of them could hold back any longer. Rowan's skin prickled with power and through the narrow slits of her eyelids she could see the same glow around Rafe. The energy was pulled off him as though by a vacuum, every bit of it flowing through her and into the stone at her back.

The heat of the Verdanith grew agonizing, in spite of her tolerance for heat. Before, it was only a hot presence that was mildly uncomfortable. Now it actually hurt.

She tried to sit, but the others moved to hold her down again.

"Not yet, Princess," Numa said. "When the pain subsides you can move. But the Verdanith is fully powered now, which means we can channel energy to the Twins."

"What's happening?" Rowan asked, alarmed both by the pain and the six immortal dragons linking hands around her. Light channeled down through their bodies and into the stone at their feet, converging beneath her with even more heat.

"It's marking you, little one," Gavra said. "You and the seed you carry will be connected to it. And through the power we're channeling now, we are forging your child's connection with the Twins. From this moment on, our child and the Twin Catalysts will have the Verdanith's power to draw from, as long as the Verdanith remains whole."

Our child. He'd said the words so casually, like the child was his.

"It will be *my* child. I hope you guys realize this. Mine and Rafe's. We will raise her. We are her parents."

"Yes, that is best, but we have a final condition," Ked said.

"Jesus Fucking Christ, you and your conditions. What is it?"

The large, black-haired man seemed amused by her irritation. "We'd like to see you again, this time each year. Not for any ritual, just to… debrief us on the state of the race. We tend to retreat when we're not needed, but we'd like an opportunity to be more involved."

"More involved with my ass, you mean?" she shot back at him.

Ked smiled. "No other ass would do."

CHAPTER NINE

Kris gently closed the door to Issa's chamber. She was still unconscious, which terrified him. With every second her energy seeped away into the children in her womb. He scrubbed his hands over his face and looked around the sitting room at all the expectant faces of the Court's mates.

"How is she?" Camille asked.

"Not good."

"Tell us what you need us to do," Dimitri said, resting a comforting hand on Kris's shoulder.

Kris looked back at his friend, at a loss for words at first. They were all here to help. To give what they could to ensure his mate's survival along with their babies. But Issa was in no condition to entertain another in their bed. He would have to do it for her—take their Nirvana and transfer it to her while she slept. He wished desperately that he was more than just a conduit. His capacity to store the energy absorbed during sex wasn't as strong as other dragons, yet he could channel it through himself for days, and what little he could store, he could give away at will.

He wished for an altar like the one in the temple, but they were far from there and nothing of the sort existed at the Monastery. Transferring enough energy to his mate would take time, so he had to be smart about it.

"You are the Udara the Council spoke of, aren't you?" He looked at Dimitri and the petite, dark-haired woman by his side. Thea, Kris had heard the others call her. Their auras were stronger than the others, which was evidence enough of what the Council had said.

Dimitri placed his palm at Thea's back and their auras pulsed with even stronger magic as though they fed off each other. If he could channel their Nirvanas to Issa, that might be enough. Or at least a good start.

"We're something, that's for sure," Thea said. "The Twins were willing to break laws to have us both."

"The Twins?" Kris asked. He looked at Dimitri and then at Thea. "You were with him and his brother before, weren't you? I remember Dimitri talking about you during the expedition. Have you always been with twins?"

Thea opened her mouth to answer, then closed it again, giving him a curious look. "What does that have to do with this?"

"My children are twins. Please, come with me."

He opened the door again and led them into the chamber. Lanterns glowed around the large bed where Issa lay. She appeared so peaceful and beautiful, her face smooth and free from worry. Kris moved up onto the bed and gestured for Thea and Dimitri to follow.

Without speaking, Kris took Thea's hand and placed it on Issa's swollen belly. Beneath his own palm, the warm presence of the babies surged and pressed outward. Thea gasped.

"Dimitri, feel this!" she whispered, urging Dimitri to place his own hands next to hers.

Issa's belly visibly shifted, the unseen lives within her seeking out their hands.

"They are killing her," Kris said. "There is only so much I can do alone. They are drawn to you. If I can transfer your Nirvana to her, it could save her life."

"Do you mean like the ritual when we woke them?" Dimitri asked. "We just have to—ah—have an orgasm while we touch her, right?"

Kris grimaced. "She's not in hibernation. She's weak and depleted of power. If it weren't for the babies, she'd have shifted to her true form, but they keep her from doing so. She needs to be conscious before sex can help her directly. But I can channel your power to her."

Thea and Dimitri shared a long look.

"What is it?" Kris asked. "You will help, won't you?"

"Of course we will," Thea said. "It's just that we haven't been together without the Twins in a really long time. And it's never been just the two of us."

"It won't be the two of you now," Kris said. "You have me."

Thea smiled and lowered her gaze. "Right, I'm still getting used to how you guys work. Um…should we just start, then?" She raised her head again and met his worried gaze. Her eyes were bright with determination and excitement.

Before Kris could answer, Dimitri wrapped his arms around Thea from behind and whispered. "Remember the first night we were together?"

Thea's eyelids drifted closed and her lips parted. Swirling eddies of power tangled with their auras, growing bright enough that Kris had to shift his eyesight to avoid the blinding glow, but even with the magic hidden from his sight, his body was aware of the power filling the air around the two. His cock swelled in response, as hard and erect as it had been in the presence of the Council's nearly overwhelming power.

Dimitri unfastened the buttons of Thea's shirt enough to slip one hand inside and tease fingertips along her breasts beneath the fabric. She gasped and tilted her head back against his shoulder. Thea's eyes drifted over Kris's chest, the gaze tracing his tattoo. The design sparked to life in response to the simple look from her. She reached out a hand, beckoning him to come closer.

Kris closed the gap, tentative at first. He hadn't been with any woman besides Issa since they had mated, in spite of her suggestions to leave the mountain once in a while for fun. Then, when she became pregnant, he had vowed to stay with her through it.

Thea's power drew him to her as much as the soft pull of her hand when he gripped it. Her lips were cool and soft under his and her fingertips gentle as she raked them through his thick hair. The kiss was both tender and patient, as though she were waiting for him to take it further. Her arousal was so undeniable he didn't have a choice and plunged his tongue between her lips in a desperate sweep. He would take everything they could give him.

Between their bodies, he raised his hands and found the buttons of her shirt, tugging at them until the garment fell open, revealing a lacy bra that held up her full, creamy breasts, her nipples clearly visible through the pale fabric. Dimitri pulled the shirt off her arms and unfastened the undergarment, then cupped both ample mounds and held them up to Kris.

He accepted the invitation, clutching at the swell of Thea's hips while he suckled at each dark-pink tip until she moaned in pleasure.

The power was a whirling bubble that encompassed the three of them. Out of the corner of Kris's eye, Issa's belly surged. Quickly, he must do this quickly for them.

He clutched the waist of Thea's pants and frantically

pulled get them undone and off her. Dimitri leaned back and hurriedly undressed himself, then moved back against the pillows, drawing Thea with him.

They seemed to sense his urgency, for which he was grateful. Yet he needed to be sure they were both as ready as he was. He reached behind Thea to Dimitri, groping in the dim light. Dimitri clutched his hand and tugged it down.

"You looking for this?" he asked in a gruff voice when Kris's hand brushed against the hard length between Dimitri's thighs. "Trust me, we're ready, but we need your help to get her ready for me if we're both going to fuck her."

Dimitri held Thea against his chest and Kris bent and swirled his tongue around her nipples once more before slipping lower. Every inch of her skin left his lips tingling from the invisible power that clung to her. It grew more pronounced the lower he went, until he reached her wet center and latched on. She jerked at the sudden contact and then sighed, sinking back in Dimitri's arms while Kris licked and sucked.

"Oh, God, Kris. You're going to make me come like that!"

"I think that's the idea," Dimitri said, his gaze avidly latched onto Kris's tongue. Dimitri continued toying with Thea's nipples, every touch increasing the concentration of power around her.

Kris decided he would use them until they begged to rest, and it would begin with her. He plunged his tongue deep into her, enjoying the way her hips rose up to meet his mouth. He remembered she was one of the Twins' lovers so she was no stranger to this kind of treatment. He fucked her pussy harder with his tongue, urging her closer and closer to the edge. He withdrew for a second, long enough to slick the length of his long tongue down over her ass, preparing for round two once he was done with this one.

Thea spread her legs and draped her thighs wide over

Dimitri's. Her pretty clit throbbed under Kris's tongue and he lapped at it, pressing and sliding back and forth, alternating between teasing at her ass and toying with the swollen bundle. She'd raised her arms and wrapped them around the back of Dimitri's head. The blond man bent and sucked at the flesh of her neck, his own hips rocking up against Thea's ass. He'd get his turn soon enough, but now…

Thea cried out abruptly. The bubble of magic around her grew even more intense, like an electrical cloud that caused the fine hairs on Kris's arms to stand on end. He latched his mouth tightly onto her pussy and plunged his tongue deeper. At the same time, he sank two fingers into her slick, wet ass. With his other hand he reached out to touch Issa's belly, just in time for Thea to arch her back, her hips twitching and her orgasmic cry piercing the air.

The magic permeating the air abruptly surged through them as though the balloon had deflated, all its air being inhaled by his lungs. Except he cleared his resistance and let it pass right through him. The power invigorated him for a moment, leaving behind a small amount of residue, but the lion's share of it sank into Issa.

The babies squirmed inside her and Kris could sense their excited need to absorb the power. Issa's head tilted back and she emitted a breathy gasp before relaxing again into slumber.

"She needs more," Kris said, raising his head.

Dimitri's eyes were feverish and unfocused. He shifted his hips, urging Thea to rise up.

"That's it, baby," Dimitri said. "Take my cock in your ass like you love it."

As Thea sank back down, encompassing Dimitri's entire length, she reached for Kris and he went. Her lips grasped hungrily at his, sucking and biting like she was the one hungry for the power. It was as though he'd never even taken what she'd already given. Her aura had returned in full force, the magic pulled to it again like a cyclone.

"Fuck me now," she said, her teeth gritted at the steady plunge of Dimitri's cock into her ass.

Kris pushed her back against her lover and hovered over her for only a second before sinking his cock deep into her. Her wet heat grasped at him, squeezing tightly enough for his vision to tunnel with the pleasure. He fucked her hard and fast, his balls smacking against the wet shaft of Dimitri's cock each time Kris withdrew and plunged back into her. The magic tingled on his skin as tangible as a Shadow's caress, seeking its way into him. Each deep thrust of his cock sent her further toward the edge again. Dimitri's harsh grunts escalated into a low, desperate groan. The pulsing of Dimitri's cock in Thea's ass as he came sent Kris beyond his own point of no return. With one final, brutal thrust he came, and Thea followed, her throat working soundlessly while her entire body quivered beneath him.

As before, Kris rested his hand on Issa's belly, letting the magic slide through him and into her.

He pulled out of Thea and sat back, watching his mate for any sign of consciousness. Her eyelids fluttered slightly and she let out a sigh. A second later her lips curled at the corners into a small smile.

"Issa?"

Without opening her eyes, she whispered. "That felt good. Do it again?"

Thea and Dimitri lay on their sides in a loose embrace, their legs tangled together. They both laughed. "I'm ready when you are," Dimitri said to Kris.

Soon Issa's energy had returned enough that she insisted on participating. Dimitri and Thea enthusiastically accommodated her, even as unwieldy as her large belly made things. She turned onto her side and reached for Thea. "Let me taste him on you," she said, shifting down the bed and shedding her sheer nightgown in the process.

Thea graciously turned onto her side and lifted one thigh to give Issa access. Kris silently rejoiced at the tiny quiver of pleasure that ran through Issa when her tongue pressed against Thea's pussy, still creamy from Kris's hot come.

The scent of his mate's arousal grew even stronger, and he lay down facing her, his head level with her bare breasts and his hard cock resting against her thigh. He cupped her breasts and sucked, pleased to sense the magic growing around her in a way it hadn't for quite some time.

Issa parted from Thea's glistening folds long enough to meet Kris's gaze and say, "I want you both now. Don't hold back, please." Her words held an edge of desperation, as though she knew she had to take as much as they were able to give.

Kris gestured to Dimitri, who nodded and moved around behind Issa. She lifted one thigh to allow Kris to ready her ass with his tongue. Dimitri wasted no time pressing the tip of his cock to her rosy opening.

Kris had by necessity coupled with Zak but had never watched another male take his mate before. He sat back on his heels and absorbed the impression of pure pleasure that Issa was immersed in. The memory of their first meeting had given him the same impression, but not to such an intimate degree as it did now that they shared the bond of mates. Every stroke of Dimitri's cock in Issa's ass incited further pleasure, making her lap at Thea's cunt with more fervor.

"Please, Kris. You too."

The violet hue of her pussy was too enticing, the memory of how she had first seduced him with it making his mouth water. He bent and pressed his lips to the soft, velvet folds and drowned in her familiar flavor. Now that she was conscious she didn't need him as a conduit so he could enjoy her again the way he used to before the pregnancy had become an exhausting ordeal. His cock throbbed again, his entire body alive with energy in response to his need to give her pleasure. The sweet throb of her clit under his tongue mirrored his own pulsing need. He kept teasing at it, swirling his tongue in the familiar pattern that drove her to distraction.

The chorus of their orgasms finally brought him back to the present. Issa's gentle touch on his head made him stop, though he was loath to leave off pleasuring her.

He looked up into her beautiful face. Her eyes glowed with love and a level of energy he hadn't seen for months.

"They need to rest," she said. "And so do you, my love."

"How do you feel?" he asked, tilting his cheek into her warm palm and resting his large hand atop her belly.

"Invigorated, but I can already feel the Twins absorbing it all. I think I can wait until these two are ready for more." She glanced behind her on the bed to Dimitri and Thea who now snuggled together, dozing quietly.

"You don't have to wait, love," Kris said. "They are all here for you. Dimitri and his lover were just the best equipped to help you replenish quickly."

Issa's eyes brightened. "All of them came here for my sake?"

"They want to help. You mean the world to all of us."

Issa shifted to the edge of the bed, exhaling a breath that shimmered into the purple gown she'd worn earlier. Before he could stop her, she strode to the door and flung it open. A moment later she was encompassed in the embrace of all their closest friends, finally getting the reunion that hadn't been possible earlier in the day.

CHAPTER TEN

With the return of Issa's energy came overwhelming cravings. She was grateful for the presence of her human friends and their willingness to sate those cravings.

"I never needed more than what Kris could give me before. I blame the babies," she said to Erika, laughing. "They can't seem to decide which of you they like the most."

"Who is it today?" Erika asked.

The pair lounged in a shady area beside the steaming pool in the courtyard outside the small temple she and Kris shared. The others were in various states of wakefulness, draped on furniture around the pool, or lounging languidly in the hot water. They had determined that a strict rotation wouldn't work to keep Issa entirely satisfied and she felt like a complete glutton requesting their attention. It wasn't until the lightheadedness and nausea that signaled a dangerous depletion of energy returned that Kris insisted she not wait that long, that they go no longer than an hour or two between sessions, and that whomever was willing should do the honors.

Dimitri and Thea together could keep her satisfied for longer, but after two days they were showing signs of exhaustion.

"The new one. Trevor. They find him quite pleasing."

Erika raised an eyebrow. "Is it the Twins speaking or Issa speaking? He is quite scrumptious, I agree. Rafe and Rowan chose well."

Issa felt her cheeks flush at Erika's observation. "It usually isn't just one of you. Different pairs appeal in different ways. The Twins always want their father's energy, but perhaps that's only a reflection of my own desire for him. But Camille and Eben together are a delightful combination, more so than just one at a time."

"What did you think of Corey?"

Issa pursed her lips, watching the brooding man where he lay in a sunny spot on the far edge of the pool with one arm draped across his eyes. "I didn't get much of a taste of him. He seems reticent and insists on only the quickest sessions."

"He feels guilty. Racha's still in the Glade with the Council and their other mate didn't join us on the trip. Jill would probably be able to pull him out of his shell had she come."

"Do you find that odd?" Issa asked. "I mean that the other female didn't come."

"Not any stranger than it was that we all hadn't seen *you* since we returned from the ritual. You showing up with a couple new passengers was a big surprise, but we all figured Kris had been hiding something all along."

"Do you think Corey's hiding something?"

Erika shrugged. "If he is, I think he'll tell us when the time is right."

"I'd like more of him," Issa said decisively. "The Twins are curious after the small tastes they did get. But he seems to hold back power the way a dragon does."

Erika tilted her head thoughtfully at Corey's prone figure. She bit her lip. "I might be able to talk him into trying a little harder. Are you in the mood now?"

"The Twins are always in the mood for more magic."

Erika stood up and adjusted the short red sarong over her breasts. Issa watched as her friend strode around the pool, first stopping at the chair where the dark-haired Hallie reclined with eyes closed. Hallie's eyes opened in response to Erika's whisper and she smiled, turning to look at Corey while Erika explained whatever scheme she'd concocted to encourage more enthusiasm out of their male friend.

Hand-in-hand, the pair of women padded barefoot to the spot where Corey dozed in one of the short sarongs Kris had conjured for him. The women lay down flanking him and pressing their bodies against his sides.

Erika bent her mouth to his ear, but Issa couldn't tell whether she spoke to him or merely teased at his neck with her lips. Issa spent a bit of energy to focus her hearing, curious what the women would do to get the reluctant male to come with them. A second later, their words were as clear as if they were speaking to her.

"You're being a little stingy, you know," Erika said. "So Hallie and I thought we'd give you a hand."

Hallie rested one hand lightly on the top of the fabric that spanned his hips just below his bare waist.

Corey removed the arm from over his eyes and turned to look at her, then at Hallie. "Oh, you think so? I did my part yesterday. By my count there are enough of us that we're only needed once a day. Besides, Issa's kind of like my sister-in-law. Don't you think that's weird?"

"Is it any weirder than Racha doing whatever it is she's doing with all the other dragons right now? Don't tell me you believe they're just in the Glade having a chat. What would Racha do if she were here now, anyway?"

Corey put his arm back over his eyes. "She'd respect my boundaries."

"Or would she urge you to contribute as much as possible for the betterment of the race?"

Corey didn't respond. Erika and Hallie exchanged exasperated looks, then Erika mouthed two words to her friend that Issa was sure were, "Plan B."

Erika's auburn head leaned across Corey's torso. Her lips met Hallie's lips halfway. The pair shared a long, sensuous kiss. Partway through, Hallie reached across and tugged the knot Erika had tied in her sarong. The fabric slipped down, revealing Erika's lovely, pink-tipped breasts. Hallie unfastened her own garment, then with her free hand cupped one of Erika's breasts and toyed with her nipple, pinching gently and tugging with thumb and forefinger.

Erika's throaty laugh echoed around the courtyard, drawing the attention of the others. Some perked up to watch, others just smiled and went back to their relaxation.

Corey's body had tensed. He hadn't removed his arm from his eyes, but Issa was sure he was watching the two women from beneath it, particularly considering the rising swell of an erection, unmistakable beneath the thin fabric that concealed it.

When the women pulled back from their kiss, Erika bent and pulled one of Hallie's nipples between her lips and sucked. Hallie's breathy sigh caused a visible tremor to ripple up Corey's stomach from his groin. He lifted his arm from his eyes and drifted the fingers of the hand over Hallie's smooth, bare shoulder, down over her breast until his fingertips swirled around the nipple that was not already being attended.

"You two are probably the second most infuriating women I know. If I do this, you have got to quit torturing me. So, you do what I tell you and we'll all leave happy, especially Issa."

His dark eyes slid to meet Issa's. She smiled at the tiny salute and nod he gave her from across the pool, though his smirk told her he wasn't the least bit irritated by the imposition in spite of his complaint. The three left their coverings behind and strolled with hands linked back around the pool to where she reclined on her comfortable cushioned lounge.

"This might be a challenge," Corey commented, eyeing the three women. "But I'd be lying if I said I wasn't up for it. Asses up, ladies. If you want me, I want easy access. That is, if you're up for it, Issa."

The contrast between his polite, accommodating tone and his lewd suggestion amused Issa as much as it excited her. Kris strolled over, seeing the activity and gave her a questioning look. She started to answer but Corey turned and said, "Hey, man. Glad you're here, I might need a little backup to keep them ready. You game?"

"If Issa wants it, I'll do anything."

"Yeah, pregnant woman cravings are tricky things to deal with, aren't they?" Corey said with a chuckle and a shake of his head. "But hey, a father's work is never done."

He clapped his hands then swirled one hand in the air, indicating they should assume the position. Issa shared a pleased glance with Erika as they moved the cushions the lounges to a clear area and bent on hands and knees, presenting their backsides to the men. Issa twined the fingers of each hand through the other women's fingers to ensure contact.

Out of the corner of her eye she caught movement approaching from the far side of the pool.

"Can I get in on this?" Camille asked, walking forward with the rest of the group trailing behind her. The other three men looked even more interested now that there were three bare, female asses catching the light breeze.

Issa's core heated under their interested inspection in spite of the coolness of the air around her. The Twins danced in her belly, sensing her excitement.

Corey nodded, his expression serious as though it was a dire undertaking and he had to make some hard decisions about how to proceed. "Yes, I think that's best. You and Thea both face Issa on the other side there so she can touch you."

Camille's heart-shaped face came into view as the pretty blonde bent down on hands and knees facing Issa. She leaned in and kissed Issa. "This is gonna be fun," Camille said, her eyes bright.

In spite of Thea's sleepy expression, the petite brunette appeared as excited as the others. With the five of them arranged facing each other in a circle, the magic of the human women's arousal seemed to pool in a concentrated bubble between them.

"Jesus Christ, that's beautiful," Corey said in an awestruck tone. He sauntered around them once, letting his hand slide over the rise and fall of the curves if their asses. He paused behind Issa, clutching at her ass with both hands. "You needed more than I gave you yesterday, didn't you? Well, I guess these two made their point."

Issa heard the loud smack of his palms as they hit the soft flesh of Hallie and Erika's backsides to either side of her. His hot palms returned to her ass and gently massaged, pushing her cheeks wide and letting his thumbs slide down between and into the wetness of her pussy. Her flesh felt like a solid knot of need until his fingertips sank into her aching depths and massaged in perfect slow strokes at the inside of her. He drew them back out and swiped slick juice over the puckered flower of her asshole. Her eyes fluttered closed with pleasure.

Around her, each of the other men had taken up positions behind the other women. Other hands clutched at hers in the center while moans and sighs of pleasure erupted from the mouths of her friends.

"Jesus, Corey," Hallie said, craning her head around. "When did you learn to flip that good-boy prude switch off?"

His deep voice rumbled behind Issa. "Baby, I always knew how. It just takes the right motivation. But when I do it, trust me, I'm all the way on the dark side. Your pussy will be heaven when I fuck it. My only regret with this arrangement is that your pretty mouth won't be taking my cock and licking your juices off me afterward."

Hallie seemed about to retort, but the only sound that came out of her was a surprised squeak followed by a groan. She lowered her head and surged backward into Trevor. At the same moment, Corey pressed his hot cock between the folds of Issa's pussy and shoved into her. She emitted her own sound of pleasure at the invasion, clenching around him as he began to fuck her.

Corey's large hands gripped her hips with a vengeance as he slammed into her. Every stroke pressed tight against the deeper bundle of pleasure that rested far inside, but just when she believed she'd reach Nirvana with one more press, he withdrew and was gone.

Before Issa could object, the familiar tingling touch of her mate rested light on her backside. "He's a different person once you get him going," Kris commented. "I think I like this version of him."

To her side, Corey said, "Don't get used to this, brother. I like to keep it at home."

"I just know my sister seems very happy. If you can keep her satisfied along with your other mate, you're braver than I am."

"The real challenge will be when Racha or Jill are pregnant. This delicious little tangle of fucking is to fulfill Issa's cravings. I hope you guys are up for the same when I need you."

Kris's hands dipped around to her front and cupped her breasts when he let his cock sink into her. "Is that what it was, love?" he whispered in her ear. "A craving to have us all fuck each other?"

"I just wanted a snack. It was Corey who turned it into a feast, but I have no complaints."

Again, she was brought to the cusp of climax before the men moved on in response to some unseen signal, likely from Corey.

In the center of the circle, the magic ebbed only minutely then surged to bright vibrancy again when another cock sank into her. Around them, Issa sensed a wider bubble of power from the men. They gasped and sweated, each stroke seeming like an ordeal after the third switch.

Instead of a cock, a teasing tongue slicked its way down the crack of her ass, sinking into her snatch. A moment later, the mouth against her backside moaned. Hands gripped her ass and Eben's familiar cock with its upward curve slid deep into her. "Sorry, I just missed the taste of you," he whispered, leaning over to press his lips against her ear. "Consider this for old time's sake."

Across from her, Camille's mouth parted in a breathless sigh as Kris gripped the blonde's ass and slid into her. Their collective lust had risen exponentially, Issa's own and Kris's glowing even brighter with each round. Thea and Dimitri looked like glowing embers in Issa's magic-filtered vision. The entire group was the most beautiful thing she'd ever seen. She almost wished to be able to look down on them from above and witness the final surge of it when they all came. But Corey seemed preternaturally attuned to the flow of it as well, and moved them along just when she felt close again.

Perhaps being the mate of a Queen had that effect on a man.

Corey met her gaze just before sliding his cock out of Thea and moving clockwise to clutch Erika's ass with a promising growl signaling his intent. The shell-shocked new addition, Trevor, placed himself behind Issa and gingerly began stroking her pussy. She was on the verge of screaming out her need when she glanced around at the other women. They were in various states of red-faced frustration and ecstasy, and all their hands clutched at hers. Through the swirling storm of magic, Issa realized they were all doing this for her, and it was time to set them all free.

Trevor's fingers shook perceptibly as he touched her. His voice was just as quavering. "I think I've fucked more women today than in the last five years since I lost my virginity," he said. "The funny thing is, you'll be the fourth dragon I've had carnal knowledge of. I hope I do it right."

"Just make me come, please? It really isn't that complicated. I need to feel you come in me."

"Oh, sweet Jesus, yes."

The desperate cling of Trevor's hands against her skin was a sweet reminder of her first few moments with Kris. Trevor was no virgin, that was clear, but he still had the hesitant caution of a man who cared deeply about his partner. Not that the other men in the group didn't, but they all knew her well and were flush with confidence in their ability to please her. Not only did Trevor have to please her, he had to give her his essence now that she'd given him permission.

Once they gave themselves over to Issa's suggestion, they all fucked with abandon. Her own orgasm had been clinging to the edge for so long, it only took a few swift strokes and his hand attentively reaching down to slide a finger in her ass and she slipped into the sweet oblivion of her Nirvana.

She quivered with the aftershocks when something happened above her that channeled even more power as the others came like a house of cards falling in slow motion. She opened her eyes long enough to see a collection of muscular arms connected above their group in the center. Kris wasn't wasting any chance at power, but the energy flowing through him was even stronger than the collective power of their small group. Her mate's eyes glowed as he soaked it in from somewhere beyond, and his face contorted. Could he even hold that much at one time without channeling it?

She no longer cared when the magic began to flow through her from the center, the bright swirling mass of it immediately attracted to her need. The entire courtyard bloomed with light, unfurling from their center of pleasure and spreading outward. Soon the women's hands left hers, Trevor's lovely cock disappeared, and a single figure rested before her on his knees.

Kris held her face in his, the power he channeled rushing into her as rapidly as if they'd just made love. The purity and strength of it was beyond anything he had given her before.

"The Council came through," he whispered. Then his sweet lips were on hers, with their hot longing.

Issa was on the verge of begging him to take her back to bed when the first spasm hit. The pleasant, sated buzz from all the energy she'd just absorbed was replaced by a sensation like a vise in her lower abdomen. She cried out at the dizzying pain. The sharp spasming clench of it sent her into a cold sweat and she doubled over.

"Issa!"

Kris's cry became a vague sound through the fog of pain.

The others spoke in alarm. Some of the women sounded more rational and she thought she heard Hallie's rough voice rise up and yell out, "She's in labor, let's get her inside!" Her friend continued to shout commands at the others just before everything faded away.

CHAPTER ELEVEN

owan and the others shimmered back into the familiar pavilion they had left from, greeted by the excited faces of Zak and Darius.

"What is it?" she shot at Darius.

"Issa's giving birth as we speak."

Echoing his words, Numa said out loud, "The Catalyst's children are imminent, we must go to them now." The immortal Green swept around majestically in her conjured green dress and walking out of the Pavilion with the others following. All of them had bathed and reclothed themselves, but remained in their human forms. Now they reminded Rowan of a line of supermodels walking down a runway with their perfect features and exact gaits.

Darius stood in a daze, mouth gaping. When the Council was gone, he looked at Rowan.

"What did you do?"

"What the hell do you mean, 'what did I do'? They're a pretty focused group of dragons. Like I could influence them?"

"I've just never seen them… like that."

"Like what?"

"In human form… and leaving the Pavilion… and…" His eyes rested at her waist, his brows drawing together. "You're with child."

Rowan wrapped her hands protectively around her midsection. "So?"

"You weren't a few days ago when you left. Now I can sense the power of the baby in you. Rowan… What did they do to you?"

His concern was endearing enough for her to go to him. Rafe clung to her hand for a moment then reluctantly released it.

"I served their purpose and they served mine. It was a trade. That's all you need to know."

Darius looked insulted. His lips creased in a hard line. Rafe moved up behind her, rested his hand at her waist.

"She sacrificed for you, brother. Everything is changing."

"They heard you?" Darius asked, his expression brightening.

"You and everyone else convinced me I had power over them. Don't tell me you had doubts all along." Rowan gave him a playful nudge. "But I get the impression they'd already made up their minds before I made my argument. My willingness to go the extra mile was just their extra little bit of leverage."

"And they agreed to everything?" he asked.

"They may be a bit distracted at the moment, but yeah, they agreed. Now I'd like to see Trevor. Where is he?"

"He's recovering from the blast," Darius said.

Rowan stared at him in incomprehension. "Blast?"

"He took the brunt of it after Issa, I'm afraid. They were coupling when the energy unleashed on the group just before she went into labor. He's fine. He might take a few days to recover, though. Corey is taking care of him now. I think he feels responsible."

"Why would the Queen's mate feel responsible?" Rafe asked.

"Well, Issa had a particular craving...pregnant dragons do, after all. And Corey was just trying to help. The rest were a rather determined group once Corey took control."

It was Rafe's turn to laugh. "Corey coordinated it? I always knew he had it in him. It seems like he's less inhibited during Racha's absences than he used to be."

Darius led them out of the Pavilion and down the hill behind the others. Rowan remembered the Queen and her mate from their trip. She and the other female had regarded each other with caution at first. After Racha's calming breath during the plane ride, they had both relaxed enough to talk and Rowan had assured Racha that she had no desire to subvert her authority. Their more formal meeting later in the Pavilion had thrown Rowan for a moment until she sensed the other woman's precarious situation. The bitter words had only been a ruse, though there had been some truth to their bite. Rowan just wasn't sure exactly what had prompted it.

When they reached Kris and Issa's chamber, the others were too excited to pay any attention to her, however. Except for Trevor, who immediately found her and pulled her into a tight embrace.

"God, I missed you," he murmured in her ear.

She sank into him, pressing her nose against his neck and inhaling his delicious, clean scent. Underneath she caught the whiff of other aromas that lingered deeper. She pulled back and looked up into his eyes. "Did you have fun while I was gone?" she asked, twitching her lips into a knowing smile.

Trevor's cheeks flushed brighter than they had when he'd

confessed the things he'd done with Roka and Rafe to get to her. "Issa needed all of us. You were gone for three days. It's not like I could sit it out when everyone else was in."

"I understand. Sweetie, I'm like her, you know. I wouldn't share you with just anyone, but these guys are the closest thing to family that I have. If they need my help, I won't say no. Besides if you can deal with sharing me with the offspring of the entire Court and Council, then I have no room to object."

"Offspring?" Trevor asked, bewildered. He turned to Rafe.

"It's true," Rafe said proudly. "Hope you're ready to share fatherhood with me."

Just then, the inner doors opened and the entire collection of waiting dragons and humans in the sitting area rose to their feet at once.

"Speaking of fathers..." Darius stepped away from the group toward the door.

The Council was the first to emerge, the six of them parting to stand on either side, each with similar elated expressions. Kris and Issa strode through next, side by side, each holding a tiny, squirming bundle in their arms.

The proud parents beamed at the group, their happiness washing over Rowan in waves. The room grew hushed when the couple looked at each other. Issa nodded once and Kris spoke.

"Friends, family, treasured mates. It is with great love and gratitude that we present our children, the firstborn dragons of the new generation. Named to honor the lost loved ones of two of you—two individuals that were valued and are dearly missed. Please meet our twin sons, Alexander and Gabriel."

They both turned the infants in their arms and held them up, letting their lavender-hued wrappings fall. The room let out a collective gasp at the tiny, beautiful creatures. Their skin was a perfect rosy pink, until Rowan shifted her vision and caught the glimmer of their scales, reminding her that they truly were tiny dragons, bound up by their parents' magic.

Rowan's vision grew blurry with tears when the room erupted into applause. She placed her hands over her womb. It had only been hours by her schedule since the events of the glade, though it had been longer in this world. She was hesitant to share the news with the others, but she shouldn't have been. A clear, sweet, feminine voice in her mind said, *"My sons and your daughter will be the protectors of our race when they come of age. Will you stay here with us so they can be raised together?"*

She held Issa's gaze for several moments, uncertain how to respond. The babies both let out sudden tiny wails of protest and the sound made Rowan jerk with surprise. They had amazingly strong voices that rang high over the din of excited conversation.

Rafe's strong hand settled at her hip. "What is it? You look worried."

"Not worried. What would you say if I decided to stay here until the baby is born? Maybe even longer?"

"I'd say welcome home."

THANK YOU

Thank you for reading "Rising Dragons"

If you're eager to continue reading about Ophelia's dragons, please look for...

DRAGON'S MELODY

Lovers of convenience.

One with a claim to a fortune, another who's already in love. And Melody, personal assistant to a black dragon, is caught in the middle.

Hearts will be broken, and alliances tested. And it all comes down to a contract, one that will rule Melody's heart and her bed.

Blue dragon Skye needs her to access his fortune, and Garen, Skye's dragon guardian lover, needs her to bond with his oldest friend. Only Garen starts to fall for Melody, and the line between convenience and love blurs.

Will Melody survive with her heart intact, or will the dragons force her away?

Author's Note: This is a complete, full-length novel with no cliffhanger. It is an extra-steamy yet beautiful story of how love can grow between three people intent on denying their own desires. Swords may cross (i.e. M/M shenanigans), so read at your own risk. Adults only, please. #whychoose

Read on for an excerpt!

The late summer heat of the San Fernando Valley threatened to suffocate Melody. It was past sunset and still sweltering. Her air conditioner had strained at the heat all day without providing any relief, so she finally gave it a rest. She couldn't afford the power bill as it was.

She wandered through her small apartment, opening all the windows and hoping for a breeze to cool the place off. The aroma of fresh Thai food wafted up from the Boulevard, along with a breeze that was barely even a whisper. She closed her eyes, imagining she was standing on a beach in Thailand with her toes in the sand.

The fantasy only lasted long enough for her brain to trip into wishing mode, then planning mode, making a mental tally of how much money she had in the bank. Even with her new job and a nice bump in salary, it would still take six more months of saving like mad before she would have enough to pay for herself and her favorite person—her mother, Julia—to take the trip they'd always dreamed of.

As a testament to her desires, a ragged map of the world graced the only wall in her apartment big enough to accommodate it. Melody had stuck pins in all the places she'd visited so far. The collection was depressingly small, with only a few major U.S. cities sporting colored nubs. As a flight attendant, she'd forced herself to stick to domestic airlines so she could have a solid home base and continue her education in between—something she'd promised her mother she would do.

So far, Los Angeles was the farthest she'd come since leaving the tiny little Appalachian town she'd grown up in. Even that distance had taken four years to achieve, but she'd known back then that she'd never earn the money to fulfill her mother's dream—*her* dream—if she stayed put.

Once she earned enough, she wouldn't go back home until she'd traveled far enough west to come full circle. Los Angeles would hopefully be her launching point in a few months. By then she'd be able to buy her mother a ticket to California, and they would leave together. Fly to Hawaii first, then from there, keep going west.

It had been several weeks since she'd spoken to her mother, which she regretted. Things had been tense between them lately—they always were this time of year. It was the end of summer, which was when the man she'd thought of as "Daddy" had left them years ago.

Even after almost two decades, her mother still held onto hope that her old lover, Alec, would return.

"Sweetie, when you find a love like ours, you know better than to let go without a fight," she'd said.

But it wasn't much of a fight if the other party forfeited.

The truth was, Melody still missed the only father she'd ever known. She absently rubbed her shoulder, reminded of the day he'd given her the silly magic tattoo. The sharp scent of her markers was just as fresh in her mind now as it had been on that day. Almost as vivid was the confusion and despair she'd experienced only a little while later.

Her memory was limited to vague images now—of a phone call during supper, Alec speaking to her mother in a low voice, strained with emotion, followed by her mother's adamant refusal to accept whatever it was he'd told her.

They'd both looked so sad. Her mother was crying, and it made Melody cry too.

"You shouldn't wait for me, Julia," Alec had said when he kissed her goodbye, "but I will be back."

And then he was gone.

A few years after that, Melody had made her promise to her mother. Alec had always planned to take them traveling around the world when Melody was old enough. She hated him a little for making a promise he couldn't keep. But she always remembered how dreamy her mother would get, asking about the places he'd been. It seemed like he'd been everywhere, too.

So Melody resolved that she would be the one to give her mother that gift. On her tenth birthday, she'd made the pledge, telling her mother not to buy her a present, but to open a bank account instead, so she could save money to that end.

The kind of trip she wanted to take her mother on had evolved over the years, and the itinerary she'd settled on wasn't cheap, but she persisted. She became a flight attendant right after high school, believing the job might give her some advantages and allow her to achieve her goal more easily. The perks were very nice, but mostly it meant fending off the advances of countless men.

Some of the offers she got were tempting—plenty of obviously wealthy passengers took an interest in her, but she always demurred as tactfully as possible. Becoming romantically entangled was not part of her plan.

Falling in love just led to abandonment and heartbreak.

Giving up that job had been a mixed blessing. She'd truly

enjoyed the job itself, both in spite of and because of the patrons. The catalyst for the change still puzzled her, even though it had been months since it happened.

During her last cross-country flight to Los Angeles, Melody had encountered one first-class passenger who'd grown exceedingly agitated. During takeoff, the woman had clutched the armrests so hard Melody swore she'd left permanent finger-shaped dents in them. And every time Melody walked past, she thought she heard the woman grinding her teeth.

"Ma'am," she whispered, laying a gentle hand on the woman's shoulder, "if you have an anti-anxiety prescription in overhead, I'd be happy to retrieve it for you once we're at cruising altitude."

The woman shook her head. "No," she said tensely. "Drugs do no good. What's your name?" She peered up at Melody with the strangest eyes—gray but flecked with red motes that almost glowed.

Her gaze had latched onto Melody's so directly it startled her. Something about it reminded her so starkly of Alec that she nearly blurted out, "Daddy?" She recovered quickly, took a breath, and pointed at her name tag. "Melody."

The sun shone through the window and into the woman's eyes at just the right angle to make the red flecks glow even brighter.

"What a lovely name. Call me Nancy."

"Would you like a pair of headphones? Listening to music might help relax you."

The woman clutched Melody's hand and squeezed, her grip strong but shaky.

"No, thank you. Just come by and talk when you can. You are a truly blessed young woman, you know."

Melody went about her business, stopping by to speak with the woman whenever she could steal a moment.

The similarities to Alec lingered, though Melody could never quite put her finger on what it was that captured her attention. The woman looked nothing like Alec, with her long, red hair and pale skin.

It wasn't a visual similarity, Melody had thought, but something in the woman's bearing. Nancy was almost majestic once the plane was finally at a level altitude, as if she actually took pleasure in flying.

As Nancy disembarked a few hours later, she paused, clasping Melody's hand and thanking her. The woman's face glowed with some odd light none of the other passengers had and Melody let out a gasp, tightening her hands on the woman's fingers.

"You see us, don't you?" Nancy said. "It isn't a mirage, if that's what you thought. Not a hallucination."

Melody glanced around the cabin. The other patrons seemed to be stalling, as though they were still waiting for the plane to land.

"What are you?" Melody asked.

Nancy shook her head. "That you can't know yet, but know you are Blessed. You belong in a higher place than the one you've found. Here …" She handed Melody a business card that felt way too warm in her fingers. "There's a place for you with us, Melody. One meant for you."

Melody had taken the card, perplexed by the woman's cryptic words. The card itself was a curiosity, stark black with only the letter "M" in light gray on one side. On the other side were two lines: "Magnus Securities. Los Angeles" followed by a phone number. She'd already considered moving to the west coast, and planned to spend the week before her next flight apartment hunting. But the card distracted her to such an extent that she found herself itching to call.

The rest had happened so fast, her mind still spun a little

from it. That had all been close to six months ago. She'd been hired as executive assistant to the corporation's CEO, with the expectation of serving as personal flight attendant on the rare occasion he needed to take the corporate jet for business.

That had happened only once, and the aftermath was what ate at her now, threatening to derail her entire plan. The job description itself seemed tailor made for her, the perfect combination of stability and opportunities to travel. She just hadn't counted on winding up with a boss as sexy and inaccessible as Kol Magnus.

Melody turned from the window and headed for the bathroom, peeling off her tank top and shorts on the way. She ran a cool bath, waiting for the tub to fill. When she finally slipped into the water, she sighed. Slowly, her body temperature sank back to a comfortable level, but her thoughts continued to blaze.

Her boss' face kept springing up. Fucking Kol Magnus. Every inch of the bastard lit her up in so many ways. The worst part was that he was married, and to a woman every bit as scintillating as the man himself.

His wife, Hallie, wasn't like the bombshell trophy brides the other execs at the firm flaunted. Hallie was a purely sensual woman: beautiful, intelligent, down-to-earth, and entirely comfortable with her sexuality.

God, I want to be like her, Melody thought.

It was her secret, the thing she'd never speak lest she give credence to a desire that ran counter to her greatest wish: the wish to discover her world before she let herself get attached to a man. It didn't help that she could never have him— thoughts of Kol still compelled her to slip her fingers down between her thighs and spread her legs a little wider, making her bathwater slosh over the side of the tub.

The fantasies were always just a little different, but in all of them she saw herself as the pet of a man like him—a bird in a gilded cage, kept for his enjoyment. The fantasies rarely involved his face, however. The sheer, sexual presence of him was what held sway over her in her mind, but the man who took her in her fantasies could have been anyone, as long as he aroused her passion the way Kol had.

She thought about the day she'd served as flight attendant on the Magnus private jet only a few weeks earlier. It was the first time she'd been asked to fulfill that part of her job description.

It had promised to be an easy cross-country flight between Los Angeles and Boston with just Kol and Hallie as passengers. That is, until she'd caught the two of them on the verge of sex even before the plane had taken off.

After working as a flight attendant for years, she wasn't exactly a stranger to passengers misbehaving. But seeing Kol and Hallie fooling around had been the first time she'd had the urge to join in.

The thick, ropey bulge of Kol's hard-on had been unmistakable at the front of his trousers when she'd told them to strap in for take-off. She walked away with her mind fixated on getting a glimpse of him in all his glory—he was such a beautiful man. All he had to do was ask, she told herself. He was her boss, after all. The gold pendant she wore at her throat was the symbol of her loyalty to him—and a reward for completing her ninety-day probationary period at his firm. Only a handful of employees were privileged enough to receive one of the gold medallions. Each one had a carved onyx emblem of the company's serpentine symbol set in the center. It had come with a token raise, too, but she'd promised herself she'd save most of it for her trip with her mother.

Melody gripped the medallion with her free hand while the other did its work between her thighs. She imagined the connection the pendant gave her to him. Her fingers were a poor substitute for Kol's tongue, but they did the trick. She'd never imagined he would actually ask. But he did. More than that, he had *commanded* her to undress and touch herself in front of him, and then he had *commanded* her to spread her legs across his face.

"I'd like to taste you when you come. To have my tongue on that pretty clit of yours."

She'd been able to see every glorious inch of his body after Hallie had undressed him. Hallie had been the only one to tend to Kol's enormous cock, but the mere sight of the massive trunk of flesh between his thighs had been a little intimidating. Not the least bit intimidating to his wife, though. Even as Kol's tongue sank into Melody's aching pussy, Hallie had taken his thick length entirely into her slick and waiting depths, then leaned forward over Kol's torso to pull Melody into a kiss.

Melody couldn't pinpoint the moment when she came, only that the sensation of Kol's tongue between her thighs had changed. He'd slipped the length of it into her, and the pleasure that followed had been so mind-crushingly perfect she'd lost control.

As much as she tried after that, she'd never been able to replicate the sensations, either with other men or with toys. Lying in the tepid bathwater with her fingers desperately working her clit and her feet up on either side of the old, claw-foot tub, all she had was the memory. It was enough for now. She cried out when the spasms took hold and clamped her thighs around her hand, pressing deeper to try to ride out the pleasure for as long as possible.

How could one man's tongue have ruined her so thoroughly? She needed more of him. Or she needed to get the hell away from him before the proximity drove her mad.

ABOUT OPHELIA BELL

Ophelia Bell loves a good bad-boy and especially strong women in her stories. Women who aren't apologetic about enjoying sex and bad boys who don't mind being with a woman who's in charge, at least on the surface, because pretty much anything goes in the bedroom.

Ophelia grew up on a rural farm in North Carolina and now lives in Los Angeles with her own tattooed bad-boy husband and six attention-whoring cats.

Subscribe to Ophelia's newsletter to get updates directly in your inbox. If newsletters aren't your thing, you can find her on social media.

http://opheliabell.com/subscribe

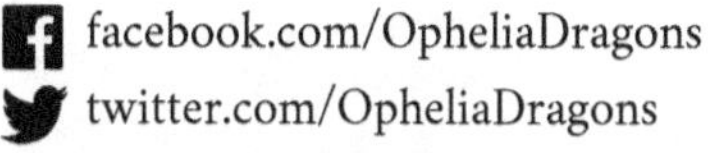
facebook.com/OpheliaDragons
twitter.com/OpheliaDragons

Dragon Void

Dragon Splendor

Dragon Rebel

Dragon Guardian

Dragon Blessed

Dragon Equinox

Dragon Avenged

Immortal Dragons Box Sets:

Immortal Dragons: Books 1, 2, & 3 + Prequel

Immortal Dragons: Books 4-6 + Epilogue

Black Mountain Bears

Clawed

Bitten

Nailed

Stonetree Trilogy

Fate's Fools Series

Fate's Fools

Fool's Folly

Fool's Paradise

Fool's Errand

Nobody's Fool

Eye of the Hurricane

Aurora Champions Series

(Set in Milly Taiden's "Paranormal Dating Agency" world)

The Way to a Bear's Heart

Hot Wings

Triple Talons

Midnight Star

Standalone Erotic Tales

After You

Out of the Cold